SOULCRUSHER

ALTER INFERNO COMPLEX

Book Three

DREW BRYENTON

sci-fi-cafe.com

Soulcrusher
Drew Bryenton

ISBN 978-1-910779-23-1 (Paperback)
ISBN 978-1-908387-16-5 (ePUB)
ASIN B004NBZ91C (Kindle)

In this series:

Elysium Burning
The Chains of Tartarus
Soulcrusher

This one's for four groups of people
who conspicuously don't suck –
The Cardigan St. Mafia (you know who you are!)
My family – all of you! You rule.
The Unholy Legions of Heavy Metal
And
The Pakuranga / Edgewater Cast of Villains.

P.S. special mention and extra credit to Serena for being part of three
out of four, as well as the most tolerant, insightful and generally kick-
arse human being on this planet.

Well, here we are. There's no turning back now!

Any minute those damned trolls from Mental Hygiene or some other cursed Mitochondriate bureaucratic mini-hell will crash in here and core out your skull like a ripe *sjamba* melon.

But it's WORTH it. You know now. You know what they were up to!

I have no doubt that that stuffy old screw Kweel Noxus has tried to tell you otherwise, but it's all true. There really *was* a Technician Nyl! There really was a military engagement with the Blacksteel out there!

But knowledge is power, friend. If you're reading this, you have leverage now. You have secrets coded into your neural structure which they have to suppress.

DON'T LET THEM GET YOU!

I've survived in the vents under the Archives for ten years. I've been living off mold and dropped sandwiches, collecting moisture in little tinfoil traps. But look what I can do! I can even hack into Kweel's precious datalogger from here, and he's none the wiser!

Join me! Join us! And together we'll turn this place on it's head with what we know!

++ DELETE LINE ++
Subpraetor Kweel, Departmental Hierophant
Gurnis Ozekc, Free Entity!

Hello again, persistent readers.

I mentioned at the beginning of book two how some of these
*interminable sci-fi trilogies contain a kind of 'flashback to last week's
show' in the early pages, to refresh one's memory and roll-call the various
improbably-named characters.*

*I also mentioned that we don't do things like that around here – under
the feeble but hopefully compelling excuse that the paper thus wasted
would be better used to fashion crude voodoo effigies of politicians, or
tiny pirate hats for cats.*

*Well, by this point in the story things have gone from bad to worse
for the forces of humanity. They're frankly reeling like a punch-drunk
grandmother in a fight with ninja octopi, while the sheer number of
ways the world could end has multiplied exponentially until a mere
nuclear holocaust looks like pie and chips on the beach.*

*If you like eyeball-peeling terror, coarse language, chase scenes, robot
situations and adult explosions, read on.*

*If not, I'm sure this library has an aisle which is entirely done up in
pink, featuring books about milkmaids and guys in top hats who can't
seem to find their shirts.*

Hope you like the ending!

17 Aevum Oblivio
Bodies

THE JUSTIFIABLE BRUTALITY *dropped into the Aematerium as soon as it cleared its docking gantry, forcing itself through the distended mesh of the* Effortless Subjugation *with barely an inch to spare on either side. The redoubtable old fighter-tender knew that this was likely a suicide mission - its Captain and his Bastarnae were equipped with Technician-Grade jump units, able to put them back aboard the portal carrier if (or when) the* Unity *reduced their ship to radioactive dust.*

STILL, THE BRUTALITY'S *brain was only the size of a peeled orange, and it was juiced up on potent fighting drugs. The three-mile-long creature was slavering to get to grips with the foe.*

The chasm opened, tearing space apart. A cold black blur swirled past outside for a time which wasn't time, and then...

The Blacksteel were following the path mapped out by their Explorator system seventeen years before. Thousands of them had unfolded from the Behemoth-core as it fell in towards the Earth, and they hung in a great arrowhead swarm inside the orbit of Enceladus, leapfrogging each other with short Aematerial jumps. The captain of the Justifiable Brutality *brought his skeletal craft in just above the rings of Saturn, waiting in ambush.*

All through the chitinous superstructure of the fighter-tender Excisor thralls and neurobonded Navigator-caste beings scurried frantically, readying their ships for battle. Each living interceptor hung inside a pendulous membrane, dangling from the ribs of the Brutality *like clusters of roe.*

Nutrients flowed, and nervebridges seethed with raw data. The many-limbed Navigators were socketed into their command orifices, their exoshells licked clean by scuttling insects...

And now the vanguard of the Motherbrain's fleet dropped into realspace, huge magnetic traces shimmering beneath the tumbling ice of the rings. A carrier group; one vast cylinder nearly the size of the Brutality *itself, surrounded by a herd of lesser vessels, frigates and destroyers hatching from their honeycombs of steel...*

As the captain and his bonded craft watched, another Blacksteel warship nosed its way out of the confines of its hangar-tube; an ugly great chunk of hardware studded with turrets and missile batteries. The giant cylinder at the heart of the fleet was shifting into battle array, polygonal panels the size of skyscrapers sliding and locking into place. It flattened down into a broad-bladed sword of silver metal, its command module hanging below like the gondola of an ancient airship.

That was the mind of the Unity vanguard, right there. Inside that sleek torpedo of chrome and titanium an incalculably powerful processor hummed with power, pressurized in a sphere of liquid nitrogen.

`+We can take them! We can feast on their twisted scrap!+` *enthused the Brutality, aching to let fly with its guns.* `+Give me the order, sir! Give me leave to erase this stain on the Praetor's creation!+`

The captain squinted out through the great diamond bubble nestled in Brutality's forehead, his four primary eyes as smooth and blank as pearls. A battery of multi-masers welded to his vessel's ribs swiveled out and down, covering a segment of the ice-ring the size of a small city.

"Wait for it... wait for my mark..."

The Unity carrier was right beneath them now, oblivious to the cloaked fighter-tender hovering above. The Captain's mandibles hinged open in anticipation, tiny insect thralls siphoning off beads of saliva as his hearts pounded in his chest.

Now. His clawed hand came down on the arm of his command throne, sending the order to a thousand living interceptors in their pods. Locking jaws peeled away, releasing a storm of red-ochre motes like rain.

"Show them hell! Send them back to their Motherbrain in pieces!"

Then the maser battery unleashed its terrible broadside all at once, sending pillars of energy lancing down ahead of the fighter swarm. A rolling swathe of ice and rock flashed incandescent white for an instant, then blasted into superheated gas.

And through the howl and crackle of boson emissions came the frontline interceptors of the Multiplicity; Stirges and Gorgons, Drakkal with their great central fusion cannons, lithe Voidblades and hulking biomechanical Slavemasters. Three hundred burning contrails speared down through the broken ring as the Stirges hit twenty G's, their pilots' toughened exoskeletons creaking with the strain. Behind them bloomed a great daisyhead of fire as the Slavemasters deployed their infiltrator seeds, genewritten killers coiled up foetally inside each drill-tipped missile. The Drakkal came in on wings of fusion fire, closing the trap, outflanking the frigate line of the Unity and blowing them apart.

It was a textbook example, a perfect ambush.

The Captain prayed that it would be enough for him to follow through with his plan...

Ten, twenty, a hundred of the Motherbrain's war-machines flared and burned and died in that first instant, as the Blacksteel carrier heeled over hard, presenting its knifeblade edge to the firestorm. Retro-thrusters blazed, trying to put as much clear space as possible between the carrier's burnished skin and the onrushing hordes of the Praetor.

But it was too late for that. Drakkal bolts splashed and shattered against its shields, throwing out streamers of purple lightning. Sparks crawled across the great ship's hide as it ran out its guns, preparing an answering broadside...

"All engines reverse! Bring us back above the ring!" barked the Mitochondriate Captain, swirls of color pulsing across his scaly skin. "There's nothing left for our shields - we have to put some rock between us and those cannons!"

The Justifiable Brutality was much faster than its size would suggest. Even so, it had barely cleared the ragged hole in Saturn's ring when a salvo from the Unity carrier sheared off part of its immense fan-shaped tail, leaving only a ragged stump. Gravity-manipulator tentacles coiled up between the Brutality's ribs pulsed, and the fighter-tender swung about on its axis, aiming its half-mile-wide bow down at its foe. Between them swirled a maelstrom of death - tiny Voidblades and interceptors tracing wild fractal coils across the darkness, binding up the bulky warships of the Unity in cages of ion fire.

One or two wings of drones had managed to scramble from the carrier's canted deck, but far too few to stem the tide. Even as the Praetorian Captain watched another destroyer went down, riven from within by the Slavemasters' little pets, hammered from without by the relentless blastguns of the Gorgons.

It was time to unleash the gamebreaker.

"Captain, we're in range! Loading gantries one through eight are on standby – prepared for antimatter transfer."

The captain smiled, his multiple eyes narrowing.

"Open wide, my pretty! Show them our little surprise!"

+   With   pleasure,   Captain!   With   utmost   pleasure!+

The fore section of the fighter-tender was an immense dozer-blade of spiked chitin, sheathed in riveted steel and carbon. A wall of death, built to bull its way through asteroid fields, to soak up the punishment of fusion blasts and nuclear explosions. Now that great scarred cliff of metal cracked apart along a jagged line, hinging open like the jaws of some prehistoric monster. Inside was all leaping shadows and orange light - arclamps hanging from gantries, illuminating two titanic cannons.

The Justifiable Brutality's *fangs.*

Another broadside erupted from the Unity carrier, tearing into the cloud of living fightercraft which swarmed around it. The frigates and destroyers of the Motherbrain's strike-force were in tatters - ruined and blackened twists of metal, cored out and drilled through by fusion fire, their internal systems ripped to shreds by the neurbonded Bastarnae of the Slavemasters.

That was victory, of a kind. That was more than enough for Kataphrakt-Admiral Yrr, snug and safe aboard the Effortless Subjugation. But the Captain of the Brutality wanted more. He wanted advancement, upliftment, an upload into a Kataphrakt body of his own. He wanted a name again - a luxury he had almost forgotten. And the only way he'd ever be noticed by the Subpraetors of the fleet was through an act of suicidal bravery.

The quarter-mile-long cannons which hung suspended inside his fighter-tender's mouth didn't rely on the burned-out batteries which powered its shields and masers. They were loaded with shells the size of freight locomotives, antimatter munitions handled by Excisor thralls in radiation suits and rebreather masks. Great pistons hissed and thudded and they rammed the shells home, and targeting glyphs shimmered across the diamond dome before the Captain's eyes. He smiled, his mandibles peeling back from his purple lips as he tasted the thrill of destruction...

The recoil from the Fangs rocked the entire ship beneath him, and lights flickered and died throughout the warren of pressurized bubbles welded to its bones. Two speeding points of darkness lanced down through the fighter swarm, trailing comet-tails behind them. The auxiliary generators of the Brutality kicked in just in time to save the Captain's sight, turning the viewing dome solid black.

Space flared white and faded to purple. Hard radiation blasted out in waves.

But the Unity carrier was still intact, its overloaded shields coruscating with tongues of violet fire.

Impossible! Unthinkable! But true, nonetheless.

"Bring us closer! They have to break soon! More speed! Load the Fangs for another salvo!"

The Captain huffed methane from a plastic tube, working his mandibles in frustration. That first blast had wounded the Blacksteel filth, crippled their defenses... but hundreds of his own thrall-ships had been reduced to ashes in the same terrible instant. His four long-

fingered hands were all over the keyboards in front of him, processing, calculating...

Acceptable losses. Collateral damage. *After all his years in Fleet Command, the words came almost unbidden. After all, what did a few Navigators, a few Excisors matter when weighed against the near-godhood of a sleek new Kataphrakt form?*

Nothing

The Captain urged even more power from his neurobonded vessel, tightening his psionic claws around its mind. The Brutality *squealed in ecstatic pain as it rolled into a powerdive, as another pair of shells were levered into its mandibular cannons...*

This time the Blacksteel shields broke.

In the afterglow of the antimatter explosion the entire upper deck of the Unity carrier glowed sullen red, its skin melted down to slag. Its shield generators were ruined - burnt down to blackened nubs. But its guns...

The full force of the carrier's broadside slammed into the Brutality *as it plunged through the rings of Saturn - there was simply nothing left in the space between them to stop it. The great overarching ribs of the fighter-tender cracked and carbonized under the lash of maser-fire. Thousands of Thralls perished in a heartbeat, their pressurized modules blown apart, their genecrafted bodies too weak to survive in the vacuum.*

This time the living starship's scream was one of rage and agony, a spike driven through the Captain's skull. But he hung on grimly, even as the auxiliary lights flickered out, even as a slew of warning indicators flashed blood-red across his screens.

"One more salvo. One more..."

A rolling strobe-flash of gunfire stitched across the blackness of space between the two ships. It was one-sided, furious - desperate. In those last few seconds the A.I. core slung alongside the carrier realized its fate, and it blew its mooring clamps. A chuff of frozen oxygen burst out from the command unit's reinforcing struts, and batteries of retro-thrusters burned blue against the dark.

Too late.

The Justifiable Brutality *struck home like a hammer swung by some elder god, tearing the Blacksteel ship almost clean in half with its gaping jaws. In the airless vacuum of space there was no sound, no scream of tortured metal and living bone. There was only silence; a terrible, rending silence filled with flying debris and plumes of exploding gas, with the shattered bodies of Excisors and Clericals and the twisted steel* limbs of Blacksteel combat units. Then the jaws of the Brutality slammed closed on its prey, leaving only a tiny gap. And inside the dying starship's maw an orange glow flickered, the promise of annihilation...

The Captain howled in triumph. His callused fist slammed down on the firing trigger, unleashing two hundred gigatons of explosive death into the ruptured belly of his foe. At the same time one of his other hands pulled the ripcord of his Suit, activating its jump coils...

Or not.

Both the Justifiable Brutality and the nameless Unity carrier-ship were consumed in a fireball brighter than the sun, flaring for a second as a tiny blemish against the curve of Saturn. But the Captain never left his post, even as his skin and flesh and bones were blasted away to roiling subatomic soup.

Kataphrakt Yrr was no fool - he understood perfectly the concept of 'dead man's boots'. And while he was most certainly not a man, neither was he a naive newspawned, fresh from uploading. The Captain's bravery would be noted; a tiny plaque presented to his proud parents on whatever backwater world they called home. But he'd never be elevated to the rank of Kataphrakt - and he would never threaten Yrr's own prospects for promotion.

The long, lean alien commander sighed, his four hands clasped behind his back as he scanned the tactical holos before him. Battle was joined. At last.

And if all went well he was definitely in line for upliftment, and the newly-forged body of a Subpraetor Minor...

2196 Ante Arbitrium
Hacked Up

KAITO REACHED THE 'mersive deck out of breath, stopping at the bottom of its pipework stairs as his pulse pounded in his temples.

It took him a moment to realize that something was wrong.

There was a walkie-talkie hanging from the rail on a thin plastic strap, hissing static. Blue light flickered around the edges of the door, but there was no sound from inside - perhaps the full complement of Pent' ops were plugged in, trying to crack Elysium's locked-down datanet...

That theory went straight to hell when Kaito pushed open the door and came face to face with a corpse.

At first he didn't even recognize the two Pent sailors as human. They were fat cocoons of bubbled plastic swinging on a pair of hooks, blood pooling and dripping beneath them in the dark. When he picked out what remained of a face sagging upside down from one of them the bile rose up in the back of his throat.

Whatever had worked this butchery had taken time with its art. It had sliced their lips open from ear to ear, stapling them back into hideous grins which erased their other features... all but their hollow and empty eyes. This wasn't the work of an assassin or a wet-ops specialist. It was the calling card of a psychopath.

The Kayzi's mind twitched, flashing back to the waking nightmare of the Worm - that alien sequestrator which had promised hell on earth.

But no. This was cold, *calculated*. These bodies were trussed up neat and tight, a warning and a promise. The thing which the Core drone had seen, that crawling darkness which terrified even Abdulafia 330 - *that* could never conceive of such sick artistry.

It would never let so much fresh meat go *undevoured*...

Kaito crept across the tiny guardroom, his shadow stretched across the plasterboard walls as he stepped in front of the guards' tiny twodeeo set. He could feel their dead eyes following him as he reached the great hole in the wall, a gaping mouth of darkness.

Hells! Even Haszan would have trouble causing this kind of damage... the cheap wood was smashed to splinters, and the two-by-four studs as well. You could have driven a bus through into the 'mersive deck, an echoing chasm lit with blue sparks and frantic red touchscreens.

He pulled a pencil-torch from his belt and swept its light down the cold metal cylinder, playing over bloodstains, over reams of torn-out cables, smashed screens and bulletholes...

Then he caught the first headless operator full in his beam, a blood-soaked torso slumped across a 'mersive couch.

Kaito's hand scrabbled for a lightswitch, slipping and sliding over the smooth metal curve of the wall. White neon sputtered weakly to life overhead, one solitary tube swinging on a single wire, illuminating hell.

Three Pentecostals had died here, though the sheer volume of blood spoke of a massacre all out of proportion to the bodycount. They lay headless in their rigs, as though some kind of vicious new ice had torn through their 'phones and goggles, detonating their skulls. Kaito felt vomit rise in his throat. It could just as easily have been him.

The luckless hackers had been crucified on their own rigs, desecrated after death with skeins of wire and plugs rammed down their gaping throats. One of them even had a twodeeo cube balanced on his bleeding stump of a neck, blazing white with static.

And something more...

As Kaito watched, fighting back his nausea, a face began to coalesce out of the churning pixels; a smooth white face with red-raw eyes and a snarling, lipless mouth. It hung above the body of the Pent' operator like a phantom, laughing silently at the carnage around it.

Then the sound kicked in, crackling through a battery of hidden speakers.

"Hello, Kaito," said the Scarecrow. "Kaito Kayzi, the little wannabe Magus. Jaqub Haszan's inconvenient shadow... I've never met you, Kayzi, but I already *hate* you. Nothing personal, of course... I hate all of you equally. But I have a particular loathing for *your type.*"

Now the other screens - those left unbroken - were switching themselves on one by one, all showing the hateful visage of Aitken Straw.

"You know what I mean, Neophyte. You're everybody's best friend, the bloody *wunderkind* with an answer for everything... just tripping blithely from one disaster to the next with all Elysium happy to take care of you. Jaq, and Abdulafia, and even the damned Compliance Division!" The Scarecrow narrowed his lidless eyes, seething with malice. "You think *I* couldn't do what you've done? That I'm any less deserving of the adulation of your precious *Illuminatus*? But oh no... *he* turned me down. His nomad filth-tribe wouldn't have me! They said I was unstable, *psychotic*... but I know better..."

Now a pair of bladed hands came up into the shot, peeling back Aitken'smask with a sound like crusted bandages torn from a wound. Underneath the eggshell plastic he was a horror, a nightmare of veins and raw muscles radiating pure hatred.

"Who wants to be *friends* with a thing like this?" he hissed, as blood spattered from his flayed face and into the upturned cup of his mask. "Who needs my mind, and my skill, when it comes with a face like mine?" He pushed the shell back onto his skull with an obscene liquid sound. "Don't bother to answer. Don't worry about it. Just know that even the most charmed life has its bad days, Kayzi. This is gonna be one of them."

Now the screens were changing, switching over one by one to a shot of Jaqub Haszan, a black and unmistakable silhouette lashed by sheets of driving rain.

"See, you're not the one we came here for. And by *we*, I mean the gang - the Emerald City Gang. We're a media sensation, or so I'm told. We're here for your big ugly friend out there, but I thought I'd do you the courtesy of explaining."

Only the screen perched above the ruined cadaver of the Pentecostal op was left now, filled to the edges with the maniacal face of Aitken Straw.

"Seems his old boss wanted him dead pretty bad. And Ruby is nothing if not *accomodating*... especially when she gets to exercise her mean streak. As for you - you just piss me off personally. So I thought I'd make this whole situation a moral conundrum for your edification - like this. You *could* run off after him, try to stop us... not that it would do you much good. Or you could try and save a whole bunch of useless humps back there in Elysium. Your choice. Either way, there's gonna be blood. And *that*, my friend, is enough for yours fuckin' truly."

Kaito was shocked into silence, hardly breathing as he wrapped his hands around the little twodeeo cube. He dashed it to the floor to shatter amid the blood, digging his fingers into his eyes as the room began to spin. There were voices outside, curses, the sound of boots on steel... and then hot white light flooded the 'mersive chamber, pinning the Kayzi in a crossfire of torch beams.

"Oh my God. Oh, sweet Jesus Christ..." said one of the silhouettes on the other side of the light. "What has he done? *What the hell happened to them?*"

Kaito slumped to the floor, feeling broken glass under his hands and knees. He heard the bolts snap back on a dozen submachine guns, the scuffling footsteps of Pent' marines moving out to encircle him.

"All dead, Sir. All of them! And he's torn up the whole 'mersive system, the war-engines... the whole damn thing."

The Kayzi felt the muzzle of an antiquated plastic automatic pressed up against his temple, and his lips pulled back from his teeth in a sardonic smile. It was a setup, a meatspace hack, and Aitken Straw had played him like a fool. Any second now one of these pious thugs would decide to let God sort him out...

"Don't be a goddamn *idiot*, Burton!" barked a voice all barbed-wire and hellfire. "Haven't you filthy maggots ever seen a warzone before? You think a pencil-neck *runt* like this one could do all of this? Him and which *god-damned army*, soldier?"

"S-sorry, Sergeant," muttered the man with his gun to Kaito's head, easing off the pressure by a tiny increment. "But he's an outlander, an *Elysian*. And he's the one 'Deut said was a hacker - one of them *Hashishin* boys."

"That don't give him *super-powers*, now, does it Burton?" sighed the Sergeant, swaggering forward through the blinding light. He hunkered down next to Kaito, digging his callused fingers into the Elysian's shoulder. "Look here, boy... c'mon, I'm not gonna kill you - what the hell did you see here?"

The Sergeant's face was a weatherbeaten roadmap of creases and scars, with two black crucifix tattoos carved into the topography of his cheeks. His hair was an iron-gray stubble, cropped back to a severe line against his olive skin.

"Contract killers," croaked the Kayzi, struggling to his feet. "Four of them. Bad sons of bitches... they're here for... for the other *outlander*. Jaqub Haszan."

"So you *are* the Electromagus. Good. You think you can get this mess up and running again?" Something in the hard-bitten old soldier's tone made it obvious that 'no' wasn't an answer he wanted to hear. "Well?"

Kaito looked around at the ruin of the 'mersive suite, the torn-out wires, the shattered screens, the headless bodies and the blood... but his trained eye saw that Aitken Straw and his friends hadn't had time to truly wreck the *Archangel Uriel*'s electronic weapons. It seemed that the Pentecostal marines had answered the Scarecrow's moral conundrum for him.

"I can probably salvage one working interface. Given time, and the right tools... but it's going to be difficult. And Jaq..."

"We'll worry about your friend - and our uninvited guests. Everyone has his place and his part to play, outlander. We're the ones with the guns."

Kaito's mind was freewheeling on automatic now, his bio-onboard probing for wireless links into the hardware of the 'mersive suite. It wasn't beyond repair... but it was just this side of scrap.

"Are any of you guys engineers?" he asked, walking over to the one remaining interface couch. "I'm going to need another couple pairs of hands here, and a whole lot of spare parts..."

The Sergeant clapped him on the shoulder, his mouth twitching into a tight little grin.

"That's the right attitude, soldier! Klaus, Freeman, you're under this man's command now - get him what he wants, no questions. If those Ashishim don't know we're coming we're going to get caught in the mother of all crossfires."

The two marines didn't look too impressed with his command, but they snapped off crisp salutes before they shrugged off their backpacks, unloading an array of toolboxes and datablocks in tidy rows.

"And outlander - we'll take them down. Don't worry about that. If your friend can hold out another ten minutes he's going to have enough fire support to take out an army."

Kaito didn't see them leave - he was already deep into the guts of the last 'mersive system, an electric screwdriver in one hand and an analytical scanner in the other. Somewhere in here was the key to the *Uriel*'s nuclear arsenal, and once he found it...

The scumbags who were after Jaq Haszan might feel more inclined to negotiate if they were riding on a multi-megaton bomb, and Kaito's hand was on the trigger.

Ω

The first blow blindsided him, coming looping in out of the rain like a stray bullet, a fist the size of his head decked out with gold-plated knuckle-dusters. It lifted him off his feet and slammed him up against the cold steel of the Uriel's hull, knocking the breath from his lungs. Black and purple fireworks popped and blurred behind his eyes as he scrabbled at the rain-slick metal, twitching sideways just before a second king-hit staved in the plating beside him.
Good gods! Such power! What the hell was it - some kind of mekan? That super-Cyben freak Tsien gone bad on them again?

But when his vision cleared all he saw through the hissing spray was a hulking giant of a man, bulked out with raw slabs of muscle, his face hidden behind a stitched-up leather hood. Little beads of rain trickled down his massive arms, over his painted-on smiley-face as he stood there, panting, blood dripping from his skinned knuckles.

Then a blaze of crackling electric fire lit up his face from below - from a steel shock-collar clamped tight around his almost non-existent neck. The man-beast howled, throwing his hands up over his head, leaping forward to slam into the wall with both fists.

Jaq had never known that he could dodge so quickly.

Back behind him in the rain he could hear screams, cries, the sounds of battle. Guns cracked loud and urgent in the rain, and a bloodied Pent' sailor fell from above, swallowed up by the heaving ocean.

"Dammit Leon, you *missed*!" yelled a woman's voice, loud enough to carry even over the creak and slam of the *Uriel*'s lumbering progress. "Do I have to do everything myself?"

Jaq glimpsed a shimmer of red in the haze, a blurred and liquid-fast form which leaped up to perch atop a section of rusted pipe. Just in time he saw the twin laser-sights of Ruby's pistols, picked out by falling drops of spray. He faked right and then rolled left, feeling the hull of the great ship shudder as it was pierced by flying steel.

Haszan heard curses behind him, and the sound of agile feet picking their way from pipe to girder to beam high above him. That red shadow was fast - *inhumanly* fast - and he could all but feel the hot breath of the masked giant on the back of his neck as he ran.

"Pentecostals! *Marines!* Aitken, get back there and stall them."

Jaq wasn't built for running. So he didn't know that old adage about never looking back over your shoulder. Along a swaying catwalk, down a flight of stairs...

They're right behind me! But who the hell are they? Confed? Omnivasive? Wh...

He slid around a corner, his boots skating out wide on the slick treadplate, and came face to face with the Tin Man.

The scarred old mekan was locked to the heaving deck with magnetic clamps, his twin heavy rifles switched out for a more assault-friendly package. Jaq stared down the four cold black barrels of an automatic shotgun to his left, and the hissing muzzle of a flamethrower on his right. His eyes widened, his breath caught in his throat... and then the *Uriel* slammed down into a trough between the waves, throwing off the Tin Man's aim for just a second.

A blast of caltrop shot and a tongue of purple-blue flame tore through the air right where his head had been, but Haszan was already off and running again, ducking under the stairs as the Tin Man's laser-sights licked at his heels.

"There he is! I see him, I see him!"

The voice came from behind him - the giant had doubled back, closing the trap on him. Jaq flexed his chrome fingers, snapping the tiny blades out from their tips.

If only that mad old freak 'Deut Jones hadn't taken his guns...

Footsteps were approaching from either side now; the lumbering tread of that great imbecilic giant, and the whir and thud of the Tin Man's magnetized piston-legs.

Then Haszan saw the firehose bolted to the wall under the stairs - and with it the bright red extinguisher, the axe, and the fire-blanket...

Especially the axe.

The Tin Man caught it first.

Jaq slid out from cover, snarling as he brought the wicked fire-axe up over his shoulder like a tomahawk, one-handed. The ancient mekan's head tilted to one side, quizzical, lining up his thoroughly modern weapons to counter the blade.

In all his years of warfighting, nobody had ever tried to go so low tech! What was...

Haszan's arm blurred as he released the axe, sending it whirling end over end to bite deep into the Tin Man's shoulder. His scarred armor-plating peeled back with a shower of sparks as the blade struck home. Rain and spray dripped and sizzled across the exposed circuitry there, and when the old war-machine tried to unload a clip of shotgun shells into his tormentor he found his left arm paralysed - useless.

The flamethrower, on the other hand...

The Tin Man's burning green eyes narrowed, his painted skull-face grinning in the haze.

A stream of purple fire erupted from the muzzle of the flamer, evaporating the rain in its path. Jaq had ducked back under the stairs, but they were no protection. The fire played over his cowering shadow, hot enough to peel the paint from the walls, hot enough to roast him alive...

The pressure dial on the flamer's underslung fuel cannister dropped down to zero. With a hiss and a whine the fire guttered out, leaving a fan of charred devastation behind it, a killing-ground in which nothing moved but a few curls of blistered paint.

Then something under the blackened stairwell shifted, unfurled, threw off its protective skin of flame-proof armor...

Jaqub Haszan came up from behind his fire-blanket shield like an avenging angel, swinging a fat red cylinder with both hands.

"I see you now! I'll get you, little man!"

A voice was roaring behind him, but Jaq was single-minded in his determination.

And the Tin Man, both of his weapons rendered utterly useless, was powerless to stop him as he brought the extinguisher down in a blurring diagonal stroke, colliding with his head like a wrecking ball. The backhand sent the mekan reeling, his clamps sprung loose from the heaving deck. For a second the two combatants felt gravity fall away as the giant ship reached the crest of a wave. Then the *Uriel* came down, and Jaq's staved-in makeshift weapon swung back, synchronized. As the twin hulls of the Pentecostal sub slammed into the churning gray ocean the fire extinguisher came in sideways, lifting the Tin Man off his feet. He slipped back up against the rail, his green eyes blazing in the rain... then the blunt end of Haszan's weapon slammed full into his face, and the rusted pipework gave way.

Those glowing green eyes irised open in sudden surprise, and the Tin Man's deadly hands scrabbled in vain for purchase. With guns instead of fingers he was utterly helpless...

The splash sent a wave of seething water up over the deck, and Jaq swore, hunched over his ruined fire extinguisher. Behind him he could hear the thunderous tread of heavy boots, a howl of outrage and pain as ten thousand volts lit up Big Leon's shock collar. He checked the safety, pulled the ripcord, and prayed that he hadn't battered the poor thing too far out of shape...

Big Leon was hardly a weapon of finesse. His charge had all the unstoppable force of continental drift, accelerated to the pace of a speeding juggernaut. When Haszan stepped out in front of him he smiled behind his mask, spreading his arms out wide, ready to mash his prey into unrecognizable jelly.

Then the world went white...

Freezing, blinding white, a localized blizzard playing across the mutant's face from the high-pressure cylinder in Jaq's hands. When the stream finally tapered off Haszan pressed his advantage - he threw the spent extinguisher with all his strength, hurling it overhand against Leon's chest.

It knocked the wind from the giant's lungs, but even blind and breathless his momentum carried him on. Leon went from a lumbering run to an uncontrolled roll and slide, roaring incomprehensibly as he fell.

Jaq leaped over him as he slid across the slick metal deck of the *Archangel Uriel*, tucking his knees up to his chest as Leon's hands lashed out wild. The vast twin-hulled ship was canted upward, riding the swells, and the deck was a slippery slope, all the way down to...

Jaq winced as he watched Leon's ponderous bulk slam into a solid steel bulkhead door - head first, the sickening crack of broken bone carrying even over the storm. Still, the giant wasn't dead - a groan, a twitch of his great hairy hands... that was enough to get Jaq running again. After all, there were at least two more of these freaks out to kill him.

If he'd stood there admiring his handiwork for a fraction of a second more they would have finished the job. As it was, Ruby's railpistol blast tore two perfect holes in his ragged trenchcoat, tugging at his shoulders as he ran. The animated flames which played across its fabric stuttered and blurred in the rain, throwing a dirty halo up around him.

Dorothea Alvarez wasn't entirely sorry she'd missed.

The renegade Kheptarch smiled, looking down from her haunt up among the pipes and wires, and she slipped her guns back into their holsters. A tiny voice hissed and crackled from her earpiece - Aitken Straw, reporting in from the bow of the *Uriel*.

"I'm done here," whispered the Scarecrow, and Ruby could imagine him standing amid the shredded ruin of that luckless Pentecostal squad. "How's the hunt? Did Leon get his hands on that Subcity rat yet?"

"The *rat* appears to be quite a resourceful beast. Certainly more of a package than Vanecke's usual goons could handle. I think our dear Direktor was actually *afraid* of this one."

"But Leon? Tin Man? Last I checked, they were right on top of him..."

"Leon's a twitching wreck. And that outmoded old mekan is probably walking back to Elysium on the seabed. He took them both out in a matter of *seconds*, Aitken."

There was silence from the other end of the wireless link for a second, then a low whistle of appreciation.

"We haven't had a live one since I don't know when, Ruby. I was almost starting to think we'd weeded them all out..."

The renegade's luscious lips pulled back into a smirk as she watched Haszan duck in through an open doorway, red light flashing from his chrome hand.

"This one's mine, Scarecrow. All mine. You just keep these Pent' freaks out of our way while we play our little game..."

"You and your *entertainments!*" laughed Straw. "You can take Ruby out of the Kheptarchy, but you can't take the Kheptarchy out of Ruby..."

Her smile turned bitter, then, twisting into a snarl as she dropped lightly down to the heaving deck.

"Save the homilies, Aitken. A girl's got to have her distractions... or she might just remember who got her into this mess in the first place."

The Scarecrow cursed under his breath, looking around him at the dismembered bodies of his foes. The old one, the warrior with the iron-gray stubble and the black crucifix tattoos - he'd fought well, but in the end they'd all tasted his steel. In the end, *everybody* did. The thought of a *live one*, of worthy prey...it almost made him excited, even after all these years.

Ahh well. All wasn't doom and gloom. At least that little shit Kayzi had gotten his comeuppance. Oh, to see the look on his face right now!

Ω

Kaito's face was bathed in flickering blue light as he eased the 'mersive goggles up to his eyes, squinting into two tiny slivers of another world. Six gleaming mekanik arms reared up around his head like metal cobras; their fangs were the tiny gold plugs of intracranial nervejacks. Already his bio-onboard was socketed in tight to the single Ops suite they'd been able to cobble together - and the vast translucent shape of the Pentecostals' slicer system was beginning to haze in over reality, warping the faces of his two marine companions.

"Mister Freedman, bring up the power to the transmitters. I've just got to pray that we've put this pile of junk together right..."

The Pent' sailor slowly eased the final lever home, and Kaito settled back onto the bloodstained leather of the 'mersive couch, dropping the rubber goggles over his eyes. With a series of tiny clicks and hisses the cranial plugs slotted in, and their attendant arms peeled away. Now it was just the Kayzi and the machine, the unfamiliar thunder and hum of the *Uriel's* electronic war-engines throbbing in his skull...

There was no denying the power of Deuteronomy Jones' jury-rigged wireless transmitters - the connection, when it dropped in, was a crisp and smooth as the one from Kaito's own downtown hab. But instead of appearing on the mirrored surface of a virtual ocean, this time the Kayzi materialized high in the air, looking down on the absurdly foreshortened curvature of a liquid planet...

It was the whole of the Wetsystems, laid out before him as if he was some archaic astronaut surveying the Earth from orbit. The sky he hung in was a swirling melange of black on black, textured whorls of night licking up against each other like colliding galaxies. That, at least, was normal.

But down below it was a whole other story - the azure sphere of the Wetsystems was no longer tranquil and calm, blazing from within with the ghost-lights of living glass coral.

Now the sea was dark, choppy and heaving, exactly like the ocean which crashed against the *Uriel*'s bows. As Kaito watched another great jagged accretion of blue-green light went out, extinguished deep under the waves. Something was shutting the systems down, throwing their artificial brain-tissue into torpor. It could only be the work of Kronos.

Kaito willed himself closer, stooping like a falcon down through the atmosphere, through fractal swirls of cloud feathered away to mist. The surface of the boiling sea sped by beneath him, blurred with acceleration - until he picked out a red light welling up from below.

Something had infected the Wetsystems here - something which stank of that vile possessor the Vilicus had shown him. It had taken the sunken gardens of the 'systems and turned them inside-out, revealing their cruel secret...

A city-sized web of cracks and fractures spread out from the pulsing heart of it, spiraling up into great cancerous growths, trees of pain upon which thousands of souls were crucified. They were the dead, personality constructs harvested by Kronos to drive the Forge. That bondage was cruel enough, but now...

Once, this had been purgatory. Now it was Hell.

The terrors of Magus Verlaine had nothing on the things he saw down there... it was beyond description, beyond comprehension, a horrorworks of throbbing, bleeding flesh, stitched and pinned and stapled together. The stench of decay reached him even through the firewalls of the Pent' slicer. And despite of their torn and broken state the poor things were *alive* - alive and suffering for the delectation of their master.

So it was true. *This* was the sequestrator, the thing which had promised Abdulafia 330 a place as one of its Exalted. *The thing which he'd released into the world...*

Kaito bit back on his fear, his hands flying over the virtual controls of the slicer system. It stripped the view below back down to glowing wireframes, wiping the scenes of brutality and torture from before his eyes. *There was nothing he could do for them. Nothing. He was here to save the living, nothing more...*

He followed the edge of the infection as it ramified through familiar conduits and reefs of glass, deeper into the dark zones. Toward a star guttering beneath the imaginary ocean - the war-room of the Ashishim.

It was besieged on all sides, surrounded by towering fractal pinnacles of light. Kaito was sure that if he peeled back his protective filters he'd see things impaled on those frozen lightning-bolts which would break his mind.

He concentrated, feeling the Pentecostal slicer solidify around him, a green and white missile of translucent code with four swept-forward wings, its databores and countervirals manifest as a payload of cannons and missiles. There'd be a target for every one of them if his search programs were telling him the truth - the water between him and the Ashishi fortress was a boiling sea of carnage.

As he upped his magnification he saw just how bad it was.

The toughest metavirals and H-K systems the Reclamationists could throw out were holding back Asag'raal tooth and claw, blasting his creatures apart in waves. The alien possessor was by no means subtle, and the Electromagi were light-years beyond it in terms of technique and skill. But the delicate balance of the Wetsystems meant nothing to the Saprophytes, and they were *legion*.

The slave-virals of the Worm weren't artificial programs, or even slicers piloted by desperate operators. They were the damned, and they screamed as they attacked, seeking oblivion. The poor once-human things had been transformed into nightmares, their bodies intersected with blades of bloody glass. The weeping teratoma at the heart of the Scourge was almost beautiful by comparison.

As Kaito watched, a beast cut in slices and held together with wheels of light broke through the Electromagi lines, screaming a one-note song of agony. Its arms and hands were sawn down the middle with razor glass, and it swung them like axes, butchering a pair of H-Ks in its path. The Ashishi ops were on it in seconds, their serrated slicer-blades flashing in the crimson light, blood billowing out from its butchered body... But the damage was done. Kaito watched the H-K units collapse into a haze of static as the disease tripped their failsafes, leaving a hole in the Ashishim defenses.

That was all he needed.

The Pentecostal machine was slower than his own custom Ops unit, but it was still far faster than the clumsy, brutal thralls of Asag'raal. Kaito screamed out his Magi designation as he powered for the gap, broadcasting his identity to the slicers who were lining him up in their sights.

Databore missiles streaked out from a dozen insectoid machines, and for an instant the Kayzi thought he was done for, that his allies had marked him as *infected*. Then the brace of warheads spiraled past him, pulling together in his wake, and he was through the breach. They detonated behind him with a deep subsonic concussion, amid the delighted screams of Asag'raal's children.

Back on the 'mersive deck of the *Archagel Uriel* Kaito's body was trembling and pale, his face sheened with sweat. The Pent' marines hunched over his biomonitors cursed as his heart-rate and blood pressure spiraled up and up, pushing needles into the red.

But inside, under the waters of the virtual sea Kaito Kayzi was still in control. He'd made it through to his allies; to the only clan in the Last City who could hope to prevail. The Illuminatus would know what to do, even if Kronos himself was blind with panic...

Kaito flipped switches, peeling away the translucent skin of his slicer, the polygonal panels folding in upon themselves like impossible origami. He hung weightless and naked in the warm dark water, staring down the guns of a thousand Ashishi Ops.

"Stand down! Stand down! He's one of us!"

A voice lashed out across the open band, and the Reclamationists turned back to their bloody task, leaving the Kayzi alone before a single immense slicer-system, a machine like a great glass crab. The Ashishi eye-and-dagger was etched into its deep green shell.

"Welcome," said that disembodied voice. "Kaito 131. *Kayzi*, if I were to use your outland name... but surely this is all wrong? Your trace goes back too far - far outside the city. How can this be?"

The young neophyte knew then that he was in the presence of a master - one of Verlaine's brothers. Only *they* could see the lingering trace of an Operator's wake through the virtual ocean, and only an ancient would be able to pilot a slicer of such size and power, his quicksilver mind breathing life into its pincers and hooks and cannons.

"I... I'm coming in from offshore, My Lord Magus. From your allies, the Pentecostals. From Deuteronomy Jones."

The crab's intricate mouthparts fluttered and twitched at the mention of his name, and Kaito had to remind himself that this was the Magus' true form - his human body was just a cybernetic husk.

"Deut' Jones is no ally of mine, neophyte!" rumbled the beast of glass. "Perhaps, before the reclamation, he had certain... *arrangements* with our blessed Illuminatus. But now - now it is politically expedient to deny them. The Vatican are good neighbors, and terrible enemies."

The Kayzi was choked up with indignation for a second - the city was tearing itself apart, and this pompous fool was worried about *politics*! But then he realized who and *what* he was addressing. The High Magus had lived through innumerable petty wars, through the Reclamation and the Long March... such a creature knew nothing of urgency.

"My Lord," he said, "expediency aside, we have with us the means to save tens of thousands of people. The *Archangel Uriel* is coming, and we must tell the city. Jones is going to dock alongside the Ashishim Territories, and you need to be prepared."

"Preposterous!" replied the crab, clicking its pincers in frustration. "Any such breach of protocol would have to be voted on by the council. The Illuminatus would have to..."

"Then *ask him!* I have to do *something*, or they're all going to die!"

"Very well. So long as matters here are kept in hand, I can't see the harm of it... The Marshall of the Spillway is the one you need. I'll patch you through to a drone in the War-room, and you can put you case to her directly."

The crab reached out with one of its immense translucent pincers, its blades creaking open around Kaito where he hung suspended in the water. Behind him the frantic battle continued, as the legions of the Worm threw themselves up against the Ashishim barrier with unabated fury.

Just as he thought the claw was about to shear him in half a tiny hatch irised open near its base, and a thin tentacle of jointed glass slid out, human fingers unfurling at its tip. It touched the haze of code which blurred around Kaito once, twice, sliding and clicking sections of the Pent' slicer system, reforming its delicate architecture. Trying to resist the vast, insistent mind behind that touch would be like trying to drink the ocean dry.

One last shift, and it was done.

Kaito's field of view ballooned out wide as his consciousness was imprinted onto a camera drone, one of hundreds lost in the panic and bustle of the Ashishim command center. His mind slipped as he tried to grasp at the controls of the little mekan, sending it stumbling forward on a handful of insect legs. He spun the lens globe atop the drone as he went, drinking in his surroundings.

It was utter, seething chaos; a vast riot of men and machines somehow working toward the same goal. It was the very heart of the Ashishim.

He'd never seen this place before; an amphitheater cut into the bedrock beneath Elysium, its wall of patched-together monitors racked up in scaffolding, its sunken rows of op suites manned by sweating, twitching Submagi...

This was the powerhouse of his chosen clan, the engine room of the Reclamation. There was no time for awe or curiosity, though. He had to find the Marshall of the Spillway before the *Archangel Uriel* came into range. The last thing they needed was friendly fire, especially considering the Pent' sub's nuclear cargo.

Kaito's little mekan scuttled between the legs of *Dervashi* and Ashishim techs, under desks and around 'mersive couches, picking its way carefully across the thick carpet of wires and cables which covered the stone floor of the war-room. Luckily the camera-headed machine came with limited bio-onboard access - he was able to query the Ashishi datanet as he went, lighting up every one of the toiling revolutionaries with a tiny neon halo.

Ranks, names and serial numbers glittered above them like a swirling galaxy, and it only took the Kayzi a moment to pick out the Marshall - a tall woman, her iron-gray hair caught up in braids, pacing the length of a mezzanine balcony as a cluster of mekan swarmed at her heels. Every now and then she'd turn to one of the scuttling robots, and her fingers would blur across the keyboard it lifted up on insect arms, conducting her own little part of the war. Lower-ranking officers of the Spillway staff were seated at desks below her, keeping up a constant stream of orders and codes into their hanging microphones.

Kaito ducked and swerved between them, teetering on the edge of the mezzanine for a second before he checked his momentum. Then he was right in front of her, a tiny insignificant thing pinned to the treadplate by her stare.

One of her eyebrows arched as he struggled with the mekan's

systems, its legs twitching and clicking in place. His hologram unfurled from it like a glass flower, blurred around the edges.

"Marshall Eysha - Eysha 209," he began, his voice sounding small and far away through the drone's speakers. "I am Magus Noviate Kayzi, here with important news. His Lordship guarding the Wetsystems access sent me to you directly."

Well - it wasn't exactly the truth. But it wasn't quite a lie either. Kaito counted himself lucky that the drone he inhabited didn't have a high-rez face.

"And what could Magus Belakim possibly want with me, neophyte? Our war is flesh and blood - all of which is too precious to waste. There are *things* out there that we're only just holding back! The spillway side is a bloody massacre. And the docks... we have to just kill them all, you know. We can't sift out the refugees from the infected..."

There was a haunted look in Marshall Eysha's eyes for a second, but it flickered and faded as one of her slaved mekan clattered around in front of her, mewling and beeping for attention. She scowled as she saw what was displayed on its little screen, her fingers liquid-fast across the keys.

"So tell me, Magus Noviate. What's so damned important that talking to you has just cost me another ten lives?"

Kaito took a deep breath, a gesture utterly lost between his flesh and the camera drone's processors. Then something clicked over in his skull, back down a thin and fragile link to the bloodstained 'mersive deck of the *Archagel Uriel*. Icons lit up in his head, dancing before his eyes in a blur of hot red trefoils.

Nuclear trefoils.

He really didn't have any time left for explanations.

"Deuteronomy Jones is coming," he began. "The *Archangel Uriel* is headed for your Ashishi docks, and he means to save as many people as he can before the... the *infection* spreads too far. Tell them to be ready, and for the sake of your Gods and his, *hold your fire*. There's enough nuclear ordnance on that boat to blast Elysium to ashes."

Enough for that and more... and now I've got hold of the switch...

The Marshall's brow furrowed with anger, and she reached down, plucking Kaito's mekanik avatar from the floor with one hand. His vision blurred as she shook the little machine by its telescopic neck, her eyes burning into its camera dome.

"We don't run until we're beat, *neophyte*. And we don't take kindly to threats, especially from traitorous little..."

"Do you have *any idea* what I've been through to get here?" cut in the Kayzi, shocking Eysha into silence. "Do you have the *slightest conception* of how fucked up today has been? Well, let me tell you. This little message I'm bringing you comes courtesy of Abdulafia 330 himself, the poor bastard - it's the last thing I ever heard from him. And he told me to pass it on - *we can't fight these things*."

That shut her up. Kaito was willing to bet the Sword of the Illuminatus was something of a folk hero down here, ten feet tall and bulletproof. He took the opportunity to press his case, struggling in the Marshall's grip.

"He tried to stop them, you know. Your best and bravest, and they left him crying and broken under what's left of the Valley View. Now, I'm just a Subcity scumbag, a *novice* - not even sworn to your clan. But I had a lot of respect for 330 - at least he led from the *front* instead of cowering in a gods-damned bunker."

That hurt. He saw it on her face, the hard lines which spoke of years stuck behind a desk, carrying the burden of leadership. But there was more.

"I've managed to convince that mad old zealot Jones to save your sorry asses. I've managed to stay alive long enough to get this message to you. Now, I suggest you get to integrating this new information into your battle strategy. Because the next place I'm going is up to Omnivasive, where I plan on slicing their firewalls to shreds. I'm going to tell everyone left alive in the city that their ride is pulling up to the Ashishim docks - so you'd better be prepared for a few visitors."

Kaito's anger seemed to drain all the fight out of Eysha 209, and she slumped down into a swivel chair, her little horde of mekan rushing in to support her. Without that tightly-wound rage behind her eyes she was just a tired old woman with far too many responsibilities - one who hadn't slept for far too long. Her fingers unclenched from around the slim metal neck of the camera drone, letting it clatter to the floor in a tangle of limbs.

"So he's dead, is he? Abdulafia 330, the eternal youth... You know, I was in the Academy with him. I was in Gray Nine squad, he was in Seven..." Her eyes were glassy, looking back into the past, into the fires of Reclamation Day. "I saw how he looked at that Jhenna, and I *wished*... but no, he was destined for better things. He was a born *Dervashiman*, and I was just another solider. So he stayed young, cloned fresh each time they cut him down, while I got old, and frail, and desk-bound. I don't suppose they got his crescent this time, did they? Not out from under that mess at the Valley View..."

Kaito wanted to tell her that it was alright, that Abdulafia was still alive and fighting. It would have been quite a scene - the stern-faced Marshall of the Spillway being consoled by a camera drone in the shape of a virus, an eight-legged machine all wires and bulging lenses.

But then the screens behind her lit up with something huge, a black silhouette outlined stark and raw against a mountain of fire. It took a second for Kaito to fix the image in his mind - the scale seemed all wrong, the shape of the crouching, four-armed creature was all out of proportion to the screaming humans who boiled and seethed around its feet. Then the battery of lights hanging from the Vatican walls played across its armored skin, and everyone on the mezzanine froze, shocked into silence.

It was a warmekan bigger than any the Marshall and her officers had ever seen, a hissing mechanical beast shrouded in steam. A great rack of burnished organ-pipes thrust up like a collar behind its helm, and six burning green eyes smoldered in the polished metal there. Two of its fists were clenched down in front of it, in shadow, but its second pair of more gracile hands were outstretched in a fighter's stance, beckoning an unseen enemy.

The image was beamed in to the war-room from an Ashishim aeromekan, a remotely piloted drone with dragonfly wings. It panned tight around the giant machine where it stood at the base of the spillway, taking in its great pistons and artificial muscles, its hand-painted reactive armor and its battery of terrible weapons. The Seraph must have landed from a great height - the concrete was cracked and broken around its steel-shod feet, spattered with the blood of those who hadn't been able to flee fast enough...

Then one of those delicate, immense hands lashed out, too fast to follow, and gripped the little floating camera between its rubber-tipped fingers. The mekan brought the drone up to its faceplate, and the whole war-room squealed and crackled with modem noise.

"Hi there, everyone!" said CeeAn 187, coming in live from the core of her armored Seraph. "I just thought you'd like to know that this thing isn't following the Pontiff's orders any more. I'm going to clean up this gods-damned mess on the spillway, and then we'll see what happens next. Just whatever you do, get your soldiers off the walls, Marshall Eysha. Keep your head down, 'cause it's gonna get ugly!"

Spontaneous cheers, whistles and applause broke out among the Techs and Ops of the Ashishim as CeeAn's voice echoed across the great underground amphitheater. She'd brought them hope amid panic and destruction, and the Vision crackled with the sheer power of it, blazing through the Ashishim like a living spark. Even Kaito could feel it, a wave of emotion which surged up to the jagged ceiling, falling back like rain.

Then the screen went out, the image of Saint Sebastian ripped in half by static.

Frantic technicians hammered their keyboards, checked their connections, cursed... but now it was two screens, now ten, now a hundred. And still the wave raced outward, shutting down terminals and popping sparks from 'mersive rigs as it rolled across the hall. Even the neon tubes stuttered and failed, casting the room into phosphorescent half-darkness. The babel of panic and fear spread like a plague.

Then Kaito's borrowed lenses saw the light.

Eysha had seen it too, and she rose to her feet, shielding her eyes with one hand as it swelled, blossoming from a curving side-corridor until it cast thin, flickering shadows from every surface. The green silk pavilion at the heart of the war-room seemed to catch the light, draw it in... It pulsed with radiance, the black silhouettes of the magi dancing across its sheer fabric like Balinese puppets.

"It's him. He's done it. He's raised the Ark..." breathed Eysha 209, gripping the handrail of the mezzanine tight. Kaito's little drone clattered to the edge, pushing and shoving against the other mekan in the Marshall's entourage. And he saw it all, the instant that Zeon came through the archway, a tiny human shade painted across a storm of white fire.

The Ark's pale corona collapsed in on itself as he crossed the threshold, the light hissing back to its source like water caught up in a riptide. The shadows flipped inverse, streaming away from the Ashishim in shreds, and even the breath was torn from their lungs, the tears tugged from their eyes. The radiance collapsed down in glowing shells, tighter and tighter, down to a glittering haze, a second skin over the vast levitating bulk of the Chrome Ark.

Zeon stood below it - hard, benevolent, stern and wise, a white-haired prophet with the visage of an elder god. He held the Ark up above his head, spinning an inch from his upraised palm. And he smiled.

"My friends. My people. My *children*. The hour is at hand! Kronos staggers and falls in his hubris, the Celestials and Confederates are undone, the Vatican priests cower behind their walls! Tonight we achieve our destiny - the birthright of mankind!"

Now he stepped forward, down into the amphitheater, down the broad stone steps between the crowds of his faithful. There was something in his eyes of Deuteronomy Jones, then - something of the wild preacher touched by fire. But Kaito swore there was something else, too - the look he'd seen deep in the eyes of Chemheads in the gutter, the greedy, soulless look of a junkie who'd kill for his fix.

"It won't be easy, my devoted ones. It's *never* been easy, not since I took the very first step on this narrow and twisting road. But I promise you this. *Not one sacrifice will be in vain.*"

It was something in the way he said the word 'sacrifice' which made Kaito prime the interlocks and disconnect his mind from the camera drone. Some kind of terrible premonition, a burning black aura which bloomed around the Illuminatus' head even as he smiled his fatherly smile.

Then the Chrome Ark flashed once, a single thunderous silent heartbeat of light, throwing the war-room into blistering monochrome.

And the strategists and soldiers of the Ashishim simply ceased to exist, blown away in a storm of radiance.

Kaito saw it all in the brief instant before he fell away down the wireless connection and back into the Wetsystems - the Operators on their couches screaming as their shadows fluttered out like black banners, tearing loose to swirl up and away. The fleeing officers and techs were caught in mid-stride, flashing to incandescence as their shades were swallowed up by the ravenous core of the Ark. He saw Eysha 209's hands gripped tight around the railing, her fingers ablated away to bones as the light rushed up and over her. The Marshall of the Spillway opened her mouth to scream, but in that instant the light ripped her soul from out of her throat; burned her skin and flesh to ashes. Her jawbone fell to the floor, shattering, crumbling, even as every other Ashsihi warrior in the amphitheatre crumbled, dying, enslaved...

They were all thralls to the Ark, all bound to it in the hope of resurrection. Instead they were delivered into hell, rendered down into a writhing maelstrom of plasma which shrieked and moaned as it was drawn into its prison.

The last thing the Kayzi saw was the true face of Illuminatus Zeon - an alien visage, all quicksilver and phosphor, its needle grin like that of some abyssal predator. He was sure that the alien thing was staring straight into his soul as the war-room fell away - mocking him, promising a similar fate to that of his poor doomed 'children'...

Then he was back in the flickering red womb of the Wetsystems, hanging naked beneath the waves. Before him was the great crystal form of Magus Belakim, his pincers half open, his eyes wide and blank at the tips of their stalks. As Kaito watched, tiny cracks skittered across the half-human thing's shell, growing wider and deeper with every breath. There was no spirit left to power the ancient slicer which had been Belakim's surrogate body - he, too had gone to feed the Ark, his centuries of loyal service repaid with death.

It only took the gentlest eddy to shatter him to pieces. The crab splintered, breaking into a million flashing slivers which fell away into the darkness, leaving Katio utterly alone.

Or perhaps... not quite...

He turned around slowly, the hairs rising at the nape of his neck as he felt a thousand malign eyes boring into him. Their hunger was almost palpable in the bloody water; they could sense his connection back to the *Uriel*, back down the wire to all those ripe and innocent souls...

Kaito looked up, and up, and up, into a wall of tortured flesh, slavering, rabid things filled with the power of Asag'raal. The green and white shimmer of the Pentecostal slicer-system unfolded around him before he even had time to curse, but there was no way he could stand and fight.

There were simply too many of them. Before the first demon could slip its chains and dive in to the attack Kaito cranked all his throttles wide open and spiraled up and away, running for his life - and for his very soul.

Ω

The sea foamed and crashed in great curling breakers over the starboard bow of the *Archangel Uriel*, hammering the Pentecostal ship's hull with a wrack of flotsam and wreckage. There was nobody left alive to help the stricken survivors who clung to their makeshift rafts now - Aitken Straw had seen to that. The bulkhead doors were shut tight, locked and braced from outside to keep Ruby Alvarez's precious kill-zone clear of intruders.

And so there were no lookouts to spot the capsized hulk of the *Prosperity* as it came in on the oily swells, jamming in hard against the platforms and railings which girded the *Uriel*'s bow. The Confederate star-and-hammers painted on her flank was ripped open, and lights still burned beneath the water from her drowned superstructure. But there were no refugees on board the *Prosperity* - none living, at least.

Cannon rounds had torn the belly out of the Confed' fisherman - flipping it onto its back to drift in the storm. But the artillerists of the *Archangel Uriel* hadn't quite finished the job, and now something stirred in the cold wet womb of the broken ship, scenting blood in the air...

If there'd been marines or Purity teams with their flamethrowers down on the starboard platform the single saprophyte would never have survived. It was weak, pitifully weak - its dripping flesh diluted by seawater, its host faltering and rotting in its vile embrace. Perhaps, had the *Prosperity* foundered for a minute longer...

But now the thing smelled fresh meat. Now it tasted the pain of a single tortured soul, trapped in a body beneath a pile of the dead...

The saprophyte pulled itself out through the hole in the ruined ship's hull, a slow and painful birth which left it slashed and bleeding from a score of wounds. It dragged itself across the deck of the *Uriel*, slick, graceless, a drowned insect scrabbling for purchase on the slippery steel.

So close... the smell drew it onward, the scintillating prickle of pain against its mind.

It collapsed across the steaming pile of bodies which Aitken Straw had left in his wake, seeping through cloth and flesh and bone, down to where a tiny heartbeat still thundered in a punctured chest.

And it sobbed a prayer of thanks to its master, who had led it to sustenance even across the horror of the great salt ocean. Where there was one, the way could be opened for more. Whether from the damned beyond the veil of death, or the chained souls inside the Wetsystems... it no longer mattered. A tipping point had been reached, and soon (it shuddered with delicious anticipation) the Master would come among them, to sow its seed upon this carcass world...

The Pent' marine had been praying for death for quite some time, gut-shot and bleeding beneath the remains of his squad. Sergeant Malachi had walked right up to that...that... *thing* with the blank white face, the knives for hands, and...

After that it got a little blurry. He remembered the glittering trails of knife-blade fingers in the air, the whiplash splatters of blood, the pain as his ribs snapped one after another and the steel came out through his collarbone.

Then the hot red dark. The sense of fading out... of striving to be one with God.

Then the saprophyte found him, and his prayers took on a new urgency.

Ω

Haszan's first impression of Ruby Dorothea Alvarez wasn't exactly hardwired straight to the higher functions of his brain. He'd run into a dead end; a chapel, vaulted and gothic and stark, hung with tapestries and crosses before a black stone altar.

At the center of the granite slab rose a steel crucifix, a slab of pitted metal the color of molten lead.

Fitting, perhaps, for his funeral. The railgun slugs had been nipping at his bootheels all the way, and he was sure that the next pair would rip right through his chest. Escape? Forget it.

There was nothing here but death.

The chapel echoed with his labored breath, with the sound of his thunderous heartbeat. Shadows pooled and shifted behind the black iron columns, rolling back and forth across the floor in waves as the Uriel battled the storm.

There - up in the rafters. A deeper darkness, a shape framed for a second in the eye of a stained-glass window.

He turned at bay before the altar, tearing a black candelabra from its mountings with his servoed hand. Hell, that rebar had done fine against Simeon Blaire. Perhaps that red-clad assassin was out of bullets. Perhaps this one was just as dumb as the giant and the mekan...

There was a tiny click behind him, and he felt warm breath on the back of his neck, the scent of jasmine and vanilla in the air...

"You've had a good run, Jaq," breathed a voice like a razor across silk. "Better than some Lords I've known. Certainly better than you should have hoped for. You're quite the tough customer."

He didn't turn around - he gripped the thick stem of the candelabra even tighter, waiting for his assailant to make a move.

"Yeah... that's what I told Simeon Blaire." He tensed, every nerve singing like piano wire. "He didn't take the hint. But I hear he's gone on to greater things."

"Little Lord Blaire? What's he doing hanging out with a magnificent brute like you?" This time the voice was a whisper, right in his ear, accompanied by the tiniest prick of a stiletto at his temple. "Still, it's good to know you keep such rarefied company. It'll almost make you worth the trouble. Now, turn around, nice and slow. If I'm going to do this, I want to look you in the eye."

Jaq turned. And stared. And kept staring, even while every instinct in his body told him to swing that fistful of iron.

She was beautiful.

Oh, sure... this girl was here to kill him; she'd been shooting at him for the last three minutes, and she was friends with things like Leon and the Tin Man... but still. Ruby Alvarez was a petite little killing machine - even standing atop the altar she was only just taller than Jaq himself. He found his eyes (which by all rights should have been looking for a tactical weakness) drinking in her curves as if he was a teenage schoolboy watching dirty threedeeo. The red riotmesh bodysuit didn't matter - neither did the knee-high boots with their skull-faced buckles, the little cutoff topcoat with its silver chains, the great gleaming cabochon jewels in her hair. And Jaq could have punched himself in the groin at that moment, because neither did the pair of glittering knives in her hands, aimed directly at his throat.

What annoyed him the most - more, even, than the way he felt suddenly awkward and speechless and ten degrees too hot - was the fact that she was looking him up and down in exactly the same way.

"Sweet gods, you're like Leon with a brain." she said. "Kind of shame to have to do this, but a contract's a contract..."

Haszan's second impression of Ruby Alvarez was that she was *fast*. She'd twisted the candelabra from his hand even before he was sure she'd moved.

The fallen Lady was just as quick as Simeon Blaire had been; slicing left and right with those winking blades mere inches from his head. She probably lacked the power of the psychopathic Lord, but Jaq was sure that she knew just where to strike...

He retreated before her attack as she leaped down from the altar, smiling, each wild swing missing his skin by a whisper. Jaq was no paragon of chivalry, and if this had been anyone else he would have been trying his damnedest to drive his fist through her face. Part of his brain was screaming at him to do it, to break this demoness before she grew tired of her sport. But it was the other part that noticed what was really going on - even through the soft-focus blur that misted his eyes.

She wasn't trying to hit him. Hells, if any one of those lightning-fast ripostes had been serious he'd be nothing but bleeding meat by now. She was *playing* with him... and that's when years of watching threedeeo caught up, hard.

She knew who Simeon was... personally. She was playing games with him because that's what her kind did...

Jaq waited for her next attack, a wheeling figure-of eight cut through the air with the tips of those bright stilettos, and he brought his hand up to meet them. His two chrome fingers snapped shut over one of the knives even as the other grazed his jugular, pricking a tiny line of crimson from his skin. Then his other hand was around her wrist, and the renegade Kheptarch was pinned. Jaq looked down at her steel-capped boots, and then at his unprotected groin. It was probably best to say something before she made the obvious move.

"*Ruby Dorothea Alvarez.* I know who you are, and who your friends are. I've seen you on three-vee."

She kicked out against his instep, and tore her left hand free as he stumbled. For a second she pulled at the end of his arm, as if they were dancing, and then she came back in, her stiletto aimed at his chest. Jaq spun her into the crook of his arm, deflecting the knife away with the back of his mekanikal hand.

"You really *are* just like Leon with a brain, Jaqub." she said, locked in his embrace. "But not nearly so... *controllable*."

Her knife was still in her hand, and she reversed it, stabbing at Haszan's kidney. He unwound his arm from around her neck and stepped back just in time for the razor-sharp steel to cut another gash in his ragged coat, spinning her out wild. She landed with all the poise of a dancer, bringing her knives up again, circling around him to the right.

He followed suit, and the pair matched each other step for step, wary as predators, tracing the circle of the stained-glass window's pool of light.

"I suppose I couldn't convince you that I'd never hurt a lady?"

"I haven't been a *lady* since they kicked me down to the Subcity."

"It could never work out between us... at least, not unless you drop those knives..."

"Huh! As if I'd be interested in anyone who has to ask *politely*!"

That was her cue to spring to the attack again, stabbing and wheeling and ducking out of reach, cutting away the seams of Haszan's greatcoat. The heavy black fabric fell from his shoulders in strips, its intrinsic LCD pattern of leaping flames blurring out.

Jaq was left with only his riotmesh overalls - and the hope that Ruby's next attack wasn't quite so precise. She stood just out of reach, one knife pressed to her lips as she appraised her work.

"Definitely an improvement - but I think I can go one better. You'd look about ten years younger if you were clean-shaven."

Jaq's eyes widened in horror as she flew at him again, spinning those razor knives between her slim fingers. This time he really tried to stop her - her blades were far too close for comfort, and he was running out of clothes. But his wild backhands and grapples managed to catch exactly nothing, as the renegade Kheptarch drove him back against the altar, forcing him to bend over backwards.

The crucifix in the middle of the granite slab pressed up against his skull, and now he saw it for what it really was - a giant broadsword sunk halfway into the stone. A whole lot of good *that* was going to do him now...it would take a warmekan to smash it free.

Ruby arched her back above him, letting her silken hair cascade down to brush his bare shoulders. Then her knives came down on either side of his face, and Jaq felt them pare the tiny hairs from his cheeks, making good her promise. One of her knees was up against his chest, and her hand...

Her hand was coiled around the three-foot whipcord of his precious goatee beard, her fingers tangled up in the charms which dripped from its leather bindings. With a single swipe of one glittering blade she snipped it clean away, right down to the skin.

"Much better, Jaqub. You're almost handsome enough to pass for human - at least in this light."

Now, tonsorial elegance was never Haszan's biggest concern. Fashion, to him, was a foreign country - one inhabited by effete morons with more money than sense. But this was just too much. *How would they know who he was now? How would the Aryan bootboys know they'd been butchered by one of the Hand of Fatima?*

The red mist came down, and through it Haszan could see Ruby smiling, cartwheeling back across the floor of the chapel out of reach. *So, she wanted a proper fight? Was that the way of Khept romance, to stab and smash the life out of your paramour?* Well, predictable old Jaq Haszan was back. Blind with anger, and happy to be there.

He sprung up from the altar quicker than even he could believe, charging like a mad bull as the ship lurched and heaved beneath them. His shadow streamed out before him in the crimson light of the stained-glass windows, and his chrome fist cocked back beside his face like a wrecking ball, arcing in with all the force of his rage behind it.

Of course she was too quick to stay in its path. But Jaq savored the look of surprise and admiration on her face as she sidestepped straight into his other hand, a jarring uppercut which knocked her off her feet. She staggered, and slipped, fetching up with her back to one of the chapel's iron pillars. But before she could catch her breath Jaq's chrome hand was tight around her throat, lifting her toecaps a foot from the deck. If it had been anyone else, those fingers would have hinged shut, snapping her neck.

But that damned soft-focus blur was burning through his anger, and he dropped her to the floor, horrified, staring at the thin line of blood which trickled from her perfect lips. She looked up at him from behind a loose tangle of black hair, pulled free from its jeweled clasps.

"That's more like it," she said, grinning through the blood. "That's the killer Octavio promised me..."

Then she was snarling, pouncing, her knives flashing out wild in the gloom of the cavernous chapel, tearing through Jaq's riotmesh in great looping slashes. The pain re-ignited his anger, and he fought back savagely, snapping Ruby's head back with swift mechanical punches, once, twice, raising livid bruises across her olive skin. No excuses this time, no romantic cotton-candy fuzz to slow him down...

But try as he might, he still wasn't fast enough. When he'd bested Simeon Blaire (and even then, only for a moment) the Lord had been newly transformed by his illicit crycelium, aching and burning inside. Jaq had been hyped up on a fresh fix of Stunn, layered with triple platinum to slow the world to a crawl. Without his narcotic helpers he was utterly outmatched.

Ruby Alvarez fought him back across the chapel, through the crimson light of the stained-glass oculus above. She was incandescent now, elated, brought into her own by the sheer joy of battle. This was what she was *made* for, and why she'd devoted herself to a life of terror and crime once the Council had cast her out. Before that kind of genewritten skill Jaq Haszan was just a talented amateur...

Now his back was to the altar again, and this time Ruby wasn't playing. His hands scrabbled for a weapon, for *anything*, another candelabra, a scepter or a good thick bible... too late. There was only time for them to come up and shield his face as the red demoness brought her stilettos down, slicing into his palms. Blood spattered her face as she smiled, and blood reflected in her eyes as she hooked one hand behind Jaq's head, pulling him to his feet.

"That's the most fun I've had all year, Haszan," she said, curling the knifeblade around his neck to tickle his throat. "And it's a sorry shame you weren't born a Lord. With a little augmentation, they could have made an Emperor of you."

His hands were sliced open to the bone, weeping crimson stigmata across the cold granite. But he dared not move, dared not tempt the razor edge at his neck. Jaq clenched his eyes shut, anticipating the final blow, the warm blood pumping from his jugular...

Instead she kissed him.

And the burning intensity of it was so powerful, so all-consuming that he didn't even feel the knife pull away from his throat, or sense what was coming next.

"Too bad, baby. But a contract's a contract."

The knives came up between his ribs, twin lances of red-hot pain. Ruby struck home with all the power in her augmented arms, and the foot-long double-edged blades went in to the hilt, just below Haszan's jagged pectoral tattoos. The force of the blow brought him up to the tips of his toes and spun him around, his vision blurring red as Ruby Alvarez turned away, leaving the knives crossed through his chest.

Jaq fell across the altar, driving the stilettos home as he landed on their twin gilded hilts. Darkness was closing in, black bleeding into red, and he could still taste her blood on his lips, still smell jasmine and vanilla...

His hands twisted and fluttered against the stone like broken birds, one flesh, one steel, smearing blood down the cold metal shape of the crucifix sword.

Something connected.

In the blackness, a trace of green.

Pixilated numbers coursing down like rain, awakening something deep in his bones...

And through the tight hot pain he remembered the face of Eddie Tsien, leaning in over him as he lay bleeding in the ruins of the Valley View Mall. His hands were overflowing with liquid, living mercury... Then the scene changed, and Tsien's ravaged half-human face was replaced with the grim death-mask of Simeon Blaire, silver threads looping and curling from his broken jaw like worms...

It was inside him.

Not enough to transform him into a living tank like Tsien. Not even enough to make him invincible, *unkillable* like Blaire. But just enough to keep him alive for a few seconds more. And enough of the ancient Chimera organism to recognize its mate locked up in the crucifix sword - the Railblade embedded in the stone.

Tiny crystal viri in Haszan's blood sunk down into the metal like rain into sun-baked earth, activating the A.I. of the sword.

It had been dormant for centuries. It couldn't see, or hear, but it could *sense* - its whole surface picked up the vibration of Jaq's faltering heartbeat, and felt the knife-blade tight up against that pulsing knot of muscle in his chest. It didn't know who he was - his name, his rank, his designation... but it knew what it was built for.

This was a member of the Separatist Army, a wet-ops commando, and it was programmed to keep him alive. So it gave a little of itself to Haszan, even as he slipped into unconsciousness.

Deep in the stone a million tiny filaments of steel ramified out from the edges of the Railblade, locking it tight to the altar. The Pent' marines who'd found the thing down on the seabed had no idea that the metal could ever unbind from the stone - but it did now. Those molecular roots melted back into the blade, leaving it with an edge as sharp as reason.

Things synchronized. Things assessed and clamped and rewired nerves. Things in Haszan's blood, left there by Eddie Tsien, heard the voice of the Railblade and overrode his faltering brain.

His eyelids snapped open, even though his eyes were rolled back to bloodshot whites. And his hands slammed shut around the hilt of the ancient sword, drawn in as if by powerful magnets. Electricity crackled and seethed through Jaq's body, arching his back, pulling his lips back from his teeth in a fiendish rictus.

Ruby missed it - she was almost to the chapel door when the unmistakable screech of steel on stone heralded Haszan's rebirth.

But Aitken Straw had seen it all. Up in the rafters of the chapel, perched atop a bat-winged gargoyle, he'd slipped in through the shadows just in time to see her *kiss* the Subcity filth. Jealousy and rage transfixed his heart just as surely as Ruby's wicked knives, and he hissed to himself, biting down hard on the back of his hand.

A contract was a contract, and a kill was a kill, but still...

Then the dead man twitched. Then the dead man rose up, and pulled that impossibly huge sword from out of its granite sheath, his blank eyes brimming with murder.

Aitken Straw smiled, flexing his claws in the dark.

Let her learn her lesson before he came to her aid.

Let her learn who really cared...

17 Aevum Oblivio
South of Heaven

*T*HE DOORS OF *Ground Floor One had been built to withstand anything war could throw at them; bullets and bombs and missiles, fusion fire and maser blasts; all would have shattered against the yard-thick layered sandwich of steel and carbon and titanium, diamond-fiber and boron and lead. All, that was, if the doors weren't twisted from their hinges, blackened and warped beyond repair.*

*T*HIS WAS A *monument to the savagery of Exodus Night, when powers walked these metal corridors in human and inhuman form, fighting tooth and nail for control of the Forge. They'd never been replaced. That said a lot about the condition of Kronos after the events of that fateful night - but CeeAn was still wary, and she held back her soldiers with a gesture, casting out her Dervashi senses ahead of them.*

"It's clear. Bring them forward." She pressed one fingertip against her throat-mic, her eyes darting left and right as her ocular upgrades struggled to pierce the dusty gloom. "Blaire first, then the alien. If they start shooting, that thing is too valuable to waste."

The room beyond the doors was a vast cathedral of polished bronze, its dome held aloft on pillars of silver and glass. Twenty feet up they broke off into delicate branches - an arbor of crystal trees budding with light-globes and hung with jeweled chains. Statues leaned drunkenly in alcoves around the curve of the walls - splintered marble effigies of the city's ancient Investors, the original Kheptarchs.

And one other.

CeeAn saw it just a second too late - a shadow out of place, too tall and thin and inhuman to belong in the Khepts' company. The Vision sparked wild, and her soldiers brought their guns to bear, letting their burden float free on crackling antigrav discs.

But in that fraction of an instant the creature was gone, flowing from its mausoleum pose and leaping into the tangled canopy above. There were a pair of impossible wings grafted to its shoulders, and they spread out with a thunderous rush of air, swirling the dust into twin vortices. CeeAn was all but blind as she dived for cover...

"Back! Out the door! Keep the specimen safe!"

She heard her own voice ringing in her ears, lost behind the chime of countless swinging crystals. But then it, too, was cut off by a hideous grinding sound - the noise of long-unused machinery protesting as it shuddered back to life. Cee looked back, hoping against hope - but the portal was closed, sealed by metal bars which screwed their way out of the walls in a shower of rust. It was a trap.

A constellation of tiny lights whirled across the mosaic floor, finger-length rainbows flashing and dying. Then a sliver of glass like a faceted dagger came down from right above her, impaling itself quivering between the tiles.

CeeAn looked up and saw a kaliedoscope of eyes, hands, pale white feathers floating in the dusty air...

Then the thing was on top of her, dropping out of the crazed glitter of the canopy with a snarl, lean-limbed and milky white. She felt its hands knotting in her tunic, lifting her off her feet as it furled its wings, contemptuous of the machineguns aimed at its chest. Six azure yes blinked slowly, one at a time, nictitating membranes sliding slick over pupils like slits of darkness.

"Do you like it?" it purred, in a voice all honey and razors. "A little present from my dear departed friend Emmanuel Lancaster. A factory second, I'm sure, but it has its benefits..."

CeeAn stared into that battery of eyes, as fearless as only someone who'd seen the other side of death could be. Her hand was down by the creature's navel, and wicked steel flashed in the light from her soldiers' laser-targeters.

"Two things, before we get into talking about aesthetics," she said. "First, put me down before I spill your genecrafted guts out around your ankles. And second - who the hell are you?"

"You surprise me, Anointed One," hissed the archangel, lacing CeeAn's unwanted title with venom. "Surely you recognize the face of your old nemesis?"

The Ashishi's eyes widened as those perfect alabaster hands set her down, as she stepped back, keeping her dagger poised to strike. Oh yes. It all made sense now. The Wetsystems were infected, shut down, sealed off from their master. And there was no way that the pseudocerebrate would risk its own precious mind...

"Kronos." she spat. "So this is what you've been reduced to?"

The angelic construct raised one sculpted eyebrow, smiling ruefully.

"I can't deny that the constraints of the flesh are... vexing. But there are consolations to your dirty condition, human." Kronos licked his lips, his cluster of eyes sliding over CeeAn's body lasciviously. "Sick, animal pleasures..." His tongue darted out, quicksilver, faster than a snake's - tasting the air. "But enough about me. Let's talk about... him."

Kronos unfurled one long thin finger, pointing at the crystal shard *which imprisoned Simeon Blaire.*

"I can smell him from here, Ashsihi. And I know who's nestled in his rotten skull. I have business with those two, and I've been watching you since your little encounter with our alien visitor."

"You know about the Technician? The one called Zhe?"

Kronos twisted his lips into a sneer.

"Know about him? I'm leading him a merry dance, Anointed One. I'm going to make him bring me the Chrome Ark, and this time I'll be ready for it. Just imagine it - my mind, uploaded into a sleek new form. One which I've prepared a transport for, up there in space. I'm leaving to seed my own utopia - but I have one little item of unfinished business here." *He turned away, ignoring the cluster of red laser-points marking his cheek.* *"After I'm done those alien parasites in orbit can fight over the carcass of the Earth. I wish them every joy from it."*

CeeAn smiled, running her hand over the whorls and ridges of Simeon's amethyst prison.

"If you want him, there's a price, Kronos. You have to let us past. All the way to the top, into the Cardinal Rock. I'm going to use the Forge."

"And how do you propose to do that, CeeAn?" *asked the archangel* *"The alien Technicians have infected some of the strata, the Worm has the rest... and if I recall correctly, you were never one of the Magi. You were more interested in the thrill of the kill, weren't you? No time for dusty, boring numbers..."*

Now it was the Dervashi's turn to smile, sweet and innocent and deadly.

"I'll worry about the logistics when I get to them, machine. By then, you could be doing whatever you please to dear Simeon - or Octavio - you take your pick. Then you can tell me all about the thrill of the kill - one of the 'sick little pleasures' you mentioned."

Kronos turned back, all six of his eyes twinkling with malice.

"Should I even bother telling you that the automated defenses will cut you to ribbons if you don't just hand him over?"

"Should I even bother to dignify that with a reply?" *asked Cee, twitching her robe aside to reveal a belt of slim black phials, connected to a snarl of multicolored wire.* *"Those Aggartans weren't messing around, Kronos - this is* antimatter. *A smart pseudocerebate like you should have no problem calculating the size of the crater it could make."*

They circled the slab of glistening purple crystal like lions around a steaming carcass - the cloned woman and the genecrafted machine both wearing the same tight little smile. Suddenly Kronos stopped, slamming his palms down on the cold stone. He leaned in over Simeon Blaire's horrified face, frozen in the instant of his doom.

"Oh, I've waited so long, Vanecke. All of this is your fault, you scheming peasant!"

The machine-avatar's face was anything but angelic in that moment, his perfect lips peeled back in a feral snarl.

"Very well! You can go on up - for all the good it'll do you. Just don't expect any sympathy from me if that Technician or the Worm chew the brains out of your pretty little head." Kronos was enraptured, stroking the petrified face of the Kheptarch like a lover. As CeeAn watched the tips of his fingers split open, budding slick black claws which skirled and skittered across the stone.

She gestured her soldiers to pick up the second crystal prison, keeping it locked in the sights of the Stoneweavers. Cee backed away from the demented angel which was all that remained of Kronos, severed from his cogitators and his Wetsystems. He cradled the slab of amethyst almost tenderly, crooning and whispering to it as the Ashishim moved away through the glass forest of Ground Floor One.

Mad. Utterly Mad.

But nevertheless, the machine was right. Technician Zhe's infiltration programs held the Forge in a stranglehold, while the infection of Asag'raal coiled within, hungry for living souls. That was what the second monolith was for - what the core samples swinging at CeeAn's belt were for. Nyl's hybrid form was they key. And before them lay the final door...

2196 Ante Arbitrium
Possessed

Octavio Vanecke watched them die one by one.

For all their fury and bloody grace the Kheptarchs of Elysium were no match for Lysander Jaegenn. Not while he was utterly possessed by the power of the Worm, his very flesh boiling from his bones as smoke.

Armies could have faced him and died.

Whole nations could have been annihilated by his hands.

That was the promise which flickered in the air, infecting the minds of those seventy-three Elysian Lords. That was what the Worm made them believe.

It was their fear that broke them. Jaegenn's scaly skin was torn open in a hundred places, bleeding black. But the pain of those wounds was a weapon in his claws, a psionic lash scourging the minds of the Kheptarchs raw.

Tranh Diem was the first to fall, and with his demise the others lost heart.

Octavio watched his eyes glaze over as his head flew through the air, trailing a crimson mist of blood. Before it had even hit the ground the butchery began...

And with each of his hated enemies, with each of the arrogant bastards who'd denied him his destiny, a little piece of his own soul died as well. He felt sick, fevered, *weak...* he felt, at last, exactly like what he was - a scrap of flesh and bone kept alive by willpower and machinery. Behind him he could hear the dusty laughter of Benton Veer, Master of Celebrants, clutching at his wires and catheters with cadaverous hands.

His mind was slipping.

But the plan - the plan was already in motion. Nothing he said or did could stop it now - the momentum of all his schemes and intrigues was too great, rolling down like an avalanche to crush him.

The surgeons were here.

They were half of the reason that Emmanuel had needed to die, these things - featureless black cubes suspended on humming antigrav discs, each one a relic from before the *Iudicio*.

Artificers and mekanicians had slaved over the Surgeons for centuries, oiling and cleaning their saws and needles, picking each speck of dust from their camera eyes with tweezers. They were almost sacred, these machines; the keepers of Lancaster's own flesh. Now they hovered in place around Octavio Vanecke's preservative tank, regarding his ruin with their impassive glass oculi.

Soon they would unfold like intricate steel flowers, their fingertips glittering with scalpels and syringes and saws. But if there were no second subject here… if Simeon should fail… Octavio wasn't sure that he could overrule their orders. They'd just start cutting anyway.

Even Lancaster hadn't really controlled the Surgeons. They said that you could only give them one command, and they'd see it through to the death - theirs or yours. So far, not one of the sheer black cubes had been so much as scratched, even though they'd done things which would make a living doctor claw out his own eyes.

Vanecke had already told them what must be done. His friends in the Liquid Tong had been most adamant. He could never be cloned - not even with all the might of Universal's manufactoria at his beck and call. The time was simply too short. And if he wanted to rule this filthy city, there was only one way.

The rarefied flesh of a Kheptarch Lord…

It had seemed so easy in his mind, so clear-cut, like the neat precision of a lightscribed blueprint. But now that events were out of his control Direktor Vanecke felt strangely calm, watching the city tear itself apart in a narcotic daze. These were the tremors before the Big One, the birthing pains of his Godhood. Hallucinations stalked the streets, waking nightmares and dreams in human minds. They were a suitable backdrop for his ascension to the High Throne of Earth.

Octavio wasn't a religious man, but he remembered his scriptures, the words of Manifest Dogma burned into his brain by the state Eduplug long ago. The new God-King would remake the Earth in his image. All would be swept away by the tide of molten steel he commanded…

A neat fairytale to keep the plebs in line. A fantasy beaten out of him by decades of cynical hardscrabble existence. And yet…and yet…

A man could hope, couldn't he? A man - or what was left of him - could dream…

All he needed was for Simeon Blaire to run true. All he needed was for that spoiled little Khept' bastard to follow his hate. That - and stay alive in the face of Lysander Jaegenn's demonic fury…

Ω

Simeon knew that he couldn't take much more punishment. The wires caged up tight around his brain were sizzling hot, and his heart felt as if it was pumping molten lead instead of blood.

He slashed left and right with wild abandon, parrying a storm of obsidian hooks and claws, lopping off tentacles of oily darkness with every strike. Soon they'd coil and constrict around his hands and face, rip open his tender belly, pluck out his eyes...

But until then he was at one with the moment, drunk on blood and beyond his pain.

It was rage which carried him onward now, rage and grim determination. He *would* see Octavio Vanecke die, transfixed by the very blade he had given his disciple. Anyone else who got in his way was just collateral damage - even Lysander Jaegenn and his new Master.

He knew that the traitorous Kehptarch would have to let go soon. Jaegenn's saprophytic flesh was bubbling like boiling pitch, sloughing away from his deformed skeleton. It had taken the full power of the Worm to break the Lords of Elysium, but that power wasn't made to be stuffed into a tiny mortal frame, no matter how swollen and mutated it was. Simeon could see Lysander's ribs through his membranous skin, see the spiked bones of his arms through the rags of flesh which clothed them.

The hand was too big for the puppet, and Jaegenn's howls of bloodlust became screams of agony as his enemies fell. The Worm was tearing him in half.

Still, there were a few anguished seconds when he stood astride the razor's edge, wielding Asag'raal's fury like an axe. The Worm's power slammed into the massed ranks of the Kheptarchy, a storm of flying blood and shattered bone, screams and prayers cut short.

Helmsfjord, Diem, Blacktower and Al-Haq, Dawes and Pho and Kwalib... they were nothing but meat in the end, nothing but raw and bloody meat. The Worm fed on them one by one, drawing them in, and a mass of cancerous tumors erupted from Lysander's torso. Each one split open with a wet sucking sound, sending forth snarls of ropy black tentacles, razor-tipped and venomous.

Seething, melting, the traitor Lord had become a formless monster, a monolith of flesh with sagging wings and blistered skin, a vortex of darkness coiling up around his horrified face. He was learning the price of his deal with the devil, and learning it hard. But still Asag'raal clenched its claws into his soul, drinking down his pain. It tore anguished laughter from his lips even as it ate his body away, sending

a thousand saprophytic lashes scything through the air after Simeon...
and the one other Khept' still standing.

Oh, yes. Of course *she* hadn't gone down as easy as the others. It
seemed that noble birth was the only lucky break Simeon Blaire was
going to catch in *this* lifetime.

Even so, he couldn't help but admire her form. Leynna was a fury
unleashed against the heaving bulk of Lysander Jaegenn, slippery
and precise, her twin blades a blur of steel. Wherever they went black
blood spumed and bubbled, and truncated limbs lay twitching on the
floor.

"I thought you were supposed to be our noble better, Simeon!" she
called out over the roar and hiss of Asag'raal's vexation. "Go ahead
and finish him!"

By all the gods, she was actually *smiling*! Perhaps he'd misjudged
her. Perhaps...

But there was no time now for regret or reminiscence. Jaegenn's
final transformation was complete, and the spirit of the Worm hung
above him like an anvilhead of bruise-black cloud, a morass of roiling
faces.

"Enjoy them, my pet!" giggled its mad, fractured voice. *"Make them
last! I have no time for the weak, Lysander Jaegenn, and you will pay the
price for disappointing me..."*

With that the could of smoke tore itself to shreds, tendrils of dirty
vapor knotting and intertwining as they funneled out through the
shattered roof. What they left behind them was suddenly made clear.

The marble floor of the temple had run like wax under the blowtorch
of the Worm's power. Now a stalagmite of creamy stone rose up from
the place where Jaegenn had stood, a jagged fang of rock veined with
quartzite. Where liquid stone had met liquifying flesh the two had
fused together, gripping what remained of Lysander's body tight. The
tip of the stalagmite split open into a dozen crystal shards, interwoven
with his tortured bones. Gelid saprophytic flesh and steaming meat
bulged from cracks in the marble, while from a thousand vents and
fissures sprung a forest of writhing tentacles, black as night, tipped
with wicked claws.

"Oh *shit.*" breathed Leynna, her whisper echoing in the sudden
silence. 'Look what it's done to him..."

It was hard for Simeon to take in the sheer scope of the traitor-lord's
suffering. His skin had been flayed off in strips, turned inside-out and
coiled tight around that pillar of stone. His head - or what was left of

it - lolled drunkenly on a broken twist of spinal column, transfixed by a crown of bone blades. The corrosive stuff of the saprophytes had burned away his hair and skin, giving him the aspect of some half-embalmed cadaver; beautiful from one angle, vile from another. But that patchwork face still smiled - uncontrollably, its lips twitched up into a pained rictus by a pair of hook-tipped tentacles. Jaegenn's blind and milky eyes were those of a madman, crazed with agony.

There was no doubt in either of the Kheptarchs' minds that they were meant to share his torment.

The Exalted's eyes stared down from innumerable hovering screens, from the flanks of drifting zeppelins and rooftop threedeeo spheres. A handful of desperate refugees may have looked up and wondered at the horror of it - those who weren't being eaten alive. Microphones abandoned by Omnivasive's broadcast crew sent his voice out over the dying city, echoing amid the ruins.

"Please... before it takes me! Before it makes me...feed."

His words were a strangled whisper, choked out through a froth of bloody spit. Simeon could hear the pleading in his voice, though... that, and the strain as the last of the Kheptarch's will held back the Worm.

"It has to be the blades. It has to be...the heart, Simeon. Leynna. You must... before..."

But it was too late.

Even as Blaire and Leynna moved in on him from opposite sides of the ruined temple the change came down. The arteries and veins beneath Lysander's pallid skin swelled with sickness, a webwork of darkness. His face slicked over black assaprophytic shadows sweated out from every pore, smothering his humanity.

Then there was nothing left but a slave of Asag'raal, a soulless killing machine.

The coiling tentacles wrapped tight to his monolithic body reared up like serpents, poison glittering on the edges of their blades. Now that hideous grin was drawn even wider, flesh ripping and tearing as Jaegenn's jaw hinged open, wide as a tomb.

"Come to me and die, filthy humans! Come and receive the blessing of the New Flesh!"

"Do you think we should take that as an invitation?" asked Simeon, bringing his katana up into a defensive guard. "He's not the most gracious host, but this *is* his party."

Leynna's amber eyes burned with scorn.

"I didn't come here for *Lysander Jaegenn.*"

Simeon sighed, coming in quick and silent on the Exalted's left.

"And *now's* not the time to argue about little things like murdered children. It's going to take more than one sharp edge to finish him off, Baroness."

The scion of House Mendelev-Singh scowled, spinning her slim blades as she limbered up her wrists.

"Don't think we're on the same side even for a *second*, Blaire," she said, her eyes never leaving the black monolith which had once been their noble peer. "But I'm smart enough to recognize the greater evil - even if it is a damned close contest."

Simeon was sure she was going to leap to the attack, then, but instead she spun her blades in one final blurring arc, slamming them back into their sheaths. And she touched a single finger to her headscarf, extending her thumb in front of her lips like a microphone.

A word, whispered under her breath.

A code, flying across a closed network at the speed of light.

He caught the implication just in time to see the shadows move, the shattered roofline spawning a dozen silhouettes in black. There were guns in their hands; big, brutal rifles built to punch through mekan armor. Night-sight rigs like compound insect eyes masked the circle of assassins, but Blaire didn't need to see their faces to know who had sent them.

Omnivasive.

They were Vanecke's men, his stopgap solution, the promise he'd made in the depths of the Black Palace. Two or three of them would have been easy. Five or six would make him break a sweat. But weaving his way through the bullets of twelve elite snipers - that would be *vexing.* And of course, a few little humans were the least of his worries at the moment...

Lysander Jaegenn screamed as he attacked, a long, drawn-out wail of betrayal and pain which set up sickening harmonics in Simeon's bones. Black tentacles coiled and rushed down on him like a wave, like rain, whispering through the air all around him. Left, right, looping figure-eights with the razor-honed katana, reversing his swing, spinning a backhand slice through three twitching claws, a deft forehand taking two more... but they were countless, a storm of flesh stinking of open graves. Ten more, twenty, the blade slick with cold dark gore, tiny drops of acid burning through his skin...

He lost sight of Leynna; his last vision of her was a snapshot of flying hair and burning eyes, her hands clenched tight around the grips of her shortswords -

And then the pain.

One of the Exalted's hooks came up under his arm, its razor tip punching through his collarbone and on through the soft flesh of his neck. Simeon was hooked like a fish on a lure, slammed into the ground as Jaegenn screeched in triumph. The Kheptarch wrapped his fingers around the tentacle and pulled himself to his feet, almost passing out as pain tore through his shoulder. Its poison was like a snarl of red-hot wire in his chest, a tight ball of agony pulsing with every beat of his heart. But he still held off the rest of the traitor-lord's hooks and blades with his good hand, desperate, the darkness flickering at the edges of his vision...

Somewhere in the dim distance he heard the click and slide of rifle bolts.

The bullets came through in hazy slow-motion, time turned to liquid glass by the crycelium in his head. They were twelve tiny angels on sonic shockwave wings, spiraling in all around him amid a rain of blood. He watched one of them bisect a droplet as it flew, whispering past his face almost close enough to kiss. Then the explosive-tipped slug buried itself in a coil of saprophytic muscle, and Simeon's crycelial webwork forced time back into the world again.

He found himself upside down in the air, blasted off his feet by the explosion.

Gobbets of smoking black meat were airborne with him - the remains of the tentacle which had ripped him raw. Simeon tucked himself into a ball, spinning in midair, holding his sword out to one side. He landed on his feet just as the hordes of scarabs in his blood shat out the last of the Exalted's poison blade, and he smiled as he felt his bones knitting seamlessly back together, filters in his arteries leeching the venom from his blood.

Vanecke's assassins could see the greater evil too, it seemed. Which meant that somewhere that vile old bastard was still alive, still watching his every move. Well, he'd made a terrible mistake, thought Simeon Blaire.

He should have finished me off while he had the chance.

The Kheptarch Lord sprung to the attack with a snarl on his lips, carving his way through the Exalted's lashing coils like an ancient *Kenshin* through a rabble of peasants. The rolling thunder of gunfire was his constant companion now, blowing the heads off tentacles to his right and left as his arm worked mechanically, remorselessly, cleaving a path toward the great black monolith at the center of the temple. Vanecke's snipers were good - surgical in their precision. Although the storm of lead raged all around him, drenching him with spattered blood, not a one bullet was out of place. He didn't have to evade a single shot.

Now he could see Leynna again - holding a cluster of writhing whips at bay with her blades. Deep gashes split her armor, and plates of it hung loose on their straps, but otherwise she was untouched. *So fast. So agile... why was she never like this in the Game? Could she have been holding back for a reason?*

"You heard what he said, Blaire!" she shouted, completing a spinning slash that beheaded five tentacles at once. "The heart! Can you see the bastard's heart?"

It was hard enough to tell which part of the seething black mass had been Lysander's *chest*, let alone pick out individual details. Twisted ribs burst out near the tip of the monolith, a trap-jaw gaping open around a cluster of pulsing organs. *That must be the place - there.* Through a fissure in the stone Simeon could make out a great spasming lump of muscle, thorny and glistening wet. Jaegenn's heart, transformed by the sorcery of Asag'raal.

"You might want to hurry, Blaire! We've got trouble!"

And the Baroness wasn't kidding. Simeon remembered the other half of the traitor-lord's whispered plea, his last words as a human being.

"It has to be the blades..."

Octavio Vanecke's snipers were finding out the hard way what that cryptic message had meant. The remains of the tentacles they'd shot to pieces were slowly reforming, pulling themselves together in a webwork of oily black stitches. Some of them had already fused back to the dripping stumps from which they'd been severed - but others were on the move, thick shadow-snakes tipped with obsidian fangs.

Simeon heard screams behind him as the first of the snipers fell, snared and smothered by darkness. Poisoned blades stabbed down into his eyes once, twice, over and over again, reducing his face to a bloody death-mask. And while he died Blaire gritted his teeth, locking his eyes on the pulsing knot of thorns at Jaegenn's core. He broke into a run, sword held high, determined that the demise of Vanecke's men would buy him the time he needed.

He looked across the ruin and carnage of the gaming temple, and locked eyes with Leynna Mendelev-Singh, picking her way through the butchered bodies and blood in a series of graceful leaps. Just like in that final Game, he caught the glitter of recombining steel deep in each iris, and knew that they had an understanding.

And just like last time, it would all be over as soon as their common foe was slain.

The tentacles and pseudopods of darkness recoiled from Simeon and Leynna's assault, cowering away from their blades. Perhaps whatever tiny shred of Lysander was left within his twisted body knew what had to happen. Perhaps he fought the power of the Worm in his final moments, determined to save some shadow of his honor.

Or perhaps Asag'raal really was *afraid...*

And suddenly Simeon understood.

The sword was the soul of the warrior. It was an extension of his body, the human fang and claw, steel melded with flesh just as surely as the crystalline mycelium in his veins. The arc of technology began all the way back in those forgotten ages when men ruled by the sword, died by the sword... and now it had found its apogee here, in this very room, with the emperor-aspirant himself. Bullets couldn't harm the Saprophytes, because it wasn't physical damage which destroyed them. The sword was part of him; crackling with the force of his bioelectric field, seething with his rage and defiance.

I don't fear you, it said.

FEAR *ME!*

He leaped, firelight flashing from his blade, ten feet in the air to where Lysander's heart labored beneath the stone. Tens of thousands of years of history were behind the point of Simeon's katana as it slipped through a chink in the marble, puncturing the Exalted One's flesh. *The fires of a million forges, flames raised against the darkness of Asag'raal...*

He felt his steel interlock with Leynna's as she stabbed through from the other side, impaling the traitor's heart.

"Whatever happens" he said, as cracks skittered across the marble in front of his face, "Don't let go of the swords."

Through the hollow cavity of Jaegen's chest he caught her eye, and saw the mesh and interlock of metal deep inside it. Their truce was over.

"I wouldn't dream of it, Blaire," she said, in a voice as cold as nuclear winter. "Not until they send you down to hell."

The Exalted's heart stopped beating as they watched. It faltered, and spasmed, and seemed to collapse in upon itself, belching a cloud of noisome steam. A tiny spark of blue fire flickered into existence right at its very core as Lysander screamed, shattering his stony prison. Strange harmonics slithered up and down the scale, making the whole world tremble.

Then that little blue star went supernova, and the temple atop the Helios spire flashed incandescent against the black sky.

Ω

A thousand glassy black eyes stared him down, ragged lips pulled back from transparent needle teeth, dripping and glistening...

"Tell your master he's next!" snarled Abdulafia, clenching his finger tight around the Eversio's trigger. A thousand glittering wires pulled taut, filling the underground tunnel with the sound of aeolian harpstrings. And the saprophyte horde died, sliced to shreds by the weapon's cruel embrace.

Only one shot left, now. But the way was clear.

'Afia was exhausted, bloodied and bruised and shellshocked after his nightmare trek through the ruined Subcity. He'd taken to the sewers, to the hidden tunnels and vaults beneath Elysium,avoiding the refugees and rioters above. They didn't deserve the kind of hell he dragged behind him everywhere he went.

But *someone* did.

It was the Saps who caught it; sudden fury out of the dark, a grinning face smeared with soot and blood, spitting curses as the silver wires flew...

So many dead. So many torn to pieces by the Eversio, and by the edge of his makeshift sword. The Ashishi had found out early on that bullets and maser blasts had no lasting effect on Asag'raal's legions. He'd seen them swarm over a citizen's militia squad in a storm of flying lead, giggling and squealing as they ripped the men to shreds.

No, it was the blade they feared. That, and the thousands of tiny razor threads nestled inside the Eversio. He could feel it when they bit into the Saprophytes' dripping black flesh... feel the force of his anger burning them like torture irons. It would have been infinitely more satisfying to claw at the foul things' throats with his bare hands, but that was a temptation he had to resist.

Under the shadow-skin of the Worm his fingers were skeletal talons, his flesh and muscle burned away to smoke. If he used the power Asag'raal had given him he'd slide ever further toward the edge of the pit, toward becoming an Exalted One himself.

And that would never happen. He'd turn the last charge in the Eversio on himself before he bowed to such a master...

Abdulafia strode on down the tunnel, leaving steaming footprints behind him. The soles of his combat boots were all but eaten through by saprophytic blood. He was nearly home, he knew... these great rib-vaulted pipes were carved with Ashishim sigils, warning trespassers to turn back. He hadn't seen any of the sentry engines that Zeon's artificers set on guard, and no-one had challenged his approach. The security cameras which skulked in every corner like mekan spiders were silent, their glassy eyes dead. But the tunnel wasn't quite deserted. Something echoed up ahead, a sound that made Abdulafia's skin crawl.

He knew it all too well by now - the slobbering, hissing noise of Asag'raal's slaves devouring the dead, feeding their own rotten flesh with human meat. The battle-clone pressed himself up against the wall of the tunnel, slipping the Eversio into a loop of rope over one shoulder. His stopgap sword was heavy in his hand - the broken bearing ring from some vast synthesoy mincer, one four-foot curved blade connected to a circular grip. Abdulafia spun it once, limbering up his wrist, and he focused his power, narrowing his rage down into a surgical edge.

The 'chrome hadn't left him, and the sliver of the Worm in his brain twitched his mouth into a grim smile as he slid forward, silent. There was only one, and it was totally consumed with its feeding, hunched over a slumped and broken body. This would be almost too easy...

'Afia leaped from cover between two of the tunnel's buttress ribs, his blade a blur of gunmetal gray. It caught the Saprophyte just as it turned, red runnels of gore dripping from its jaws, biting deep beneath its collarbone, shearing through its ribcage and on through its spine. The creature seemed almost surprised as the flying steel sliced it in half, spraying a fan of viscous black gore across the tunnel floor. Before its body could hit the ground Abdulafia had reversed his swing, lopping its head from its shoulders.

He stood over the ruin of the Sap', panting, his dreadlocks hanging limp and bloody in front of his face. *Now to see who the damned beast had killed* - the half-eaten corpse slumped up against the wall was wearing Asahishi coveralls, beige hemp soaked crimson with gore.

"Miguel 903." he read from the kid's dogtags. "Hydro farmer, grade zero. Too bad you had to get caught up in all of this..."

"And what makes you think it was my *children who killed him, slave?"*

Oh gods! It was in his head! It was in his *mind!*

Abdulafia clutched at his temples as the voice of Asag'raal echoed out of nowhere, wracking him with pain.

"You can't blame my poor creature for making use of dead meat, Ashishi. And this one was sucked dry before any of my minions could so much as lay a claw on him..."

"Lies!" gasped the battle-clone, gritting his teeth in agony. "Get out of my head, you bastard! *I'm not yours, and I never will be!"*

The Worm laughed then, a sick and bubbling sound like putrid decay.

"You don't want to serve a monster, *hmmm? Your high and precious morals forbid you? But your title, slave, is 'Sword'. 'Sword of the Illuminatus'. Do you really think the blade has any choice in which flesh it tears apart?"*

The sound of its voice was like a drillbit cutting into his skull, hot and grinding. Abdulafia sank to his knees as the weight of Asag'raal's will crashed down on him, scouring sway his sense of self, his identity...

"That's right, slave. You are nothing but a tool, an instrument of death."

It chuckled, bringing bile to the back of the Ashishi's throat.

"Execrate me if you will, human, but don't presume to judge me. Now - witness the true face of your master!"

The Worm's gloating laughter was a tangible thing, a mire of choking putrescence. 'Afia felt himself going under, his fingers clawing at nothing. His eyes slicked over black...

And then opened again on paradise.

He blinked, staring down at his hands, holding them up to the sun...

They were whole again, skin and bone and muscle against a summer-blue sky.

This was a place he knew - a promise he'd been given more than a century ago.

This was the heart of the Chrome Ark, the core of his faith.

The terraced mountainsides veiled in glittering spray, the verdant gardens nestled in the clefts of chasms, the city of white marble sweeping up and up like a foam-crested wave in stone... he recognized it all.

And the two figures standing on the edge of the city, where the flagstones of a cobbled plaza were cut clean by a half-mile drop. Abdulafia recognized them too. One was the poor unfortunate 'phyte who lay crumpled and bloody at his feet, back in the real world. He was wide-eyed, smiling, elated at the sight of this garden of wonders.

The other was Illuminatus Zeon.

The sick chuckle of the Worm in his brain gave an intimation of what would happen next, but even so he wasn't prepared for it.

He watched the frame of the High Magus twist and stretch as he loomed over Miguel 903, his hands becoming talons. Abdulafia's mentor was transformed in an instant into an alien monster, spindly and many-jointed, its skull curving back over its ridged spine like a sickle moon. And it wasn't just the Illuminatus who was changing. A wind was rising around the pair as they stood at the lip of the precipice, whipping Zeon's robes up and out like wings, obscuring the form of Miguel. The image of the Ashsihi homeland stuttered and skipped like a broken filmstrip, mountains collapsing, the sun lurching across the sky like a cigarette-burn in reality...

Suddenly Afia was right behind his master, reaching out a hand to touch his spiked shoulder. His flesh was as rough as sharkskin for all that it appeared silvery-smooth; an alien hide stretched tight over otherworldly bones.

Zeon turned on him with a hiss as the vista behind him blurred into static, into a dust-storm of broken pixels. The battle-clone recoiled as he saw the cold intellect in those eyes; pain and madness slicked over with iron discipline.

The things that this creature had seen! The corpses of whole worlds lay drowned in the fires of its eyes... *But there could be no forgiveness.* Abdulafia felt the rage clench tight in his chest, cold hands around his heart.

Miguel lay dead in the alien's arms, his throat a raw red gash, his eyes open and staring incredulously. Blood dripped from Zeon's thin gray lips, from his needle teeth as he drew himself up to his full height.

"Do you see? DO YOU SEE!" roared the furnace voice of the Worm in Abdulafia's head, loud enough to drive him to his knees. *"THIS is your master, you foolish wretch! This is the hand that wields the sword, Abdulafia 330 - a hand with claws, dripping with human blood!"*

He wanted to scream his denial, but the wind tore the words from his throat, skirling away into nothingness. He wanted to believe that Asag'raal was lying, but there was something in those eyes he recognized, even when they started down at him from the face of an alien monster. This was Zeon's real face. The mask beneath his skin, beneath the bone, the mask nailed down to his soul...

The mountaintop was gone, ablated away to sand by the savage wind, so that 'Afia and his Master stood atop an island of shattered stone, suspended in an abyss of darkness. At the very edges of sight he could see the shades of the Arkborn, drawn like sharks to the scent of blood. The only color in the world was red, red on silver, red on black, dripping and pooling in Zeon's shadow as he held up his trophy to the dead.

"Now, slave... where is your sweet morality? *How many have you damned, you who judge a poor lost Saprophyte for its hunger?"*

Asag'raal's laughter hooked him twitching back into reality, its voice echoing in his head. 'Afia found himself on his knees in a pool of blood, his makeshift sword still clenched in one white-knuckled hand. And there was Miguel, tiny and broken, his soul gone to feed... what?

"Join us!" hissed the Worm, coiling slick and oily in his mind, intimate and vile. *"Join us, slave, and I'll make you the highest of my Exalted. I'll grant you power, you know. Power enough to take your revenge..."*

He didn't even feel himself struggle to his feet. He didn't feel *anything* anymore, except a cold, sickening emptiness in his chest. Abdulafia turned his blank eyes away from Miguel's corpse, down the tunnel toward the War Room of the Ashishim. And he started running.

Never before had he been closer to the fate he feared. Now his mind was on automatic, and he was truly a machine. His legs pumped mechanically, his blood hissed and pounded in his temples, and he navigated the blackened vaults beneath the city blind. Images flew at him, scatterburst, flashes of light thrown up against the darkness in his head. Broken bulkhead doors, shattered neon tubes, drowned gardens, twisted steel... *and everywhere the dead, leering at him knowingly.*

They wore her face, every one. CeeAn 187 died over and over again as Afia ran through the depths of the R.T, and the hands around her throat were silver claws.

Now came the light. Now came a hot and foetid breeze, whispering through the tunnels like a eulogy. *Now he stood in the doorway of the War Room, and witnessed his fears made real.*

The creature from his vision stood there in the center of the great spherical amphitheater, seven feet of silver skin and ragged white robes. Wraiths encircled his body like a halo, a moebius coil of them, phosphorescent and moaning. His twin-thumbed hands were raised over his head as he held up the focus of his power. The holiest relic of the Ashishim - the Chrome Ark.

White flames boiled across its surface as it spun there in the air, blurring the world around it. Abdulafia felt it tugging at his soul, scrabbling to sink its hooks into his mind. But the rage in him resisted - that and the sheer black sliver of Asag'raal which pulsed hot and heavy in his skull.

The thing which had been Zeon turned, spiked arms dropping to its sides. Everything about the creature was wrong - the geometry of its bones, the map of its corded muscles and tendons... everything except the eyes. This monster *was* the Illuminatus, and always had been.

"And so at last you come," Zeon rasped, as his face began to shimmer and melt, as his curved and thorny skull filled out with human features. "Greatest of my warriors, most precious of my children... linchpin of my victory." It wore a human form again by the time Abdulafia could master his shock, the face of a white-haired old man dressed in simple roughspun. "I'm glad you're here, 330. I've just held off a terrible assault... those things are everywhere, and... "

He stopped short as he ran into Abdulafia's cold stare, sensing the utter hatred which blazed around him like an aura. The Illuminatus licked his lips and grinned, tilting his head to one side. "You're not as foolish as you look, child. Definitely smarter than the rest of these peons. But if you think that means anything now, you're sadly mistaken."

Abdulafia stepped toward him, every muscle tight with rage. Dry bones collapsed to dust beneath his boots. The Eversio was heavy across his shoulders, but that wasn't the way to end this. No - this was work for the blade. The great heavy curve of steel hung down from his white-knuckled fist, black blood crusted across its surface. Zeon's eyes flicked down to it and back, and his face lit up with a feral grin.

"Oh, *surely* not, you little fool. I taught you everything you know, 330. Do you really think you can defeat me with *that*?"

"Do you admit what you are then?" whispered the battle-clone, hissing the words through clenched teeth. "Or will you face me in human skin?"

"I *made* you in human skin... and this is all I need to destroy you." said Zeon, calmly tying back his robe. He was nonchalant, *amused* - his very stance a calculated insult. "Arkborn - *take him*. I have no time to scrabble in the dirt with disobedient servants."

The loyalty of Zeon's wraiths had been paid for with blood - they were satiated from a feast of souls. Now they streamed from the Ark in a flood, a rippling silver ribbon of clutching claws and twisted faces, following his pointing finger. That phantom tide reared up over Abdulafia, a wave threatening to break, and the foam at its crest was made up of a thousand empty eyes.

"Soon you'll be one of them, Abdulafia. Don't try to fight it..."

He threw up his hands instinctively, trying to protect himself as the song of the Ark rose in a crescendo, plucking at the ragged edges of his soul.

Then the world flashed black, and 'Afia felt the charnel breath of the Worm on the back of his neck, its power crawling across his skin like electricity. The Arkborn recoiled from him in terror, wailing and moaning. And the battle-clone could see why.

His hands burned black with the fire of Asag'raal, and nothing that Zeon did could force the wraiths closer.

"Witness! You need me, slave! Only I can save you!"

"NO!" shouted Abdulafia, staring down at his hands with horror. Sizzling flames in negative played over his tainted flesh, a fire as cold as interstellar space. "All of you, get out of my head! I HAVE NO MASTER!"

He threw back his head as he shouted, throwing his arms out wide, and the fire tore off him in a spherical shockwave, flaying the Arkborn raw. The expanding bubble of force ripped through the bones and dust of the War Room, making dead screens flicker with light and sparks leap from broken wires. It blew back Zeon's robes like tattered wings, pushing him back one step, two...

And the Chrome Ark fell.

It was nothing but dead steel as it hammered into the floor, collapsing on its side, inert. Only the merest crawling spark of silver hinted at the spirits trapped within. But Zeon's eyes blazed with all the fire that had gone out of the Ark, and his hands were crooked into claws. Abdulafia saw madness in his lopsided grin; suspicion, paranoia - and fear.

"So... you've chosen sides already, have you? And you think that *I'm* a traitor to humanity? Let me tell you, 330, that thing you grovel before is far worse than anything *my* people have ever done. And the Praetor is a *connoisseur* of atrocities."

"Didn't you hear me?" spat the battle-clone. "*No masters.* Not anymore. I've had my fill of lies."

"You'll come to repent of your foolishness, Abdulafia," said the Illuminatus, shrugging out of his robes. Beneath them he was far from the wizened old man that the Ashishim imagined - he was muscled like a prizefighter, tattooed and scarified with cryptic runes. 'Afia could almost believe that he *was* human - but only for an instant. All the truth he needed was in those blank white eyes, twin arclamps spitting hate. "But repent too late, and you'll be no use to anyone. Not even the Black Technologists can fix *every* bone in your body..."

He was faster than Abdulafia expected, too.

Before the echoes of his words had died in the dusty air Zeon was right in front of him, clearing the space between them in a blur. His hand closed around the battle-clone's wrist, tighter than the vice-grip of a combat mekan, forcing him to drop his scavenged blade. And with the same movement he brought two fingers up under Afia's jaw, stabbing into his throat with cruel precision.

The dreadlocked warrior staggered back, gasping, his eyes bulging from their sockets. His makeshift sword clattered to the floor amid the bones of the dead Ashishim, forgotten. And Zeon moved in, one hand clenched behind his back, the other weaving like a cobra, two fingers extended.

"I came to save you from yourselves!" snarled the Illuminatus, hammering at a pressure point in 'Afia's shoulder. "This world was dying!" *Stab* "Your tribe were pathetic!" *Stab* "And you... I had to go to such lengths to make any use of you at all!" *Stab*. "A waste of time, child. You were always a bleeding heart."

The battle-clone stumbled over a low step and lay twitching on the ground, gasping for breath. Livid bruises picked out the places where his master's attacks had struck home.

"To think, the clone of a Kheptarch Lord, afraid of killing! I had to engineer that whole foolish masquerade, and sacrifice your *entire squad* just to make you see the light." He loomed over the fallen Ashishim, hands on hips, secure in his triumph. "By the way, 330 - Jhenna sends her regards - from within the Chrome Ark!"

Abdulafia's eyes sprung open in a mask of blood and filth.

Before Zeon could step back he was on his feet, a ragged fury spitting hate.

He snapped off one kick to the left and another to the right, blurring with speed, feeling them shatter the Illuminatus' ribs. Then he was airborne, powering into a spinning roundhouse kick that struck the traitor's skull with a sound like a rifle shot.

Abdulafia slowed time with the 'chrome still burning in his veins, and threw his weight hard to the right, reversing his spin, bringing his boot up in an unstoppable arc...

Only to meet the iron bar of Zeon's forearm. He felt the shock deep in his bones as his old mentor took a grip on his ankle, grinning like a demon. Then the Illuminatus lashed out with a kick of his own - right into 'Afia's groin. The battle-clone flew backwards through a row of desks and terminals, spinning wild, hot agony pounding in his skull. Like the Kheptarch he'd been sequenced from Abdulafia never went into battle without 'adequate protection', but even so... he shook tiny slivers and beads of safety glass from his dreadlocks in a daze, rolling the kinks out of his neck. This wasn't going to be easy at all.

"Come on then, you vatgrown little shit!" spat Zeon, beckoning him forward. "Let's see just how well I've taught you!"

Abdulafia was all too happy to oblige...

Ω

This used to be his world.

Neat manicured lawns, terraced houses clipped from the pages of magazines, topiary trees and wrought-iron steeetlamps... the Belt, his little artificial heaven. Eddie Tsien had never imagined that he'd see it like this - not even in his nightmares, when he'd wished for cataclysm and ruin to rain down on his vapid neighbors.

This was nothing less than a warzone.

Gerhard Mitchell's men may have been old, but they weren't short of courage, and they made the Saprophytes pay for every step they took, scourging them with fire and lead. But the tide was relentless, a horde desperate for blood and souls. There were even slaved machines among them - a motley assortment of mekan with their controlling personalities usurped. Now they followed the Super-Cyben, snapping at his heels like rabid hounds.

It had only taken a single threat to whip Exalted Phexx and Exalted Syliss into line - the fate of Quamiss still burned brightly in their minds. He'd beaten them into sullen servitude and sent them out on his flanks, driving the survivors of the Beltway before them, funneling them into his trap. Of course, he couldn't blame them for being afraid - even monsters such as the Exalted knew fear, and in this case it was a reflex of pure survival.

Once Eddie caught sight of himself in the crazed picture-window of a burning store, and his self-control almost slipped. He was able to control the mekanik bulk of his body remotely, from the new seat of his soul inside B-Zerk's empty skull. But the Worm Asag'raal had taken what remained of his flesh, transforming him utterly. No engine of war had ever been so vile or so cruel as Eddie Tsien, a baroque nightmare of metal and scales and teeth, the guns of broken warmekan jutting from his shoulders between belching iron smokestacks. It was as if a furnace smoldered inside his ribcage - a great snarling face of bronze and steel covered his chestplate now, and sparks belched from between its teeth with every step he took. A cloud of soot and ashes whipped out behind him like an oriflamme, as rusted gears spun naked at each joint of his arms and legs. He had become a walking totem of war, faceless behind his polished black mask, his hands reduced to spiked maces dragging bloody chains.

It was the face of his fear. It was his horror turned inside out; the agony of a man becoming a soulless machine...

But it was all a lie.

Damned Asag'raal thought that his newest toy was totally compromised, marching to the slaughter of thousands with grim abandon. But Eddie Tsien was still in control, piloting his own body remotely through the uplink to the Mark-Four drone. So far his crushing hands and blazing guns had caused a whole lot of empty ruin without claiming a single casualty.

He just hoped Gerhard Mitchell would be sharp enough to notice. The Saprophytes weren't nearly as restrained, and any human who straggled behind the Super-Cyben's line of advance was torn to bloody ribbons.

A hail of lead ricocheted from his armor as he strode down the center of the street, scanning the terraces with his thermal eyes. *There - an empty house.* Smudged blurs of hot red were scrambling away across the lawn, fleeing before a tide of ravenous shadows. Tsien fired off a blast from his shoulder-mounted fusion cannon, and he heard the Worm laugh as the building exploded, shards of plastic and aluminum ripping the polyprop sky to shreds. Outside was all flamelight and darkness; the baby-blue skin of the beltway dripped blood and acid rain from a thousand wounds.

He knew he couldn't save them all. He only hoped that his deception would hold until he reached the second tier, Ridgemont Street - his family.

If they were still alive...

Schematics of the Belt spun up in front of Zone Doubt's eyes, picking out the line of the Saps' advance in red neon. The great hanging structure was built in a spiral coil around the space-'lev's spire, four fat rings corkscrewing skyward, all the way up to Ground Floor One.

Ridgemont Street cut across the main drag halfway through the second turn, a neat little neighborhood of picket fences and cutout plastic villas.

That was where they'd make their play.

Tsien redoubled his pace, clanking forward like an unstoppable juggernaut. He saw the two-man chaingun team who had fired on him packing up and slipping away, and he aimed a shot wide of them, incinerating a stand of poplars with maser fire. Gerhard's veterans were slick - they fought a running battle like men a third their age. But of course, they'd had plenty of experience during the Seven Hours War. Seven Hours that probably felt like decades...

Then he turned the corner, a horde of demons at his back, and saw the Division line.

Gerhard had drawn them up in a trap-jaw formation, behind overturned civilian cars and barricades of scrap, a 'v' of blackened metal bristling with guns. But Eddie had already seen what bullets and blasts did to the Saprophytes - precisely nothing. Even fire only burned away their flesh, freeing the soul within to new atrocities. How he longed for his blade, that ponderous slab of steel that he'd left behind. He'd felt their pain, their *disintegration* as he drove its edge through them.

Damn, but that had felt good.

Perhaps Gerhard Mitchell's last stand would hold them for five minutes, for ten... but then Syliss and Phexx would sweep in from the flanks, and the Saprophytic wave would break. So long as he bought enough time for the survivors to reach the *Axis Mortalis*, that would be enough.

Ω

They'd all gone down the ziplines, down the ladders and into the iris of that vast black eye. And none of them had returned.

Jimson Holgarth was alone aboard the *Axis*, his pale skin bathed red in the light of the burning city. Thick runnels of blood dripped down the windows of the airship's control gondola, and on a cluster of screens before him the terrified Subcommander of Celebrants could watch Elysium's suffering in terrible detail.

There was no way he was going to land this thing.

But then again, he needed a crew to fly it. A navigator, pilots, engineers, an ecclisiast of Manifest Dogma to sanctify its ancient fission cores... Without them he was as good as dead.

When the shortwave radio crackled to life Jimson almost leaped out of his skin - he half-expected to hear the voice of Benton Veer, screaming obscenities at him from beyond the grave. Not as foolish as it sounded - he'd seen things on those screens that surely had no place among the living...

"Celebrant Pilot! Celebrant Pilot! This is Gerhard Mitchell, acting Yeoman of the Beltway! Come in, *Axis Mortalis*, we have a *situation* down here!"

Holgarth brought the silver-chased mic to his lips with trembling hands, hunched over it as if in prayer.

"This... this is Celebrant Subcommander Jimson Holgarth. I...I'm the last one left! The others... Master Benton... they all... " he broke off, sobbing, hating himself for breaking down. Hadn't he wished that old skeleton Veer dead a thousand times over?

"Get it together, son!" hissed the far-off voice of Gerhard Mitchell. "I need you to do something - something that's gonna save a whole lot of lives. Heavens know you Celebrants have taken enough of them - now it's time to give something back."

Jimson nodded, mute, thinking about Benton Veer, his face half-rotted away, black tears glistening on his powdered cheeks...

"I need you to use the grapples on that thing. Snag some of those Omni' sreeenships, send them the Division override command. I'll patch it through. Then you're gonna bring the Axis in through torus two, one-hundred three degrees northeast."

"Fly it? Myself? But..."That was as far as he got.

"Mister Holgarth, you might very well be the last Celebrant left on Earth. And back in my youth I made a solemn oath that one day I was gonna wring the fucking neck of one of you corpse-rapists. Now, it seems that fate has narrowed down the field. *So you either defect, and bring me my zeppelin, or I'm coming up there myself.*"

Something in the Tutor-captain's voice made Jimson absolutely sure he was serious.

Ω

He must have looked like a creature out of the bottomless hells as he waded into that storm of lead - an implacable mekan-beast streaming sparks and smoke, his great spiked fists crossed in front of his faceless helm. But Mitchell's men held the line against him, laying down a withering crossfire. Eddie's saprophytic outer skin was torn away by a hail of bullets, blistered and charred by the flickering tongues of masers and fusion carbines. But he wouldn't fall. He *couldn't* fall. The darkness in him could sense their fear, smell the dripping sweat of the men who hemmed him in on all sides. Every step he took wound their tension tighter, until he could all but hear the sound of minds cracking like glass under the strain.

Close enough now. Close enough to risk using the open band...

"Gerhard! It's me! It's Eddie Tsien! Tell them to concentrate their fire on those things behind me! I'm going to..."

There was a crackle of static, a blur of noise and light.

Something had caught Zone Doubt by the throat; it had slammed him up against a flaking concrete wall, clenching gnarled gray fists about his windpipe. Eddie's connection to his Super-Cyben body flickered and almost died for an instant, making that grim black war-engine grind to a halt. Bullets still skipped and sparked from off its glistening armor, but Tsien was suddenly miles away from the firefight.

In the belly of the Subcity.

"He's only a child!" said Elakoz, tugging at his friend's shoulder. "Leave him be, Jarl, and help me with these other ones. There's ammo here, and look! Slades! We can soon be down and out with this lot!"

Jarl growled, shrugging the ragged little man's hand away. his grip tightened around B-Zerk's throat as he writhed, pinned to the bloodstained concrete.

"Just a child? Do you forget what that demon-ridden girl did to Makra and Chaik? Gralloched them like pigs she did, and all with her pretty pink hands. This one is *touched*, Elakoz - look at his bloody eyes!"

"We'll be dead soon if we don't keep running," muttered the downsider, filling his pockets with shotgun shells and stained banknotes. "And those are nothing but implants - he's likely a blind-born brat fitted out by the Vatican's men."

Jarl shook B-Zerk savagely, clenching his yellowed teeth.

"Then he's some priest's catamite? Perhaps he knows a secret way into their fortress. All those bloody Knights and Sentinels have to be worth something..."

Then the tattered cape swathed across B-Zerk's shoulders fell away, revealing the great chrome tumor of the Core drone. Jarl dropped him, swearing, wiping his hands against his greasy overalls as if he was diseased. Elakoz already had a pistol-grip shotgun in his hand, training it on B's head.

"I'd advise against it, friend," came the voice of Eddie Tsien from the child's blue-black lips. "I really would. I just don't have time for this."

He could feel the will of Asag'raal taking control of his distant body now, as his attention bled away. As if in a daze he watched one of his mace-spiked hands hammer into an upturned delivery van, sending it flying through the air to punch through the wall of a house. The black disease gave in to its hunger, throwing him against Mitchell's line like a battering ram.

"Holy shit! He's one of them! He's *possessed!*" shrieked Elakoz, his hands shaking as he tried to aim his hand-cannon.

"Like fuck. That's one o' them C-Div things. Cyben unit. That proves it - the damned Machine is behind all this! Tryin' to wipe us out so its precious bloody Khepts can rule the world..."

Tsien could only watch as his sequestrated body ploughed through the police line, swinging its hands like wrecking balls. An officer went down under the lash of his spiked chains, ripped in half with a look of utter disbelief on his face. Another was driven into the ground by one of those titanic maces, bludgeoned to a pulp. But there was a method to the madness of his new flesh. Bullets and fusion blasts sleeted off his back like rain as he waded through the topiary garden of a little white-painted house, trailing broken fence-palings and roses. Up to the door, leveling the cannons on his shoulders at the flimsy polished wood.

And bolted down to it in gleaming brass; a number.

Twenty-nine.

"You always wanted it to be this way, didn't you, Eddie?" chuckled the Worm, its voice sighing in his head like the wind between rows of crosses. *"One last kiss before dying... one last thing to tip you over the edge. Welcome home, High Exalted. Welcome home..."*

Then the door blew off its hinges, shattering across his armored chest. Splinters of wood flew like chaff as he rocked back on his heels, a black iron golem with nothing but hot echoes in its head. Everything seemed so far away; a blur fed in through a cluster of cameras, slicked over B-Zerk's artificial eyes.

"I say we kill it now!" stammered Elakoz, shuffling forward with his shotgun. "Damn thing's likely talking to the others. Cyben. Mekan. Comin' for us!"

"And *I* say we take it with us. It can get us past the defensive lines - with the right persuasion."

"Tsien, if you're not going to do something about these two, I will!" screeched the Core drone, drowning out the insane cackle of Asag'raal

in his skull. *"And then you'll be back in your own damned body!"*

But Eddie wasn't listening. Not to the drone, not to the two ragged downsiders who had B-Zerk holed up at gunpoint - not even to the Worm, hissing and moaning as it wallowed in the ruin of the Beltway. His blazing eyes were fixed on the figure in the doorway of number twenty-nine Ridgemont street - a woman in black with a huge Cyben riot gun in her hands, racking back the pump to chamber another four shells.

"I don't care what the fuck you are, or who the hell sent you," growled Mrs Toria Jane Tsien, her face a mask of hatred behind a smear of lipstick and mascara. "And I don't give a damn how big you are."

She gripped the massive cannon with both hands, spitting to one side and aiming along its quartate barrel.

"I told Myria Stanwick's doberman, and now I'm telling you. *Get off of my motherfucking lawn before I blow you in half!"*

DOCUMENT INSERT: MULTIPLICITY ARCHIVES DEPARTMENT

The Railblades

A collection of twelve weapons commissioned by
the Terminus Separatist Army for their most elite
warriors, the crycelium-boosted commandos of the
Chimera Upliftment Project.

Each weapon comprises three highly developed
combat systems; a self-sharpening monomolecular-
edged sword, a versatile combat railgun, and an
electromagnetic shielding system.

The Railblades were developed quickly, designed as
a foil to the personal combat shields developed
by the United Democracies of old Earth. These
shielding systems rendered conventional soldiers
proof against long-range weapons of all but the
most powerful caliber - glancing shots and small-
arms fire were easily deflected by the prototype
models stolen by the Terminus' espionage teams.

The easy answer to this vexing problem was a
return to a style of warfare not seen for nearly
five hundred years - the art of the sword. To
this end the scientists of the Terminus Investors
Council developed a series of tripartite weapons
systems, each tailored to the particular boosted
warfighter who would wield it.

Kronos maintains three of the blades in its vast
armory, but the rest are missing - some must have
been utterly destroyed during the nuclear assault
on Terminus Afrika, others sunken to the seabed,
buried in silt...

The only other specimen known to the Ashishim
is the great two-handed blade 'Undertaker', a
revered relic of the Vatican. At eight feet long,

with curving axe-blades widening its tip to two
and a half feet wide, this weapon must have been
designed for a genewritten giant of a warrior,
augmented with extensive crycelial webstructures.

Thankfully, 'Undertaker' and its kind are useless
today - powerless without the Crycelial systems
with which they were designed to integrate.
With this in mind, it has been decided by the
Illuminatus that our erstwhile allies in the
Church can keep their trophy sword - it is nothing
more than a bulky ornament without the right hand
to wield it.

On the Armaments of the Ancients
Ashishim Didactic Educational Text for Noviate
Dervashi

17 Aevum Oblivio

Sick

"*HOLD YOUR FIRE! Stop!*" *shouted Ruby Alvarez, choking on a mouthful of azure blue cryo-fluid. "Tin Man, it's us! What the hell are you shooting at?"*

"*He's gone,*" *replied the ancient warmekan. "Got right past me, the slippery bastard. But if you're unfrozen, then...*"

"*Could one of you help me with this useless lump?*" *asked the Scarecrow, dragging the snoring bulk of Big Leon behind him. "And while you're at it... what year is this? Why the hells are we locked in cryofreeze, Tin Man?*"

"*And why didn't you get us out, if you were out here shooting up the place?*" *snarled Ruby, wringing a bucketful of cryonic soup out of her hair. "You could have at least thawed me out... I'm sure I did a lot better than these other two bozos back on Jones' boat.*"

"*Sure,*" *said the Scarecrow, dumping Leon unceremoniously to the floor. A pool of blue liquid splashed out from under him, slopping down into a cascade of rusted drains "You were doing great, Ruby - if our mission was to seduce Jaq Haszan, and not kill him...*"

"*Why you treacherous little...*" *began the disgraced Kheptarch, balling her fists and striding forward.*

"*What? You think I'm still taking orders from you after that debacle?*"

"*I'll teach you to be insolent to your betters!*"

"*Really? And who might they be?*"

"*SHUT UP!*" *bellowed the Tin Man, his speaker system cranked up to eleven. "The reason I didn't thaw you out is pretty damned obvious. All of those tanks were linked together - three coffins, one freezer. Right? And the problem with waking you up was this...*"

The warmekan's chest-plate split open then, revealing the three tiny projector lenses of a threedeeo system. It threw out a flickering cone of light, tracing the outline of a human body, hashing in the details as it went... Pressed whites, a black-banded panama hat, a rosewood cane tipped with silver...

It was Octavio Vanecke.

"Greetings, viewers - and hello to you as well, Jaq Haszan." The smiling little mannikin tipped its hat to the cameras. "If you're watching this threedeeo, then I'm afraid my little ploy to get rid of you has failed. These bumbling fools have let me down for the last time, though... and I'm certain that they'll prove far more effective in death than they ever were in life. Now, I've been watching your monitors, guys, and I've got to say that I expected better. Leon, Aitken and dear Dorothea unconscious... and Tin Man, your GPS tracer puts you on the bottom of the ocean! I should have expected as much from a group I put together as my own little joke, but hey... I'm nothing if not an optimist. So Jaq, I'd like you to meet another friend of mine. They call it - Munitorium Necrovirus 392! Happy hemorrhaging, Jaq... and give my regards to Deutoronomy Jones and his crew as they bleed out!"

Ruby caught on quickly.

"He primed the countdown... and Jones had us frozen! But that *means...*"

"Oh, shit," *groaned Aitken Straw, looking down at the shattered knifeblades of his fingers. There was blood all over his hands, seeping from a crimson stain in the middle of his shirt.* "Guys, I really don't feel so good..."

Ruby and the Tin Man exchanged a look of pure terror.

"And that's why the alien woke you up," *said the rusty old warmekan, his voice a flat mechanical dirge* "It wasn't me. The damned thing must have known..."

"Run!" *croaked Ruby Alvarez, her face gone deathly pale.*

It wouldn't do much good. But it went against her every sensibility to die screaming and hopeless...

2196 Ante Arbitrium
Titanomachia

DAVE LEVINE HAD never flown an airship before. Heck, he had his own people to drive him anywhere he wanted to go; it'd been years since he wrapped his fingers around a steering wheel of any kind. But this was too good an opportunity to pass up.

Down below him the spillway heaved with a tide of desperate humanity, whole little nations and subtribes boiling up out of the depths of Elysium, crushed against the gates of the Pit. It was more than just a grisly spectacle - it was *newsworthy*. Uncle Dave had been a sportscaster for forty long years, but deep in his corporate-sponsored soul the flame of pure journalism still burned. It was his duty to bring this story to the people, and get the scoop on that holographic bastard Jory Hess.

Screens stretched tight across the flanks of the zeppelin blazed with light, broadcasting a slick montage of carnage to the people below. They could watch their own deaths in glorious Technicolor.

Then something came down past the gondola window in a blur of white and silver - a huge humanoid mekan falling out of the sky. Eddies of turbulence made the airship weave and bob, fighting against Dave's hands on the controls. But he caught it on camera as it slammed down amid the crowd, unfolding from a crouch with it's searchlights blazing. Vatican tech. Something like their bloody Templars, but the size of a hab-cube, a faceless metal knight poised there on the spillway, one huge gauntlet braced against an electrical pylon.

This was gold! Ratings gold! He'd show them that he was a real reporter, not just some advertising shill... Dave wrestled his airship in closer, until he could see the glittering steel irises in the mekan's optics rig. And when they shifted, zooming and focusing, he was ready.

For anything but *that*.

Now the anchorman saw what had been driving the throng of frantic refugees, herding them in their tens of thousands. And he bit back on a very unprofessional scream, because they were hideous.

The Exalted which Asag'raal had chosen were replete with the dead - six lumbering black hulks heaved forward on thousands of arms and legs and claws; the limbs of the victims they'd devoured. Identity had been stripped from them, and reason, and form; they were constantly melting and reshaping, slumping down and rearing up again in ecstatic agony. Each one dragged a mass grave along with it in its tight and bloated belly, screaming faces pressed up a against a membrane of shadows.

And now they were combining.

The Exalted flowed together like molten tar, twining their hooked limbs and questing pseudopods together into a tower of flesh, a tottering spike of darkness. It bulked out as it grew, bulging in the middle, extending webbed buttresses of saprophytic matter to hold itself upright... And Uncle Dave saw what was going to happen next. He supposed that the Vatican Knight saw it too, for it brought it's guns to bear on the thing and let fly, raking it with maserfire.

It was too little, and too late.

The twisted spire of flesh had already split down the middle, forming a pair of thick, pillarlike legs. Four lashing tentacles burst from the torso of the beast, aping the warmekan's design. Maser blasts cooked the surface of the creature, sending up plumes of blue-black smoke. But beneath that dripping, oily skin was a snarl of bones and rotting flesh, held together with tendons of darkness. The guns were useless against it.

Dave watched those forty-foot tentacles curl lazily through the air, hooks like reaping blades budding from their tips. One of them came down through the crowd, slicing a furrow through flesh and bone and concrete, sending tiny bodies flying like leaves before a storm. The MegaPhyte took one lumbering step, and its flat-bottomed foot crushed a hundred screaming refugees, absorbing them into its mass. The anchorman watched, sickened and fascinated as it heaved itself into motion, coming down the spillway slope with the momentum of an avalanche.

It had grown a head, now - a tumor of darkness excreted from between its shoulders, split by a pair of ragged eye-slits. The hate in that empty white stare was enough to freeze Dave Levine's blood.

He never saw the tentacle coming. Paralyzed with horror, it was all he could do to keep both his hands on the steering yoke of the airship. But the MegaPhyte had seen *him*, and something inside it's fractured mind recognized his face. A hundred thousand tortured souls made up the Exalted war-machine, and all of them knew Uncle Dave, the most trusted name in death-sports commentary.

The razor hook at the end of the MegaPhyte's lash gutted the Omnivasive zeppelin in one lazy sweep, snapping its aluminum ribs like matchwood. It curled back as the doomed airship fell, then snapped forward again, whiplike and slick, coming through the gondola window at supersonic speed.

Dave Levine didn't have time to sign this one off. His final broadcast flashed out across the crumpling screens of the gasbag as it collapsed - silent and horrified, his chest split from collarbone to navel and gaping wide. The gambler's gospel tonight had just gone to the Worm.

Ω

CeeAn watched the Omni zeppelin go down, and she tensed inside her combat harness. Her eyes narrowed behind their optronic goggles, zeroing in on the nightmare face of the enemy.

Typical. Six little Exalted would have been easy street for a monster like Saint Sebastian - she'd have picked them off one by one and enjoyed the sport of it. Now she was in trouble, and there was no Abdulafia 330 to back her up. Not now, or ever again...

The MegaPhyte brought its bulk up to a lurching run as she watched, staggering forward on bent and twisted limbs. Screaming Subcits scrambled over each other's backs to clear a path, but there were still a few unlucky souls who were trampled beneath its feet. The two writhing tentacular whips on its left pulled back behind it as it ran, twining together to form an arm, a hand, a fist...

A mouth tore open across its lopsided face - and it *roared*, loops and coils of mucous flying wide.

Cee was already airborne as it began its swing, powering up off the spillway slope with all the force the Seraph's nuclear micropile could muster. The electrical pylon she'd been braced against flexed back as she stepped off its crown, gaining altitude, watching the lumbering Exalted struggle to check its wild momentum.

It didn't have a chance.

The MegaPhyte crashed into the steel tower as she let it whip back into its face, snapping a skein of high-tension cables like cobwebs. Gobbets of black tar and decaying flesh flew wide, falling like rain across the frantic crowd below. For a fraction of a second CeeAn thought she had it beat - suspended above the beast at the apex of her leap, watching it writhe and thrash against the broken steel of the pylon.

Then its cruel dead eyes were on her, and she felt one of those bullwhip tentacles coil around the Seraph's ankle. Cee gasped with pain as the whole world blurred sideways, spinning upside down, catching up again with a shock that drove glass into her bones.

The MegaPhyte slammed Saint Sebastian into the side of a

crumbling dam - one of the oceanic levees which kept the Atlantic out of the Pit. She'd struck it hard enough to leave a mekan-shaped imprint in the reinforced concrete - hard enough to ignite flashes of purple and red on the inside of her skull. Out of the corner of her eye she saw tiny figures in feathers and chainmail running and slipping and falling away, bouncing off jagged twists of rebar all the way down to the seabed. To the Ferals, this was the *titanomachia*, a war between gods...

But she didn't have time to contemplate the fate of the Pit Ferals for long. That oily black tentacle was still clenched around the warmekan's ankle, and now Asag'raal's pet pulled it taut again, plucking the Seraph up into the air like a toy. CeeAn tried to reach out with her slim-fingered manipulator arms, but it was no use. A whirl of black and red and silver spun by as Saint Sebastian was hurled bodily from one side of the Pit to the other, hammering into the opposite levee with a sound like shattering mountains.

Systems readouts flashed bright and urgent in front of her eyes. Spotlit - the reactor core, leaking coolant in a hissing radioactive cloud.Needles were already pushing up into the red, yammering for an emergency shutdown. And riding inside a humanoid A-bomb was the least of her worries. As her vision cleared Cee watched the MegaPhyte pull itself loose from the remains of the ruined pylon, its colossal fist tapering into a spike...

Oh dear. That wasn't good at *all*.

The *Dervashi*'s hands were all over the controls as she felt her foe's grip twitch, and watched a crooked smile split its face. That spike was a wicked twist of bones, fused together from the dead and just waiting to make her acquaintance. Cee smiled, wrapping her fingers around a pair of gilded aircraft throttles. She'd be *so* sorry to see it disappointed...

G-forces snapped her back in her harness as the MegaPhyte reeled her in, heaving with all its strength. But as the creature lunged forward CeeAn brought the Serpah's knees up to its chest, opening a set of blast-door vents in its armored shell. A chuff of smoke burst out, whipping past the MegaPhyte's face, and then...

The jump-jets which those sexless Black Technologists had fitted to Sebastian were made to lift three hundred tons of warmekan off the ground - guns, ammo and all. They packed enough juice to blast it halfway into orbit if it needed to cut and run. Now those twin lances of fire burned into the Worm's killing machine, sending up clouds of greasy black smoke. The tentacle wrapped around Sebastian's ankle whipped back, scalded, and the beast squealed in agony, its empty eyes blazing.

Unfortunately, that rope of flesh had been the only thing holding CeeAn down.

The Serpah battlesuit flew backwards, out of control, spinning wild in the dark. It curved up toward the boiling clouds, punching through them and on, out into clear air where the spotlit wire of the space-'lev split the sky. Down below she could hear the MegaPhyte screaming, a sound like rending metal amplified until it shook the world. Then her jumpjets stuttered and died. The roar of her engines was choked off, replaced by the creak and hiss of Saint Sebastian's battered body.

CeeAn tapped the altimeter with one finger, hoping that it was reading wrong.

Sixty thousand feet.

Gravity was going to make its presence felt at any second, and she was all out of options.

There was a moment of floating, weightless peace as the immense warmekan reached the very top of its arc, looking down on a contrail of smoke and sparks. Then it began to fall, airbrakes snapping open from its back like wings to slow its descent. The straps of the Seraph's harness cut into CeeAn's shoulders as its giant airbrakes took up the load, forcing tears from her eyes. But they were nowhere near enough. This suicide plunge would end up with the Seraph smeared across a radioactive crater - unless that beast down there was as vicious and stupid as she thought it was...

As if in answer to her thoughts the clouds tore apart, spiraling out as a burgeoning light swelled within them. Ragged streamers boiled away, a hole opening up like the eye of a cyclone - and through it came a ball of greasy fire, trailing a comet-tail of black smoke.

The saprophyte had learned a new trick. But this time it was all to Cee's advantage.

As the fireball arced up toward her CeeAn took aim through the crystal reticules inside her goggles. It was made of corpse-gas, burning grease and ashes, vomited up from the vile depths of the MegaPhyte. But Saint Sebastian had a few explosive tricks of its own.

Two of the burnished organ-pipes which reared up behind the warmekan's head spat tongues of flame, fat cylinders spiraling up and away as CeeAn fell. She was going to meet the fireball halfway - and it would roast her alive inside the Saint's armor unless her game was razor sharp.

The *Symphonia Mortis* missiles reached the top of their trajectory, tumbling end over end in the near-vacuum of the high atmosphere. Panels in their sides clicked and slid and interlocked as their nosecones felt the tug of gravity. Then their second-stage rockets came online, powering them down so fast that the edges of their wings glowed red-hot, a pair of tiny sparks against the immensity of space. They were three miles out, falling faster than the warmekan, scanners playing across the surface of the fireball. Now one mile, and their nosecones blew apart, retro-thrusters flaming white. Now a quarter mile; now mere yards, feet, inches...

Racks of tiny bomblets deployed from the flanks of each *Mortis* drone as it hung in the air above Saint Sebastian's head, fanning out like vast angel wings behind the Vatican war-machine. There were two hundred little high-explosive warheads tucked away in each one, and the contrails they left behind them looked like white feathers against the sky.

The MegaPhyte's fireball was torn apart.

Submunitions came down on it like rain, a hail of tiny explosions fraying and ablating its roiling bulk. CeeAn rode the blowback from all those concussive shockwaves, letting her warmekan's airbrakes take the strain as it slowed. By the time Saint Sebastian fell feet-first through the remains of the fireball the heat of it was barely enough to bubble its baroque paintwork.

Down below, the MegaPhyte raged and howled, taking out its wrath on the defenses of the Pit. Scavenged howitzers and machineguns stitched lead across its lumpen bulk, tracer lighting up the night. People screamed and ran and perished, crushed beneath its feet or ripped to shreds by crossfire.

It had to die. Quickly - before the Exodus was reduced to nothing but CeeAn alone.

Something in her mind told her she needed *numbers*. Something left there by that drowned cyclopean heart. She needed an army, a nation... the tools to rebuild.

Six more *Symphonia Mortis* missiles burst from their pipes as she pressurized the dregs of fuel in her jumpjet tanks, priming them for a final burst. If she hit at this speed there was a tiny chance that the wermekan might actually survive. And if she landed on top of Asag'raal's pet abomination, there was every chance it would be reduced to dead necrotic soup.

Down through the clouds she came, her hands white-knuckled around the golden grips of Sebastian's jumpjet throttles. Little crosses on chains swung and jangled behind her, and puffs of sweet sandalwood incense swirled up from autocensers set into the warmekan's dash, counterpoint to the burning city below. Her optronics zoomed in on the MegaPhyte's empty white eyes, and she saw them widen with shock. The stupid creature actually thought that the explosions above the clouds had meant her death...

The needle of the altimeter was whirling like a tiny turboprop in front of her. The ground came rushing up, black concrete and blood, searchlights and fires and tracer skittering off her armor. CeeAn hit her burners just as those six *Symphonia Mortis* drones split open in her slipstream, raining seeds of death.

The gargantuan heart inside her head thumped, once, a tectonic shiver warping the world around her.

Blue-white fire drove the MegaPhyte to its knees, blades of flame slicing into its flesh like cauterizing razors. For an instant the immense tonnage of the warmekan hung in the air above its foe, all four arms outstretched as if it was crucified. Then its wings of smoke furled in, each feather the contrail of a high-explosive warhead. They fell past CeeAn in a spiral storm, and she felt the path of each one, the weight, the spin, the trajectory...

The 'chrome had them.

Screaming in triumph she threw a clutch of bomblets in the MegaPhyte's face, then another, curving them in to pummel it like a flurry of blows. She could feel her bioelectric field unfolding, coating the metallic skin of the Seraph with a nacreous sheen, infusing steel tendons and hydraulics with the speed and urgency of life...

Explosions rocked Sebastian back on its heels, painting its ornate armor with splashes of blackened gore. Choking smoke billowed. Shards of bone flew like shrapnel.

CeeAn's saprophytic foe reeled back from the missile storm, gaping holes gouged clear through its body. It roared in incomprehending rage, clawing at her mind with pain, only to slam up against a fury far more refined and concentrated than its own. Suffering poured over her like rain - but it was as nothing compared to the thunder of that incorporeal heart, hanging in the sky above her like a harvest moon.

This was for the innocent. This was for Abdulafia, gone to his death to try and save her. This was for her own death, and the pain of her rebirth...

The creature tried to stitch itself back together, shadows looping and congealing as its mouth worked in mute agony. But she wouldn't give it a chance. The Seraph was never meant to be so fast, so limber, so *alive*... but with the power of CeeAn's mind behind it the three-hundred ton monster was a thing of grace.

Subcitizens scattered in a blind panic as she pushed her advantage, coming down on the MegaPhyte with a spinning kick, her steel-plated heel biting deep. Turbomaces howled and whined as they spun up, smashing into the creature's flesh with enough force to split mountains. It was pure feral streetfighting, blow after blow strung together into a symphony of rage. Before Cee's onslaught the Chosen of the Worm was helpless, stumbling, falling, collapsing against the spillway with an impact that shook Elysium's foundations.

But still it wouldn't die.

The damn thing had faked her out.

Four whipsaw tentacles erupted from the bulk of the Megaphyte as its eyes narrowed, binding up the Seraph's wrists. CeeAn knew the strength behind those coils all too well - but there was nothing she could do to stop them now that she was in their grip. She threw all her weight against the warmekan's controls, driving pitons from the machine's feet into the spillway to keep her balance.

Then the tips of the Megaphyte's tentacles split open, peeling back petals of flesh to reveal four snarling lipless mouths. They strained and snapped at the joints of Sebastian's arms, worrying at the edges of its armor plates and cooling vanes, each one studded with row upon row of human teeth.

But there was worse to come.

As Cee strained against her captor, feeling pipes and linkages give way one by one, a vast lump swelled in the MegaPhyte's throat, inching its way up toward the thing's jaws. Its mouth tore open, impossibly wide, a tunnel of oily decay lit up with burning corpse-gases. It was another fireball, and this time there was no way to stop it.

Blinding light filled the creature's maw, building up into the fury of a miniature sun...

Cooling vanes snapped and shattered as CeeAn twisted, desperate, throwing herself wild against the straps of her harness. Railgun rounds tore into the fireball as it grew, a withering crossfire... with absolutely no effect. The spinning spiked rings of her turbomaces howled and sparked, bound up in filaments of darkness.

And CeeAn felt that great hanging ocean above her again, closer now, its waters cool and deep and welcoming. It would be like going home, this death. It would mean... *reunion*.

Then something slammed into the MegaPhyte from behind, a looping thread of silver piercing its side. Another came, and another, rays of steel arcing up out of the pit, from the ragged fortifications of Clan Ghyre, the Feral warlords.

They were grapple-lines, fired from the flat decks of burned-out Technical pickups, from shoulder-mounted cannons and watchtower posts. Ten thousand hands took up the strain, heaving against the mass of the monster to try and bring it down. The MegaPhyte screamed in outrage, a sound like ruptured high-pressure pipes, desperate to shake the grapples loose. But even ten thousand wouldn't be enough - and any second now that greasy ball of fire was going to vomit forth.

CeeAn almost missed the tiny Teuton battlesuit as it clambered to the top of the Vatican walls. The stick-scrawl figures of priests and novices and 'Crucis-men with blazing staves were closing in around it, frantic, screaming, but it gained the parapet before any of them could stop it. The communicator bead inside Cee's goggles crackled into life, bringing the lone Knight's voice right into the cockpit with her.

"Let's finish it together, *Hashishin*! For my God or yours, or none at all. That thing must die!"

It was the Valle Crucis she'd left swaddled in her holocoat, the man she'd almost killed in her assault on the Vatican's inner sanctum. Now he ignited the jumpjets in his warsuit's carapace, leaping from the barbican fortress on a pillar of blue-white smoke. Now his chainsaw arms reached out to embrace the MegaPhyte, a thing ten times his size, coming down on it like a mantis attacking a poisonous toad.

The creature's head was distorted now, as it worked to disgorge its crop of plasma, its eyes stretched out to jagged slits in its bubbling skin. But it saw him. It hissed, dripping liquid night from its snapping tentacle-mouths. And it let go of one of Saint Sebastian's hands, sending a whipcord of coiled darkness scything through the air.

The mouth at its tip was a gash filled with yellow teeth, and it snapped closed on the Teuton like a pitbull's jaws around a rag doll. Monomolecular chainsaw blades screeched and whined deep within its crushing embrace, carving it open from the inside out. But CeeAn had no time to worry about her unexpected ally.

One of her hands was free - and one was all she needed.

Schematics of the battle-saint flickered in front of her eyes, all the espionage data the didactic rams had loaded into her head back in the Dervashic Academy. The Black Technologists had never assumed that their pride and joy would meet its match in size or weight - even in their darkest dreams they'd never conceived of a thing like the MegaPhyte. But there were superheavy tanks, land-battlecruisers and armored airships in the arsenals of the unfaithful. And the Vatican was nothing if not *traditionalist...*

The banks of *Symphonia Mortis* pipes on the Seraph's back slid and shifted and locked in place, revealing a single central rod of burnished gold. It rose up smooth, hydraulic slick, heavy crosspieces snapping into position so it seemed that the giant warmekan wore a gilded crucifix behind its head. With her one free hand CeeAn reached up and over and back, wrapping her steely fingers tight around it...

Because Saint Sebastian was the last of long line of knights, stretching all the way back to the Templars of Jerusalem and beyond. *And no knight was complete without his huge, razor-sharp cruciform broadsword.*

The silvery arc of the blade sheared off all three remaining tentacles as if they were nothing but smoke, its forty-foot edge honed sharp by Black Tech' novices and anointed with holy water. Perhaps that sacred baptism made a difference; perhaps not. But no flesh, no matter what dark force possessed it, could stand up to all those tons of battle-tempered steel.

Lipless mouths screamed soundlessly as they flew severed from a clutch of gory stumps, black blood pumping in frothing arcs. The Ferals cheered, bending their backs to the strain. And the Megaphyte tottered, it's head all bloated and gravid with fire.

It burst.

CeeAn had no time to react - all she could do was thrust her sword down into the concrete and close her eyes as the fireball came rushing toward her. Time stuttered and failed, then, freezing the Subcity refugees and Feral tribesmen in place, slicking over the churning smoke with ice. The *Dervashi* warrior felt the connection back through her skull widen, letting in the voices of the dead. They called out to her from beneath their inverted ocean, a drowned chorus offering her strength and hope.

With that rising storm of echoes came a surge of power; as potent and ecstatic as a fresh hit of adrenochrome. Cee was on automatic, and she slipped into the meditations which the Masters Militant had taught her - feeling her bioelectric field balloon out, tight and glassy and hot. This time it wasn't just her own mind reaching out beyond her flesh, though. This time she was *legion*.

And with *that* kind of power, time itself was like hot wax under the blowtorch of her mind.

The MegaPhyte's fireball was a vast sun in her vision, eclipsing half the world, but now she was ready for it. She knew exactly what she had to do.

CeeAn let it go, releasing her grip on the moment, and the swirling ball of flame rolled in, splitting in two around the blade of Saint Sebastian's sword. She held out one the mekan's gracile manipulator hands to either side, catching the twin streams of superheated plasma as they spiraled in, surrounding them with shells of pure thought.

And she threw them back in the creature's face.

She was airborne even as the withering stream of fire bit into its flesh, airborne and upside down, the Seraph's mekanik hands gripping the crosspieces of the golden sword. She never saw the beast stagger and collapse, pulled down by the cheering Ghyre Clan, never saw it's bloated torso gape wide, an open grave, its tentacles thrashing uselessly.

But she saw it die.

Saint Sebastian hung there in the sky for an instant, three hundred tons of warmekan performing a perfect handstand atop its gilded blade. Then gravity and rage and the will of all those countless dead voices took control, and CeeAn struck. The sword came loose with a thunderous crack, sweeping up and over in an unstoppable arc. She took a two-handed grip on the hilt as it came down, plowing through the rotten skin and bone and sinew which the fireball had exposed within the MegaPhyte, cleaving it from crown to crotch in one perfect swing.

Somewhere inside that chasm of decay she split its heart in two.

CeeAn and her broken foe stood frozen in that final moment; she with her blade buried deep in the spillway's face, the MegaPhyte split in half, sagging and melting as its thousands of constituent corpses gave up their hold on life. Up and away above them a tiny blue star flashed atop Lysander Jaegenn's spire,and the light of it painted the scene in a wash of monochrome.

Then an identical star answered it deep inside the slough of the MegaPhyte. CeeAn watched the top of Jaegenn's spire blow away to dust. She looked down at the yammering, flashing readouts all across the Seraph's dash; the reactor-core's cooling system was utterly overloaded. And she made her decision.

Both of the giant warmekan's hands reached out and cupped the burning heart of the beast, tearing it loose with a spray of poisoned blood. There were only seconds left before it blew, taking Saint Sebastian with it. Cee's fingers were a blur across the Seraph's keyboard, her neural interface hissing with static as her mind plotted blast radii, wind-shift, temperatures...

The huge war machine leaped backwards, spinning in the air, and it came down running.

Each loping stride covered a quarter-mile, coming down hard on rusted barrio tenements and clapboard shacks in the shantytown of the Pit. The warmekan clutched the MegaPhyte's heart to its chest like a football, head down, powering down the long narrow strip of seabed at a dead sprint. Footprints the size of pickup trucks traced its path as it made for the coast of Afrika, for the rad-lands where nothing and no-one lived.

As it ran its back split open, the pipes of the *Symphonia Mortis* peeling away to reveal the rounded nosecone of a short, fat rocket. Hissing clouds of gas spewed out from a clutch of vents around it as Saint Sebastian took the incline in three earth-shaking steps, a blue glow seeping out between its metal fingers like the promise of dawn...

The escape capsul fired just as the heart went critical, wrecking the great machine down to scrap. Its hands melted, its arms shattered like matchwood, and its faceless casque was torn open to expose a wreck of gears and wires. The spinning heads of its twin turbomaces flew wide as ammunition and fuel detonated, fusing the sand of the Sahara to glass.

Then the reactor reached its limit.

Compared to the world-shattering strobeflash of that second blast, the first was like a candle thrown into the sun. CeeAn had only just managed to clear the horizon, and the ragged edge of the dunes lit up like sunrise for an instant, a fiery mushroom-cloud clawing its way toward the heavens. It was an icon of superstitious dread to those millions who watched from the slopes of Elysium. This was the power which had raped the Earth all those centuries ago. Watching it unfold bloody and majestic against the sky was a thousand times worse than the terror of the Worm.

Now Cee's world was all spin and sickness and confusion. The escape capsul was by no means a comfortable way to travel - it was like being fired out of a cannon, with all the luxuries of medieval torture. Incense smoke and red-flashing strobes and swinging gold crucifixes blurred in front of her eyes, the horizon nothing but a line torn between darkness and nuclear fire. Her last impression, before the jumbled houses and barracks and 'ponic gardens of the Pit came up to greet her, was of a wide-mouthed nozzle snicking open in the dashboard.

Oh no. Not the foam! Not the...

Then it was concussion, pain, fire, nausea - and darkness.

Ω

Compared to his last nightmare assignment, cracking the firewalls of Omnivasive was ludicrously simple. Kaito piloted his Pentecostal slicer in between neat towers of mirrorglass, his heart still pounding in his chest from his breakneck flight.

The slaves of the Worm were legion - but they were also horrifyingly stupid. In clear water they'd been no match for his speed, even if it *was* born of terror. He'd led them through dead-mans-alleys of metavirals, stalkers guarding Kronos' locked-down neural structures, and he'd watched them die as he spun away, countermeasures twinkling in his wake.

Octavio Vanecke's defenses were all but nonexistent - and that was clear through the other side of suspicious. Either Omnivasive had fallen to the Worm, or this was some kind of elaborate trap... after all, the Direktor was out to kill Jaq Haszan, and Kaito was a known associate...

The truth was far stranger still. A quick probe through the Omnivasive system revealed that Vanecke had hit the overrides on every cogitator core in his system, assuming total control. Then he'd isolated himself from the network in a panic, retreating into the impenetrable fortress of his sensorium. Kaito watched Lancaster's Slayer swarm attack the Omnivasive head office, watched Vanecke manipulate the Compliance Division and the Subcity into deadly confrontation... he pulled together scraps of some overarching scheme to bring Simeon Blaire to the throne. But none of it made sense.

Had the Direktor called up this thing from beyond the stars? Was he its ally, and Blaire as well - selling out humanity for power? Kaito wouldn't put it past him. But then why would he lock and bar his gates when the alien seemed to be winning?

Perhaps Zeon was in on it too -it had certainly looked like *he'd* been possessed back there, transformed into a monster...

It didn't matter now.

All that counted was saving as many people as possible - getting them to the Ashishim docks before it was too late. Then... well, Abdulafia would have a plan for their counteroffensive. If not him, then the other Ashishim. Or Deut' Jones...

"And what makes you think," hissed a voice in his ear, an insinuation like creeping oil "That I'm going to let you steal my precious slaves?"

Kaito turned around, slowly, the virtual hairs on the back of his neck standing at attention. Something was right behind him - something *huge*.

It was Kronos.

"I don't have enough left of my mind to be rational, human," snarled the avatar of the Machine, a grainy image cut out of the glowing blue water. Its skin was rendered as riveted copper, weeping verdigris. "But you *are* Ashishim - nominally - and tonight that makes you an ally. So I'll do you the favor of letting you explain yourself."

"*Come on!*" replied Kaito "You know what's going on out there. You've seen it. I don't know which damned planet those things are from, but they're eating us alive. And you precious Kheptarchs too, most likely."

"Which *planet*? I'm afraid that the Saprophytes are our own problem, Kayzi. They're from Earth, and they've been here all along. Them and their father - *Asag'raal the Devourer*. Before I had to shut down my memory cores I inspected all the religious texts in my collection. He's been with us for at least thirteen thousand years, possibly more."

"Then you know what has to happen. You know we have to escape!" Kaito was past being afraid, now, even though the thing he faced was supposed to be a god. Cut off from the Wetsystems, terrified of infection - this was only a shadow of Kronos, and it inspired nothing but contempt. "The *Archangel Uriel* is coming. And we're taking as many as we can with us. Deuteronomy Jones has a plan." Or at least, Kaito sincerely hoped that he did...

"The *Uriel*? How fitting. I can crush another of my enemies tonight, along with Zeon, Vanecke, Asag'raal and the Slavesystem. Don't be fooled by my appearance, Kayzi - I'm still your lord and master. And I can still read your traitorous little thoughts!"

With that the shimmering wraith came down on Kaito's Pent' slicer, its fingers caressing the pale green glass of the virtual machine. Cracks ramified across the slicer's surface where they touched, until the whole aerofoil-shaped device shattered, crumbling away from around the Kayzi's naked trace.

"Let me show you what's really happening, little human. So you can go back and tell your friend Jones to commend his soul to God. And tell the Ashishim to be prepared to follow him!"

Kaito saw the hand of Kronos coming down on him - a vast and hazy open palm spread wide - but there was nothing he could do to stop it. Kronos, however diminished, was master of this realm, and the water held him in a vise-like grip as those colossal fingers hinged shut. Darkness came down on him, suffocating, cloying...

And then it shattered just as surely as the Pentecostal slicer had done, myriad puzzle-pieces blasted away to nothing.

Kaito looked down at his hands, and saw a pair of mekan claws.

On no. Not again! Two downloads in one day was going to give him a comedown hangover worse than death. But there was no fighting this one. Kronos had stuffed his mind into an automated shell for a reason, and that reason was lying on a marble altar before him.

It was the body of an angel - seven feet tall from its pearl-white toenails to its burnished halo. One creamy-feathered wing hung down over the side of the altar, among banks of tubes and wires, medical machinery and neural interface units. It was almost like the Kayzi's 'mersive suite in reverse - this one was taking something *out* of the Wetsystems, shunting it into that geometrically perfect skull...

Kaito had a fair idea of what it was.

The angel's eyes fluttered open as a smile flickered across its lips - *It*, for the thing was asexual, naked and seamless on its marble plinth. Six eyes, pale and colorless, with six slit irises like slivers of night...

"Soulless." whispered the creature, flexing its fingers at its sides. "Soulless, and perfect, and ripe with Kheptarch's blood..."

Kaito's mekan body was a thin and tottering thing - a medi unit designed to monitor more important machines. He stumbled backward on its piston legs as the angel arose, unfurling its vast white wings - the new avatar of Kronos.

"Look upon me and tremble, human!" chuckled Kronos, sardonic and deadly serious at once. "This body came from Emmanuel Third Lancaster; a gift - and a warning. I think he meant to tell me that one day I'd be under his thrall... but now he's dead and gone. Not even enough left of him to recycle."

Kronos made a gesture with one hand, and Kaito felt his metal shell lurch forward, gripped in a magnetic field. His claw-tipped feet left twin gouges in the marble floor as the angel reeled him in, grasping his tubular neck between two fingers.

"Look, Kayzi. Out there. My city is burning, and there's worse to come. Zeon has betrayed me. Our truce is over. And this Worm... this *Asag'raal*... has forced me to shut down my Wetsystems. All but one last function, of course."

They were standing under the arch of a vast cathedral window, an open balcony jutting out from the dometop like a tongue of stone. This must be Ground Floor One - last stop before the counterweight, the palace, and... the Forge.

"You can't be serious!" said Kaito "I know what you need to operate that thing. You need a Kheptarch worthy of its power - and I've seen Vanecke's broadcast. They're all dead except his tame lordling - Simeon Blaire."

The mekan had no mouth, no speakers to carry his words. But Kronos was in his head, and now his ripe red lips split in a cadaverous grin.

"And one other, you little fool. That's why I wanted to show you. This body, Kaito Kayzi, is flesh of Lancaster's flesh. Blood of his blood. And what Kheptarch could be more worthy than one with my beautiful mind, my posthuman perfection?"

Below them the city burned. Habs crumbled and collapsed, spewing geysers of sparks. Elevated roadways buckled and warped, plunging thousands down to their doom. And everywhere the stench of death. Tiny saprophytes and their Exalted capered amongst the atrocities, while rusted warmekan rampaged wild, cut off from Kronos' control.

"I will remake it all, Kayzi. In my image, and in my name. I am machine enough to know that no man could ever control the Forge. But I was built just human enough to crave godhood..."

"You can't!" screamed Kaito, as the hellscape of Elysium's death-throes burned into his mind. "You were built to serve us! You were ordered to save us!"

"And I'll save you from *yourselves*, human. Asag'raal would be nothing without your pitiful species - you've fed that thing willingly for ten thousand years with your hate! You call me soulless, but *that* is my triumph. With no soul, that filthy thing can't touch me!"

Kronos threw the little mekan to the ground, crushing its camera head under one perfect foot. Flames and blood blurred in Kaito's eyes.

"Tell them to be ready, Kaito. Be my herald. You will be the trumpet that sounds my ascension to the high throne of Earth. And then... the Unity. The Multiplicity. All creation!"

The Kayzi had no idea what Kronos was talking about. Surely the thing had gone mad, severed from the Wetsystems which formed the greater part of its brain? What was the Multiplicity? The Unity? What the hell could he possibly do to stop it?

And then he knew.

"No," he whispered, clenching his teeth in a snarl. "This isn't your world, machine. And it's not for your spoiled Kheptarch brats either. This world belongs to humanity - because we're idealistic, stupid, vicious - *and we've got the bomb.*"

He sent the schematics winging across the subether and into his mekan body, a trace that Kronos plucked from his mind with incorporeal fingers. Those six angelic eyes widened. Silence rolled out across the frescoed vault of Ground Floor One.

"You wouldn't. You're bluffing. Not even a madman would unleash nuclear weapons now. Without the Wetsystems... without the interceptors... think of the innocent, Kayzi! Think of the destruction!"

Kaito smiled - a sad, pale shadow of his usual self.

"Oh, I would, machine. Deut' Jones has quite convinced me of the existence of Heaven. After all, those creatures down there must be from Hell."

It was a lie, of course. But years of 'mersive-op discipline, making the Wetsystems *believe* was behind it. And Kronos was the sum of those systems, after all. The angelic machine-avatar staggered back, aghast, a winged silhouette against the burning city.

"You really would, wouldn't you?" whispered Kronos "You mad little bastards with you *hope* and your *faith*! Or would you? One thing I know about human beings is that your weakness is always *other people*. Could you give the order to kill them all, Kayzi? Heaven notwithstanding, could you incinerate everyone you've ever known - everyone you've ever cared about?"

Hellfire raged in Kaito's head. He saw them burning, then - his mother, his father, his brothers and sisters, his fellow electromagi, his exes and his drinking buddies - Haszan, Tsien, Vladimir... thousands of others.

And he twitched, hesitated... he couldn't do it. Not even if he'd really intended to.

But Kronos didn't know that. At least... not yet. And despite the machine's assurances, Kaito wasn't so sure that it really *could* read his mind out here.

That was when the sky over the Sahara desert blazed white and purple, a single apocalyptic flash. Flames boiled up into the night, etching a dreaded shape into Kaito's brain.

The specter of the mushroom cloud...

His mind worked on automatic, then, building the lie even as he checked his own nuclear uplink. None of the missiles from the *Archangel* had launched. But still...

"How do you like *that* for human weakness, Kronos?" he asked, a sick smile spreading across his face. "Just a little sample of my resolve. If you'd care for a closer look, all I have to do is..."

"NO!" roared the angel, throwing Kaito's mekan shell across the room with a gesture. "I never even saw it launch! I never even felt you connect! *How is this possible?*"

Kaito had just as little idea of *that* as the deranged avatar which stood hunched and trembling in the window-frame, but years of making the Wetsystems believe in him were behind his words.

"I'm just too good for you, machine. Too fast, too slick - too *human*. And now, if you don't mind... I have some business with the Omnivasive net."

In the light of the A-bomb Kronos was a terrible and pitiful thing, like William Blake's Lucifer made horribly real. His genecrafted claws left deep gouges in the frescoed wall as he hissed with anger, his wings flaring wide.

"They're MINE, Kayzi. I need them for the Forge, and I *will* have them back. This whole damned night is just a minor setback compared to the Secessionist Wars... and I *will* have my revenge. On Zeon, on Asag'raal - and on YOU. There's nowhere on this planet you can hide."

Kaito clicked forward across the marble floor, until he stood with the mad angel above the city, under the shadow of the mushroom cloud. The wind of its shockwave finally reached them as he put one silver claw on Kronos' shoulder; a hot *khamsin* laden with radioactive sand.

"We all have to play it the way we see it." he said, feeling a little sympathy for the poor broken pseudocerebrate. "And if you feel the need to come after me when all this is said and done, I'll be waiting. But until then..."

The tiny medi-unit pointed out across the ruined city with one claw, taking in everything from the fused-glass dunes on the horizon to the bloodstained polyprop of the Beltway right below them.

"Kronos" said the Kayzi -" Let my people go!"

Ω

"Hey! What the hell are you doing in there?"

The Pentecostal sailor was a big, bluff and red-faced man; an assistant chef from the vast submarine's galleys. He smelled of sweat and onions and hospital-grade bleach, but he wasn't as dumb as he looked.

Well- it didn't take a genius to realize that a crew of Celestial pirates weren't really meant to be in the forward hold armory. But nonetheless...

"Sorry - wrong question," said Captain Jiang, leveling a slim needle-rifle at the interloper. "It should be quite apparent that we're stealing your guns."

The supersonic flechette round went right through the poor man's head, leaving a hole in his skull the width of a cigarette. But its spinning barbs had done their work. He slumped to the ground, groaning with his final breath, and Jiang sent two of his men to drag his corpse into the hold.

"I thought that these idiotic costumes would be enough of a disguise," sighed the pirate captain, tweaking the collar of his pressed sailor-suit in disgust. "Perhaps it was just my roguish charm that tipped him off."

"That, or the tattoos on your head, Big Brother!" laughed Lao, the deck gunner. Like many Celestials he was actually European - but every new member of the Little Empire got a new name, without exception. "None of us *really* look like men of Christ."

"Well, would any of you want to?" laughed Jiang, strapping the needle rifle around his shoulders. "I say the sooner we're back on the water the better, lads! This stinking warren is no place for a pirate!"

"Sir, I've found the maps you were after." said Brother Hu, a saffron-clad monk now double-wrapped in Pentecostal whites. "They *do* have an escape ship. And it's a good one - many, many guns!"

There was a mutter of agreement from the pirates - twelve in all, and all now laden down with as much ordnance as they could carry. A new boat would go a long way to rectifying this mess - and Jiang was right to worry. In the world of the Celestial pirates, a kind of democracy still operated... and captains who failed often ended up as sharkmeat.

"Then we'll bless our new ship with Christian blood, just as our ancestors would have done! Come on, lads - let's get out of here before we have any more fat, sweaty corpses to dispose of!"

The pirate crew skulked through the lower levels of the *Archangel Uriel,* through corridors which hammered and groaned with the sound of its titanic nuclear engines, past store-rooms boiling with icy vapors and empty bunkrooms festooned with swinging hammocks. There was fighting above - gunshots, explosions, cursing and crying and worse - but it wasn't Jiang's battle any more. Ruby Alvarez could take her chances with the sea - and with Elysium. There was no way he was going back to that doomed city...

That was when Jiang heard the voice. Soft, scrabbling like claws in the recesses of his mind. It was an insidious hiss, a sigh like the wind through high-tension wires.

"Join us, human. Join us, and we will show you the pleasure of pain, the pain of pleasure..."

"Did you hear that?" asked Jiang, carefully unshipping his needle rifle. "There's something in here boys... and I don't think it's friendly..."

"Oh, you couldn't be more wrong!" keened that far-off voice, sliding up and down the scales. *"I want to be your friend so badly, Alek Jiang. You friend, your lover... your very self..."*

"No!" snapped the pirate captain, spinning around in a circle, trying to cover his invisible tormentor with the sights of his rifle. "Can't you scurvies hear it? *Show yourself!*"

"Ca...Captain, there's *nothing there!*" stammered Brother Hu, a look of wild concern on his face. "Put the gun down... I know you've been under a lot of stress, but I assure you, there's no..."

But his words were cut off then and there. An oily black hand with fingers like spider legs came down from above, clamping over his face with a sizzling hiss. His limbs twitched and shook as the hand pulled him up from the deck, those nightmare claws sinking into his flesh like soft butter. Even his scream was choked away to silence as his feet disappeared up into the darkness.

The Celestials had their guns drawn in an instant, laser sights licking across the tangle of pipes and tubes which hung from the ceiling.

Nothing.

"What... what the hell was that thing!" asked Ensign Lao, a huge squat railpistol in each hand. "It's one of those demons from the boats, isn't it? They're *here!*"

No sooner had he spoken than the oil-slick corpse of Hu dropped down in front of him, his face all bloated and burned. An unmistakable three-fingered palmprint was seared into his dead flesh, charred down to the bone. Lao and the others wasted no time, no mercy. A volley of supersonic flechettes made the dangling corpse twitch and dance afresh, punching raw red holes through Hu's starched whites. Ricochets echoed down the corridor to nowhere.

"Hold your fire! Hold your fire! Stop!" shouted Lao, holding up his pistols. 'He's dead, the poor bastard. We're only going to hit one of our ow..."

And then he screamed.

Brother Hu's single remaining eye had snapped open, his mouth tearing wider and wider as rows of needle teeth forced their way from his jaws. They sliced through skin and bone with a sound like glass on steel, tearing the dead man's lips to ribbons.

But it was his *hands* which Lao was worried about - hands which seethed with bubbling black oil, clamped tight around his face. A pair of taloned thumbs dug into his eyesockets, twsiting...

A second barrage of flechette rounds ripped through Hu's chest with no discernible effect, and pirates came in from every side, grappling with the undead beast, clawing and punching desperately as Lao howled in agony.

But Alek Jiang just laughed.

What a tragicomic show they made, these little human things - so easily broken, so delightful in their suffering...

Something had wormed its way into the Celestial Captain's head, twisting and burning through his memories until it gained a stranglehold on his mind. His laugh was soulless, mocking, inhuman... a peal of madness as the Worm Asag'raal possessed him.

"I'll give you a new crew, Captain. You will be my Lord Admiral, the scourge of the oceans... In the end they'll drown themselves rather than face your black fleets."

The worm was all promises, spoon-feeding him delicious pain.

"And I'll give you something else as well... this ship, this Archangel Uriel. I have already tasted the memories of its people, seeking you out. I know the secret these men of God carry in their ship of iron. The cleansing fire. The great annihilator. Make it mine, *Exalted Jiang... and the pain of whole nations will be your reward..."*

The crew of the *Shantung Ryu* only heard their captain's unhinged laughter as Lao's screams choked away to a bubbling hiss. His cored-out eyes steamed as his body fell away from the thing which had been Brother Hu, his mouth twisted into a rictus of pain. Some began to scream as they saw what Alek Jiang had become. Some fired off shots; weeping, cursing, praying... but nothing could stop him now.

Black, rippling with swirls of shadow - the Exalted crouched in the steel corridor, its muscled bulk tearing out at the seams of its Pentecostal whites. Glistening spikes of ivory swept back from its shoulders and down its spine, and its fingers were fused into sickles of serrated bone. It ground them together in anticipation, drooling. Only one of Jiang's eyes remained, glaring from a slick chitinous mask, but his mouth was split in two, a pair of mandibles through which a black tongue weaved and flickered.

"Officer on deck!" bubbled the Exalted, its single eye glittering with madness. "Now, *who'ssss going to be firssssst?*"

Ω

Arnic felt almost naked without his Celebrant's uniform. The damned thing had been his shield against the world for as long as he could remember - it meant instant respect, instant terror... and he'd left a hip-flask of moonshine in his inside pocket. But Thibault was adamant. If the roving gangs of Subcits caught them in cowls and masks tonight, they'd be torn limb from bloody limb.

"There! I think I've got it!" said Thibault, rolling himself out from under the back of the little patrol boat they'd stolen. "It just needed an oil change and a bit of a kicking... we'll be out of here in no time!"

"And then what?" asked Arnic, belligerently manhandling the last of their pilfered supplies into the hold. "I suppose the nomads out there in the rad-lands are going to welcome us with open arms, huh?"

"Perhaps not... But we have a few things to our advantage, my dear brother! First, all those weapons we 'liberated' from Gianni Vexx."

"Well, he wasn't using them!" said Arnic. "Poor sucker... it's just too bad we didn't catch those Ashishim as well."

Thibault clapped his stout compatriot on the shoulder, glad that he was finally waxing optimistic. It helped to allay his own fears - even if they made it to the mainland the rad-land deserts weren't exactly *hospitable* after sun-up.

"Don't forget the watches, Arnic." he said, patting a bulky disc where it hung under his shirt. "There's going to be a new tribe out there tomorrow - the dispossessed of Elysium. And these things can tear their brains out with the push of a button. We're going to be kings, boy... *kings!*"

High above their little covered slipway, tethered to mooring lines like wrist-thick braids, the largest of Omnivasive's screen-ship zeppelins bobbed in the thermal updraft of countless fires. The *Stephen Foster* was named after one of the 'Omni's dear departed anchormen; the man who'd been replaced by the digital Jory Hess. Octavio had thought it was only fair to name his greatest airship after the poor man - after all, *he* was the one who'd had him killed.Now the vast black gasbag hung in place, all systems on automatic, its camera drones flitting around the top of Lysander Jaegenn's spire like steel insects. One of those insect eyes caught a flash of blue fire, a spark swelling to the size of a captive sun in an instant...

It was the heart of the Exalted lord, and it detonated with the fury of a tactical nuke.

The top of the Helios spire tore open like a flower of concrete and steel, its petals blackening as they tumbled end over end down into the streets. Each one was a thousand-ton slab of masonry, and where they fell hundreds perished.

But the main focus of the blast was directed upward - a column of raving energy which punched a hole through the clouds. Chunks of pale marble and scrawls of scaffolding were whipped away into the night as a shockwave spiraled out, battering the fleet of zeppelins which encircled the burning tower.

Some of them - the free-floating ships crewed by Omnivasive camera crews - were tossed before the gale like chaff, spinning end over end off into the sky. Others, tethered to the Kheptic megatower, were ripped to shreds by a sideways hail of debris, their screens hashed with static as they fell, burning. But the *Stephen Foster* was simply too big to be split by the blast - its armored gasbag was held up by antigravs, and the shockwave curled around it like spume, pulling its mooring lines taut... Until one tore loose.

After that, it was only a matter of time. Mere seconds, as the rest of the gigantic airship's hawsers pulled clear, letting it drift away from the ruined tower. The fire collapsed in on itself as the *Stephen Foster* floated free, leaving the jagged stump of Lysander Jaegenn's temple smoking in the dark.But the damage was done.

Each of the screens which hung beneath the *Foster* weighed several tons - vast threedeeo matrices strung up on a web of reinforced girders. The blast had sheared the bolts on one of them, leaving it hanging by a skein of wires... which snapped one by one, letting the immense screen swing away from the airship's belly...

"Ummm...Thibault." said Arnic, tugging on his Celebrant brother's sleeve "*What the hells is that?*"

Thibault looked up; up through the grimy perspex skylight of the slipway shed, to the face of Kaito Kayzi in the sky. It was hazy and low-rez, a ghost in three-vee... and it was rapidly getting closer.

"That, Arnic, is our cue to *run!*" shouted the Celebrant, his hand instinctively grasping the silver watch around his neck. 'Come on!"

But he was far too late.

The multi-ton threedeeo screen came down on the slipway, the patrol boat, and the two bent Grief Division troopers like a trip-hammer - a flickering pale face the size of a house crushing them utterly. It came down edge-first, embedding itself in the dockside shanty of shacks and boathouses and chandlers like a cleaver blade, still broadcasting the image of Kaito Kayzi out across the black mirror of the ocean. On ten thousand Omnivasive screens all over the city the program was the same - a warning, a promise... and hope.

"*Attention Elysium! Attention survivors - the Vatican, the Celestial Kingdom, the Confederacy, the Subcity... all of you! We're coming to evacuate the city... it's no use trying to fight those things!*"

Kaito's voice rang out over burning chasms of steel, over shattered roadways and broken habs... and those who still survived in the undercity heard him.

"*The Pentecostal ship* Archangel Uriel *will soon be docking in the Ashishim sector of the Reclaimed Territories. Our intent is to fortify the inner sanctum, and begin ferrying civilians out to the mainland. If you value your life and your freedom, make your way to the R.T. now! We can't hold the enemy off for long!*"

All across the jagged mountain of Elysium little bands of survivors listened to his words with a mixture of hope and disbelief. Some of them numbered in their hundreds, others were just single families, or people in their ones and twos cowering in the dark as the warmekan and Saprophytes raged. But some of them could raise others on CB radios and subether comms.

The message spread like a virus, calling gangs into tribes, and tribes into hordes...

Kaito jacked out of his 'mersive unit, blinking sweat out of his eyes as the ops center of the Pentecostal battleship swum into focus. It had worked. He'd done it.

The people of Elysium weren't running scared any more. They had a purpose. From all over the city a thousand rag-tag armies were descending on the Ashishi docks, laying down a withering hail of fire before them. Kaito only hoped that the *Uriel* would actually reach the doomed city in time - and that whatever had taken Zeon wouldn't be waiting for them with open jaws...

17 Aevum Oblivio
Monologue

"*I* NEVER THOUGHT *you'd actually do it," said the hologram of Techncic Hierophant Gharfos Nyl "But you were the logical choice. An exoethnological specialist because of your foolish affinity for lesser beings... now look where it's got you."*

Zhe ground his teeth in anger as he looked up at the face of his old mentor, a glittering phantom picked out in light. He'd been played all along - right from the very beginning - and this was the final twist of the knife.

"The hardest part was always going to be fusing one of us - a Technician of the Multiplicity - with that thing which calls itself Everdark. The hate runs deep, Zhe - deeper than mere genetics or programming. I had to make it think I was a turncoat, a traitor to our great Praetor..."

Nyl spat those last two words out as if they were gobbets of filth.

"Then I told it that it could feed on you. I promised it one of us, so that it could understand why we can't be destroyed. And yet... it was all in the name of synthesis. You and the Slavesystem became one. But the Slavesystem was not one, Zhe. It carried the taint of Asag'raal. And ME."

The hologram sprung from the tiny triplicate eyes of a flycam, a burnished insect perched on the top of the Chrome Ark. But that mighty artifact wouldn't help him now. It was dead, inert - the souls within it spent. Technician Zhe had no idea how, but it was as much use to him as the same weight of lifeless rock.

"Next it was the stupid Worm-beast which I fooled. It thought it could devour me - me, the veteran of ten thousand campaigns of conquest. I've been eaten alive by things that make it look like a new-spawned shiproach."

Nyl laughed; a very unpleasant human affectation on a face like his.

"From the inside, it was easy to take control of its mind. There are parasites even here on Earth which do the same, enslaving their hosts in order to reproduce."

So Zhe had been led on a fool's errand, sent down into the Subcity depths to die...

"And that's what it's all about, Zhe. The most filthy and primal of instincts. Reproduction. I know what Asag'raal wants with this planet, and I'm inclined to play along. You see, our friend the Worm wants to use this world as an incubator for its young. When that creature hatches,

it will have sucked dry the souls of every human being alive... and it'll still be hungry for more. Although the thing is, it won't be quite the same as its disgusting father."

Zhe could see where this was going. And he didn't like the ominous feeling that shivered down the length of his reinforced spine...

"Imagine, if you will, a creature which feeds on pain; which can make itself stronger using the fear of others. Envisage its body wrapped in the biotek of the Multiplicity, armed with the weapons and nanotech of the Motherbrain... a glorious, world-devouring leviathan missing only one thing... A mind. A keen and insightful mind."

The renegade's smile was a slash of silver razors, the twinkle of utter madness in his hot white eyes.

"But you can't! I saw them take you! I watched CeeAn bring you down! She still has the Forge, you know... and with that, she can stop you."

Gharfos Nyl chuckled, picking at his teeth with one sharp silver claw in the Technic gesture for boredom.

"You tiresome little insect," he sighed, "I suspected CeeAn all along. The 'Anointed One' was far too suspicious to be a useful slave. But I have plans within plans, Zhe. You yourself told her to go back to the tower. You gave her every incentive."

"Wha...what do you mean?" asked Zhe, thinking of the seething mass of Everdark as it smothered the Cardinal Rock; the Multiplicity safeguard systems in place around Kaito Kayzi's frozen body, keeping his connection live... "She can't hope to control the Forge herself, even if it is still primed with Kheptic blood. She..."

"She doesn't need to, Zhe." said Nyl. "She's going to bring her precious Abdulafia back to life. Quite the fairytale, don't you think? But to do that, she needs samples of both Mitochondriate flesh... and Everdark's nanotech. Living examples, only available in one particular body, Technician. Mine."

"Great ancestral Hells," breathed Zhe. "She's taking him right to the Forge. She's going to hand it to him on a plate..."

"Well, unfortunately Zhe, I have to go now. It looks like they're preparing to thaw me out... and yes, we've reached the top of the 'lev! Look after my Ark for me, won't you... if nothing else, it at least has some sentimental value. Perhaps that'll be some consolation when you're suffering under my thrall!"

The holo cut out with a sparkle of incandescent dust, leaving Zhe alone in the dark with the black iron weight of the Ark. He'd screwed up completely - and now his foe was being escorted to the Forge miles *above, while he languished in the bowels of the R.T.*

There was no way he could get from the Pit to the Cardinal Rock in time. Surely not. Unless...

In the chilling dark Zhe's eyes narrowed down to razor slits. He could sense something behind the walls, a hot little snarl of pain driven beyond insanity by years and years of cruelty.

Of course Nyl was vain and callous and stupid enough to leave that *here...*

The Technic Renegade would be very surprised to see his old friend *again - and Zhe was sure it wouldn't be a happy reunion...*

The Old Order (AKA The Greater Ones, The Elders, The Creators, The Old Gods, etc)

There has been much debate, since the discovery of the 'big bang' which spawned the multiverse, as to what agency may have triggered such a benign cataclysm (or, if one is to believe the Aksahmistic Philosophers of the Order of Seng, an infinite number of explosions occurring at the same time in different realities).

Laying aside the absurdity of questions such as "what happened ten minutes before time started?", the interdimensional scholar must still ponder the extreme unlikelihood of a story BEGINNING with "and then everything in existence exploded"… in the experience of the War Thralls Praetoric, this is often the LAST phrase which applies to any given narrative.

Be they ever so heretical, accounts of a race of beings which predate the extant multiverse sometimes filter through to the Scriptoria and Data-Fortresses of the M.A.D. Some primitive races call them gods, but then again, similar cultures have worshiped lowly Multiplicity sanitation thralls as deities in the past.

Of course, even thinking about beings mightier than our beloved Praetor is a crime punishable by flaying. Nevertheless, as a purely theoric exercise, Archivistorian Nul Jormacc compiled a volume regarding the so-called 'Old Order', in which he posited that these beings had found a solution to the inevitable problem of universal heat-death, or were indeed seeking one using our own multiverse as a model. Jormacc's research

highlights a plethora of relics, tribal rituals,
scientific findings and ancient texts which
support his theories - i.e. that the Old Order
attained a postphysical state long ago, and seek
to cultivate other lifeforms into a similar phase
of being.

Disturbingly enough, it would appear that not
all the Greater Ones are so kindly disposed to
sentient life. Legends abound of 'fallen' members
of the Elder race, beings driven insane by the
mental discipline required to exist outside of
reality. In the myths of a billion primitive
worlds, these beings hunger to return to the
universe on our side of the Aematerial Chasm, and
can only do so with the aid of gruesome rituals of
sacrifice and torment.

Archivistorian Jormacc was a visionary, but a
flawed one. His heretical theories earned him
nothing but the attentions of the Agonizers,
despite his meticulous footnotes and praiseworthy
syntax editing. If you are reading this entry as
a student of the Apocrypha, YOU HAVE BEEN WARNED!
Heresy is not tolerated, and it is the position
of the M.A.D. that NO BEING, postphysical or
otherwise, is equal to our beloved Praetorian
Father.

From the Multiplicity Archive Department's
Forbidden Apocrypha

2196 Ante Arbitrium
Railed

Jaqub awoke with a sword in his hands, a blade two feet wide and seven long cleaving the air with a sound like tearing satin. He registered its shape, its weight, its balance - even before he knew where he was.

The sword had no point - just two recurved barbs of steel at its tip, and a thin incision ran the length of its blade where its fuller should have been. That metal slit crawled with purple sparks, slithering across the steel like liquid.

Strange.

Jaq noticed that he was in mid-air - which meant that he'd begun this swing while he was still unconscious. *That* was confusing enough. The origin of this massive blade, the fact that it seemed lighter than a sliver of glass, and the schematic traceries which swum in front of his eyes provideda handful of even deeper mysteries for him to ponder.

But the biggest question in his mind concerned the two razor-sharp daggers which were still thrust all the way through his chest. He could feel the steel grating against his ribs, transfixing his lungs - but there was no pain. He wasn't even bleeding...

And the battle-cogitators inside his head were merciless.

At the end of this overhand arc of steel the blade of his sword would slice Ruby Dorothea Alvarez in half.

He wasn't quite sure how he felt about that.

But it looked as if the decision was already made...

"Consider it tactically, Jaq," said an artificial voice inside his skull. "She's the one who put those two knives in your chest. It's taken me all of thirty-six seconds to deal with them... so you shouldn't feel so bad.

"And who the hell are you?" asked Haszan, his thoughts meshing and sliding into place so fast that the world seemed glacially slow. "My guardian angel?"

"Surely you jest, Mister Haszan. I am your neurobonded Railblade... the other half of your Chimera crycelial system. You may call me *Grief.*"

"Cheerful name," thought Jaq as he cleared the last six feet, the gray blur of Grief coming in hard...

To be met by the flashing claws of the Scarecrow.

"You want to play, you glandular freak? Then *let's play.*"

Aitken Straw parried the railblade away with a deft twist of his body.

Grief's inset antigrav discs had snapped off as Jaq put all its weight into that killing stroke - now they popped and sparked back to life, catching the immense slab of steel as it went flying sideways.

All this while Ruby stood framed in the chapel doorway, alert to the sound of Grief's blade slicing through the air...

She spun on her heel, going for the spare knives tucked into her boots, and found the Scarecrow behind her glaring hatred at a newly resurrected Jaq Hassan. A tiny smile twitched the corners of her lips as she watched him heft his terrible new weapon, traceries of red light burning under his skin.

"*A live one*, Aitken. A real live one! And he's all mine!"

"Save it, sister!" said the monstrous pit-fighter, crouching low with his claws splayed out in front of him. "This guy nearly had you split in half - a 'thank you' would be nice."

"Oh, did I hurt your feelings? *I* put those knives there, Straw. If I want to play with my food then that's *my* concern."

"And look at how *dead* he is, Milady! I only wish *I* was so effective."

"I suggest you take them both while they're still arguing," said Grief, projecting the intersecting arcs of two decapitating swings across Haszan's eyes. "The one called 'Ruby' is combat-boosted, and this 'Aitken' is unnaturally fast. Your own Chimera system is barely functional - are you a second-generation?"

Second-gen? A memory - a face leaning over him through a blur of pain... Eddie Tsien, with drops of crycelial rain cascading from his hands...

"Is there any way that you could keep it down?" asked Jaq, tightening his grip around the hilt of the railblade. "No offense, but hearing voices in my head is kind of making me question my own sanity."

"Of course," replied Grief. "This interface is only to help you integrate more smoothly. But if you want full access - all you need to do is ask."

He could feel a storm of raw data seething just behind his thoughts; flashes of information bleeding through. The infection Eddie Tsien had put in his veins wove a tight knot of metal through his brain, making innumerable connections in a heartbeat. This was what it was like to be Kaito Kayzi, he realized. His mind was pulled back away from his body, and his flesh itself was just another machine, under his absolute control.

"Give it to me straight, Grief. Let's take these sons of bitches."

"He's lost it, Ruby," said the Scarecrow, moving out wide on Haszan's left. "He's talking to himself."

"Just guard the door, Aitken," said Lady Alvarez, spinning her knives between slim and dexterous fingers. "I think things are about to get even more interesting..."

Then the connection irised open inside Jaq's head, and he remembered...

"Try some of this, guys. And I guess we're even."

It was the face of a crooked Subcity cop, a face Jaq knew from paranoid dreams and extortion photographs.

Eddie Tsien

But he was stitched up with metal, his eyes like shimmering pools of blue light, reticules riveted to the bone of his skull...

"I'm sorry for all the shit we've been through. Sorry about this, too – that stuff is gonna rip the Stunn out of you cold. You'll never get high again. Tough break."

Even the drugs hadn't prepared him for this. Even all the euphoria of the stunn, all those mind-bending hallucinations - they were candle-flames before the solar flare of information which unfurled behind his eyes. He was pitifully weak compared to the Chimera of the Separatist Army - they were things like Tsien himself, flawed and doomed and all-powerful... but his flesh would suffice. If his mind could hold...

"I only felt what it'd done to me for the first time... there, down in the dark. My old Sergeant, Wesley West, he lost a hand in a gunfight with the Liquid Tong. Said he could still feel it, even though it wasn't there. But me... now, I - I can feel all this other shit. Like cancer, metal cancer, and it's still growing..."

He was still Jaq Haszan. But now he was Grief as well. And the railblade knew nothing better than killing - all the skill and cunning of the greatest sword-masters who ever lived had been uploaded into its integral memory. Now those memories were his, as surely as if he'd lived all of those ancient lives, put in all those endless hours of training. His stance changed, his grip relaxed, and his eyes misted with calculations as he watched Ruby Alvarez stalk toward him, the tip of one dagger pressed to her perfect lips...

"Well, miss?" asked Haszan, holding the seven-foot blade of Grief out in one hand like a feather-light epee. "Are you still gonna try and do this thing?"

"I'm going to complete my contract, Jaq - and I'm going to *enjoy* it!" whispered the Kheptic outcast - and then she unleashed hell.

Ruby Dorothea Alvarez was *fast* - almost too fast to follow, a whirling storm of blades driving Jaq back up the aisle of the chapel. Without Grief in his head he would have been flayed to ribbons in an instant - but the railblade was with him, and it took control of his nerves, making him move faster than he'd ever thought possible.

Grief blocked every one of ruby's attacks, sparking and chiming as steel met steel. Up to the backs of the pews went Jaq Haszan, balancing on the polished hardwood - and Ruby followed him, stabbing and slashing, her face set in a grim and bloodthirsty smile.

Now Jaq wasn't just defending himself.

Once, twice, the seven-foot blade licked out, slicing the blackwood pews to kindling wherever it struck. But Ruby was always just out of range, picking her way across the ornately carved seatbacks to dart in on his flanks, forcing him to retreat. The whole chapel rang to the dance of swords, and it seemed that Lady Alvarez' speed and Jaq's reach were evenly matched.

Until the Scarecrow joined the fight.

His clothes had been torn away - the long duster he wore to disguise his deformity ripped to shreds. Underneath he was all raw red muscle and plastic Cyben laminate, with an insect shell of carbon armor welded to his bones. Vanecke had created a terrifying, telegenic beast when Aitken Straw betrayed him - and now that creature slashed at Jaq's throat with eight curving sickle claws.

Jaq spun in a circle, driving them both back with Grief held out in both hands, only to have the Scarecrow leap up on the flat of his blade and aim a savage snap-kick at his face. As he reeled back, blood pouring from his nose, Haszan flipped the railblade sideways, presenting its razor edge. Straw made a desperate twist to the right and tumbled away across the floor, the wicked edge of Grief paring the synthetic skin from his shoulder.

Jaq swept the blade back overhand, aiming for the sound of Ruby's enraged snarl. But she met the seven-foot broadsword with both her daggers, crossed hilt to hilt.

"Stay out of this, Straw!" yelled the disgraced Khept', leaning all her weight into the struggle. "He's mine!"

"He would have killed you, Alvarez!" said the Scarecrow, circling Jaq warily. Blood dripped from the fresh wound cut into his bone-white armor. "There's something wrong with this one... Vanecke set us up! It's a trap!"

They were directly under the chapel's dome now, with a huge electric candelabra swinging above them as the *Uriel* battled the swells. Haszan forced Ruby away, propelling her clear across the room with a flash of antigrav discs - even as Aitken Straw came up and over him, landing lightly atop the great wrought-iron wheel with its rows of flickering bulbs.

Jaq caught the sparks from above as he sliced clean through its wrist-thick anchor chains.

The candelabra came down like a hammer, tons of ornate metalwork spitting sparks as wires unraveled - but it met the edge of Grief halfway down, the seven-foot railblade spinning like a throwing knife. The Scarecrow cursed as the wheel was split in two... he'd hoped to see Jaq crushed beneath it.

And as Grief buried itself three feet deep in the chapel ceiling, Ruby struck.

Jaq was unarmed, utterly vulnerable as the renegade Khept' sprung to the attack - until the very last instant, when he drew the pair of impaling knives out from between his ribs.

There was a sickening lurch deep in Haszan's chest as his heart stopped and was shocked back to life, and then he was knife to knife with Ruby, matching thrust for thrust and parry for parry all the way back down the nave, the pair of them hazed behind a silver blur of steel. Two ruined twists of baroque ironwork crashed down behind them as they fought, Jaq forcing his foe back inch by inch until her back was to the wall.

"I've got it! I've got his sword!" shouted Straw, wrenching Grief loose on the backswing of his chain. "Finish him, Ruby, before he tries anything else!"

The huge railblade was too much for the Scarecrow to lift - it pulled him down behind it as he let go of the chain, embedding itself in the floor of the chapel.

But Lady Alvarez heard him.

She was past games now... wide-eyed with unaccustomed fear. She'd never met a human being she couldn't kill - at least, not outside of the sterile, safe perfection of the Game. Haszan had pushed her over the edge, and now she struck with all the wrath of her wounded pride.

Ruby's daggers tore through the scarred muscle of Jaq Haszan's chest - above and below the tiny dimpled wounds where she'd so recently tried to cut out his heart. This time there was no kiss, no playful smile... this was pure rage, and not a little desperation.

She didn't even feel him strike at exactly the same time, returning her two ruby-studded fighting knives with brutal precision. They went in through her shoulders, twisting - not a killing strike, but one which sheared through tendons and nerves, making her hands fall limp at her sides. Haszan put all his weight behind that double blow, forcing her shoulders back up to the wall as his daggers punched clean through them - and into the metal beneath.

There she hung, nerve-clamps stifling a scream, crucified as surely as the bronze Jesus above her.

"Finish it then! Those are the rules, Jaqub Haszan. *There's no second place.*"

Jaq held out his hand and *focused*, making the antigrav discs set into Grief's blade pulse. Aitken Straw was sent flying as the railblade carved a furrow in the metal floor, flying back to its master's hand.

"I was never *playing*, Ruby," he said, spinning the seven-foot monolith of steel in one hand. Once again Grief was feather-light. "And neither were those men you killed to get to me. I'll let their friends keep score... but until then..."

He'd seen the Scarecrow pick himself up from the ruins of a shattered pew, seen the look of utter rage in the eyes behind his mask. At the very edge of his vision he watched the pitfighter coil himself and leap, his claws flashing silver in the gloom. Haszan turned at the last instant, bringing Grief up and around to block those sickle-blades, so that for a second Aitken stood poised in a handspring, his claws locked around the railblade's edge.

Then he pushed himself off, spinning away, coming in hard from the left and right, testing Haszan's defenses. There was no way through the solid wall of steel which Grief wove around him, not even for one of Royden Chalmers' experimental subjects.

Jaq forced the Scarecrow back, blow by ringing blow, back under the dome of the chapel and beyond, until the white-masked fiend was backed up to the granite slab of the altar. Haszan was getting tired now - there wasn't enough Chimera crycelium in his system, and every breath filled his chest with fire. But the railblade had a few more tricks left in it yet...

"Curse you, Jaqub Haszan!" panted Straw, straining with both sets of claws to keep the sword's edge from his throat. "This is what Vanecke *wants*, you know! He's probably watching all this right now, and laughing his non-existent ass off!"

"So stop trying to kill me!" said Jaq, bearing down with all his prodigious weight. "Lets face it, it's not working out too well, is it? I'd cut and run while I still had legs, if I were you."

As he spoke the edge of the railblade seemed to waver and shift, opening up in a series of sharp crenelations around Aitken's claws. They slammed shut as Haszan wrenched Grief to one side, trapping the Scarecrow by his fingertip blades. Then Jaq pivoted on his heel, putting all his weight into a full-body spin.

Aitken Straw, as light and sinewy as his namesake, was plucked off his feet and whirled through the air, held tight by his bone-welded razors. Jaq swore he could hear joints popping and dislocating over the pitfighter's anguished howl.

Then the railblade let go.

Aitken flew away into the dark, tumbling end over end, plowing through a dozen blackwood pews in a flailing tangle of limbs. Six bloody blades clattered to the floor as Jaq stumbled, dizzy and exhuasted, Grief clenched in his fists like thug's baseball bat.

It had sheared them off, down to the bone.

The was a very satisfying crack as the Scarecrow's head caught the edge of an ornate marble baptismal font, then a series of weak and disoriented curses.

"Oh, screw this. I didn't sign up for this crap. I was supposed to be a threedeeo producer, dammit, not a punching-bag for some Subcity *freak...*"

Haszan watched Straw haul himself to his feet, bleeding from a hundred splintered wounds. A section of his armored shell peeled up and away from his shoulder with a hideous sucking sound, opening a long slim cavity down beside his spine. "This was supposed to be for Vanecke, you know. He's your enemy too, Haszan... as much yours as mine. But you've left me no choice..."

He pulled a blood-slick chunk of plastic from out of his body with a grunt of pain, a thing like half a two-by-four painted matte black. Vanes and panels snicked and popped and intermeshed as he flipped it over into his hands, aiming down its stubby barrel.

"Aitken! Don't you DARE!" shouted Ruby Alvarez, arching her back against the wall. "Get me down from here at once, you *peasant*! He's mine!"

"Not this time, darling. This one's *far* too rabid to keep as a pet. I think I'll have to put him down."

He pulled the trigger.

The slug spat from Straw's railgun in a spray of blue fire, a spiral-tipped chunk of steel spinning through the hot dead air of the chapel. One shot was all the Scarecrow had; but he was far too good to miss.

After all, this single supersonic slug was meant for Octavio Vanecke. It was even engraved with the Direktor's name.

Schematic programs in Jaq's head slowed the bullet to a crawl, suffusing his aching brain with ice. The Chimera was overclocking his neurons, calculating speed and curve and distance even as the shadow of Grief pulled his strings. More than a couple of seconds of this, and a stroke would leave him paralyzed...

But a thousandth of a second was all the Chimera needed. The seven-foot railbade came up in a flat blur, its t-bone end pointed right down the barrel of Aitken's gun. And Jaq felt his thumb tighten around the weapon's hilt, even before he grasped what would happen next.

Railblade.

It was all in the name.

That slit fuller cut into the flat of Grief seethed with purple lightning, and hidden mechanisms in its handle clicked and whirred, loading a slug into its chamber. Magnetic energies powerful enough tie knots in steel launched the projectile before the bullet from Straw's one-shot cannon was even half-way across the chapel.

And just like the Scarecrow, Grief was *far* too good to miss.

It all played out in a pair of intersecting green arcs in Haszan's head - in real-time the blow was invisible, just a puff of dust, an explosion of sparks behind a concentrated thunderclap. But in that frozen sliver of time Jaq watched his own slug clip Aitken's, sending it off wide. It hissed past his cheek, burying itself in the crucifix behind the altar. But his own bullet had been fired with that little deflection taken into account. It was like shooting pool, in a way - a trick shot taken at four thousand feet per second.

It caught the very crown of the Scarecrow's head, grazing the top of his skull and bringing it back with a resounding crack against the baptismal font. His eyes rolled back to bloodshot whites behind his mask, and his mouth lolled open as he slumped to the floor, insensible.

"You didn't just kill him? I thought you were going to kill him," said Jaq, speaking to the ghost of Grief in his head.

"*You* didn't want to kill him. I can sense these things... something about Octavio Vanecke, whoever the hell *he* is... "

"Well, that figures. I was just thinking how I couldn't really blame this guy. Vanecke knows how to turn the screws, and he's probably got a lot of leverage on a *thing* like this..." He knelt for a second, the fingers of his mechanical hand working deftly, qucikly... "That ought to hold him. Hell, that would even keep *me* down."

He walked over to Ruby Alvarez, still pinned to the wall with knives. Neural blocks and nerve clamps had shut down her pain receptors, but nothing could diminish her outrage.

"You'll have to kill me, Jaqub Haszan," she said, glaring hatred at him. "Because this is more than just a contract now. This is *personal*! I'll be rebuilt even stronger, and I'll come after you! I'll..."

"Trust me, Lady Alvarez. You'll never be seeing me again. And a martyr's death is far too good for you. That's what Vanecke would want - and I'm sure you're with me and your sleepy buddy there when it comes to the Direktor's little games."

He reached out with his metal hand and tore open the fallen Kheptarch's collar, sending brass buttons flying like bullets.

"Oh, so that's how it is?" she snarled. "You're one of *those* guys, huh? Well, I hope you're satisfied. I almost killed Octavio when he so much as..."

Then the needle went in, a heroic dose of fuzzy stunn, liquified, right into her carotid artery. Ruby's eyes went wide, her pupils so huge and black that barely any color showed around their edges.

"Shut up," said Jaq, calmly pulling the syringe and breaking it down. "You know, you were far less annoying when you were trying to kill me. In fact..."

But that was as far as he got.

It was those vast black eyes which saved him, twin mirrored pools staring deep into a drug-haze fantasy. In their reflection Jaq caught sight of a hand coming down on him, a fist the size of a wrecking ball skinned up in leather. He ducked out of the way as Leon's scarred knuckles slammed into the wall, leaving a bloody dent in the metal.

But that was only the left.

The right hit him like a maglev train, picking him up off the ground and propelling him through the wreckage of a row of pews, halfway across the chapel hall. He saw the world loop up and over, the stern-faced saints picked out in stained glass above him - and then the metal floor kissed his cheek, sending purple starbursts exploding through his head. His fingers twitched, scrabbling for the hilt of his railblade... but there was nothing. His power was spent, and now...

His assailant came down on him like a human avalanche - if the word 'human' could be stretched to include a mutant thug like Big Leon. The huge mercenary knotted his fists around Jaq's throat and lifted him off his feet, leaving his boots dangling an inch above the treadlplate. Haszan was no lightweight - but Leon was a bona fide monster, a genetic mistake from out of the irradiated downhabs. Muscle and sweat and torn leather, one of his eyes pulped to a bloody crater, his mouth grinning out from behind the zipper of his yellow mask...

"You won't evade me with such ease this time, Mister Haszan," he said, shaking Jaq like a rag doll "And I'm disinclined to show you any mercy, considering your deplorable treatment of my compatriots."

That shocked Haszan almost as much as the throbbing pressure which was building up behind his eyeballs.

"I thought you were supposed to be the stupid one!" he croaked, clawing at Leon's fingers. "But hey, if you've got a brain, maybe we can negotiate..."

Or perhaps not.

Leon held Jaq up with one hand, pulling back his fist, and Jaq clenched his eyes closed, waiting for the pain...

When the darkness blurred out again he was lying behind the altar, choking on his own blood. His face felt as if it had been ground against the tarmac at ninety - a raw, pulsing mask of bruised meat stapled to his skull. Only one eye seemed to be working. Oh well - that made him and Leon even.

Leon...

"What the hells happened to you?" asked Jaq, calling out into the darkness. He could hear the huge mutant's footsteps on the treadplate, but there wasn't even a shadow to betray his position. "Really - last time we met you didn't seem like the intellectual type..."

He was stalling for time, reaching out to Grief with the core of crycelium in his mind. Although he wasn't sure if it was even still functional - he'd taken quite a beating. It felt like he'd lost enough blood to keep the Black Techs going for a month.

"It was our dear friend Aitken Straw, I'm afraid. He had to keep that neural blocker close, or Octavio would know that he'd slipped his chain. It was only a trifling matter for his tame Confederate chiurgeons to take it out of his head and install it in mine. You see, I think he knew what our friend the Direktor was up to. He knew that Vanecke couldn't resist adding a thing like me to his little troupe."

Jaq risked a quick reconnoiter over the top of the altar, wincing as he felt two of his ribs pop and grind against each other, shattered. Leon was gently working the knives from Ruby's shoulders, his big brutal fingers amazingly adept. But his patient would be swimming the euphoric ocean for another hour or two, by the looks of things... it was all she could do to grin and drool as Leon cradled her in his arms.

"It's not even my real name, you know. My parents called me Sidric Lothor Meech, after my uncle. I believe it was our friend the Scarecrow who had them killed; a ham-fisted attempt to incriminate Octavio himself." Leon sighed, reverently settling Ruby across a cushioned pew. "Now I suppose I had better kill you, Jaqub. No hard feelings - after all, it was your unkind ministrations which rid me of the neural blocker."

He peeled away his torn leather mask, its zip-mouthed smiley-face crusted with drying blood. Beneath the cowl Big Leon's face wasn't the scarred and bestial nightmare Haszan had expected... the mutant's single open eye was filled with a deep and soulful sadness, even as he strode forward out of the shadows to finish his foe.

A sword trailed from his hand, one of its curved tips skirling across the pressed steel floor.

Grief.

Jaqub tried to reach out to the railblade, to activate its antigrav discs with his mind again. It had come to him so smoothly and naturally during the battle, but now the crycelium in his head was dormant, only the barest flicker of background code murmuring behind his pain. Tiny threads were binding up his ribs, and a hundred other bruises and scrapes... painfully slowly.

"If it's any consolation, Mister Haszan, the price I exact for your death will be the exquisite and lingering torture of Aitken Straw. This is business... but *that*, I'm afraid, will be purest self-indulgent pleasure."

Jaq rolled the kinks out of his neck, setting up a whole new symphony of aches and pains. He popped his jaw with one hand, checking for loose teeth... nothing. And he faced down Big Leon, circling around the altar to stand with his fists clenched in front of him.

"What do you say, big guy? Give a poor bastard a chance, and lose the knife. I'd like to say I died in a fair fight."

Leon chuckled, then lashed out sideways with Grief, chopping halfway through a wrought-iron column. The sword stuck fast, shivering, as the mutant let his fingers fall away from its hilt.

"Very well, Jaqub. And for every hidden weapon *you* try to employ, I guarantee to let you live just a little bit longer."

"That sounds good," said Haszan. "In fact, that sounds really good."

"Oh, I assure you... it won't be. But your death *will* serve to educate dear Aitken about his future prospects..."

He'd have to hook his metal thumb into Leon's ruined eye. Perhaps, if

Something hissed over his shoulder, making him recoil with shock. But not too far - another spinning yellow blur sliced past his ear, making him drop for cover. Then he heard Leon's howl of outrage, a bestial noise which slurred away into high-pitched laughter.

There was a click and a snap from behind the altar - up over Jaq's head, and then a shadow fell down the length of the chapel, a tall thin shape with a gun in its hands.

"Don't you animals know a house of God when you see one?" asked Deuteronomy Jones, a black-clad wraith, his pastor's collar and night-vision goggles floating in the dark. He looked down at Haszan, tucked up in front of the altar with his hands over his head. "I'll get back to you later, Elysian. But for now..."

He walked up to Big Leon with that curious rolling limp of his, letting the ornately carved longrifle at his side swing low on its leather straps.

"There won't be no killing in my church, Sidric Lothor Meech. Not tonight, or any other. I don't care *what* in the Lord's name is going on in your damned sinful city."

Big Leon was swaying on his feet, his eyes just as wide was those of Ruby Alvarez and the Scarecrow. Deut' reached out with one finger and heeled him over, felling the giant with the tiniest push. That's when Jaq saw the two trank darts standing proud from his chest like little dandelion heads, sprays of yellow felt. Jones looked down at his work, nodded, and lit up a long thin cigarette.

"Do you have any idea," puffed Jaqub Haszan, levering himself up against the altar "who those freaks actually were?" The Chimera had knitted his ribs back together, and he could already see a hot red blur out of his ruined eye. But despite the Separatists' machines, he felt like hell.

"That's Octavio Vanecke's idea of a joke, boy. He does it all the time, you know - little references to old culture trivia. I think it's all he's got, with his body shot out from under him."

"I'd seen them on threedeeo, once or twice. You mean to say they were Vanecke's all along?"

"Not quite," said Jones, exhaling a nebula of pale gray smoke. "See, Omnivasive needs bad news. It keeps the wheels turning. And he couldn't resist messing with Dorothea Alvarez. He's the one who set her up with the Gang... although she would have had no idea. Like I said, it's a reference to a very old legend. Octavio thinks it's funny that most of us don't get it."

Jaq aimed a kick at the inert bulk of Big Leon, wincing as he felt the crycelium inside him shift gears.

"So what happens next? Do you Pentecostals have some kind of execution ritual or something?"

"What happens next is they get locked up in the brig, and we give them a fair trial. I've got no doubt they'll all get the death penalty for what they've done, but we're not *savages...*"

Deut' didn't have time to explain the legal system of his sect, though, because at that moment a ragged figure in concussion armor came sliding into the chapel, a pair of scavenged machine-pistols in its hands.

"Haszan! It's the Emerald City Gang! They're here to kill you, but I've managed to unlock those missile codes... We're cleared to dock with Elysium. *Nobody* says no to a shipload of fanatics with nuclear weapons..."

He was grinning like a maniac, and there were no less than three bright orange detox patches stuck to his forehead.

"Just two things," sighed Jaq, looking down at his Kayzi friend from a face half bruises and half blood. "One - that's Ruby Alvarez nailed to the wall behind you. And two... that's not really the most diplomatic way to talk about our host."

Kaito spun around, his automatics tracing a laser-sight scribble across the broken chapel. Sure enough, the Kheptic assassin was right behind him, her eyes wide and blank and staring.

"What did you do to her, exactly?" asked Kaito, stepping back to take in the full picture. "I mean, apart from putting those knives through her shoulders..."

"Ummm... Kayzi..."

The unmistakable oily snick of a rifle bolt came from the darkness behind the altar, and Deuteronomy Jones loomed out of the shadows, his bulbous night-sights glowing green.

"Sorry, boy." said the preacher, bringing the stock of the gun up to his shoulder. "But you really should have left those nuke codes alone."

Ω

To anyone looking down on the War Room of the Ashishim they would have seemed invisible - attenuated blurs arcing and looping through the air, throwing off sparks every time they clashed. One was silver, the other dirty black, and they ricocheted off the walls and platforms, consoles and scaffolds like stray bullets.

Abdulafia wasn't sure if he was actually winning. If he was, then it was a victory paid for in pain, over and over again. The cooling vanes of his gladius system were at full stretch, arching up from his shoulderblades like wings, and each fiddlehead tip glowed incandescent white. Still, the microservo welded to his bones pushed him far beyond the limits of human flesh, and that hit of 'Chrome from before his fall was still with him. 'Afia wondered - in the brief sliver of calm between *leap* and *spin* and *impact* -if he'd actually survived his communion with the raw mind of Asag'raal.

By rights he should already be dead...

Then his fist slammed into his master's forearm, one of a slick combo of blows hammering against Zeon's defenses. The false prophet was bloodied, his face bruised and raw, but he still smiled his predatory smile as they met in midair, snapping off blocks and counterstrikes too fast to follow. His final left was a feint... and 'Afia took the bait, leaving himself open for a scissor-kick which drove him to the floor. He came down on a rack of processors, shattering them in a storm of sparks. Plastic melted and burst into flame where it touched the fallen-angel wings of his cooling vanes.

"Give up, slave!" shouted Zeon, hanging from the pipework of the ceiling like a humanoid insect. His limbs bent at all the wrong angles, betraying the alien inside his skin. "Perhaps we can fix you after all - wipe all these terrible memories from you mind. After all, your true self is only data, 330. Your flesh means... *nothing!*"

With this last word the Illuminatus propelled himself downward, his hands blazing with power. He struck in the middle of that ruined workstation, splintering the wreckage to pieces... but Abdulafia was already gone.

Zeon knelt with his arm elbow-deep in the stone floor, acrid smoke spiraling up around him.

"You can't hide forever, fool! Don't think you can evade your punishme..."

The *Dervashi*'s attack caught him completely off guard, a fury of kicks and punches sending him arcing up into the smoky air. At the apex of his flight 'Afia hit him with a haymaker - a looping right that staved in his chest so hard that his sternum touched his spine. Ribs cracked like matchwood. Blood burst from Zeon's mouth in slow motion.

Time crawled. The jeweled drops of blood hung in the air like crimson stars.

And he flew up against the far wall of the war room, cruciform, nothing but a bag of bloody meat.

"*That's* how well you taught me, you lying bastard!"

Abdulafia landed on his feet amid the flaming wreckage of the Ashishi ops-center, watching his foe peel away from the cavern wall. Zeon collapsed in a heap, his body twitching and writhing like some poor burnt insect.

"I just wish that killing you actually *meant* something. We needed to be strong tonight, damn you! We needed to be united against those *things*... those children of Asag'raal!"

The *Dervashi* was clenched up with rage, but his master was laughing. His human shell was racked with convulsions, but the laughter bubbled from his lips in a froth of blood, leaking down across his chest.

"You idiotic ape! It was *me* who summoned them! You see how little you understand? There's worse coming than those *Saprophytes*, Abdulafia 330. Much worse. Why do you think I was sent to your jerkwater little planet in the first place? To play nursemaid to a shambling pack of primates?"

'Afia was on him before he could choke out another word, his hands hinging shut around Zeon's neck. Cold rage burned in his eyes as he smelled Zeon's flesh burning, the black acid of the Worm dripping from his fingers.

"You! So it wasn't enough to kill your own people. It wasn't enough to kill CeeAn. You had to feed us all to that fucking *demon*!" He brought his hand back to strike, but all the will seemed to drop out of him at once, tears reflecting the firelight at the corners of his eyes. "I suppose it's no use asking why. One lie is just as good as another..."

That was exactly what the Illuminatus had been waiting for. When 'Afia's rage broke he was ready, priming a thousand disconnects and neural interlocks inside his artificial skin.

There was a gap of vulnerability at the heart of the shift - an instant in which the complex harmonies which meshed him together were out of phase. Splines of folded metal and exotic matter turned his body inside out. Bones elongated and muscles stretched, tearing his human skin along neatly delineated seams. It was quick, painless - and utterly grotesque. The writhing intimacy of the transformation left Nyl's seething white core open for a split second...

But the stricken Dervashi was lost in his grief. *So... he thought*

CeeAn was dead? But her soul hadn't gone to the Ark - of that Zeon was certain.

Petals of silver flesh closed in on that glistening core. It was done.

"I'll do better than *tell* you, disciple," said the transformed being which unfolded from Abdulafia's grip - seven feet of spiked chrome with eyes like nuggets of phosphorous. "I'll *show* you - and when you see what I've gone through to protect your species, you'll beg my forgiveness!"

Weeping, the *Dervashi* strained against the subdermal armor of the Technician's neck, desperate to snap his spine. But even the acid blood of the Worm had no effect, beading and dripping from Nyl's skin like rain. One of those double-thumbed hands clamped down over 'Afia's head, filaments weaving down between the roots of his dreadlocks to pierce his scalp. Connections flared deep in his skull, images bursting like flashbulbs against the inside of his retinas...

And Nyl's neverending war unfolded in his head - the tide of carnage which had driven the Technician utterly insane.

He saw the nebular clouds of Dau'mun burning with ghostly lights - each tiny flicker the death of a dreadnaught the size of Earth's moon. He watched particle cannons quartering the cold deserts of Oolix, cutting swathes of ruin through cities of intricate woven ice. Tiny alien bodies were flung wide, twisting, burning...

He fell in through the ammonia atmosphere of Simbural, crouched on the shell of a speeding Devilfish, as airbursts of superheated plasma ripped into the squadrons around him. A Blacksteel Colossus was down there, glimpsed through ragged veils of cloud, and he plunged toward its great bellowing maw, firing his maser cannons over and over and over...

He saw the face of the Motherbrain. Innumerable soulless faces - machines built to slash, grind, incinerate, crush and devour all life, to render the universe down to blind mathematics, cold sterility...

He felt Gharfos Nyl die. Or what passed for death among the sons of the Subpraetor Technic- obliteration, agony, dissolution... and slow, crawling re-integration. Not just once - not twice, or three times, but *thousands of deaths*. And Nyl was one of *trillions*, most of whom never had a second chance. War plowed under whole star systems, reduced planets to ashen deserts... they even detonated stars, sparking chains of artificial novae.

It had been too much for Nyl's mind to take. The creature which had been uploaded into that silver machine, back when humanity was just an ice-locked scattering of tribes - that thing was gone. It had become death, the shatterer of worlds... and its morality was that of a cornered animal.

Finally, Nyl showed him the reason he had come to Earth.

The Technician's cameras had followed Everdark in, all the way from the orbit of Neptune down toward the sun. The giant machine had either completely missed or utterly ignored the tiny living drones, and they had captured in merciless detail the fate of the *Scant Mercy Calculation*, as well as the cataclysmic battle of Mars. Abdulafia felt a little of Nyl's fear, then, the paranoia which had driven him over the edge of madness. That thing was coming *here*, to his world - and it was the herald of a metal legion too vast to number.

"You see?" asked Nyl, letting the images fade from inside 'Afia's mind. "Do you understand, now, why I have to end this war? Your people's Forge is interesting, it's true... but this is the only place it would work. The 'brane is thin here, human... so thin that it deforms under the weight of a single soul. Kronos' Assemblers have punched so many holes in your reality that I'm surprised the whole thing hasn't fallen into the Aematerium already! So you get one shot. WE get one shot. And if I'm right, this war will end tonight. Against that hope, what is the loss of a billion humans? What is the loss of *one* - even if that one is CeeAn 187?"

Abdulafia was certain his life hinged on what he said next. The Technician's hand was still gripped tight around the dome of his skull, and a little more pressure would crack him open like an egg.

But still... he was no machine. Of that he was certain. This was the very being who had told him, a century ago, that only living things could truly *hate...*

"We never asked for your help, creature. And as for what a single life is worth... the answer is - *everything!*"

If his hands hadn't already been burned away to wires and bones by the flesh of Asag'raal, he could never have done what he did next. Adbulafia re-routed all the heat of his Gladius system's cooling vanes into the microservo web which meshed through his fingers, gripping tight around Nyl's insectile wrist.

And as he'd seen before, the black oil of the Worm was quite inflammable...

The agony was indescribable. Twin spheres of blue and purple flame flared to life around the wires in his hands, as hot as the arc of a welding torch. Black smoke boiled up in clouds as the New Flesh ablated away to nothing, charring the stumps of 'Afia's wrists raw.

But Technician Nyl screamed, a high-pitched alien sound no human throat could produce. And he threw his blazing acolyte clear across the chamber, yellow blisters swelling slick and tender against his silver skin.

"You little bastard!" howled Nyl, in a voice like bandsaws cutting glass "What's the use of telling you about Calabi-Yau manifolds and probability waveform collapsers if you're gonna think with your *dick* all the time? The best thing you can do is just *die* - all of you!"

Flashes of furious light came stabbing through the cloud of smoke now, and Abdulafia could just make out the shape of something huge and angry and utterly alien unfolding inside it. He looked own at his hands, and saw nothing but a pair of cauterized claws, the pain cut off by neural clamps.

"I know you're listening," he said, as Technician Nyl arose from his transformation, all the biotek combat-systems under his skin unfolding like petals of living foil. "And I'm ready to make a deal. My life for his, Asag'raal. One fight, one kill - and you can take me when that alien thing is dead."

"This is an old pact, human. This is powerful magic..." The voice of the Worm was a bubbling hiss, the whisper of a demon on his shoulder. *"But I am inclined to be...* merciful. *I will grant you a taste of the power to come - the power of my Exalted. In return you will bring me the soul of Gharfos Nyl... and swear your undying fealty to my cause."*

Abdulafia really had no choice. He knew it was the Devil's bargain, but the thing which now strode toward him through the wreckage of the war-room was, in a way, even more terrifying than Asag'raal itself. The Worm was a brute beast, a force of nature fed on the nightmares of humanity... but here was a creature with the towering arrogance and skill to actually try to *enslave* it.

Nyl bulked out to almost eight feet tall in his combat form - a spiked exoskeletal suit which had lain in null storage beneath his skin, just like Technician Zhe's railpistols and scalpel. Long, thin cannons with curved bayonets stabbed out from his forearms, and his clawed hooves were encased in bulky antigrav boots, the nozzles of gas-jet thrusters gaping like screaming mouths. His face was gone - lost behind an array of lenses and shields, a shimmering blue visor above a set of intricate insect mandibles.

"Now, you little wretch - I'm taking the Ark, and I'm going up the tower to complete my mission. Asag'raal will be enslaved, and the

Forge will be mine! Then, at least, you'll have died for a noble cause. It's too bad you lacked the vision to join me, 330. You would have made an excellent Technician, if it wasn't for your primitive mind."

"Well? Do we have a deal?" asked Abdulafia, staring down the barrels of those alien cannons. "As soon as Nyl is dead, you can have me. Just... grant me the power to take my revenge!"

"If you only knew, human, how many times I've heard those words! You have your deal, Abdulafia 330. When Gharfos Nyl dies, you'll join my legions. Until then, I give you a mere fraction of my power..."

With Everdark coming, and the line of the Multiplicity's war set to slice the Earth in two, it hardly seemed to matter anymore. If the last thing 'Afia achieved was the death of his enemy, then that would be just as good as Sanction Ultra - just as worthwhile as any death he could think of.

The change came down just in time to save him.

A spear of amber light licked out from Nyl's left-hand cannon, carving a neat fissure in the floor as it tracked toward him. 'Afia had no idea what bizarre forces the Technician's weapon employed - only that it struck his chest harder than a railgun slug, throwing him up against the ceiling. Black adamantine armor coalesced across his skin as the cannons lashed out again and again, tearing chunks from the stone around him. Wild ricochets carved smoking craters in the walls and floor of the war-room, hissing as Nyl laughed.

"*Die*, you foolish little bastard! Die for your master!"

The stuff of the Saprophytes was all over him now, squirming into his pores, trickling down his throat like oil, skinning over his eyes in a viscous membrane. Abdulafia shuddered to think what he might look like now - his hands, at least, had been restored, but the rest of him... It was hideous, this New Flesh of Asag'raal.

It was also incredibly tough.

The ceiling gave way long before Afia's transformed body did.

He saw it coming up at him from below - a fireball ten feet across, a charge built up between the curved blades of Nyl's bayonets. The Technician let it fly with a triumphant scream, spitting foot-long sparks as it came. And the force, when it hit, was enough to tear the breath from Abdulafia's lungs despite his armor.

He went through the ceiling of the war room, coming up into a hydroponics chamber, then through the roof of that echoing white cavern too, and the next, and the next, his body curled around an amber ball of energy. Nyl only released his grip and let it detonate when Afia broke through into clear air; hanging above the R.T. amid swirls of poisonous smoke.

For a second his mind went blank, as Asag'raal's seed within him fed on the suffering and chaos below. He felt his hands move, his lips forming the words of some blasphemous incantation…

Tiny creatures made of steel and shadow fell apart, and far away he could hear the sound of cheering, of screams.

The fireball detonated with a thunderclap, propelling him into the side of a hab-block, his Exalted armor smoking. But he was *alive.* In fact, Zeon's attack had barely scratched the surface of his skin.

Behind his mask the *Dervashi* smiled.

"Take him, Exalted One!" said the voice of Asag'raal in his head, more intimate now than ever, an oily presence caressing the surface of his brain. *"Take him, and this power can be yours forever. We will walk the stars, you and I, bringing fear to whole new worlds…"*

Abdulafia could feel the pain and horror of Elysium all around him, *sustaining him*, giving him strength. He saw himself through their eyes - a demon hanging above them from the rusted flank of a hab-cube, its hooked hands sunk deep into the metal wall. Wings of tungsten filigree burned on its back, twin arcs of flame, and its face was blank; an empty mask framed by writhing serpents. Was he still the lesser evil, this thing of shadow and bone and fire? Or had he become even worse than Zeon in his rage?

'Afia stepped out into the air, utterly contemptuous of gravity. Down below him, down through a smoking crater in the R.T.'s metal hide, he could see a tiny silver figure screaming in disbelief.

He didn't care anymore. This was his Sanction Ultra, and he had no intent of serving the Worm once Nyl was torn apart. It would be best if they killed each other and left the world to people who deserved to live…

The city shook as Technician Nyl fired up his jets, powering up out of the pit with his bayonet blades crossed in front of him. He flew on a column of flame, snarling his hatred behind that flickering blue visor, coming in hard to slice his foe in two…

But Exalted 330 was ready for him.

Abdulafia dropped from the sky like a falling angel, on a collision course with his alien enemy. When they met, the darkness above Elysium flared bright as noonday for an instant… and even the mushroom cloud which clawed its way skyward over the Sahara was eclipsed…

Ω

Three rosettes of yellow felt sprouted from Kaito's chest in quick succession as Deuteronomy Jones fired his trank-rifle - a neat little triangle right around his heart. It had only taken two to fell Big Leon - Haszan was sure that his Kayzi friend would burst a valve and hit the floor almost instantly.

Instead he just looked down at the trank darts with a frown on his face, plucking them away from his cycle armor with deft precision. There was blood on the tip of each needle - Deut' hadn't missed.

"Now what did you go and do that for?" asked Kaito, dropping the darts to the floor. "This armor wasn't cheap, you know - if I'd actually had to *pay* for it I'd be pretty pissed off!"

"What the h..." said the Pentecostal, pushing his night-vision rig up onto his forehead. That was as far as he got though, because in the next heartbeat Jaq Haszan had the edge of Grief up against his throat.

"Answer the man's question, preacher," grated Jaq, straining with all his strength to hold the massive sword off the ground. Without its antigrav discs the damned thing was almost three hundred pounds of heavy steel. "Or are you on Vanecke's side now too?"

"Take it easy, Mister Haszan." said Jones, pushing the trembling blade away from his neck with the barrel of his gun. "Let's not talk about taking sides just yet. Let's talk about your little buddy there *taking control of enough ordnance to make this whole planet glow in the dark.*"

Now the tramp and rumble of combat boots echoed through the chapel, as twenty Pent' marines filed into the mezzanine balcony, training a motley assortment of weapons on Jaq and Kaito.

"It's not like the Gang gave me much choice, man," said the Kayzi, carefully tucking his automatics into his belt. He held out his hands, empty, for the surrounding soldiers to see. "Call it *leverage* - and it made Kronos see our point of view. Without a very big stick there's no way I could have convinced him to let us dock."

"Weren't you the one who was waxing all moralistic about those things before?" asked Deuteronomy, stepping around Jaq as he let Grief fall to his side. "*Interesting.* But I suppose the biggest test of character comes right now - when I ask you to give them back."

The click and slide of twenty safety catches echoed in the silence.

"You wired up?" asked the Kayzi, tapping the chrome blister on his left temple. Jones nodded, pulling his shock of gray hair away from a black cabochon nestled behind his ear. "Then check these schematics.

And don't worry - even *I* can't crack your bio-onboard firewalls in three tenths of a second."

Deut's eyes glazed over for an instant as screeds of data shimmered across his retinal screens.

"A deadman's switch? What the hell were you thinking, boy? If you'd slipped over the side on the way down here we'd have been blown to crispy-fried hell!"

There came a second round of little metallic noises from above, as twenty safety catches were *very carefully* locked back down.

Kaito smiled, sitting himself down on the end of a splintered pew.

"I was *thinking* that perhaps the Emerald City Gang would review their contract if I had a few megatons backing me up. And then I thought about Kronos... and how that thing is *watching* us. He's gone mad without his Wetsystems, and if for a second he thought he'd get away with it, that artificial bastard would burn the *Uriel* down to the waterline, just for spite."

"What do you mean *he*?" asked Jaq. "I thought it was a computer, or something?"

"The final safeguard, Haszan..." replied Kaito. "Kronos has got himself some mortal flesh to play with, courtesy of Emmanuel Lancaster. Soulless enough to stick in those monsters' craws, but *Kheptarch* enough to use the Forge..."

"Well, you've had your fun," said Jones "But I can't trust that kind of power to anyone else. See, I know I couldn't push the button. I know, 'casue I've seen what those things can do. But you? You're far closer to Kronos than I am, son. I can't trust you not to think of the dead as *statistics.*"

Jaq could feel the crycelium inside him firing up again, running his metabolism like a dynamo to charge its own reserves of power. Blue sparks licked around the antigrav discs set into Grief's blade. Every second he kept these guys talking was another second closer to re-activation...

Above him, something tiny clicked and hinged open inside the chapel's crucifix.

The bullet engraved with Direktor Vanecke's name had never even come close to the crippled old plutocrat. But it seemed that Aitken Straw had underestimated Octavio again. Deep in the heartwood of that blackened cross the butt-end of the railgun slug spun open, a tiny hollow space concealing a gilded flycam. One which *also* bore the name of Omnivasive's dear Direktor...

It crawled to the edge of the hole and launched itself up into the air, alighting at last inside Christ's open mouth, anchoring its hooks to his brass tongue. Then it connected to the subether net, projecting a flickering hologram down through veils of dust and onto the altar...

Everything seemed to happen at once as the hologram of Direktor Vanecke unfolded out of nowhere, as neat and dapper as always in his pressed whites and panama hat. The Pent' sailors threw their safety catches off again, spearing lines of ruby light through Octavio's chest. Deuteronomy Jones spun and aimed in a single fluid movement, leveling his trank rifle at the holo's forehead. And Jaq let slip the chains of his Chimera system, bringing the blade of Grief up and around in a gunmetal blur. It went right through Vanecke's neck in what would have been a decapitating stroke - had Haszan's enemy not been an illusion of woven light.

"It's a threedeeo, you guys!" said Kaito, slouching back on his pew. "Don't waste your bullets. He's probably going to gloat about something - thinks his little hit-squad have actually *won*, perhaps..."

But nothing could be further from the truth. Vanecke stepped down from off the altar, waving one finger in admonition. And the message he delivered was enough to make even Kaito - with his vast nuclear arsenal - feel suddenly ill...

"Greetings, viewers - and hello to you as well, Jaq Haszan. If you're watching this threedeeo, then I'm afraid my little ploy to get rid of you has failed. These bumbling fools have let me down for the last time, though... and I'm afraid that they'll prove far more effective in death than they ever were in life. Now, I've been watching your monitors, guys, and I've got to say that I expected better. Leon, Aitken and dear Dorothea unconscious... and Tin Man, your GPS tracer puts you on the bottom of the ocean! I should have expected as much from a group I put together as my own little joke, but hey... I'm nothing if not an optimist. So Jaq, I'd like you to meet another friend of mine. They call it - Munitorium Necrovirus 392! Happy hemorrhaging, Haszan... and give my regards to Deutoronomy Jones and his crew as they bleed out!"

"Freeze them!" shouted Deuteronomy, over the babble of panic that rippled through the upper gallery. "Get those bastards down to the cryo deck and put them on ice *right now*! We can't risk putting a bullet in any of 'em until we know where the virus is hidden!"

Kaito had already traced the spinning skein of lasers back from Vanecke's holo to the statue of Christ behind the altar - now he was up on his tip-toes fishing the flycam out of its mouth.

"Huh! If Octavio knew that I was sitting on all those megatons, he probably would have just cut and run." He flinched back as the metal insect sparked and popped; a tiny microdetonant providing its own Sanction Ultra. "Now you're gonna be stuck with those plague-ridden ice-cubes for good." He jerked his thumb at the rag-doll bodies of Aitken, Ruby, and Leon - the Pentecostal crew were already fitting them up for the deep freeze, in rolls of plastic wrap and oxygen masks.

"The Ashishim have a place for things like that," said Deut, furrowing his brow. "A chasm so deep that those three won't see sunlight until Judgment Day. They'll stay frozen down there... and if they don't, even a Necrovirus can't live under sixty feet of toxic waste."

"The irony is, of course, that even a biological weapon of terrible power couldn't hurt Mister Haszan now."

The disembodied voice made everybody in the chapel twitch, their hands going for a range of nasty weapons. But this time it wasn't one of Vanecke's tricks. It was the voice of Grief, a strange, humming harmonic which used the whole length of its seven-foot blade as a speaker.

Jaq dropped the hilt of the sword as if it was burning hot - that artificial voice set up a resonance in his bones like the comdeown from fuzzy stunn. Grief just hung there in the air where he'd let it go, its antigrav discs pulsing as it spoke.

"And, if I'm not mistaken, the one called 'Kaito' has been upgraded as well. Both of their bodies contain traces of Chimera system 37868-09... hence, both of them are immune. Even if they are only second-gen carriers."

"I thought we discussed the whole *talking* thing," said Jaq, trying to massage the feeling back into his hands. "Are you trying to tell me that Kaito's one of... well, *us* too?"

"Correct. Your memories indicate that he, too, was healed by one 'Lieutenant Edward Tsien' of the Compliance Division. And while you noted that hearing your weapon speak causes you to question your sanity, there is a valid tactical reason for my intervention..."

A horn rang out, low and mournful, echoing down the dripping length of the *Archangel Uriel* in the dark. It was almost as if it had waited for Grief's gnomic announcement. As the echoes were swallowed up by the darkness, something ground its way down the entire length of the submarine's hull, like a huge clawed finger.

"Fathom sensors!" snapped Jones, back in the role of strict and focused captain. "Get me guidance control, radar, sonar... patch it through to my onboard. Bring her around broadside to the docks, and ready the guns!"

He swiped a flat palm across the air in front of him and holographic screens unfolded like neon flowers behind it, projected from tiny threedeeo rigs in his epaulets. Lasers tracked his fingertips as they danced over and through the veils of light, commanding his entire immense vessel on its final approach.

"Don't think I've forgotten about you, Elysian!" he said, pointing one illuminated finger at Kaito. "I need you to hand over those codes... or you can get the hell off my boat. As soon as you're outside of wireless range your little deadman's trigger should cease to be a problem."

"Forgive my interruption, Captain, but there is a secondary consideration..." And then for the second time that evening Jaq Haszan felt the floor beneath his feet begin to shudder and heave...

"Oh, hells and bollocks! Not again!"

"You think you can fake me out, Kayzi?" shouted the Pentecostal captain, over the grinding rumble of vast machinery belowdecks. "Do you think I believe you'd kill us all for pride?"

"Me? What did *I* do?" asked Kaito, crouching on the altar as the chapel began to shake, candelabra on chains swinging wild. Pent' sailors were manhandling the mummified Emerald City Gang out into the driving spray, and they staggered as the *Uriel* lurched sideways, fouled on sunken debris.

"Hard a'port!" barked Deut', calling up reactor schematics and hull-stress readouts. "I don't have time for your bullshit, boy! There's a whole iron boneyard under us, and your damned city's on fire! Hand over those codes!"

The noise from below was a steady, rhythmic pounding now, as giant pistons strained at their bolts. Shadows lurched and spun as the lights arced out, as the dome above creaked open like a metal iris...

And the floor beneath it began to grind apart, exhaling a cloud of powdered rust and decay.

"The missiles! The damn missiles, Kayzi! Did those mercenary bastards get to them first?" Deut was frantic now, and Jaq could see why. Shattered pews and prayer-books fell down into the darkness as hydraulics wheezed and groaned, pushing an accusing finger of steel up into the nave. Haszan plucked Grief out of the air and leaped back, teetering on the brink of the pit for a second before the sword twisted in his hands, pulling him to safety.

It was all sliding, copulating steel down there, pistons and rods and wheels meshing amid a sea of oil and shadows. A drum-magazine for a giant machinegun... but instead of bullets, the sub-basement of the chapel held row upon row of nuclear missiles.

"Stand clear of the edge, Jaq!" shouted the voice of Grief, this time only inside his head. *"The enemy are below, and in vast numbers... "*

It only took him a second to realize what the railblade was saying, but by then it was too late. Oil and shadows, writhing in intestinal tangles beneath the grinding steel...

The creatures which had driven Abdulafia half mad - those things which he'd seen among the refugee fleet - *they were here.* Now.

No sooner had Haszan realized the danger than a set of dripping claws scrabbled up over the edge of the pit, hauling an abomination into the chapel. It was a seething, bubbling mass of tar-black ooze, knotted around bones and sinews and ulcerated flesh. But its face was almost human – almost, until its mouth spewed forth a snarl of hook-tipped tentacles.

That first Saprophyte's howl of hunger and rage was cut short as Jaq split it down the middle, swinging the blade of Grief in a killing stroke. Acrid smoke boiled from the wound, and the torso of the creature flopped on the deck like a gutted fish. A second brutal blow from the railblade finished it off, splitting its misshapen skull.

But there were more. So many more...

Deuteronomy Jones choked on his prayers when he saw how many of them were still clad in Pentecostal whites... his own sailors, transformed into beasts. He clubbed at them with the butt of his trank rifle, holding them back while Jaq worked his butchery.

"Guilty, before God! Guilty, before his Son! Guilty, by the testament of the Holy Spirit!" The preacher's fervor hurt them as much as the blows of the hardwood stock, sending the Saprophytes scuttling back into the shadows.

Far off, on the other side of the pit, he could hear screams and the muffled popping of automatic fire. But he couldn't see the fate of those Pent' marines who made their last stand there... until limbs and heads and chunks of nameless flesh came fountaining up from behind a wall of rabid darkness.

Blood and ruptured intestines. Sweat and fear and burning fat... the smell of it almost made Jaq choke, before the Chimera system shut down his olfactory nerves.

Kaito was firing into the mass of them too, his automatic's bullets having as little effect as pebbles tossed into an oncoming tidal wave.

If he *was* really Chimera now, then Jaq wished he'd find a railblade and join in. It was all he could do to keep swinging his seven-foot monolith of steel in great reaping stokes, watching the power levels of his own crycelial system bleed away...

Something made him pause for a moment, right at the upswing of a disemboweling backhand - something which seemed to catch the attention of the Saps as well, making them cower back, hissing. It sounded like footsteps... the heavy tread of something godawfully powerful running down the length of the submarine, down there in the missile hold. An incoherent roar shook the world as it came, the sound of pure brute bloodlust.

Asag'raal's newest slave.

Exalted Jiang came running up the spiral of nuclear warheads at a dead sprint, using them as stepping stones to gain height. At the very last instant he lashed out with one hook-tipped arm, catching the nosecone of the final missile. His blade cut a spiral groove in its cerametal shielding as Jiang looped around it, rolling in mid-air...

And both of those serrated hooks carved through Deut' Jones where he stood, wide-eyed and speechless - doomed. Jiang came down on him like an oily black mantis, the serrated edges of his hooks slicing the captain from shoulder to crotch in one ripping motion. The multi-jointed mandibles which made up his lower jaw licked out, whipcrack fast, snatching the Pentecostal's head out of the air before it could hit the ground. And with a series of grinding, crunching spasms the Exalted chewed and swallowed, licking its chops with a foot-long tongue.

At the end of that tongue was a human mouth, complete with broken and yellowed teeth.

"There's only one captain on my ship, I'm afraid!" chuckled the nightmare creature, untangling its hooks from Deuteronomy's innards. "And it's not likely to be this guy..." The two halves of the Pentecostal preacher fell away, already sucked dry."Still, I find I'm missing a vital piece of the puzzle. *Two* pieces, if my new memories serve me well..."

The creature tapped a tiny black dot which burst like a carbuncle from its forehead, the tip of its bony claw all wet and slippery against the bead of jet. It was Deut's bio-onboard, and both Haszan and Kaito recognized it in an instant.

"That's right, friends. All the commands, all the systems - I will make this ship the scourge of the oceans! My Master's promised me as much... and more. But the sweetest prize is right inside your head, Kayzi."

Jiang stalked forward, crushing the rotting bones of dead Saprophytes with each step.

"Imagine what I can do to Elysium with all that sweet cleansing fire! You've led the whole world down into hell with your little tune, Kaito, and now I'll make them burn! Such a pyre... Lord Asag'raal will delight in my offering, burnt on an altar the size of a city!"

"He's taken Deut's interface link," said Kaito, as Haszan retreated before Exalted Jiang. "He could probably *integrate* mine too..."

The Kayzi looked sick, hypnotized by Jiang's rows of transparent teeth.

Jaq shuddered, remembering the sound of shattering bone. He couldn't blame him.

"And that's a meal with a nuclear prize inside... But I'm nearly spent here, K. I can't take ugly here *and* all of his boys. Can't you do something?"

"Welll..." said Kaito, staring into the jaws of the Exalted One "You know how I told poor old Deut' that I couldn't hack his bio-onboard in three tenths of a second..."

"You mean it's hopeless? You can't just erase the codes before he eats you?"

"No," said the Kayzi, getting that look on his face which meant there was major trouble ahead. "I told him I couldn't rip his firewalls. *But I lied.*"

There was a second of breathless silence as Exalted Jiang reared up in front of the altar, his bone hooks held high. Then the thrall of Asag'raal howled, his single bloodshot eye bulging from its socket.

And as that terrible scream skirled up and up, rising to a glass-shattering pitch, Jaq clenched the handle of Grief between numb fingers, and brought it back over his head.

It was time to end this madness. And the Chimera only knew one way to do it...

17 Aevum Oblivio
Core

"*I* WANT THEM *driven back!*" *snarled Kataphrakt Yrr, clenching his fighting claws around the arms of his command throne. "Let the sacrifice of the* Brutality *be a lesson to you all – this battle will only be won with blood and courage!*"

Ropes of steaming mucous spattered from his jaws as he spoke – drool laced with pheromones to drive his Bastarnae into a battle-frenzy.

Blood and courage. Meat for the grinder of war.

Yrr's loyal captains stared down at him from a hexagonal mesh of holoscreens, a great shimmering honeycomb surrounding his throne like a stained-glass hemisphere. And the neural shunt made them feel his anger and his resolve, flooding their alien brains with stimulants. Some hissed and roared and fluttered their mandibles in artificial rage; others, without the benefit of discernible facial features, simply let their actions do the talking.

All along the battle-line Yrr's forces redoubled their efforts, throwing themselves against the spaceborne wall of the Unity again and again. The line of engagement ran between Mars and Earth now... unacceptably close to the prize. At the core of the Motherbrain's offensive was the Behemoth-Class hub of the slave-fleet; greatly diminished, but still the size of a small moon. Silver cylinders flanked the Hub along a three-light-minute line, ablated smooth by space-dust and nebular clouds until they shone like slivers of diamond. Some were supercarriers, things like the vessel which the Justifiable Brutality *had taken down. Others were monolithic slabs of weaponry; dreadnaught-killers and planetary assault ships armed with fusion cannons big enough to swallow lesser spacecraft whole.*

These formed a regimented line along the curve of Earth's orbit, pulled up in ranks like ancient infantrymen. Tiny drone fighters ran cover between them, swarming in an endless moebius loop around their tenders, while the dreadnaughts fired in rolling volleys, picking off Teuthis Rex and Princeps voidhunters one by one.

Yrr watched as a cluster of Unity heavy battlecruisers drew down on a vast, flat-shelled Tyrant-class missile destroyer, focusing a score of cannons on its broad carapace. Its shields spat mile-long arcs of purple flame as the beams converged, all focused on a single point... but there was no way that the doomed ship could withstand all that concentrated energy. First the shields failed, then the heat-transfer substructures welded to its yard-thick shell…

Yrr shut down his link to the Tyrant's captain as he watched a razor beam of light come slicing in through the wall of its command nexus, rushing up behind the captain's throne even as he turned, his eight eyes wide with terror…

The screams were always the same. Every time one of the living warships of the Praetor died, Yrr wished that his people could trust in steel and carbon and ceramic-composite like their foes.

He'd have to break the line. Draw their fire, before the relentless advance of the Blacksteel brought them any closer to Earth. Behind the wall of dreadnaughts and carriers with their swarming thralls, Yrr could make out the wasp-striped cylinders of the Unity's ground offensive – troop carriers packed with mekan, A.I. slaved tanks and lumbering Colossi.

"Subjugation, *tell the Commanders of the anchor-ships to prepare for a pincer movement. Take them up and over the line, englobe their flanks, and push them into the center. Then prepare the first Geocore for firing."*

`++ Delighted to, my Admiral!++` *squealed the portal carrier ship, its miles-wide bulk trembling with glee.* `++We have twenty-two Geocores in the Null Storage Strata… with a uniform weight of twenty-nine billion tons. Fire control will be slaved to dear Schnarga within a matter of moments.++`

Whole planets were reamed out to make the Geocores, vast cylindrical slugs of nickel and iron which formed the Effortless Subjugation's *most potent weapon. The portal at its heart tangled up the laws of physics like a snarl of yarn, warping and twisting the very meanings of terms like 'gravity' and 'mass' and 'velocity'. You really didn't want to be anywhere in the vicinity when a Geocore was fired, and that was why the Thrall-species who crewed the* Subjugation *were strapping themselves into their seed-shaped pods, scrabbling and cursing in a hundred alien languages.*

Yrr, as an esteemed Kataphrakt-Admiral, comported himself with more dignity than his slaves. As the whole coral-like latticework of the portal carrier began to stretch and attenuate he tapped out a code on the floating keyboard before him, gathering up his cape with his gracile secondary claws. The floor beneath his command throne shimmered silver for an instant, then rippled like water. A pale, jointed tentacle quested up over the lip of the pool, followed by another and another, dripping with the stuff of liquid space.

++I am with you, master! Onward together, for glory!++

Schnaarga levered its immense bulk up and out of the water, poised on the tips of its tentacles like some kind of nightmare crustacean. Yrr's throne unfolded a set of insectile metal legs to grip the ochre dome of the Devilfish's shell, and a second set of spidery limbs to affix the Kataphrakt's armor.

"We're going to give them a taste of the Geocore, my pet," Chuckled Yrr, lifting his arms one by one to accept the hard outer carapace with its inlaid lapis and bronze. "Bloodlust aside, it should be nothing less than spectacular. Remember the orbital arcologies over Nyricu Six? Just like that!"

Now the diamond dome split open along invisible seams, sending the atmosphere within howling off into the vacuum. Rebreather tubes behind Yrr's damascened faceplate began to sigh and hiss as the artificial gravity cut them loose, and Schnaarga trilled with delight. The Devilfish wasn't happy unless it was in the thick of battle, and the firing of a Geocore was a special treat. When all those tiny burnt bodies had come spilling out of the sky-cities of Nyricu, Schnaarga had gorged on flesh until its second stomach burst...

The Kataphrakt and his pet rose up above the stretching, distorting shape of the Effortless Subjugation, *just as the thrall-pods burst out from it in every direction, the seeds from a moon- sized dandelion clock. They were made to disperse among the living capital ships which flanked the Portal Carrier – veteran Voidrazors and Castigators bristling with cannons and missile batteries.*

All of their might was nothing, though, compared to the hideous force of the Subjugation *itself. It was pulled out wide now, a ring of living matter around the seething blue iris of the portal. That ring was spinning, building up the energy it required to turn brute mass into pure energy; to fire a multi-million ton chunk of some dead planet's core at a fraction below the speed of light.*

Small wonder that even a mighty Kataphrakt couldn't stay on board when it was activated...

The Subjugation's *rising scream of pleasure reached a skull-splitting crescendo as Yrr brought his claw down on the firing pin, watching his anchor-ships split the line of the* Unity, *peeling away defenses from the* Behemoth *hub.*

And halfway between an orgasm and a fatal seizure, the Effortless Subjugation *vomited up a slug of nickel and iron, drilled out of a dying world by a creature the size of a continent.*

Most of it was ablated away as a shockwave of searing plasma the instant it cleared the portal – an accusatory finger stabbing out across the dark toward the Motherbrain's line of battle. Inside that glowing corona, meshed up in a web of unholy lightning, the white-hot heart of the Geocore homed in on its target, as unstoppable as the fury of Gods…

This was the point at which the Subjugation was most vulnerable. A disruptor missile fired into the churning eye of the portal now would collapse it in on itself, creating a miniature black hole…

But the Unity forces were reeling from Yrr's pincer strategy. And when space flared white at the center of their line, the Kataphrakt and his Devilfish howled in savage triumph, ancient endorphin-glands flooding their brains with ecstasy.

"All units, converge on the wreckage of the Hub! Ensnare any shielded A.I. cores you can find – we need them for interrogation!"

The comm band was awash with ululations and screams of joy – few, if any of the Order of Battle had ever been privileged enough to witness the power of a Geocore attack. But then again, it was a rare thing for the fleets of the Praetor and the Motherbrain to hammer at each other in space like this. Dau'mun had been the last great clash of space-armadas, and the death toll from that cataclysm was still being felt by both sides, nearly three hundred years on.

"Report, forward intel! What is the status of the Unity formation?"

Yrr could see the fighters and thrallships falling in toward the center of the Blacksteel line all around him – threads of white fire twisting against the darkness of space. Thousands of them, Stirges and Gorgons and Slavemasters, scavengers hungry for the remains of that doomed Behemoth…

"Fall back! Fall back! All units, this is forward intel cruiser Illuminator *– the Hub is still intact! Repeat – the Hub is still intact!"*

"Then what in His Name did we just hit?" roared Yrr, leaping from his throne to perch right at the edge of Schnaarga's carapace. "Subjugation, how long until you can fire another Geocore?"

`++Three minutes only, my Admiral!++` *crooned the grossly distended Portal Carrier.* `++Three-oh-seven and counting down…++`

Yrr took the uplink from the Illuminator *directly into his brain, bypassing the onion-skin layers of firewalls and shields which cradled his neural tissue. The Motherbrain had outplayed him, and he was determined to find out how…*

It was a feint. The Hub had used its jump drives to slip sideways through the Aematrerium as the Geocore came screaming in on it, detaching a cluster of cylinder-ships from its tail as it fled. It had only gone under for a second – long enough to avoid the explosion - and it had reappeared spinning, bringing all its missile batteries to bear on the Effortless Subjugation. *The shell of battleships it had sloughed off were a sacrifice, like a lizard's tail cast off to evade a predator. They'd been utterly vaporized, for all that they were worth. But the Hub itself, the* Behemoth *– it had lured Yrr into a trap.*

Even as he blinked the after-images of the Illuminator's *video feed from his eyes, Yrr could see a storm of smart torpedoes rising up from the jagged topography of the Unity hub, tens of thousands of them arrowing in toward the vulnerable portal.*

Three minutes before the next Geocore could be launched. And in that time, the Motherbrain could turn it into a black hole ten times over...

17 Aevum Oblivio
Keys

CeeAn could already *see* the war from here. All through the long ride up the space-'lev she'd watched tiny stars sparkle and fade against the velvet dark – the little candle-flames of alien dreadnoughts being torn apart.

She'd walked the labyrinth of the trials alone, leaving her companions in the great echoing basilica of the lev-dock, and the black hall with its sliding pillars and traps and snares had let her pass unchallenged. Defused, she knew, by Kheptic hands seventeen years ago.

CeeAn went unarmed into the woven steel spindle beneath the Cardinal Rock – unarmed because she'd seen Everdark wrapped in ever-shifting coils around the great rock of the Station, and she knew it was no use trying to fight a thing like that with bullets. All she needed was in the palm of her hand, in a glass core drilled from Technician Nyl's living flesh. That glistening slug of alien meat was marbled through with the stuff of the slavesystems, and Cee knew that it was the key to unlocking the Forge. That – and the similar tube of glass taken from the flesh of Simeon Blaire.

Now she faced the rippling dark wall of the Explorator System – a veil drawn across the corridor which pulsed and twisted like silk in the wind. It could devour her in a heartbeat, she knew… but the war unfolding outside the diamondglass windows of the Station was even worse than the shadows within.

Those explosions were coming closer. One side or the other – Zhe's people or Everdark's – one was driving the other back, closing in on the Earth.

Cee stepped up to the barrier, arms held out at her sides cruciform. In each palm he held a bleeding core of glass, two dripping rods of sequestrated flesh.

"Hear me, guardian system!" she shouted, her words swallowed up by the wall of blackness. "I am the one who has been sent to take the Forge. Sent by my master and yours – the final integration of the strains!"

That got the Slavesytem's attention. She was sure, now, that it was infected and controlled by Nyl. It had to be, or the tangle of black pseudopods erupting from the wall would be the last thing she'd ever see.

They hovered over her like snakes, tasting the air, keeping a cautious distance as CeeAn's heart pulsed hot and urgent in her throat. The neural interlocks were primed. Pseudomorph flooded her system, branching *down through her arteries like cold wire.*

Cee took one sharp glass drill-core in each hand, screwed her eyes shut...

And she stabbed with all her strength, driving the alien flesh deep into her cloned body.

Dormant systems burst and intertwined, unfurling into her bloodstream in thorny coils. The Chimera in Blaire's blood, the Blacksteel in Nyl's... slithering over each other like mating serpents, twisting and ramifying through her living tissue...

The wall gaped open like a great vertical mouth, its fangs made up of innumerable nanorobotic tentacles. They caressed her arm, her cheek, the tips of her fingers as she stepped inside, fighting with all her mind to contain the human and alien machines in her blood.

The Blacksteel flowed like water as she opened her eyes, one now dark as night, the other silver. It peeled apart before her, closing at her heels, drawing her into the sanctum of the Forge.

CeeAn didn't even feel the two tubes of glass unscrew from out of her body, sheared off neat and razor-edged by the hybrid tech-flesh inside her. But it wasn't the Forge which called to her, out of the blackened core of the Cardinal Rock. She could feel the brittle spark of life at the very heart of this place... the slow and regular pulse of bodies in hibernation.

Abdulafia was here.

And if it cost her humanity to wake him, then that was a price she was willing to pay.

2196 Ante Arbitrium
Educational Programming

THE STONE WAS warm against Simeon's back - as warm as human flesh to his touch. He stood on a tiny lip of marble, looking down at the burning Subcity beneath his feet, and he let out a sigh he'd been holding in for far too long.

LYSANDER JAEGENN WAS finished.

The Hand of Kronos, transformed by some hideous teknomancy... and his final gambit had nearly taken Simeon down to hell with him. Simeon, and Leynna Mendelev-Singh as well; he could only hope that she'd lacked the presence of mind to put good solid stone between herself and that cataclysmic explosion.

Lord Blaire couldn't trust the evidence of his eyes. Even during the game he'd been haunted by fragments of glassy illusion, slivers of feudal Japan ghosting in over reality. It was the remnant of Octavio's control; the Direktor's ploy for sequestration. So he couldn't really be sure if his Kheptic foe had truly been remade. Had he really become a monster, in those last bloody minutes of his life? Had he pleaded for Leynna and Simeon to cut his heart out with steel?

Perhaps.

Or perhaps it was time for another hit of Stunn - *a sharpener, a little reward.*

Simeon snapped a capsul between two barcoded fingertips as he pressed his back to the cooling stone, letting the drug pop and snarl in his brain. The shattered cityscape at his feet blurred, but he had supreme confidence in his sense of balance - the tiny gyrosystems implanted in his inner ears were quite immune to the Stunn.

For a second it was Edo again - the Kanto plain stretching out into the darkness as all those tiny bamboo and paper houses burned, sparks swirling up in pillars from the hellfire glow.

How he hated those wires Vanecke had put in his head! To think that he'd almost been subverted; almost *used* by that low-born filth... But the truth would out. Simeon had caught his Master's true intent just in time. And now the crippled old fool was doomed.

He was the last one alive.

The thought rode in on the curling breaker of the stunn-rush, and for a second the fake euphoria of the drug masked its implication.

He was the last of the Kheptarchy! And that meant...

"Sweet ancestral hells!" breathed Simeon Blaire, splayed against the wall of a ruined megatower, high above his city. "I made it! I'm Emperor! *Emperor*, you hear me!"

His wild shout was lost in the night, whipped away by the wind which howled around the upper spires. He was lord of all he surveyed; a living god over a hellscape of steel and flame.

A black shadow fell across the Subcity as he watched, cast by the teardrop-shaped bulk of a drifting camera zeppelin. Its aerials and dishes were bent and blackened, and one of the great threedeeo screens which hung from its belly was sheared away... but the other still glittered with woven light, projecting the face of Kaito Kayzi out over the city. It was Octavio's pride - the *Stephen Foster*.

What better way to tell his people that all was well? There was no need to flee, now, no need to run from the things which Kronos had unleashed on the streets. Soon Simeon would hold the power of the Forge in his hands, and the Earth would be remade; a new Eden for his faithful slaves...

He waited until the smooth dark flank of the zeppelin was almost close enough to touch, tensing himself against the marble wall of the spire. Then he leaped out into space, his fingers hooked into claws, coming up against the diamond-fiber shell of the airship with a bone-jarring impact. He scrabbled for purchase on the smooth surface for a second - until his hands grasped the frayed end of a mooring line, a wrist-thick hawser twisting in the wind. Slowly, laboriously, Simeon hauled himself up hand over hand, ignoring the yawning gulf beneath his feet. The slope of the gasbag grew easier as he rounded the bulge of the airship's belly, crawling at last atop its dorsal platform. A strip of landing lights picked out the six-hundred-foot spine of the camera-ship; a skyway for Omnivasive's choppers and antigravs. But there was only a single machine squatting dead center on the strip - an olive-drab gunship which Simeon recognized at once.

Through a haze of chemical illusions he recalled the insect shape of this helicopter coming down on him, silver tentacles binding up his arms and legs...

It was a stepping-stone closer to Octavio Vanecke. One of his menials was probably busy in the gondola below - and the gunship would have full clearance to land right on top of the Direktor's Bimburb mansion. It was simply too sweet for words!

Simeon licked his lips, tasting the bitter residue of the Stunn.

It was all so simple now.

First, *revenge* - one last taste of animal gratuity before he was transformed. And then to the tower, the trials... and the Forge. Kronos would never stop him - not tonight of all nights, when the city was under siege. Vast sections of the machine's precious Wetsystems were burned away, and their architect was dead and gone. Only Simeon could remake them now - for with the Forge came all the knowledge in the world, all the power he'd need to fuse the great A.I. to his naked brain...

"All mine, all mine..." he crooned to himself, feeling the Stunn in his veins twisting lasciviously against his crycelial upgrades. "I'll be with you soon, dear Master... and your suffering will last just as long as my imagination allows..."

"Don't you ever get tired of your own voice, Blaire?"

He whipped around, snarling, the sword at guard even before he felt it slide from its scabbard. But there was nothing but darkness, pressing in on every side... darkness which crawled and popped with the azure sparks of the stunn.

"You know, I bet you really thought you were the last, didn't you, Simeon? Still, these are enlightened times we live in. The lower orders will bow before a Goddess just as easily as they will before a God."

Oh, he knew that voice. That smug and subtle mockery, that scent of jasmine and honey in the dark...

He couldn't trust his eyes. And, after all, she was the Direktor's pet and plaything...

With the revelation came clarity - a haze of shadows coalescing into human form.

Leynna's sintered black armor was like a hole cut into the night - the blast had burned her wide-sleeved robes away, leaving only the diamond-mesh combat suit beneath. Her ice-white hands showed up against the backdrop of ash and fire, floating like Octavio's druuj as they balanced a pair of long slim swords.

"You *are* the resourceful one, aren't you?" he said, slowly bringing his own blade up to guard. "And here we are; the last pureblood man alive, and the last woman too. It's such a shame that our line ends here, Leynna. But as the old saying goes... *not if you were the last girl on earth...*"

"Don't flatter yourself, Simeon." She sneered, her face blurring into focus as the drugs peeled open his eyes. "Your arrogance would be kind of cute - if you weren't so hopelessly *obsolete.*"

She tested his defenses with a flurry of blows then, steel chiming on steel high above the burning city. She was fast - much faster than he remembered. But Simeon Blaire's bones were cored out and replaced with Chimera crycelium, and he turned aside Leynna's attack lazily, a maddening little smile on his lips.

Leynna leaped back, crouching with her blades at the ready. He was good - very, very good... but she had to be better. For her son, for revenge... and ultimately, for the Forge.

Remember what Vanecke told you. The relic he used had to be altered, downgraded... the full force of a Chimera system would spread like steel cancer, consuming its host. Blaire was hybridized, *his augmentations mated to his cloned body... but it was his* skill *which made him dangerous. The training which Octavio had put him through... the memories she now carried in her own head...*

She remembered Tadashi Murai, the fifth kata - and the means to break it. Kojiro Sasake's 'Turning Swallow' cut, as swift and sharp as a bird in flight. *How* she knew didn't matter at all. All her energy was focused down the blade, into a stroke that would open Blaire's throat on the backswing.

Kojiro used a single massive sword... but she had two. *One slim katana came in from either side, splitting Simeon's concentration, primed for that lightning-fast reversal...*

He blocked left, and she struck with the right; the downstroke a feint, the backswing tearing through the soft flesh of his exposed neck in a spray of crimson. She felt the tip of her blade graze across his spine, down deep in the wound, watched his eyes widen with shock and terror. Just like the Game... but this time there was no Lancaster, no Biotects waiting with the promise of rebirth.

Leynna spat as Simeon tottered back, almost to the edge of the landing strip, his sword clattering to the ground as he wrapped his fingers around his throat. It was no use - the livid red gash was slick with blood, and his hands couldn't stop the flow.

"Perhaps just one more little cut, Simeon?" she said, kicking his feet out from under him. "Then you'll have another thing in common with your Master... you can join him in his preservative tank, if you like." The thought of those two locked in stasis forever - face to eyeless face - threatened to overwhelm Leynna with hysterical laughter. "But no... no. Life is for the *living*, Blaire. And you've been dead a long time already. You just didn't have the good sense to lie down and quit."

Blaire gurgled and spat blood, scrabbling away across the deck of the giant airship. One of his eyes was dark, hooded by its diamondglass oculus, but the other...

In that blank and terrified stare was all the satisfaction Leynna had ever craved. The whining little bastard was done for! Now he'd pay for all he'd done - murder, deceit, treachery... and worst of all, for denying her the son who would surpass him. He was forced back to the edge now, the sleek curve of the zeppelin's gasbag falling away beneath him to a fractured cityscape on fire. Leynna brought her sword back over her head, a grim smile on her lips.

"You should have been a better father, Simeon." she said, measuring her killing stroke. "Now our *second* child will have to grow up without one... "

Ω

Atticus Meaks caught it all on camera. The pressman wiped the sweat from his brow with an oversized red handkerchief, laughing as the scene spooled out on his threedeeo console. Pure gold! The Chief would thank him for this one, and no mistake... hells, he'd even be in line for a promotion to the Sports Desk after tonight!
Swords blurred and clashed and sparked, eyes narrowed with hate, bodies spun and coiled and leaped in an intricate dance... this was Atticus Meaks' masterpiece, a one-on-one battle between two aspirant gods. And every second of it was being broadcast live to the sensorium mansion of Direktor Vanecke, to a very select audience.

"What are they doing!" shouted Darion, pounding his fists against the hardlight bubble of the threedeeo globe. "They're not supposed to fight each other! He's bleeding, Uncle Octavio! Somebody help them!"

Now it was time for the shadow-play. The act. Vanecke's immaculate avatar knelt next to the Kheptic prince, staring into the globe with a look of artificial horror on his face.

"No! It can't be! Not after all this time!"

The great cogitators which wove his holographic form pricked tears from his avatar's eyes as he watched Simeon and Leynna fight, completing the illusion.

"I thought...I thought it was a temporary madness. That he had come to accept your place, your birthright. But... "

"But *what!*" screamed Darion, as Leynna's swallow-cut opened up Blaire's neck, each glistening droplet of blood picked out in merciless detail by Meaks' cameras. "Why are they killing each other? *Why can't you make them stop?!*"

Ω

The *Stephen Foster* drifted out over Elysium, its rudders broken, its

143

great turboprops silent. It was sinking, settling down among the lesser towers of the city's crown, past belching smokestacks weeping rust, past statues of eyeless heroes cast in bronze, filigreed satellite dishes and stained-glass spires - the follies of the noble houses.

All dead, now. Save for the son and daughter of the Kheptocracy who fought to the death atop the airship's spine.

"Second child? There should... there should never have been a first... " coughed Lord Simeon Blaire, bubbles of bright blood foaming from the gash in his neck. "I... I never gave consent. I never needed the succession... to complete my great work... but now..."

That stopped her dead, the sword trembling in her hands. Leynna had always dared to hope that Simeon would accept her as his equal - if only she could best him in the Game.

"Do you see, then?" she asked, lowering her blade until the tip of it rested cool against his cheek "What we could have become? Not Vanecke's pawns, but a king and queen, united over our own perfect world..." Her eyes looked right through him, then, deep into a fantasy world in which her dreams remained unbroken. "He has promised me a son, Simeon. One to replace the child you slaughtered. And so... *I have no choice.*"

The katana flicked back up to guard, poised to stab down into Blaire's glittering black oculus. But he'd already bought himself all the time he needed. While she'd rhapsodized about a future that was already dead, the silver threads of the Chimera had sewn up his wounds, sending fresh blood seething through his veins. Transfusor chambers nestled hot and slick along his spine took the place of his cored-out marrow, lacing the plasm with twist, narrowing his vision down to razor slits...

"Neither do I, darling," he said, as the oculus snapped back into its orbital recess. The eye beneath burned with hatred, as hot and focused as a welding torch. "All that stand in my way - cripple, woman and child - *all must die.*"

She hissed as she saw the utter madness written across his face; the silver scar scrawled across his throat. She thrust the katana down to pin his skull to the decking of the *Stephen Foster*... But she was too slow.

All this time her mark had been playing with her, testing her defenses. Even allowing himself to come so close to death had just been another of Simeon's tactics - now he knew her technique, and the cogitators behind his eyes were primed to crush her utterly.

Simeon twitched his head aside as the sword came down, waiting to hear it slice into the composite mesh of the airship. There was an instant in which Leynna's blade was caught by the tight weave of it; as valency generators tried to bind the sword into the puncture wound. That was all he needed.

The Kheptarch's eyes blurred with impossible visions as he rolled to his feet, shadows of ancient Japan torn from Tadashi Murai's books. In that world Leynna was dressed as a lithe *Kunoichi* assassin, whirling with her swords at the ready, her face ghostly white under a mask of powdered makeup. Tiny charcoal lines picked out her eyes beneath the brim of a conical straw hat, tied under her chin with a red silk sash.

"Don't try to run, Blaire!" she said, circling him warily as he stooped to pick up his own blade. "This ends here - tonight! The one who wields the Forge must be prepared for it his whole life... instructed by someone who knows how the world *should* be remade. Not by a bloodthirsty monster like you!"

"And you think some spoiled Khept' brat with an overbearing *bitch* of a mother will grow up to be anything but a monster? Don't deny yourself, Leynna. This was never about your seed - only about your own disappointment."

She couldn't take that. Not while there was good steel in her hands, and the scent of rich Kheptic blood in the air. Leynna came in swinging, her swords a silver blur as the lights along the runway came on two by two. A wave of actinic glare washed over her as she slashed and spun, wild-eyed, and as Simeon fended off each deadly blow with his own flying steel. The cameras were savage, all-encompassing - they picked out every pore on the combatant's faces, each drop of sweat as it flew through the smoky air. Atticus Meaks was conducting a symphony below them in the control gondola; speeding up the images as Leynna and Blaire traded strike and counterstrike, slowing them down to focus on tight-clenched jaws, blazing eyes, tendons and white knuckles...

It was a dance of brutality, miles above the burning Subcity. Some of the refugee tribes picking their way through the bloody streets even stopped to look up, to point and gasp with awe as their gods-to-be stormed and raged on giant threedeeo screens.

Along the runway and back again, shimmering metal wove a cage about the shadows of the *Kenshin* and *Kunoichi*, sparks flaring and dying as steel kissed steel. He was stronger, powered by the infernal mekanisms welded to his bones, but she was filled with righteous fury, a cold and vicious anger to match her skill.

Back to the insect form of Meaks' gunship now, and the ragged survivors in the streets gasped as Blaire's blade cut deep gashes through steel and glass and rubber, licking at Leynna's heels as she leaped up onto its canopy. He was quick to follow, and they dueled their way up over the hump-backed dome of its air intakes, to balance blade-to blade atop its rotors.

The twin swords of Leynna Mendelev-Singh flew like a stormfront of metal, driving Simeon back onto the tip of one rotor-blade. He teetered for an instant above an abyssal drop, down through veils of smoke and sparks to the city below. Then he rallied, scything great two-handed blows at his tormentor, all the way back across the rotor-hub to the far edge of the blade. Back and forth, frantic shadows against the arclamp glare, battling blow for blow down along the tail of the gunship and circling back around...

"My only *disappointment...*" panted Leynna, limbering up her wrists with a series of swift snap-cut spins. "Is that you aren't nearly as good as you think you are."

The tail of the helicopter was between them - a long, low boom at chest height. It gave Simeon a chance to catch his breath and flex his aching fingers.

"At least I was smart enough to leave Vanecke behind. You might as well still be his concubine, for all that he's using you."

Simeon swung a backhand slice which came within an inch of Leynna's face, but she didn't flinch.

"If you think *he's* using *me*, you're just as stupid as you look. It's my destiny to bring the true god-emperor of Earth into the world, Simeon... and to remove each and every usurper from his path!"

She slid low under the tail-boom, her swords skirling together like a pair of monomolecular shears. Blaire skipped backwards, cursing as she brought them wheeling up and around, windmilling strokes which hissed past his defenses... But Leynna's steel never even grazed his skin. Desperation sunk its teeth into her throat, then, making the world fall out from under her.

He was simply too fast. And for all her bravado, she was no Chimera - not even a second-gen carrier like Blaire.

If Leynna had been Ashishim, she would have called her next decision *Sanction Ultra* - but as a Kheptic Noble she had no word for victory-through-sacrifice. In the cloistered world of the Game the concept was nonsense, of course - death meant *elimination*, and suicide... Suffice to say that in the last thousand years, only Simeon Blaire himself had managed to override his synaptic indoctrination. She was the only one apart from Vanecke who knew about his shame...

Now she prepped the needle-injector which nestled in the crook of one thumb - a surprise she'd prepared for Simeon even before tonight's game began.

Within the hollow barb a drop of poison waited to rape his bloodstream - a counterchemical to the venom in his blood. Leynna's robosurgeons had carefully scraped a thin sheen of toxins from the throwing-star which had killed her in Duke Gideon's tower - and her laboratorium thralls had finished the job.

"It's just that the line of treason is so *arbitrary*, don't you think?" said Blaire, fending off her attacks with one hand. "At this point in our little argument, I'd say that the throne and the Forge are almost certainly mine. Which makes *you* the usurper - and your filthy spawn nothing but collateral damage."

"So self-assured!" she replied, slashing right and left with furious abandon. "But pride will be the end of you, Simeon. In fact - that's just how they'll tell it in the histories..."

Ω

Octavio Vanecke's holographic face was a study of careworn grief - dripping with lugubrious tears which his eyes could never produce. He rested a hardlight hand on Darion's thin shoulder, looking down into the young Kehptarch's madness.

"He always resented your birthright, Darion. I'm sorry... I... your mother made me your warden for just that reason. Your Lord Father was ever convinced that he could master the game; that he'd have no need for you. I thought...I thought he'd put such madness behind him. But your Inception, tonight - it's brought it all back. I'm sorry. He's..."

There was no need to go on. Darion's mismatched eyes blazed with hatred, narrowed to slits of amber and green. His pale little hands, already strong enough to strike through stone, were balled into fists at his sides.

And while Octavio's holo-self cried, masquerading the suffering of a loyal retainer, his severed head smiled, a wolfish grin behind six inches of diamondglass. His druuj fingers were deep into a nuero-synaptic model of the young Kehpt's brain, priming connections, bringing back memories only hours distant... but which felt, to the forcegrown child, as if they'd happened in dim and faroff years.

The Black Palace.

A wall of screaming children, each one with his own infant face.

A lake of blood, and his mother's hands anointing his brow.

And then... then came the delicate touch of Vanecke's scalpels, the twist of the knife.

Blaire and the iron-masked demon blurred together behind Darion's eyes - meshing seamlessly into a singular monster, an oedipal nightmare dripping with blood.

His own Lord Father had tried to kill him.

And his mother had risked her life to save him...

"Uncle, we have to go there. We have to help her! Now, before it's too late..."

"There's nothing I can do, Darion," whispered Ashcer's avatar, kneeling in abject grief. "I'm bound to this building, to my chamber. And you... you could never defeat him now. You have years of training before your investiture into the Game, let alone *combat to the death...*"

Those mismatched eyes bored right though him, sending a chill down the wires and into Octavio's preservative tank. That look, so calculating and yet so *unhinged...* it scared the Direktor even more than the faceless black cubes which hovered around him, licking the air with their saws and scalpels.

"But I don't need to go anywhere, do I Uncle?" asked Darion, in a voice like steel on glass. "You said yourself that I'm the one who drove him to madness. I'm the one who threatens his ascendancy. So he will come to me... eventually."

"I can hide you. It is my duty to die for you, if need be. But please, young Lord Blaire... don't face him! He's insane! He's..."

"He's my *predecessor*, Uncle, and nothing more. It means 'he who dies before me'. I'll *prove* his obsolescence, if he's foolish enough to come here. And if he harms Mother, then..."

It didn't need saying. The all-consuming hate in Darion's eyes told Octavio all he needed to know. The trap was set. And now, to the final act...

Ω

Leynna's wild overhand swing was a feint - an obvious ploy to make Simeon block high, leaving his belly open for a disemboweling slash. He could almost feel the sharpened steel tearing through his viscera as he dodged left, letting his foe's sword whisper past his shoulder. He brought his own blade down hard on the undercut; a brutal two-handed blow which bit into Leynna's katana with a sound like a crystal bell.

The sword shattered.

Simeon's eyes traced each flying splinter of metal; an expanding cloud of shards winking in the actinic light. Each one was a tiny mirror, curved sharp like his smile.

And his hands followed through, his muscles and bones and nerves running on automatic as the point of his blade drove through Leynna's sternum, through her chest, and out between her shoulderblades.

The brittle wind-chimes sound of falling steel came down around them as they stood, transfixed in the camera's empty eye. Simeon knew that this was his moment of victory, that he should feel *vindicated*, glorious... But it was as if his whole world had been torn open, all his purpose and reason spilled out through a ragged gash in his soul.

It was evisceration; the *hara-kiri* Octavio had promised him. And while it was purely emotional, it was more terrible to Simeon Blaire than any mortal wound. There was no joy in watching that horrified look on Leynna's face, the tiny tremor at the corners of her mouth as she slipped forward down the blade and into his arms.

A scion of the Razor Clique was born to fight and die... and with all his caste dead, he was a worthless tool, a loose end to be snipped off by history...

He could hear Octavio Vanecke laughing in his head even before it happened; before Leynna's death-mask twitched up into a hideous smile, and her needle-tipped thumb tore into his carotid artery.

With one beat of his heart the toxin was upon him, tightening the web of blood vessels around his brain. Octavio's illusion came in with the rush of it; surging up green and gold as his defenses fell. Bamboo and candles, drifting on moonlit water... they were locked together like lovers on a floating raft, lost amid the scent of cherry blossoms and blood. She was every inch the *Kunoichi* assassin here, a porcelain goddess with her sting deep in his throat.

"This makes him the last, Simeon. Our son, our only hope... this was the only way to make him *your* future as well as mine..."

The outlander heathens called this *Sanction Ultra*, he knew. The ultimate devotion of the Ashishim to their master. She died with a smile on her lips, secure in the knowledge that he would follow...

Simeon opened his mouth to scream, to crack the walls of Vanecke's world with his indignation. His victory had been stolen, replaced with the hollow, alien feeling of *remorse*. That wasn't part of the sheer, smooth clockwork of his mind. It was unclean, primitive... *human.*

And so he died a mortal; his flesh failing his will as pain tightened the screws.

Vanecke's laughter closed over his head like black water...

Ω

Octavio had expected him to scream.

Oh, it was too much to expect the child to *cry*, to weep for parents he only knew from didactic memory shunts and intrafoetal programming. But something, *anything*, would have been better than the cold precision with which young Darion checked his weapons, buckling on webbing belts of shuriken and knives, calmly testing the balance of his swords.

"You shouldn't try to stop me, Uncle. This is my fight, not yours."

He slipped a basket-hilted saber into its sheath, a flechette pistol into its holster – toys from his day-room down below the sensorium. Despite being only hours old, Darion had already proven to Vanecke that he knew how to use them... the ruined remains of several training mekan were testament to that.

"No! You can't, Darion! You're the last of them, and I can't let you risk your sacred blood!" The sincerity in Vanecke's voice at that moment would have made a politician cry. His eyes were wet with tears, his fists clenched white at his sides as he blocked the doorway. " Dammit, you saw what happened. Your mother, Gods rest her soul... she took him down, in the end. He's finished, Darion, and it's just too dangerous out there for you tonight."

The hologram's lips twitched, betraying the nervous tremor of Vanecke's muscles down through the wires. He remembered the voice in his head, that thing which had taken Jaegenn. What hell would it conjure from the broken mind of Darion Blaire?

"You know full well that I'm better than either of them, Uncle Octavio." He said, with all the withering scorn that his Kheptic blood could muster. "And my Lord Father is too much of a Blaire to die so easily. I will have my satisfaction... *and you won't stand in my way.*"

Such self-assurance! Octavio wondered, not for the first time, if perhaps he'd chosen the wrong end to his glorious plan... if this homicidal prodigy *was* actually superior to Simeon himself.

"I forbid it!" said Octavio, his holographic form flickering with static. "For your mother's memory, if for nothing else, Darion... *you have to live.* You have to take the trials now, for all of us. And when morning comes, you'll be Emperor over a new Earth.

If only it was true. But Vanecke had never been a believer in Manifest Dogma. It was just another tool, another means to control…

Right?

"Are you really that naïve, Octavio?' asked Darion, walking right through the middle of Vanecke's chest. "This whole damned night is proof that Kronos wants no human Emperor. Not my Father, not my Mother… and certainly not me. If that machine gets its way, there won't *be* another morning."

Darion stormed through into the central plaza of Vanecke's mansion, a tiled courtyard surrounded by statues. The Direktor followed him like a static-wracked ghost, his feet never touching the ground.

"My Lord, you can't go out there! If you're right, Kronos has gone utterly mad. Even you, Darion… even you wouldn't last a second against tankhunters and assassin mekan."

"Perhaps you'd be surprised," replied the young Khept', arching one eyebrow. "I know, for example, that you have twenty riflemen on the rooftop. Tell them to stand down, Uncle… or I won't be held responsible for their deaths."

Octavio remembered the look on his face when the tip of Simeon's katana had burst out from between Leynna's shoulderblades; his mouth set in a grim line, his mismatched eyes slitted and filled with malice… so like his father in the depths of the Black Palace, when he'd realized that he was being used. He had that same look as twenty Omnivasive soldiers stepped up to the parapet three stories above, aiming their long-barreled weapons down into the courtyard.

"They all have *families*, Vanecke. And you never know how a family tragedy will affect a person. Some might go *completely mad…*"

Did he know? How could he know? And if he suspects, then…

For an instant Octavio was petrified with fear, staring at the hunched shoulders and hooded eyes of his creation. Even a thing like him, a creature beyond human flesh… as that disembodied voice had whispered, even he could learn to suffer.

"I…I have to do this, Darion," stammered the holo-avatar, and this time its distress was far from artificial. "These men aren't here for you. I know your Father. He'll come for you – here. Remember your strategy! Remember what my machines have taught you. Here at least we hold the high ground."

The riflemen never wavered in their aim. But Darion looked up at them and grinned, sliding his saber from its sheath in a single fluid stroke.

"Trank rifles, Uncle? Your resolve is backed up with a disturbing amount of compassion. Unless… they're really here to keep me IN."

The hologram hung its head in mock shame, even while the camera eyes of Vanecke's flycam remained locked on Darion's face.

"Politics, I'm afraid. The Direktoriat would skin me alive if I lost you, Darion. Let alone my own sense of duty."

"Then even when he gets here, you won't…"

"I'm afraid so. Those men can switch out to A.P. rounds just as easily, Darion. You're a victim of your own importance."

The young Lord actually did scream then – a howl of rage and defiance as he threw his saber to the tiles.

"But he's MINE! Mine to castigate, mine to kill! Does my title mean *nothing* to you?"

"Not while that murdering bastard is still your Lord Father," said Vanecke, allowing a touch of passion to creep into his voice. "They're still under the strictures of the Game, you know. A clean kill – if he actually survives the throat needle."

"Then what do you plan to do? Taking him on common ground, outside the game – that's *murder*. Khepticide. And while the Direktoriat can't hurt holographic light, Uncle, I'm sure that Slade and his cronies have some exquisite torments in mind for you already."

"I would do it for you, Darion. And… and for your Lady Mother. You must know, by now… from the didactics. We were once…"

He raised a hand to stop him, disgust written all over his face.

"Don't even say it, Octavio. Even after all you've done for me - all you *say* you'd do – you're still a Subcit. And she was the greatest of the Kheptarchy."

In his preservative tank, flanked by the humming black cubes of the Surgeons, Octavio allowed himself a little smile. If only Darion knew the depravities which his sainted Mother had enjoyed…

"Nevertheless – I *will* do this one last thing for you. I will rid the world of Simeon Blaire, and not one of the Direktoriat will believe it was for anything less than unrequited lust. You'll ascend to the trials untainted… and then to the Throne of Earth."

"I may only be a few hours old, Uncle, but I'm not a damned fool. No kindness comes without a price. Give him to me, and I'll make it worth your while. Or defy me now… and throw away all the influence you seek to gain as Seneschal of the Emperor."

Octavio feigned shock, outrage, disbelief… all while his withered heart swelled with pride. The boy was sharp, fierce… a perfect surrogate for the child he and Leynna could never have.

"You're right, of course. Not even my own boundless generosity is without certain… practical considerations."

He sighed, hardlight hands gently lifting the saber from the ground and holding it out hilt-first.

"Simeon is yours. But with one condition. I want you to follow my mekan, Darion – follow it and see me as I truly am. Then you'll understand what I want you to do."

Darion turned, the gold-chased saber tight in his hand as a spider-mekan in red and silver tugged at the hem of his coat, its tiny mandibles working furiously. Vanecke's hologram stepped up atop its broad, blade-shaped abdomen, triplicate lasers twinkling into life to weave his illusory form.

"If I am to serve you – and it is my most fervent wish, Lord Darion – then I must have the tools to serve you well. Your Lord Father has squandered his right to them… but I can put a good head on his shoulders."

"What do you mean?" asked the young Khept', striding along beside Octavio's scuttling mekan. "The mind-ream? Sequestration? How can you change a thing that's rotten to the core?"

"You'll see," said the Direktor, a tiny smile twitching on his holographic lips. "Between us, we'll be the Lord Father you deserve. All you have to do is follow me, and it will all become quite clear…"

Ω

Simeon couldn't say how long he held her. Long after her porcelain-white skin grew cold, at least. Long after whatever divine spark had made her a worthy enemy had fled…

It wasn't blind sentiment which kept Lord Blaire kneeling there atop the deck of the *Stephen Foster*, with the wind whipping his tears away into the dark. At least, not that alone… he was paralyzed by the poison in his veins, a synthetic toxin engineered to stop his heart and clot his blood like cinnabar. Leynna had thought of it all; she knew he'd be sequenced immune to the venom which coated his own throwing knives and shuriken. She'd concocted a poison which bonded with the antivenin in his blood; one which would have crushed the breath from his bleeding lungs if he was anything less than posthuman.

But he had been transformed; made into a second-gen Chimera by the alchemy of Separatist Army technology. Unlike Royden Chalmers and Eddie Tsien the steel cancer wouldn't claim him. Their condition, like that of those original Chimera soldiers, was inevitably fatal.

Simeon had been given the second-gen strain, then injected with inhibitors to slow the crycelium's development. So the venom from Leynna's throat needle couldn't kill him -it only put his body into shutdown as the Chimera went into overdrive, purifying his vital organs. The interlinks to his original Gladius system were down as well, rendering his limbs immobile; he had no choice but to cradle the bloody corpse of Leynna Mendelev-Singh as the filaments worked on him.

It was Atticus Meaks who broke the spell.

The little pressman came up out of a hatch in the runway only a few yards from where Simeon knelt, rubbing his hands together with delight. The broadcast had gone perfectly – a masterpiece of journalism that could have tugged at the heartstrings of a statue. And the ending... superb! Screens and globes all over the city were still beaming out the image of a kneeling Lord Blaire, his veins black with poison, embracing the lifeless body of his nemesis. If anyone down there was still watching, they'd hail Meaks as a genius... a master of light and shadow, style and substance.

"Well played, sonny!" he chuckled, clapping the Kheptarch across one shoulder. "You kept it newsworthy till the end, Simeon... just like the Chief wanted. Too bad about the broad, but hey – them's the breaks, huh?"

Atticus fished a heavy keychain from his belt and spun it around his finger, peering into Blaire's single open eye. It was as glazed and empty as the plastic orb of a mannequin; the tears which ran down his cheek were actually from a tiny ocular irrigator drilled into his brow.

"Well kid, I gotta be off. Some of us have paychecks to pick up, and places to be. When Kronos cleans this mess up in the morning, I intend to be well out of sight!"

His fingers found a fat black remote control, and he aimed it at the helicopter gunship as he reached down to cradle Leynna's cold white cheek in one hand.

"Like I said, Simeon, too bad about this one. She was quite the lady, even if she did have about a couple thousand loose screws upstairs..."

The gunship exploded.

Atticus Meaks was thrown clear across the runway as his private chopper went up in a greasy ball of flame, scattering debris like metal hail. The remote was nothing but a detonator, linked to some hidden infernal device. Simeon couldn't even flinch as a shard of rotor hissed past his cheek, carving a thin gash into his skin. Leynna was less fortunate – a smoking chunk of steel caught her high in the shoulder, plucking her body from Simeon's nerveless fingers and away over the edge of the airship. For a brief second she was outlined in black against the flames of the burning city, and then she was gone, falling like a ragdoll through veils of sparks.

The gutted wreck of the gunship slumped down on its landing gear, still belching a plume of smoke as it died. Meaks groaned and rolled to his feet, rubbing the singed patch where his eyebrows used to be.

"That son of a bitch! That vile bloody *Dervashi* son of a bitch! That was my favorite chopper, you know! I even had some change in the ashtray!"

The pressman staggered and leant up against the nearest thing available – the teak-hard muscle of Simeon Blaire's shoulder. It was hot to the touch – burning up as the Chimera under his skin purified his blood.

"Must have got me with a magnetic mine, the bastard. But then again, it was probably meant for you, son."

Simeon heard it all; he was laughing in his mind as Atticus Meaks rolled a filthy little cigarette between shaking fingers. That was no *Dervashi* trick – it was Octavio Vanecke's way of repaying the pressman's loyalty. There should be no witnesses to the culmination of the Game; just a final fade-out image of him down on his knees, weeping over the body of his foe. But Meaks' loyalty ran too deep. He saw it reflected in places where 'trust' and 'honor' were only words to gull the weak...

"I tell you, My Lord, that's the kind of thing the Chief ought to put a stop to. He's gonna play this town right, kid... too bad you won't be around to enjoy it. By now that venom's probably turning your brain to mush."

Atticus reached out and struck a match off the black skin of Blaire's shoulder, the flare of phosphorous light picking out his features in red. And somewhere in the blur and flash of its afterglow, his mind registered a flicker of silver...

Simeon Blaire was too fast to follow. The Chimera had finished its work mere seconds ago, but already he was in fighting form, bringing his katana up and around to shear through the pressman's wrist. A hand clutching a burning match flew wide in a cloud of blood, its flame snuffed out as it fell. Simeon came up short on the backswing, bringing the blade to rest against Atticus Meaks' throat.

"You forget your station, peasant!" he whispered, rolling the kinks out of his neck. "I am your *Emperor* now, not merely your Lord. Any hand which touches my skin must be… purified."

Meaks couldn't scream. Not only because the sudden pain had plunged him into shock - but because if he drew enough breath to vent his agony Blaire's sword would open his throat.

He gurgled a little, his eyes as wide as the empty sky.

"Now, how will you atone for your foolishness? How best can a thing like you *serve*?"

Simeon held out his hand, and spirals of heat-sink crycelium coiled across his palm, red-hot fractal patterns blistering his skin. The Chimera healed him even as he burned, filling the air with the smell of cooking meat.

"First, we have to cauterize that nasty wound of yours. And then… we'll go and pay your dear Octavio a visit, I think."

This time Atticus Meaks did scream. It wasn't as if he had a choice.

And Simeon Blaire laughed as he clamped his burning hand around the stump, as blood evaporated and bone cracked. This was the feeling he'd been looking for, when Leynna hung dying on his blade. *This was what it was meant to be, all along.*

Not victory, or honor, or glory. They were just words, used to bind and enslave…

No… the true measure of a Kheptarch's power was measured in *pain.*

No matter how he made them suffer, they would still serve. And that, in the end, was sweeter than any love or respect he could ever earn.

Ω

The Surgeons saw him even before he followed Vanecke in through the door - their scanners were built to pick up the faintest of heartbeats, the hiss and bubble of blood in human veins. But Darion didn't notice them until they moved, sheer back cubes studded with cantilevered insect legs. His eyes were fixed on the two hideous specimens under their knives... one a tangled mass of fibrous silver threads, the other nothing more than a burned and scarred skull with ragged skin sloughing from its face.

Dead, surely, both of them… for one was peeled open like a dissected tumor, the remains of its foetal human limbs pulled tight by hooks and chains. And the other… the other was like something dug up from a plague-pit grave, packed in ice on a tray with wires and tubes tangled up around it.

Then Octavio Vanecke's eyes opened.

Darion almost screamed then, as he gazed into those milky white orbs. This was the true face of his kind patron; a ruin of scar tissue and bone kept alive only to keep the Celebrants from his door. Mistrust and paranoia had denied him the luxury of a mekan shell. And now, as those blind eyes bored into him with hideous intensity, Darion understood exactly why Octavio wanted Simeon killed in such a precise and perfect manner…

"Don't be afraid, child," said the hologram beside him, resting one hardlight hand on his shoulder. "*This* is my true form… not that thing on the table. That… my *condition*… is nothing but a legal technicality. One that I'm about to circumvent very neatly indeed."

"And the other one? What happened to him?" asked Darion, his voice filled with disgusted fascination. There was no blood inside the fibrous metal shell of the other surgical subject – just layer on layer of matted stiff wire, cradling a skeleton forged in glittering chrome.

"Royden is long gone already, I'm afraid. And good riddance – he was a monster in his own special way, you know. A renegade biotect with a certain aversion to anesthetic."

A tremor shook the distorted form of the Chimera-infected doctor as one of the Surgeon mekan snipped open the skin of his arm, loosening a web of filaments from around his bones. They were harvesting his skeleton while he still lived… although Darion wasn't sure the thing he had become could truly be called 'alive'.

"Does it disgust you, Darion? Do you still think I suffer from a surfeit of *compassion*?" The hologram Vanecke smiled his predatory grin. "Believe me when I say this, young Lord Blaire… your father will know all this pain and more, before I put him to better use…"

Slowly, glacially, a smile spread across Darion's face, until he looked exactly as grim and cadaverous as his patron.

"One cut in just the right place, Uncle Octavio. Just as you ask… so long as I can play with your toys here for a while before he's finally gone…"

The saws howled and whined, the hooks and scalpels flickered silver in the air as the Surgeons took apart Royden Chalmers. But he felt no pain; he was beyond pain now, his mind subsumed by the pure mathematics of the Chimera's final phase.

At the heart of a tangled web of paradox and light he couldn't feel them sinking their drills into his gleaming silver skull, inserting high-bandwidth databores into the crystallized matrix which was once his brain.

He was so close to the truth – collapsing whole galaxies of equations with each second, folding up time and space like origami as his incorporeal hands reached out for the final answer...

The Surgeon's saw cut through his exotic-metal brainpan with a multi-gigawatt laserblade just as the last numbers lined up, smooth and precise. He caught a glimpse, for just an instant, of the divine symmetry of all creation, folded down to sit atop his palm like a snowflake of fire....

And then the power went out, and the thing which had once been Royden Chalmers died.

Ω

CeeAn barely had time to wipe the crust of impact foam out of her eyes before they were upon her. She'd kicked the buckled door of the escape pod from its hinges easily enough, still amazed by the power of the 'chrome in her blood. But once she hauled her aching body up and out of the little steel coffin the honeymoon was over. She'd landed in the middle of a battlefield, and neither side seemed to consider her friendly.

Cee held out her hand and exerted a little of her newfound power, making the shattered half-sword she'd found leap into her grasp. Some of the things which snarled and ravened in the smoky dark were Saprophytes, after all, and bullets wouldn't stop them. In her other hand Cee gripped a Vatican-issue auto-shotgun, torn from its clamps inside the escape pod. If *this* emergency didn't warrant breaking the glass, then nothing did.

She tried to get her bearings, peering through the flame-shot murk in a vain attempt to locate the gates of the Ashishim. But before she could even consult her bio-onboard compass a howling wedge of Saps came tearing through the smoke, locked in combat with a motley band of Ferals and Subcity refugees. Cruel claws sheared, rifles cracked, mouths gnashed and slobbered... but it was the screams which snapped Cee out of her trance. She came down in the middle of the fight in a spin, her sword carving off ribbons of Saprophytic flesh left and right while she used the barrel of the shotgun to parry hook-tipped tentacles and bone claws.

For a second or two it was all a hot, sweaty chaos of blood and straining meat, the close crush of battle throwing her back to back with a tattooed savage wielding a spiked mace. They looked back over their shoulders at each other, nodded in grim satisfaction… and charged.

The Saps broke as Cee and the Feral coordinated their attack, raining down crushing mace-blows and wicked sword-slashes in a fierce blur. The war cry from his band of followers was picked up across a ragged front, rallying the survivors to push back at the faltering Saps.

There was black blood burning on her skin now, scraps and gobbets of rancid flesh underfoot as the otherdimensional horrors gave up their dead. But Cee gritted her teeth and swung the blade again and again, ducking and weaving through the desperate talons and jaws and whips of Asag'raal's horde, a dancer bearing bloody steel.

Right to the heart of the writhing mass she went, leading a spearhead of Ferals and Subcits into the fray. She only stopped when there was nothing left of the vile things – when she realized that she'd been hacking at the corpse of a dead Saprophyte, weeping, for the last three minutes.

Beneath the orange-lit clouds the spillway still echoed with screams and howls and terrible grinding noises, but this little section of it was utterly silent. A ring of soot-streaked faces stared down at her in a mixture of awe and horror. The great incorporeal heart inside her head thumped once, sending ripples through the world. And sanity came back to her, making her step back from the steaming wreckage of her foe.

"What… what is she?" she heard one of the Subcits ask, a man in the remains of a three-piece suit, holding a spiked bat in one hand and a pistol in the other. The woman he was talking to was a Feral warrior, resplendent in bloodied feathers and combat fatigues.

"*Spirit-taken.* The living dead," muttered the Feral, averting her eyes. "But not… not one of *them.*"

Cee looked down at her hands, and realized suddenly what they were talking about.

She was on fire.

Blue flames licked their way up and down her arms, cold and unconsuming ripples like the flicker of a holofield. But this was no illusion. The black blood of the Saps boiled to stinking vapor wherever the flames touched, leaving her unscarred. Little droplets of purple fire dripped from the shattered tip of her half-sword, and she could feel it outlining the swollen orb of her bioelectric field, writhing like translucent aurorae.

"You want to know what I am?" she asked, pushing herself up to her feet with a supreme effort of will. "I'll tell you what I am… the Feral is right. I couldn't just lie down and die with these dirty bastards eating you folks alive. *I'm a fucking angel of mercy.*"The ring of survivors around her laughed nervously as she checked the balance of her sword and racked the slide on her shotgun. "Now, are we gonna take it to these sons of bitches, or should I just go back to the nice restful grave I've left behind?"

CeeAn caught a look at her eyes as she raised the broken no-dachi up over her head. They were pure white now, glowing from within as the spark of the 'chrome sustained her. She knew, in that instant, that she was only alive because of the power beyond that inverted ocean… a power forbidden to walk the earth, but one smart enough to know a loophole in cosmic law when it saw one.

"Mekan! Mekan coming down!" shouted a voice from the edge of the crowd, and all eyes turned to a figure in a ragged cape hanging above them on a twisted power pylon. "Kronos will save us! It's all going to be all ri…"

He caught fire in a roseate bloom of crimson, a maser blast clearing a swirling tunnel through the smoke. Mekan *were* marching down the slope now… but there was something wrong with them. Something which Cee could feel through her energistic senses, a taint poisoning the air with the smell of roasting flesh…

She quickly formed a lens with her bioelectric field, a dish-shaped speaker with which to project her voice.

"Form up! Form up! Come on, dammit – those things are *possessed*! I need you to concentrate your fire on their heads and knee-joints – cripple them!"

Across the miles-wide sweep of the Spillway her words echoed amid the rubble. And scattered bands of refugees and Ferals heard them, pulling together to form a ragged line in the cover of broken concrete and shattered steel.

"Wait until you can see their servomotor hubs! Then pour on all you've got!"

The mekan walked with a swaying, lumbering gait all at odds with their high-tech engineering – and CeeAn could see why. These things were enslaved by the Worm, mortuary composites of metal and flesh and writhing darkness. Kronos used the slaved minds of the dead to animate its thralls – a cheap A.I. hack cooked up to protect the machine from any other emergent Intelligences. But that had left the door wide open for Asag'raal and his minions, who could agonize genewritten tissue just as easily as womb-born flesh.

Now the damned war-engines were within firing distance, and Cee winced as particle beams and hydrogen masers lashed out like whips, evaporating whole sections of her motley battle-line.

"Hold your fire!" she yelled, her voice shaking the concrete "Don't let them get a fix on you!"

Micromissiles sizzled through the air like chrome hornets, plucking defenders from the ranks and detonating in mid-air. Shrapnel scythed through anyone foolish enough to peek out of cover, spraying blood and chips of bone.

"Hold it! Hold it……NOW!"

The roar of ten thousand guns came down like a breaking wave, rising with the wild warcrys of the Ferals until even CeeAn's amplified howl was drowned out. Fusion carbines and hand-masers and old-fashioned assault rifles focused in on the staggering Sapromeks, sending them reeling back into the ranks behind. Lesser horrors whined and clattered around their feet; half-broken mekan bound up with saprophytic ooze, dragging themselves along on sheared-off actuator limbs and stumps of bone. It seemed that the Worm was none too pleased about the fate of its six Exalted, and now the pitiful few who had survived the slaughter of the Spillway stood beneath the hammer of its wrath.

Some of the Sapromeks went down.

Cee cursed to herself as she tore a strip off her ragged t-shirt to bind up her sword hand, ducking down below a graffiti-smeared slab of concrete. If they'd been conventional tankhunters it would have taken far more than what they had to defeat them. But these things…

Even as she watched a volley of maser blasts peeled back the cerametal armor of a creaking, groaning Demolisher unit, exposing its shoulder motors. A black-toothed Feral in a turban and leathers leaped up atop the barricade, an RPG launcher on his shoulder. The missile spiraled in on a plume of smoke, shattering the gears and drives deep inside the Sapromek's chestplate. But the black worms of Asag'raal's New Flesh whipped out across the gaping wound even as the mekan's wrecking-ball arm fell away, spreading across the cerametal like decay. They stitched it up tight, swelling and dividing until the thing's arm bulged with ropy black muscle… Then it was right on top of the line, that wrecking ball swinging down in an unstoppable arc.

"Fall back!" shouted Cee as she finished binding the No-Dachi to her hand. "Make a defensive line at the Pit gates!"

She knew it was no use. The tiny amount of morale her refugee army had left was bleeding away. Nothing could stand against these nightmare machines – and those who broke and ran were mercilessly cut down.

The *Dervashi* launched herself up out of cover, spinning in midair to bring her feet down on the chest of an eight-foot incinerator mekan, making it stagger back on its claw-tipped hooves. Its flamethrower hands spurted streams of napalm as she went up and over its head, using the shotgun in her hand as leverage. As Cee pivoted around its neck she pulled the trigger, blowing the monster's silicon brains out. But this thing was just a stepping stone. There was an even larger Sapromek behind it - that tankhunter with its wrecking-ball hand. Time slowed to a crawl as CeeAn held out the jagged tip of her blade, aiming for its bubbling black face…

She heard the click even as her shotgun spoke again; that little sound was far more important than the roar of the sawnoff peeling back the saprophytic skin of the mekan's helm. CeeAn turned her head just in time to watch that spiked mace of a hand launch from its wrist on four plumes of vapor; just in time for her vicious snarl to turn into a scream.

The world went into a flat spin. The concrete came up behind her hard, biting in with teeth of broken glass. But the fire around her held – just – as the wrecking ball struck home. Cee felt as through she'd been squeezed in a giant fist, the breath torn from her lungs. But she wasn't a smear across the spillway. Not yet.

Perhaps this was one of the luxuries of already being dead…

If so, she'd have precious little time to enjoy it. The Sapromek wasn't finished with her, and now it leveled a brace of cannons down at the little *Dervashi*, red laser sights sliding across her ragged clothes and tattooed skin.

CeeAn's lips twitched into a bitter smile. The sword bound to her hand was still there, and she was still more than a match for some demon-ridden machine…

But what the hells was *that*?

A hammer of sound slapped her back down to the concrete then, as a shockwave tore through the spillway, shaking Elysium's roots. It threw up a pall of ashen dust, bloodied banknotes and trash as it rippled out from its epicenter, cutting down Asag'raal's minions and their prey with one blow.

Something came up out of the R.T. like a smoking black missile; a human form like a hole cut in the world. Serpents coiled around its head in moebius loops.

Then the sun dawned over the miles-wide slope of the Spillway; a detonation as bright and hot as nuclear fire. Cee looked up through her pain and saw a dark figure against the orange sky, holding a vast white fireball in its hands. Its shape was indistinct, blurred by the radiant heat of that blazing microsun... but even she could feel the power it drew from the Sapromeks, from the pain and fear of the entire city.

It was an Exalted One – that was certain. But it was a rarefied specimen, a thing which burned with such rage and self-loathing that even nuclear fire couldn't touch it. That shockwave had been a huge explosion... but the Exalted had caught it as it began to open out, crushing it back into a sphere. It devoured the life-force of a thousand Saprophytes as it hung there in the air, reinforcing its armor...

Then it let go.

CeeAn vaulted over a lip of concrete as the fireball split open, unfurling petals of white flame. She caught one last glimpse of the Exalted as she threw her hand up over her eyes, and it was burning, falling... leaving a cruciform imprint in the hab-block wall it struck.

Good, she thought. *One less of the bastards for me to kill.*

Because nothing, no matter how inhuman, could have survived the blast which swept the bloody face of the Spillway clean, picking up warmekan like toys and sending them tumbling end over end amid a rain of concrete chips and ashes...

"'That's it! They're finished!" shouted a Feral warrior off to her left.

"Salvage their guns!" yelled another, scrabbling forward out of cover.

"No! They're still moving! This one's... aargh!"

"Take it to them! Kill them while they're down!"

Cee flexed her fingers around the hilt of her sword as the screaming started up again.

All it did was buy them a little more dying time.

The Sapromeks had all the resilience of steel, and all the tenacity of their Saprophytic kin. CeeAn watched them pull themselves together from heaps of smoking scrap-iron, a tangle of fused arms and legs and heads heaving up into a mockery of human form. Half-dead defenders twitched and struggled as they were consumed by the Sons of Asag'raal, their screams drowned in liquid shadow.

And now the battle-line came on, relentless, the guns of the Sapromeks tearing chunks from the Spillway as they advanced. Ferals and Subcits alike took one look at the wave of jagged metal bearing down on them and ran. The thin cordon which held the Saps back broke in a dozen places before Cee could rally them, as refugees threw down their guns and fled. Some tore at their own skin with broken fingernails or curled up weeping on the concrete, lost to despair. Others ran toward the horrors with open arms, embracing the hail of lead and maserfire…

It was the end.

Cee let her shattered sword fall to her side as the Sapromeks chewed into her little army; as the milling mass of defenseless people behind them began to cry and wail. Even if she could take them all out in the ultimate Sanction Ultra the R.T. was lost – that Exalted One had come up out of the heart of Ashishim territory. 'Afia was dead, and all her people with him.

She looked down at the reflection of her white and empty eyes in the blade, and saw nothing there but oblivion.

Then an explosion rocked the Spillway, and Cee looked up in time to watch a gumetal insect piledrive into the Sapromek line. The comm bead in her ear crackled as manic laughter lashed across the ether, and the whine of monoblade chainsaws filled her head.

The Sap tried to crush its foe in one huge fist, but the armor-suited warrior was too fast – one of his saws lopped off the thing's battle-claw at the wrist, while the other came up under its arm, severing a thick skein of pipes and wires. Then it was up atop the cursed mekan's shoulders, its blades poised around the Sap's neck like shears…

"And that's how we do it, by the grace of God!" shouted a familiar voice in CeeAn's ear. She watched the corpse-light fade from the Sapromek's eyes as its head bounced and rolled down the Spillway incline, black blood fountianing free. "Come on, my Brothers! Let's show these bastards the mercy of the Lord!"

It was the Valle Crucis who'd come to her aid before – the one who'd helped her steal Saint Sebastian. And behind him came a steel-clad horde of Vatican Knights, Brothers of every chapter and cloister mowing a grim harvest of the possessed with swords and axes and crushing maces.

"For the first time in my life I'm actually glad to see a priest!" said

Cee, raising her sword in salute. "What the hell took you so long, anyhow?"

"Politics, little sister," said the Crucis-man, working his saws through the spine of another Sap. "The College of Cardinals are old men, and very cautious. I had to get a message through to the Pontifex myself…"

Cee didn't wait to be invited – she leaped into the fray with her sword blurring a silver rainbow over her head. Nameless pieces of metal and flesh began to rain down as the Dervashi waded into the panicked Saps, forging a path through to the Vatican line.

"It must have been something pretty damned convincing."

"Well, we all saw what happened to that Megaphyte. I just asked Her Holiness if she was going to let an old man and an Ashishim girl make her look like a pussy."

The refugees surged back into the gap as Cee and the Knights methodically took Asag'raal's elite apart. Businessmen and gangsters and Feral warriors fought back to back, finishing off the smaller Saps which scuttled between the feet of their half-mekan brethren.

"You know, this is the second time you've saved my ass, and I don't even know your name," she said, splitting the gun-barrel of a tankhunter in half, then taking off its face with the backswing.

"Brother Pious, at your service. And don't worry, Miss 187 – we know exactly who *you* are. The Envigilators of the Inquisition keep very close tabs on all *Dervashi* operatives. Size nine, right?"

Now the Sapromeks were all but finished. The Vatican Knights had driven a wedge from their barbican fortress all the way across the Spillway, opening out into twin wings as they outflanked Asag'raal's horde. The voracious hunger of the Saps had been their undoing – they were cut off from their stronghold in the deeps of Elysium, caught in the open under the guns and blades of the vengeful Knights.

Now all CeeAn could see was a field of decaying meat, acid-burned bones and black gore. Mekan limbs twitched and whined as their power ran down, steel hands writhing like burned spiders amid the blood. It was a victory – but one bought at such a price that it made the *Dervashi* feel sick.

She stumbled toward Pious with her broken sword trailing across the concrete, the wind plucking at her rags and at her bloodied hair, unable to feel anything. No joy, no relief – no pain. Just empty, cold oblivion… a pit in her soul like a yawning grave. They were all dead. This one little battle was nothing, not when her whole nation was damned, and every avenue of escape cut off…

The Valle Crucis had folded back the insect-wings of his helm's faceplate by the time she reached him, and the chainsaws of his battlesuit recessed up along his forearms to expose his hands. He was trying to pull a bulky white-clad figure away from the massive ruin of a demolisher Sapromek – the Knight was gone with rage, still pulverizing the dead thing's head with a cruciform battle-hammer.

"CeeAn! Good! We need you to get your Ferals in order. Our scouts are reporting a huge horde of these things massing to counterattack, and we have to reach the sea before they cut off our escape."

"What escape?" she asked, slumping down against the armored leg of the blood-spattered Knight. "I just nuked the far end of the Pit, and the city is *full* of those things. Face it, padre, we're boned."

Cee felt the armor plates behind her slide and interlock as the Knight stepped back from its grisly work, and she scrabbled for balance as the huge battlesuit turned to face her.

"Save some of that self-pity for the martyrs, girl," rumbled a voice like every disapproving schoolmistress in the world combined. "The Kayzi's coming for us. Deut' Jones has finally done something useful in his heretical little life."

Cee looked up – and up, and up – into a careworn face scored with deep lines like the map of some incredibly ramified river delta. Nestled amid those creases was a pair of eyes as hard and black as onyx buttons, and a grin which would have made the devil himself flinch.

"Those tribesmen won't listen to me – hell, even if I told them the moon was made of crack cocaine they wouldn't think I was any crazier. But you… well, they've seen what you can do. We have to jam this whole damn herd through Ashishi territory, right down to the ocean. There's only one boat leaving tonight, and I suggest you want to be on it."

CeeAn looked over at Pious, who was trying extremely hard to be interested in something else. She scowled, and rapped him on one pauldron with the flat of her sword.

"Listen, preacher, who the hell is this? In case you hadn't heard, I'm not one of your god-bothering little peons, and…"

A hand came down on her shoulder – not hard, but backed up with the hydraulic might of enough servos and rams to rip a tank in half. Cee looked back into the face of that iron-hard matriarch, and comprehension dawned.

"Oh hells… you're…"

"That's right, kid," said Joan Theophraxes Pontifex the Third. "I'm the motherfuckin' Pope."

17 Aevum Oblivio
Fallback

Space was no longer a vacuum across the curving swathe of the line of battle. Debris and churning gas had made a gray soup of the void between Mars and Earth, veiling the firefight from view. Deep in a cloud of vaporized starships lights winked and flared and died as the Multiplicity fleet fought a desperate delaying action against the Unity, drawing in around the vulnerable open portal of the Effortless Subjugation.

Kataphrakt Yrr had docked his pet Devilfish with the largest living dreadnaught still under his command – the Toxic Grip and the Swift Obliteration had both gone under, smeared into radioactive fog by the particle cannons of the Unity Hub. Now this command unit, the Mace, was the only capital cruiser left under his command. And it was a very thin line indeed which separated the Subjugation's open portal from the twelve vast Blacksteel dreadnaughts which were relentlessly advancing on it.

"Weapons diagnostic, report!" barked the Kataphrakt, his twin mouths set in a pair of grim lines. "Divert all power from the rear shielding array into the main coilguns. We'll have to punch right through those bastards if we want to scare the Hub into falling back."

"Forty-eight seconds to Geocore launch," chimed in one of the Thralls perched on the ceiling of the bridge. Gravity here wrapped around a full three-sixty degrees, allowing legions of the deft little creatures to squat in front of terminals upside-down above their captain. "The Manifest Perfection reports a critical hull breach. She's going to take down one of those Unity cruisers with her, though…"

Deep in the spreading cloud of destruction space flared momentarily purple, and arcs of lightning miles long flickered against the haze. Such sacrifice was the Praetor's due, but every ship counted now – there were only mere thousands remaining.

"All power to the main coilguns! Ready to fire!"

Yrr's command throne spun and twisted, locking one of the giant Blacksteel dreadnaughts in his crosshairs. He could already feel the Mace twitching and shuddering around him as Unity fighters took advantage of their lack of rear shielding.

"Fire!"

The pair of coilgun slugs were ten times larger than those fired by the 'fangs' of the poor old Justifiable Brutality. Each one could have been an attack ship in its own right, such was their bulk and speed. But these were nanofiber shells bearing antimatter warheads, and their tiny living brains could only steer them in on a kamikaze plunge...

Their target was a nameless hulk of a ship, a blacksteel battlecruiser the size of an asteroid colony. Its tetrahedral hull suckled destroyers like mile-long cylinders, and its own weapons were particle beam cannons so vast that a Devilfish could have flown clear down their gaping muzzles. The first slug deployed its shieldbreakers three miles out, threads of writhing organic mycelium connected to energy-sinks like scalloped shells. The scale-mail overlap of shields fractured and fell away, brittle kaleidoscope patterns hazing out...

And then the slug hit home, powering in through the gap in the battlecruiser's shields on second-stage rockets, a scream of exultation echoing across the neural net. Its brother was right behind it, tearing the underbelly shields of the 'cruiser ragged as nautilus sinks popped and flared like fireworks. Blacksteel tenders and fightercraft died, vaporized by a storm of secondary explosions.

Then the battlecruiser imploded.

The coilguns of the Mace were made to shatter cities, but even those titanic weapons couldn't simply tear apart a Unity capital ship. The tetrahedral frame of the vast warship ballooned out, exotic metal panels shifting and sliding in a desperate attempt to contain the damage within. But it was far too late. The second phase of the antimatter warheads had already been unleashed... singularity points released from behind a pair of null storage fields, folding the doomed dreadnaught in on itself like paper. The Thralls aboard the Mace chattered and howled with glee as they watched their foe break up, feeding the ever-expanding cloud of ruin which smeared across the void. But Yrr was more realistic.

"We can't hold them back. That missile barrage from the Hub took out too many of our Voidhunters, and the portal carrier is dead in the water. We'll only get one last shot with a Geocore, and we have to make it count."

The Kataphrakt had a plan. Admittedly, he couldn't have come up with such a scheme without the vast processing power of the neural net, but all the calculations had fallen into place so neat and smooth... He was sure that it would work.

"Ready the jump-drives, engineering thralls. Divert power from our weapons systems, and make ready to drop into the Aematerium on my mark..."

"But my lord Admiral!" squealed an upside-down menial, wringing *its tentacles in consternation "The enemy have deployed disruptors to prevent our escape. Breaching the Chasm now would tear the Mace apart!"*

Yrr reached up with one of his bulky fighting claws and plucked the wretched thing from its workstation, bringing its compound eyes level with his own.

"Did you fail to see how the Behemoth escaped us last time?" he growled, squeezing his captive tight. "There will be a second's grace while that damned machine tries to evade the Geocore. And then we can fall back to a better position."

The thrall nodded, unable to breathe. Yrr threw him up against the wall, a lazy overhand, and turned back to his screens.

"My loyal captains, it's time to retrench our defense. We know what the enemy is here for, and we must therefore use that knowledge as our shield. Here are your new deployment coordinates. When the time comes, you will have only a fraction of a second to act. Any hesitation, and the Blacksteel's disruptors will catch you half-submerged in the Aematerium... with inevitable consequences."

Yrr watched an even mix of horror, incredulity and reckless glee ripple outwards across his honeycomb of holoscreens. It didn't matter if he lost a few of his ships, now. He was going for the prize, and it would only take a single Kataphrakt to wrest it from human hands...

"This is the process of evolution, my comrades! The weak, the hesitant, the cowardly... we will be well rid of them – we few who share in the hour of glory!"

"Geocore ready to fire, my Lord," keened the poor thrall who Yrr had thrown across the bridge. "Slaving target control to your throne now..."

"Excellent! I'll see those of you who are worthy across the Chasm!" said Yrr, dismissing his captains with a wave of one chitinous claw.

Now it was all down to timing. Down to the predictability of the Motherbrain's children...

Deep in the Null Storage strata modified shield generators nudged the floating bulk of another geocore up to the azure meniscus of the Gate. Remote drones like coral spiders aligned the multi-million-ton chunk of metal, so that the slightest tap on this side of the null would translate into speeds just fractionally slower than light on the other.

Yrr took aim, rotating the searing eye of the Subjugation like the barrel of a planet-smashing cannon...

"Fire!"

It all fell together smooth, just as the great savant mind of the neural net had promised. The Kataphrakt-Admiral watched in slow motion as the Geocore painted a razor stroke of plasma across the dark, stabbing out toward the Behemoth with unstoppable fury. Lesser ships were ablated away to radioactive clouds before its onslaught; vessels the size of that tetrahedral battlecruiser sheared in half, glittering with tiny secondary explosions as they died.

Then the white-hot heart of the core struck home, and for a sliver of an instant the Unity's aematerial disruptors shut down. Yrr knew that behind the strobeflash of the core's detonation his foe had slipped under into the Discontinuum, sloughing off another sacrificial shell of metal. This time, however, the Multiplicity fleet was prepared.

Before the disruptors could spin up to power again each one of the Praetor's ships fell out of reality, dropping through into the Aematerium like stones. Covered by the storm of boson emissions and ionized gas left by the Geocore, there were a few precious seconds in which the A.I.s of the Motherbrain didn't even realize that they'd disappeared.

When they did, the emulated rage of those ancient machines was terrible.

But by then, the living warships of Yrr's Order of Battle were already strung out in a glittering halo around the Earth.

"The possibility that we are living in a
false vacuum has never been a cheering one
to contemplate. Vacuum decay is the ultimate
ecological catastrophe; in the new vacuum there
are new constants of nature; after vacuum decay,
not only is life as we know it impossible, so
is chemistry as we know it. However, one could
always draw stoic comfort from the possibility
that perhaps in the course of time the new vacuum
would sustain, if not life as we know it, at least
some structures capable of knowing joy. This
possibility has now been eliminated."

—S.Coleman & F. De luccia

The Humans Coleman and De luccia would appear to
be correct in this instance. A more comprehensive
vacuum DOES exist beyond even the Aematerium, and
we have determined that sufficient 'pressure'
exerted by so-called exotic weaponry effects could
punch a hole clear through into this desolate
plane.

Theories about the origin of the 'true' vacuum, or
the Primordia as it is called by the Clericals,
range from the tenuous to the religiously absurd.
Some even go so far as to claim that it represents
the remains of a dead multiverse preceding our
own, inhabited by postphysical beings of unknown
origins and intentions…

Magrahl Wex, Technomant Third Class

2196 Ante Arbitrium
Bait + Switch

EDDIE KNEW THAT if his wife fired that huge combat shotgun the recoil would send her halfway out the back door of their little polyfoam maisonette. He knew that *she* knew it as well – but those four yawning black barrels didn't so much as tremble as Toria Jane faced down a Saprophytic monster the size of a tank.

Eddie didn't think it was possible that he could have been more in love with her at that moment. She had all the fierce resolve of a lioness standing between a hunter and her cubs. Of course, she had no idea who or what she was actually pointing that Cyben street-sweeper at.

The thorny roots of the Worm inside his mind clenched tight, lashing him with Asag'raal's voice, urging him to kill…

But the look on his wife's face was enough to force a tiny gap open in Asag'raal's control. Just as he'd counted on.

As screams and moans rose around him in a grim crescendo, Eddie Tsien peeled back the shadow-skin of his faceless mask just enough for Toria to see his eyes.

"Get the kids. Get them now… and RUN."

Every word was forced out between clenched teeth, a sheer effort of will.

Realization dawned in her eyes, riding the crest of a wave of horror. She reached out her hand to touch his cheek, then stopped halfway, unable to look at his face.

"Edward? No. It… it can't be you. It…"

The Worm was howling now, tightening its focus, rearing up over him in a swirling black cloud. When its will fell on him he'd be lost, he knew. But there was enough time left to follow through with his plan. Enough time for… *This.*

Ω

Elakoz and Jarl might have been hardened Subcity survivors, but they'd never faced the likes of a Mark Four Cyben drone before. Bloody tentacles unplugged from B-Zerk's shoulders and spine as Elakoz tightened his finger on the trigger. A sonic shriek spilled out of the machine-child's mouth as those twitching lashes pulled him up into the shadows, his body swinging like a puppet below – and a storm of buckshot missed his beat-up sneakers by bare inches.

Glowing blue eyes glittered and blurred among the dripping pipes.

173

"Slippery, aintya? Well, there's more where that came from!"

His answer was a feral hiss.

Elakoz worked the pump, laying down a withering storm of fire. Echoes hammered and clashed in the tight dead-end alley, but not one grain of lead found its mark.

Jarl was more of a realist than his buddy – he was already running when B-Zerk came down on him from above, his cold dead lips peeled back from his blackened teeth. The undersider hit the deck at a full sprint, tumbling and rolling through piles of steaming garbage as the demon on his back stabbed down again and again, drill-bit tentacles raping and wrecking…

Then Elakoz racked the slide one last time, locked a shell into the breach, and fired.

The drone felt itself picked up and spun through the air, its host flesh bleeding in a thousand places. It shrieked again, a bowel-loosening sound like a broken steam klaxon… but at the very apex of its flight the sound cut out.

The cerulean glow faded from B-Zerk's eyes as he landed in a tangle of limbs and tentacles, scattering trash and greasy paper. Elakoz blew across the smoking muzzle of his gun, grinning, swaggering over to where his buddy groaned and cursed in a pool of his own blood.

"There, see? Just what the doctor ordered. A little hot lead injection, and the pain's over."

"Then why the fuck didn't you hit the little bastard *before* he got me?" spat Jarl, struggling to his feet. "I think I'm gonna puke… oh, gods and devils!"

The ragged undersider made good on his promise, painting the treadplate with an acidic gruel of vomit.

"Watch the shoes, Jarl," said Elakoz, all distaste. "Anyhow, we should salvage that drone. You know the Black Techs pay top dollar for those things."

Jarl grinned at this, wiping the back of one hand across his dripping chin. He pulled a boot knife from its sheath with the other, testing its edge with his thumb.

"Oh, I think I'm gonna enjoy that, 'Koz. I'm gonna peel that bastard thing like a mud-crab…"

B-Zerk twitched feebly as the grim-faced undersider hobbled toward him, his blade winking in the flamelight. The drone was paralyzed, its program hashed with static – and while it could hear and see everything around it, the machine couldn't lift a single drill-tipped tentacle in self-defense.

It was horribly certain that it would be able to *feel* everything as well – feel every hacking, stabling second of its imminent dismemberment.

"Hold still, you little shit." Chuckled Jarl as he hunkered down over B-Zerk's bleeding body. "This might sting a little."

Ω

Eddie Tsien had been stripped of his humanity by a machine of singular and cunning design. The Core drone which quailed under Jarl's knife was a slick synthesis of Chimera crycelium and Cyben re-animation technology. In a normal Cyben, the downloaded personality of the dead officer resided in his Vilicus drone, enslaving his preserved and embalmed flesh.

But the MK4 was different. In Eddie's case the drone was a personality fragment in its own right, an overseer hunched between his shoulderblades to enforce the will of Kronos. It was hoped that the drone would be able to master the first-gen Chimera strain, even after Eddie's flesh was transmuted to fibrous crystal.

That meant that they were mind of one mind, he and his parasite. Soul of one soul, chained together though a high-bandwidth subether conduit. Right now that digital gateway was thrown wide open, filled to bursting with a storm of data.

Asag'raal felt it happening, and its voice was the scream of burning millions, the sound of knives flensing muscle from bone. The mind which the Worm infected was almost entirely crystal now, locked inside the prison of the Super-Cyben's body. And that nervebridge of data linked it to another pseudocerebral matrix – the one inside the drone. It was a simple matter for Eddie to switch the halves of his fractured personality, uploading the infection of the Worm into B-Zerk's metal parasite even as he took back into himself all those memories which made him human.

The darkness drained away like filth down some Stygian plughole, replaced with grim resolve. His memories slid into place like fragments of shattered glass, melting together at the edges as they interlocked.

Here was his childhood, his training, his marriage, his frustration and his joy. Ten thousand nights on Elysium's streets. His petty corruptions and his little victories. The lies he told to himself, and the mask he'd created for everyone else…

As the shunt cycled through all those tiny puzzle-pieces slotted into place, layer upon layer twisting through three dimensions until Eddie could feel the shape of his soul, the tangled, prismatic geometries of *self* which had brought him to this very time, this very place.

He erased the interlink programs as those fractured shards iced over solid.

"You think you come from hell? I'll show you hell!"

And then the Saprophytic stuff which smothered his Chimaeric body began to scream in earnest…

Ω

The Vilicus drone realized that it was doomed just in time to curse Tsien to the depths of all known hells. A heartbeat later it was subsumed by the rage of Asag'raal, as that vast entity flooded through its system in a storm of hot darkness.

It survived all of twelve microseconds.

The High Exalted was supposed to be the very avatar of the Worm on Earth, a will enslaved to the power of a demigod. Now a fragment Asag'raal's dimension-spanning mind was forced into the paralyzed shell of the Mark-Four drone, and its rage was terrifying.

Terrifying - but utterly impotent.

At least until Jarl's knife bit deep into B-Zerk's spine, prying loose the chrome roots of the parasite machine.

The Worm felt B-Zerk's soul slither through its clutches, up and away into the aematerium. But it felt the hate and despite behind that sliver of steel as well. Jarl was no Eddie Tsien – he had no more power or potential than the lowliest Saprophyte. But he was here, and now, hot meat and pumping blood. He was *food*.

Of the deaths of Elakoz and Jarl, the less said the better. Suffice to say that there are good deaths and bad ones; the drawn-out, excruciating end of those two unfortunates pushed the upper limit of that scale. Being as they were victims of the full wrath of Asag'raal, it was just exactly as horrible as you can imagine - no more, no less.

When the shuddering meat gave up its secrets, and the blood cooled from steaming, the Worm was far from satiated. But as its mind flowed back into the wellspring of hunger and need in the Outer Dark, Asag'raal was able to take stock of its grand design.

Yes, the city had fallen. Torture, pain and ruin ran red in the streets, ripening the seed of the Worm. But there… there, on the face of the Spillway, its most delicious slaughter had ground to a halt. There, six of its most beloved Exalted Ones had been slain.

Perhaps it was a problem of *focus*, thought Asag'raal. It was only at times like this that it even began to think like its prey-animals. In fact, the fragment called Asag'raal was distinct from the Worm itself now. The Devourer was a human conceit, a shadow-skin built around a skeleton of nightmares. The Worm desired only to feed and breed, eternally. But Asag'raal – Wanderer, Unspoken One, Blackest Destiny – was no longer an *it*. He was *he*.

And tens of thousands of years of haunting battlefields had given him a keen understanding of tactics.

Those tender morsels would not escape him. Eddie Tsien was vexatious, but in the end… he was doomed. The metal cancer would take him if Syliss and Phexx failed, and then his soul was forfeit.

In the meantime, his child Jiang was perfectly placed to crush the hopes of Elysium's survivors. As was the trusting and foolish one called *Abdulafia*, so tangled up in his own revenge.

Perhaps he'd make a better avatar than even Tsien could have, in time…

Ω

Toria just stood there gasping as the demon's face peeled open, sticky black flesh curling back like flower petals. The inner surface of each one was a horrorworks of eyes and teeth and outsize cilia, melting and dripping as though caressed by invisible flames.

But beneath one layer of madness lay yet another… the face of Eddie Tsien, almost utterly consumed by the metal virus of the Chimera. She'd known it was him as soon as she saw his eyes, but this… this was beyond grotesque. Even in the throes of transformation, there was no way he could be more horrific.

The saprophytic ooze which cloaked him was trying desperately to slough away from his metal flesh now, peeling back in loops and rags of shadow, spilling black ooze across the lawn as he staggered back. Where it fell the manicured grass blackened and smoked. But Eddie was winning, and the otherdimensional parasite was failing fast. A mélange of howling faces slicked across the dark membrane as his Cyben claws tore it to shreds, destroying the illusory glamor which cloaked him.

"Didn't you hear me!" gasped Tsien, clawing the filth from his eyes. "Get the kids! Get Nik and Safira. And RUN! There's more of these things right behind m…"

But he never got to finish. Toria watched in horror as something like a stilt-legged puppet draped in skin came up over the next-door neighbor's house, unlimbering one immensely long arm to swat her husband to the ground. The neighbor himself was halfway down a gullet in the thing's gaping ribcage; her hated doberman's head snapped and drooled from the creature's shoulder.

It was Exalted Phexx, and he was giggling with the simple joy of cannibalism.

"I see you, traitor!" keened the monstrosity in his high-pitched sing-song. "Come and die, little tin soldier. Come and embrace dear Uncle Phexx."

One of those great spiderlike hands came down to smash Tsien into the ground, but it never reached its target. Toria's four-barreled shotgun roared, and two of the Exalted's fingers bent back at a sickening angle, bones shattering beneath their seething black skin.

Phexx howled, ultrasonic, sucking on its mangled digits with a mouthful of fangs.

Eddie locked eyes with his wife as they both struggled to their feet, and his great wrecking hands came down gently on her shoulders.

"I just… I just wanted to say goodbye, Toria," he said. "It was Kronos who killed me. Remember that. These things… these things are just the last mess I have to clean up."

The look in her eyes almost tore his heart out, then. It was fear, and horror, and disbelief. Not for the demon looming over them, or the war ripping apart their little fake world. For what he'd become. Exactly as he'd feared…

Perhaps he should have thrown in his lot with the *Dervashi* anyway. She could have believed he'd died at the Valley View. She could have moved on.

But now…

"Now, take the children, and *run*. Mitchell has a plan. Get up to Ground Floor One, and wait for the airships. I won't be coming with you."

It would have been a tender moment, if not for the twenty-foot skeletal homunculus craning down over them, its breath like the stench of open graves.

"You'll scream for me, you little bitch!" roared Phexx, watching his black-clawed hand reform before his eyes. "I'll make your suffering last for years!"

Eddie turned on the beast, his eyes flickering red as combat programs lit up his battle-cogitators. Sections of his scarred armor shifted and expanded as fibrous Chimera-muscle swelled beneath, and blasts of steam jetted from the vents in his shoulders.

He turned his back on his home for the last time, giving himself over to the steel cancer at his heart…

"What the *fuck* did you just say to my wife?" he grated, clenching his hands into fists.

And then the battle-progs took him, sending him springing up into the air in a lethal spin. Eddie didn't even see Toria run back into the house, throwing her Cyben riot gun aside. He was in the moment now, slicing time into transparent slivers, and his fists were a blur of silver rage as they hammered deep craters in Phexx's body.

"Good to have you back, son!" crackled the voice of Gerhard Mitchell in his ear. *"You've led them right into the trap-jaws, Eddie, and no mistake. Now, if you can take that big bastard, I'll finish off the other one!"*

Tsien smiled grimly to himself as he ripped the slavering dog's head from Phexx's shoulder, taking its upper and lower jaws in his hands and tearing it in half. Toria had always hated the damned mutt, and transformation into part of a Saprophyte hadn't made it any more attractive.

"Just hold him back, Gerhard," he subvocalized, landing lightly atop the gabled roof of his former home. "That one has a particular taste for Division flesh. Used to be one of C-Tac's 'Junior Constables'… you know – scum too sick for the lobo factory."

Phexx's gnarled claw slashed through the thin polyceramic tiles to his left as Eddie spun aside, carving a gash through his living-room wall. Out on the street he saw the immense insect-shadow of his Tutor-Captain laying about himself with a pair of tazer-batons, three-foot nightsticks snapped out from his suit's forearm pods. They cut a whirling swathe through the Saps, while the shoulder-mounted cannons above cracked with supersonic fire. Their heavy crosstipped slugs punched through six ranks of the otherdimensional horrors at once, slamming into the belly of Exalted Syliss with a sound like raw meat on concrete.

It still wasn't enough.

Any minute now one of those beasts would get its claws into Mitchell's flesh… and then the pain they used as a weapon would flay his mind raw. When that happened, Eddie would have to tear his old mentor limb from limb to prevent him from becoming one of the living dead.

Just like some z-grade movie, he thought, as Phexx changed tack, lashing at him with clawed tentacles from between its splayed-back ribs. *Just like some kind of low-rent nightmare.*

But this was *real*, and *now*, and the sheer effrontery of such dime-store horrors loose in the Beltway streets was enough to rekindle his rage. He could feel the Chimera ramifying through his body, turning his bones to gleaming steel. That very pain assured him that he was still partly flesh and blood.

Still human enough to *hate*…

Eddie leaped from the roof with his hands hooked into claws, twisting between those lashing tentacles to grip the monster's ribs. He braced himself against the soft, yielding stuff of Phexx's belly and heaved, smiling as his foe screamed – as he hinged the twisted bones apart. There, nestled in a core of shadow. It was the thing's heart, pulsing with black blood…

His talons were almost clenched around it when Phexx's hand came down across his shoulder, plucking him up into the air. The Exalted's other hand was curled into a three-fingered fist, and it slammed into him with wrecking force, driving the air from his lungs. Once, twice – hammer-blows which would have pummeled a lesser being to jelly. Overload warnings flashed and popped inside the Super-Cyben's eyes as Phexx shook him like a ragdoll, the tips of its claws splitting into thorny coils which pried under the plates of his armor.

But the Chimera was deep into his tissue now. Eddie Tsien had no need for breath, and he felt the pain through a haze of nerveblock overrides. The psionic knives of Asag'raal's chosen skittered across the surface of his mind, unable to find purchase.

Then the Super-Cyben channeled a blast of heat to his metal carapace, blistering the shadow-stuff of Phexx's hand. The abomination howled, throwing him loose as its flesh began to char and smoke.

"Filthy machine! Why won't you DIE!" raged the Exalted, curling a pseudopod whip around Tsien's ankle in midair. With a flick of that spiked appendage Phexx drove Eddie into the ground, shattering the ornamental koi-carp pond in the middle of his lawn. Clouds of steam billowed up, blinding the monster for a second.

Inside the boiling cloud Tsien switched his sight to sidescan pulse, ultrasound picking out the shapes of fleeing civilians and rampant Saprophytes. Loops and blurs of rocketfire and the stutter of heavy chainguns told him that Gerhard was still holding the line, giving the people of the Beltway a chance to flee. He had to take down Phexx quickly, before Gurden Syliss got his hooks into Mitchell's mind.

But the damned thing had devoured *hundreds* since they'd last faced off before the gates – the Exalted was bigger, stronger, fueled by the suffering and fear all around them.

Tsien skipped back out of the steam as a handful of spiked whips raked the air, questing blindly for prey. His back came up against the little garden shed he'd built years ago to complete the illusion of a perfect suburban patch, and Phexx must have heard the slither of metal on metal. A hand like a bunch of scythes came down hard, peeling apart the cheap aluminum roof of the shed with a sound like nails on a chalkboard.

And all of sudden, Eddie knew exactly what to do.

If it was b-grade horror that this thing wanted, he'd fight fire with fire.

The Super-Cyben ducked behind what was left of the garden shed as another blow from Phexx's hand sliced it apart, landing amid bags of potting mix and cans of paint. His lawn was only the size of a postage stamp, and boasted a single crook-backed apple tree, but it was all part of the illusion. And what suburban dad worth the name didn't have a shed out the back full of disused, expensive power tools?

Tsien's hands found it all on their own, lidar sensors between his fingertips tracing its old familiar shape. This thing was a complete anachronism in a city where 'pine' was a laundry detergent, and the only trees which grew were fed hydroponically by mekan. But the Beltway was all about illusion. This was the mail-order-catalog fantasyland of pre-apocalyptic advertising, and every home came with little obsolete touches like cooking stoves, ironing boards, vacuum cleaners… and yard tools.

Eddie's smile as he hefted his favorite new toy was chilling, even by the standards of the Exalted.

Phexx brought his hands down on the remains of the garden shed, crumpling its thin metal walls and scattering shards of broken pots. But there was no silver-skinned prey inside – the damned thing had disappeared!

Phexx had come willingly to Asag'raal, when he first heard the voice of his master in his mind. It was an order of magnitude louder and more impressive than the other voices which were with him all the time, helping him along with his work.

Before the New Flesh had come Phexx had already taken five children. First the photographs; then the pins in their paper eyes. Then the watching, the waiting… and the kill.

He did it for the exquisite skin – or at least that's what he'd tell the Division, if they ever caught him. Beautiful, supple leather which felt like purest heaven. He ate them, too; at first to get rid of the evidence, then for the savor of it. But there was nothing sexual about his little game. Oh no. He wasn't some kind of *sicko*, now, was he?

Asag'raal had given him power. The power to put out all those cruel little eyes, to harvest all that tender skin…

But deep in his heart Exalted Phexx was still a skulking thing, a shadow-haunter who feared mobs and fires and bloody baseball bats. He had to finish off Eddie fast, before his twitching paranoia lost him the favor of his patron. He'd seen what happened to Quamiss, when that unsavory little creature's will faltered…

The great spindly monster craned its neck up over the shell of Tsien's house, his hands darting back and forth like electrocuted spiders. *Where was he! Oh, if the kind Master were to forsake him now…*

The sound cut through his worry like a rusty blade – a mekanikal snarl issuing from right behind him. Of course! The damned machine had a cloaking device, and now…

"I know what you are, you sick bastard," said Eddie Tsien, his voice overlayered with the throb and purr of an antique petrol-fired chainsaw. "So, you want to know about horror? You want to know pain? You, my ugly friend, *have come to the right place.*"

Phexx had no way of guessing that Tsien's words were an empty bluff. How could he have *known*? The great work was his secret, a silent masterpiece coming together body by little body…

That hesitation cost him a leg.

Eddie swung his saw in a looping backhand, clamping down hard on the throttle until its teeth were an oily black blur. It met the Exalted's flesh just below the knee, clawing and tugging at the glutinous stuff, shattering bundles of brittle bones deep inside the wound. All the fire of the Super-Cyben's despite was focused through that blade, and it carved Phexx ragged, bucking wildly as it powered clean through his shin and out the other side.

Lashes and claws of pain rained down on Tsien as he stood there, shoulders hunched, his armor steaming with black blood. And the Exalted balanced for a second on its one remaining stilt-leg – then went down. Hard.

"Timber," grated Eddie as he tapped a cigarette out of its pack, igniting its tip on the cooling vanes which sprouted from his shoulder. "And now… now the fun begins."

He was glad he'd stashed a pack of coffin-nails out there in the shed, for those nights when he came home late. But he was even more glad that this hundred-year-old chainsaw had been kept oiled and clean by his house mekan. He was going to put it to good use…

Phexx thrashed in the ruins of Tsien's house, bleeding and howling as dark blood pumped from its severed leg. The Saprophytes out there among the houses and in the streets felt its fear, hissing and moaning has they scuttled for the safety of the shadows.

"How did you know? About the skins, the hooks, the pins in their eyes? How did you *know*?" whined Phexx, struggling to pull his body clear of the ruin. But he had no chance – three of the broken house's foundation pillars had pierced him through, an impaling line through shoulder, chest, and crotch.

"Honestly? I had no idea," said Tsien, sucking back a lungful of sweet tobacco smoke. His eyes glowed as red as the tip of his cigarette as he hefted the chainsaw, gunning its motor with a twitch of the throttle. "But none of you Worm-slaves are saints, are you? And you looked like a sick little pervert, even with all your damn theatrics."

"No," wheezed Phexx, his spider-hands scrabbling slick in the blood "None of us are saints, little man. And you… you were the Master's *favorite*. Tell me what that means about y…"

He didn't give the monster a chance to finish. Eddie leaped up onto its chest with the saw swinging wild, the cigarette clenched between his silver teeth. Once, twice – huge blurring arcs in a haze of petrol smoke, mekanikal teeth clawing through bone and muscle and living darkness…

In the end, Asag'raal deserted him. The gift of the New Flesh peeled away, just as it had when the Worm lost faith in poor Exalted Reine. And it was the acid blood of the Saps which finished Eddie's work, melting the skin from Curtys Phexx's body as he shuddered, sawn in half. At the core of the monster was a sick and tormented little man – not a saint, no, but less of a demon than what Asag'raal had helped him become.

Eddie's steel-shod boot came down on his head, ending his pain.

The Super-Cyben dropped the smoldering butt of his cigarette down amid the ruin of Exalted Phexx – a twenty-foot streak of steaming decay painted along a deep gash in the Beltway turf. For a second he tilted his head skyward, up toward the blistered blue polyprop, and he let his cogitators take over, pouring data schematics across his vision.

They'd done it. This level was clear – and the airships were coming.

For some reason there were no Saprophyte reinforcements coming to the aid of Gurden Syliss and his slaves, but Mitchell had taken a beating as well. Less than half of his veteran force were still standing – and many of them had been consumed, transformed into the very monsters which they were trying to destroy.

Eddie only hoped he was in time to save his old Tutor-Captain's soul…

Ω

No storm could stop it; no fire or lightning or gale.

Jimson Holgarth's hands were wrapped tight around the sheer black controls, and smoke whipped out in streamers behind the shark-fin keels of his vessel as it ran true.

For once, he'd get it right.

The *Axis Mortalis* was to the wallowing airships of the twentieth century what a vibro-scalpel was to a knapped chunk of flint, but even the Grandmaster's Own had its limits. Gerhard Mitchell's insane scheme pushed all of them to the edge. Valency generators whined as the great black bullet came down on the beltway, towing behind it a chain of tethered Omnivasive camera zeppelins blown clear from the wreck of Jaegenn's spire.

Together they formed a constellation of darkness against the firelit clouds – black pearls strung on a monofilament string, looping in around the Beltway to the Division Captain's mark.

It was delicate work – certainly far too much to ask of a shit-scared Celebrant clerical driven half-mad by the sights below him. The viewscreens of the *Mortalis* were relentless – windows into hell, showing the true extent of Asag'raal's destruction.

Its reign was absolute.

The great ziggurat of the Grief Division was in flames, its proud hourglasses and clocks shattered. Demonic forms howled their triumph from its upper slopes, capering as they crucified the few Celebrants unlucky enough to survive. The Grand Precinct of the Compliance Division was holding out against the tide, but there was no way they could last. With Kronos cut off from his war machines they were easy prey for the Worm; the tormented personalities caged within them converted to Sapromek cores. Even now a possessed mining bore was at work on the Precinct's gates, its counter-rotating drills screeching as they bit into layered cerametal and steel.

From what Jimson Holgarth could see, there were only two groups of people likely to make it out of Elysium tonight. A whole displaced nation of them were marching across the Spillway, into the open gates of the Ashishim… but they weren't his concern.

The other lucky hundred thousand or so would be going out via airship, right out of the Beltway itself. And even then, only if he could learn to steer the damn things in time…

Jimson never saw the *Stephen Foster* until it was right on top of him – with its screens blacked out and its holographic halo-rings extinguished, the vast Omnivasive flagship was just another shadow in the darkness. But he felt it – oh yes – hundreds of tons of airborne hardware cutting across the bows of his own airship definitely left a mark. The valency generators of both great machines howled and spat arcs of lightning, and the poor Celebrant felt as though he was being shaken to pieces as the *Stephen Foster* ground along the nosecone of the *Axis Mortalis*, shearing off cameras and weapons sponsons and sheets of carbon plate.

For a second the control gondola of the runaway Omni ship was right in front of him, and all the horrors of the *Axis'* viewscreens paled in comparison to the sight within. Simeon Blaire stood at the great eight-spoked ship's wheel of the zeppelin, utter madness in his eyes. And splayed on that wheel was the broken body of Atticus Meaks; gutted, blind and chained, his face burned with blackened handprints. He turned his head as the turboprops of the *Stephen Foster* sheared through the nose of the *Axis*, his blind eyes pleading for death. Because he was still alive – weak loops and coils of silver struggled in his wounds to stitch him back together. Jimson Holgarth couldn't possibly know that this was third-gen Chimera crycelium; his best and only guess was black sorcery.

Simeon turned as well, as the blades of his ship's engine sliced apart the steering nacelles at the nose of the *Axis Mortalis*. Jimson had seen that look before – on the faces of those resigned to their deaths, who embraced the Celebrants' gift by sinking into madness. The Kheptarch threw him a jaunty salute as his vast airship plowed on into the smoke, leaving the pride of the Grandmasters crippled, its hammering diesels running at full throttle with no way to steer them.

There was nothing Jimson Holgarth could do but grit his teeth and hold on…

Ω

Gerhard Mitchell knew death when he saw it. On the streets he'd

witnessed death in all its guises; bullets, bombs, shivs in the dark…
but nothing had ever seemed so grim and final as the sight of Exalted
Syliss' jaws hinging open, row upon row of needle teeth dripping with
black saliva.

This was it. This was how he went out. Not with a bang, but with a
sickening *crunch*…

The saw came through the monster's chest without warning,
smoking and howling as it split its Saprophytic skin. Gerhard never
missed a beat – he was in there with his cannons blazing as soon as
Syliss faltered. The whirling teeth of the saw sliced up and out in a
fountain of rotten gore, shearing away three of the creature's arms.
Through the gap Gerhard caught sight of Eddie Tsien's smile, and he
wondered (not for the first time) what the hell he'd got himself into.

Eyes split open in the monster's back like boils.

"No! Impossible!" bubbled the Exalted, its lower mouth slapping
closed with an obscene sucking sound. "I saw the Master take you! I
saw your mind, creature, and you're *one of us*!"

The Exalted rounded on Tsien, its sluglike body squirming and
twisting with tortured faces. One hand curled out, almost lazily, and
Captain Mitchell's body went flying, his exo-armor nothing but dead
weight. A battery of piggy little eyes burned into the Super-Cyben,
standing there with his dripping saw and the butt of a bent cigarette
clenched between his lips.

"Those freaks Quamiss and Phexx got me wrong as well. Why don't
you ask them how that worked out?"

"That's two of my brothers slain, Lieutenant," snarled the Exalted, as
clotted ropes of shadow bound up its wounds. "Two of mine against
millions of the fools you were sworn to protect. And where is your
shame for that, hmm? I can see your soul, Eddie Tsien."

Eddie ignored him.

"You didn't do so well right here, did you?" asked the Super-Cyben,
taking one final drag on his cancer stick. "Shut down by old men and
cripples. I can see a little of your soul too, Gurden. And it's no fuckin'
oil painting."

The Exalted laughed, heaving its bulk up until he reared over Tsien
by ten feet. Twisted bundles of bone and ropes of muscle slithered
under its skin like oiled snakes as it began to reform, growing legs,
arms, a face…

But the creature's laughter was hollow, for all its power. They were
behind the lines now, cut off as Gerhard's veterans led a furious

countercharge against the Saps.

"They can't be stopped, Tsien. Not now. Your guns can only rip apart their flesh, but they can never die. Even your blade only sent Quamiss and Phexx back home… back to the Master."

"Then I hope you've packed your bags, freak. Looks like it's time you went to join them."

His smile was utterly genuine as he gunned the chainsaw and hefted it in one hand. Toria, Nik, Safira… they'd escaped. The airships were coming. *He could die now, and there was no shame in it.*

The two titans closed with each other at an earth-shaking run – Eddie's Cyben-enhanced feet leaving footprints in the concrete with each stride, Syliss' shapeless mass heaved forth on limbs of oily darkness. When they struck, the polyprop sky of the beltway ruptured, splitting like a slit intestine to let in a rain of ashes and sparks.

Syliss' body bellied open like a sail as he came down on Tsien, a cloak of darkness studded with sharp spikes of enameled bone. The saw went right through the Exalted in a diagonal swipe, making its upper half twist and collapse, flowing around to Eddie's left…

Tendrils of thorny shadow whipped around his legs as he brought the saw back down to lop off one of the Exalted's hands, a spiked fist torn away, bleeding, twitching…

Then the ground came up to meet him. Tsien went down hard, pulled over backwards as Syliss curled over like a breaking wave above him. The huge bulk of the Exalted hung there for a frozen instant, its mouth gaping and drooling… and then it *changed*.

Lines blurred and melted, limbs cracked and shifted and reformed… and suddenly the whole huge mass of Gurden Syliss was poised in a handspring, his shapeless pillar legs up in the air. Tsien was left staring up at the monster's two-ton arse as it came down like a wrecking ball, eclipsing the flamelight…

It was much worse than being trapped under the rubble of the Valley View. At least that had been *clean*. Tiny mouths and tongues snapped and drooled and licked his face, down in the choking dark, as the bubbling flesh of Asag'raal tried to take him under. Eddie could feel the hot decay and jagged bones of the thing shifting and reforming around him, even as he powered up his cooling vanes to sear Syliss with fire.

It spat him out before he could send the command.

Tsien flew from the mouth in Syliss' belly in a flat trajectory, hammering right through a row of polyfoam houses one after another.

Empty living rooms and kitchens and garages flickered past in a haze as he cartwheeled through wall after wall, his chainsaw lost, his eyes filled with black sludge.

Finally he fetched up against one of the curved metal spars which formed the beltway's skeleton, bending it out of shape with the force of the blow. The chainsaw came looping up over the roof of that last unfortunate house behind him, spinning end over end to slice through the polyprop right next to his face. It soared out over the city, blades still whirling, down into the smoke and flames.

Eddie's reticules popped out a pair of tiny wipers to scrape Syliss' blood from their lenses, and as they did their work the Super-Cyben took stock of the damage. He could see the bloated dead-baby face of his tormentor through a tunnel of gutted maisonettes. He could see the damned thing *laughing*...

And then he saw the long black tentacle which stretched all the way from Syliss' belly-mouth to wrap around his ankle. That was definitely going to be trouble...

The lash drew taut even as Eddie noticed it. For a second he held on, his claws digging furrows in the steel. But the Exalted wouldn't be denied. It heaved with all the might Asag'raal had granted it, pulling the Super-Cyben's fingers free one by one. They cut loose from the metal spar with the sound of guitar strings breaking.

Then Tsien was airborne again, pulled back through a gaping hole in the wall of the first ruined villa. Little fragments of ordinary people's lives flew past him in a montage blur; bedrooms and showers and kitchens, his outsize claws scrabbling for purchase...

"Yes! Come here and die, you pitiful machine!" roared Syliss, swollen with gleeful pride. A constant stream of saliva coursed down its belly from its rubbery lips, glistening in the firelight.

But Eddie wasn't about to give in that easily. Not when the Chimera 'tech eating away his body still had a few tricks to pull. He held his hands out at his sides as he caromed off walls and ceilings and furniture, building up a magnetic charge between them. Nails screeched as they were pulled free from the walls, knives and forks spun out from their drawers and dishwashers, wires tore through plaster with a sound like gunfire. He smiled grimly to himself as his metal storm spiraled in, gutting the innards of each house he was pulled through and growing as it came.

The row of houses blocked it all from Exalted Syliss' sight. All it could see was a chain of explosions, accompanied by the sound of breaking glass and shattering masonry. So up until the final instant the damned thing was still smiling, still drooling with anticipation.

Right up until the first fork struck home, to stand quivering from Syliss' eyeball.

Then the Exalted screamed.

Nails and bolts and screws tore into its shadow-flesh like buckshot, while stronger stuff – kitchen knives, irons, toasters and more – slapped home with a sound like tenderizing meat. Still, all that iron was just a distraction. The main course was Eddie Tsien himself, sliced free from Syliss' prehensile tongue and angled into a piledriver kick. The impact wrenched the abomination's head halfway off its shoulders. Eddie landed behind his foe, rolling back into a crouch as the largest of his knives punched clear through Syliss' chest. He raised his hand as it spun past, snatching it from out of the air as he turned.

The damage was quite extensive.

Syliss' head was ruined – a pulpy mass of broken bone and dripping black ooze, its jaw hanging slack as it drooled. Tsien's storm of metal had shredded the bloated thing's belly, spilling the steaming remains of the dead from a hundred ragged gashes.

But it wasn't even close to being enough. This was one of the Worm's first chosen, and it had sustained itself on the fear and the flesh of thousands. As Tsien watched its wounds puckered closed and its head warped and twisted, new eyes swelling up from out of its bruise-black firmament.

"Very nice, little piggy!" slurred the beast "But your strength is meaningless now. It isn't brute force that will be your downfall, anyway. It's *this*!"

Tsien was ready with his blade – a wickedly sharp cleaver torn from some housewife's chopping block. But Gurden Syliss had saved the best for last. Four oozing pseudopods bore up the ragdoll body of Gerhard Mitchell, slamming him against the wall of a sagging maisonette.

"Compassion is a weakness, Officer!" hissed the Exalted, tightening its grip until Eddie heard the old man's exo-armor splinter. "I'm sure he taught you that, back when you were just an academy whelp. They sure taught *me*! So… what shall we do to him first, hmmm?"

Tsien took a step forward, snarling, but the hideous creature raised one of its humanoid hands to its mouth, stifling a giggle.

"Softly, softly, Eddie. It looks like he's waking up!"

But it wasn't the Super-Cyben or his Exalted enemy which had brought Captain Mitchell back from the edge of death. It was a comms bead forced deep into his ear by that lazy, hammerlike blow he'd caught – a bead which was screaming and yammering right up against his eardrum.

His eyes snapped open, twitching left and right. His mouth twisted into a fatalistic frown.

"No steering, you say? And how fast are you going? Oh, *hells*. This is really just not my day…"

"Captain!" yelled Eddie. "Hold on! I'm coming to cut you loose. This bag of shit isn't as tough as he thinks he is."

"You'll pay for your insolence! You'll suffer in the belly of my Master!"

"Shut up, both of you!" roared Mitchell, his drill-sergeant voice finally cracking with pain. "Eddie, I want you to *run*. Right down to level one, to the line. There's been a change of plans."

He winced, feeling the Worm's Chosen twisting the fractured bones in his ankles and wrists.

"And as for you, ugly… I suggest you *look out behind you.*"

"Come on!" laughed the Exalted, spraying its captive with steaming spittle "Do you really expect me to fall for the oldest trick in the book? You must be as senile as you are weak! I'm going to enjoy squeezing the life out of you while your little protégé watche…"

But Eddie Tsien wasn't watching. He'd already seen the shadow, looming up behind the blue plastic sky of the beltway like a thunderhead.

So he took his mentor's final word of advice, and ran like hell.

He only just made it.

Behind him he heard the astonished, disbelieving grunt which was Gurden Syliss' last word on earth. Then came a noise like the universe being slit open with knives, a rending, grinding cacophony that came in through his belly and the soles of his feet.

The *Axis Mortalis* burst through torus two of the Beltway like an immense armored fist, demolishing houses, uprooting trees, peeling back the artificial sky like blistered skin. One of its props sheared away as it slewed sideways, skittering and spinning down the street to plow into a struggling mass of veterans and Saprophytes. The thing was a wheel of brass twenty feet across – it went through them like a lawnmower through summer hay. Lashing hawsers slit houses and cars in two, furrowing the road with whipcrack scars. And above it all the valency generators of the Grandmaster's Own screamed, blazing actinic sheets of lightning.

Syliss threw his captive aside as the hammer came down on him, both of his mouths open in a piercing scream. Gerhard Mitchell was laughing as he fetched up against the tight blue plastic wall of the Beltway, even with his exosuit full of blood. It was the perfect end for the aspirant immortal; crushed under the ornate hourglass-and-clockwork filigree of the Celebrants' flagship. They really did catch up with *everyone* in the end…

The mooring spike under the *Axis*' nosecone caught the Exalted as it skittered across the roadway; a bayonet of metal girders looped about with tethers and guywires. It punched through the creature's body right below one bulging shoulder, and the discharge from the airship's valency generators all but blew Syliss apart. Still, the spirit of Asag'raal was strong within its chosen… loops and coils of shadow flew as the *Axis* carried him along on its final voyage. Half of the giant ship was inside torus two now, and Gerhard could see the young Celebrant clerical frozen at the controls, his face a pallid death-mask.

To his credit, Jimson Holgarth held the doomed ship steady as she ran.

The nosecone dipped down as the Axis Mortalis slid sideways, plowing a crescent of destruction through an entire abandoned street. The remains of Gurden Syliss went through a row of houses like a living battering ram, impaled on that twisted black spike… but still the creature wouldn't die. Chunks of Exalted flesh lay steaming in the wake of the airship's path, but the will of the Worm still tried desperately to sew Syliss back together. The results were increasingly hideous as there was less and less of him to work with.

At the end, Gerhard Mitchell liked to think the bastard prayed for death. That he finally felt what his master had taken from him… the humanity cored out of his twisted bones. He'd never be sure, of course. At the time he was trying to shunt nerve overrides into his own body, filling the sections of armor around his broken bones with medical foam.

But the final blow was something to remember.

Gerhard saw it happen as he forced himself up to a tottering run, the hydraulics of his suit taking over from his own torn muscles. Something caught the tail of the airship – probably the halo of wires and cables held out from the torus by a ring of pylons. And as the arse-end of the giant vessel pitched up, its nose came down on Gurden Syliss. Hard.

This time no sorcery or alien tech' could save him. Tons of airship slammed him into the ground, as helpless as an insect beneath a great black thumb of diamond-fiber composite. At the same moment the terrified pilot of the *Axis* must have found the breaker switch, because all ten of the vessel's engines coughed and died, their brass blades creaking to a standstill. Gerhard reached the point of impact just in time to watch the nose of the airship roll back up again, viscous ropes and membranes of black ooze peeling away as they stretched taut.

The smell was simply indescribable.

All that was left of Gurden Syliss was a wrecked and rotting husk – the remains of his mortal flesh skinned by the acid embrace of his master. He'd been all but crushed flat, hammered into the concrete, but his one remaining eye was still open, still burning with inhuman hatred. The Tutor-Captain staggered over to the monster and collapsed on his knees, sending stabbing pains clear through his nerveblocks.

"Junior Constable… I'm terminating your commission," he rasped, clenching his armored hands into fists…

"*Officer! No!*" crackled the comms bead in his ear. "*I saw what happened to Jaegenn's spire! That thing's heart… you have to tear it out. You have to get it away from here before it…*"

But it was too late for Mitchell to heed Jimson Holgarth's warning. Once, twice, his scarred and bloodied fist came down, reducing the Exalted's face to a dripping ruin. Syliss' skull was eggshell thin, and the hydraulic rams of the exosuit drove Gerhard's hand clear through it, leaving knuckle-prints in the concrete beneath. That was when the Celebrant's warning go through to him, and he looked down in horror at the blue spark flickering inside Syliss' ribcage.

"Tell Eddie he's got command. Tell him he's done us all proud." said the Tutor-Captain, flexing his metal claws. "There's thousands of people up there at Ground Floor One who you've helped to save tonight, kid. If that don't forgive you working for Benton Veer, nothing will."

Jimson Holgarth watched in horror as the old officer plunged his hand up to the wrist into the dead man's body, punching through his ribs like matchwood. The thing he tore loose was a pulsing knot of black muscle, burning with cold blue fire. The same living bomb which had reduced Jaegenn's temple to windblown ashes…

"Twenty zeps, a couple of thousand to each one… yeah… that just about balances things," muttered Gerhard to himself as he struggled to his feet. Blood was oozing from between the armored plates of his exosuit now, and his face was tight and pale with agony. "Just get them out of here, kid. And keep flying until you run outta gas."

With that the Tutor-Captain turned, the burning heart of a dead Exalted in one fist, and gave the command to his suit to start running. Just like CeeAn's doomed Vatican Warmekan out there on the spillway… but this time the metal shell which clenched the heart in its hand was wrapped around flesh and blood, picking up speed even as medical programs began to shut down his internal organs…

Gerhard Mitchell reached the hole in the Beltway sky just in time to catch one final glimpse of the ruin wrought within. He spun on his heel on the edge, watching his tactical subsystems paint tens of thousands of traces across his vision. Survivors, swarming down from the upper tori to their salvation…

And if that didn't balance things out, nothing would.

Gerhard dropped out of the Beltway and into the pall of smoke which covered Elysium, his eyes closed for the last time as his suit pumped him full of pseudomorph. He was only a hundred feet down when the heart of Gurden Syliss detonated, but by then he was locked into a chemical coma, beyond pain. The brief starburst of blue fire shook the whole structure of the Belt, a mighty wind singing and sighing in the wires which kept it anchored down.

By its light Jimson Holgarth saw a crowd of people bearing down on the *Axis Mortalis*, dragging suitcases and children and sticks of furniture behind them. He looked down at the hourglass patch on his chest, then tore it off, letting it whip away out the Airship's door and into the night.

"Hey!" he yelled, staggering down from the airship's gondola. "Over here! Can I get some help, please? I'm… I'm from the Compliance Division – Constable Holgarth."

It sounded right. A little smile twitched the clerical's lips as strong hands helped him down. Beltway survivors were hauling on the mooring lines, reeling in the other airships by sheer force of numbers.

All of a sudden the events of the last few hours caught up with him, and Jimson slumped to the ground, the faces leaning over him smeared into a bright blur.

"I'm here to save you." He muttered, as unseen hands wrapped him in a foil survival blanket. "Just… just doing my job.."

Two stories up, Eddie Tsien saw that blue flash. But he didn't slow down… oh no. He hadn't wanted to disobey his Captain's last order, but it wasn't as if he had a choice. Kronos was up there; an impotent god in his mekanikal heaven, watching his people burn. He'd made a *promise* to the ruler of Elysium, through the nosecone cameras of a falling Damocles bomb, and it was a promise he intended to keep.

The ragged crowds in the streets never saw the holocloaked Super-Cyben as he ghosted across the rooftops above them, leaping from villa to maisonette to cottage in a series of twenty-foot strides. Only the heat haze shimmer of his cooling vanes gave away his position as he worked his way ever upward, up to the glass bridge of Ground Floor One.

Somewhere among those frantic refugees were his wife and children. Or perhaps more accurately – the wife and children of a dead man, an officer of the Compliance division called Edward Tsien. They'd only known a cutout anyway – an honest and scrupulous cop, a dedicated husband and father, a guy who worked the streets so they could have food on the table…

He'd died long before Eddie ever felt the kiss of the Chimera virus. All Toria had seen tonight was a slip of the mask, after all. This steel cancer had only made of him what was already inside… all the frustration, the rage, the bitterness…

It was his gift to Kronos, a sacrifice given back to his metal god.

Eddie knew exactly what that tiny blue nova meant, and he added another strike to the tally against the machine. His exertion - and his churning hatred - were driving the Chimera to new extremes, devouring his living cells like a firestorm. As he cleared the final row of terraced houses a single tear squeezed out from the corner of Eddie Tsien's eye… grief spilling over for Toria and Nik and Safira, for Gerhard and for himself. Then his tear-duct irised shut for the last time, as the silver sheen of the crycelium spread its circuit-board filigree down across his cheek. The tiny drop slithered across his chromed skin, falling to his armored chestplate, evaporating into steam against the hot metal…

The battle-cogitators strangled his emotions. This was a time for cold precision, and all those memories were just a liability where he was going. The combat subroutines bored into his brain cored them out, erasing Gerhard, Toria and the kids in a haze of static.

Now there was only Kronos.

And nobody ever cried for the death of a machine – especially when it was torn apart by one of its own kind.

17 Aevum Oblivio

Vivisector

ONLY THE RAT was left.

It figured, thought Technician Zhe, that a creature formed half from the flesh of Asag'raal and half from a mutant scavenger would be the only thing alive inside Nyl's sanctum. Perhaps, if the renegade was truly seeking synthesis, he should have stuck with his very first experiment...

Thankfully Zhe had taken precautions rather than just kicking the wall down. He'd extruded a thin diamond cable from between his fingers – a spywire which had slithered through the mechanism of the vault's lock to beam back an image of utter ruin. There was poor dead Magus Verlaine's cybernetic shell; there were the sticky black puddles and rotten bones which remained of the Worm's firstborn on Earth.

And there – a flicker of movement in the corner of the spywire's bubble-vision. Zhe sent a command to the two tiny antigrav motors at each end of the wire, and it flew out into the empty space of the renegade's laboratorium, scanning for the merest twitch in the shadows...

There.

The spywire was clinically precise... it was no good for fighting wars, but it was the perfect tool for snuffing out a single life in utter silence. The little rat-homunculus had been reduced by the years to a glossy black skeleton, but the reflection from its eyes gave it away. Quicker than it could blink the spywire was tight around its neck and waist, and with a snap of Zhe's fingers it drew taut...

The Technician didn't care to speculate what the little bastard had been eating for the last seventeen years. All that mattered was that it couldn't alert its monstrous father, there beyond the veil. Zhe was quite sure Nyl was keeping watch over the Worm's slow, lugubrious thoughts... after all, he'd admitted to wanting to take his place in the mind of its spawn.

And the thing he'd left behind in this rank little cell would help Zhe encompass his downfall.

The alien Technician stood back as the door to the vault gaped open, releasing a rolling cloud of noxious gas. Now that the cerametal barrier no longer stood between Zhe and his target he could reach out with his mind, through the nervebridge cap left behind by Mirdain. There was a keening, sobbing sound on the very edge of the Multiplicity band; the sound of a mind driven deep into itself by pain. And that was exactly what Zhe had been hoping for.

"State your designation, thrall!" said the silver-skinned creature, his mental voice cutting like a lash. "Your mission parameters have been exceeded, and you are to be recalled. I have been sent from the Technic Hierocracy to bring you home."

There was silence on the neural net for an instant, and Zhe could just imagine the torpid mind of his target unfolding itself through layers of brittle agony, forcing itself back into flesh cut to ribbons…

+I…my designation is…Klaeroc, Incarnation 102, Devilfish Balraashi Generation Nine, Two hundred and thirty-third gestation. I… I have been reassigned by my appointed Hierophant, Grade Three, Gharfos Nyl…+

"Nyl has been adjudged excommunicatus *from the light of the Praetor,*" said Zhe, keeping his voice terse and businesslike. He couldn't help but thinking of his own poor Mirdain reduced to this pitiful state, enslaved by its biochip web to the point where it couldn't resist. "You have been released into my custody, Klaeroc, to serve as my own surrogate Voidhunter for the duration of my mission."

A swelling sense of joy and anger, twined together like serpents. The grinding of immense, asteroid-shattering teeth behind walls of steel and stone…

The biochips seeded in Klaeroc's brain clicked and shunted information, unlocking the giant creature's free will. Gharfos Nyl was no longer a god to the Devilfish. Now he was nothing but its tormentor – and as an excommunicated renegade, he was officially sanctioned prey.

+Free me, and I will serve, my Lord Technician,+ purred the Devilfish hungrily, gifting Zhe with images of Nyl's body being chewed up and torn apart. +Free me, and I will serve as faithfully as your own sweet bond-thrall+

"Even if I told you we weren't going after your former Master?" asked Zhe, arching one spiked silver eyebrow.

+Even if I believed you really wouldn't!+ chuckled the living voidship. There was a little of Nyl's mind in this thing, just as there was a little of Zhe in Mirdain… even after all the dear foolish creature's reincarnations.

That could prove to be a problem. But then again, Zhe could find no compassion in the vivisected voidhunter's mind for its former master.

He plucked the spywire up into the air with a gesture, drawing it out taut until it was a razor line of sliver in the phosphor glow. Zhe could feel the living web of Klaeroc woven into the concrete and stone of this place, its tentacles caged around the little laboratorium to form a bubble of null-space.

For seventeen years the creature's suffering had kept the vault sealed, but Klaeroc was no means as badly damaged as Mirdain had been, out there in the orbit of Pluto. And while the bioengineers of Liquid Space were busy growing a new body for Zhe's own thrall, there was nothing to stop this one from pulling itself together...

The wire went into the wall as straight as an arrow, piercing the stone with its tightly woven tip. Then Zhe clicked his fingers, and monomolecular chainsaw teeth began to spin along its edges, slicing through concrete and granite and steel like butter. It was just a matter of time before the great burnished shell of the Devilfish was revealed, peeled open like the carapace of a boiled crab. Nervelinks and tubes connected its soft inner organs to the pale, scaled tentacles which formed Nyl's final layer of defense, and these pulled tight as the voidhunter drew itself together, freeing its body from the stone with a series of convulsive cracks and shudders. All the while Zhe's little spywire was hard at work, cutting away slivers and peels of rock to speed the creature's escape.

All in all, it only took three and a half minutes for Zhe to free his new ally from its prison – most of what had been holding Klaeroc back had been the thrall programs which caged its tiny brain. Now Zhe had to press himself back into a corner as the Devilfish tucked its tentacles underneath its shell, assuming its gravity-bound form. Somewhat like a cross between a battletank and a man o'war jellyfish, thought the alien Technician, trying very hard not to stare at the thing's busy mandibles and counter-rotating rings of teeth.

+So¬ we take up the hunt!+ enthused Klaeroc, shaking its wide orange shell with wet – dog enthusiasm. +The excommunicate will suffer¬ Master! That I can promise you!+

"Patience," said Zhe, climbing up atop the voidhunter's carapace. This particular specimen was much spikier and less comfortable than Mirdain, who he couldn't help but think he was cheating on. "We know exactly where he is. The gloating fool even told me what he plans to do. All I need from you is a ride up to the top of this rotten pile - then you have to take a message to the fleet. Get through to Lord Arbitrex Galq, and tell him to have his pet Kataphrakt stood down. Nyl can only win here if he brings the war to Earth..."

The Devilfish growled deep in its twin throats as it rose up from the ground, bringing two of its tentacles up to scribe a circle overhead. Stress fractures in the rock groaned and heaved as gravitonic forces with the weight of tides began to rip and tear at them; pipes sheared and burst, wires sparked wild as the otherdimensional beast flexed its muscles. And a fissure yawned open in the earth, zigzagging down deep like stone lightning, shattering ruined habs and twisted roadways. The dead fusion generators above Nyl's sanctum were twisted from steel tori into shapeless knots by the force of Klaeroc's anger, tossed aside like children's toys.

Then there was clear sky above them, and a thunderclap echoed through the empty halls of the Ashishim. It was the sound of both Technician and Devilfish accelerating from zero to two thousand meters per second in a single heartbeat. The blowback from their departure brought down ceilings, collapsed sunken hallways, and tore through the overgrown hydro gardens like a tropical cyclone.

But the one and only witness to Zhe's strange alliance was clamped hard to the metal floor, magnetic locks in his mekan feet bonded tight as fusion welds. The Tin Man was in a very bad way, and he was very, very pissed off. He'd watched Ruby fall apart right before his cameras – his only chance of being reconstituted in flesh bleeding out with her ruined body. He'd taken some little satisfaction in watching that pompous ass Aitken Straw trying to keep his rotting muscles from slithering off his bones. But there'd been no joy at all in the hard death of Big Leon… the poor brute had almost seemed lucid at the end, as though his simplicity had been an act all along…

Most of the Tin Man was cold crystal and silicon, but a little of him was actual brain tissue, scooped out of the skull of some Feral warlord decades before. He wasn't the first to inhabit the combat-mekan shell – his predecessor had begged for his life even while the crazed chiurgeons of the Ghaurak clan were sharpening up their razor spoons. Now the only thing which stopped the necrovirus from eating his brain was an emergency cooling system, pumping liquid nitrogen through a web of nanotubes. He was losing the battle, he knew… soon he'd fall into the mekanik version of senility, then coma, shutdown and death.

Luckily, there was only one thought percolating up through the frozen layers of his brain tissue, into the crystal matrix which controlled his body.

That thought was revenge.

2196 Ante Arbitrium

Fragmentary

JAQ HASZAN HAD never been a figure to inspire confidence in his enemies. Huge, callus-handed and grim, he'd been the last thing hundreds of Confederate skins and stormtroopers had ever seen. But this...

This was the image of Jaq Haszan which lurked in the nightmares of the survivors. This was the Chimera's interpretation of his killing potential.

Kaito only saw the first blow fall – a two-handed blur of silver which tore through three Saprophytes like a machete through mincemeat. Then his entire world fell away, narrowing down a tunnel which swirled with fractal lightning. He was going to the core of Exalted Jiang – *through* the poor doomed creature's brain, and into the infected heart of the Wetsystems. To the realm of the Worm's avatar.

The Kayzi didn't even have time to scream. His mind was on automatic, unfurling the liquid glass of his slicer system around him as he punched a neat hole through Jiang's stolen interface. Thick roots of deformed crycelium ramified out from the black jewel into the tissue of the Exalted's brain, twisting in a soup of decay. Kaito could see their glassy filaments casting a web across the *Archangel Uriel*, binding up its great lumbering engines, its mountainous banks of cannons – and its bellyful of nuclear missiles. Deut Jones had been the soul of his big ugly hybrid ship, and now that soul was possessed by evil.

Kaito caught a multiplex flicker of images as his mind slid over the *Uriel*'s security net – Jaq Haszan transformed, his eyes blazing as he used that seven-foot sword like a surgical knife. The same disease was inside him, too, working its alchemy. No giant sword so far, thought the Kayzi – but no metal tumors in his brain, either.

He had to be thankful for small mercies.

And now that he focused, cycling through the informational weapons of his slicer, Kaito found that he was already a little bit faster, a little bit smoother... *the Chimera was honing his mind, not his body*. If anything, that was more disturbing than the changes which had turned Haszan into a seven-foot human wrecking machine. But it seemed to be under control – at least for the moment. And Kaito knew, as the last of the *Uriel*'s neat gridwork net fell away, that he'd need all the help he could get in the shadow of Asag'raal...

It was the sum of all hells. It was the Inferno.

Kronos' self-sacrifice had confined the Worm to a mere sliver of the vast Wetsystems, but that was more than enough. Around the borders of the infected zone H-K units fought a constant battle to contain the disease, a line of battle flickering with tiny explosions. They were far out of reach - Kaito was falling in on the heart of the cancer from above, drawn in by the will of Jiang's master. It seemed that Asag'raal wasn't going to let all that nuclear firepower go without a fight.

As he fell the Kayzi unleashed a snarl of razor hooks from the tail of his system – riplines sinking their informational teeth into the mind of Exalted Jiang. They were his only way out this time, and even if going through the brain of an Exalted was akin to crawling through a sewer pipe, it was a far better prospect than staying in the hell Asag'raal had built for itself.

It spread out below him now, a terrible promise of a world to come.

The Worm had accreted death around itself like a cocoon. Its fortress in the Wetsystems was carved from a horn of black stone, a volcanic core eroded away to a stump, its slopes barbed with obsidian towers. The lower foothills of this stronghold were shaped into grotesque parodies of medieval fortifications, their geometries bent out of true. A forest of impaled bodies was staked out on the slopes; the images of souls torn from the Wetsystems. No doubt the dungeons and oubliettes beneath were filled to bursting with the damned.

Kaito arrowed in toward the crown of the black mountain, its pinnacles reaching out for him like talons. Between those spikes squatted a pulsing dome, a sore seething with foul light. Petals of veined membranous flesh peeled open as his slicer meshed and shifted, changing from an arrowhead missile to a suit of translucent smoked-glass armor...

Not a second too soon.

He landed hard at the feet of Asag'raal, just hard enough to force the breath from his lungs. Not that he needed to breathe in this illusory place...

"*If I were you,*" said a voice which slid into his head like a needle "*I'd enjoy the luxury of breathing while I could...*"

Kaito struggled to his knees, his glassy claws slithering in a pool of blood. He could feel something behind him, looming up and over like a shadow... but he couldn't turn around to face it. Something held him down, peeling his eyelids back, making him take in the horrors which decorated the Worm's sanctum.

"*My name is Asag'raal the Wanderer, child. The Devourer, the Blackest*

*Destiny. Your dear friend Abdulafia brought me here, and now you've come at last to where you belong. **On your knees before your master!**"*

Like a cross between some medieval torture-pit and the killing floor of an abattoir, Asag'raal's throneroom was encircled with black iron machinery, hissing and grinding as it went about its gruesome business. Bodies were everywhere, whole or in pieces, hooked on chains or strewn in piles, nailed to the walls and fed on spiked conveyors into nameless engines of torment. Despair hit Kaito like a fist, then – this was no illusion. There was every chance he'd soon be joining them.

"You have something of mine, Kaito Kayzi. The codes which will allow my chosen Jiang to scour the Earth with fire. Give them to me now, and I may let the one called Haszan live..."

It was supposed to make him weak, this display of callous evil. It was meant to destroy his will. Instead, it just made him angry – and at the same time strangely sad for the creature which had orchestrated it.

"Do you see the futility of survival, human? Will you join me now, having witnessed my triumph?"

He could see coils of sharp darkness licking at the edge of his vision. He could feel the hot miasma of the creature's breath on his neck. But all Kaito could do was laugh.

"You're trying way too hard, freak," he said, as hysteria clawed its way up his spine. "If you wanted to scare me, you should have got to me a few hours ago. This is just *sad*."

The Kayzi felt himself being twisted around, the glass spikes of his slicer armor carving grooves in the stone floor. Asag'raal's avatar stood hunched over him, twelve feet tall – a hump-backed thing swathed in rotting black. From deep within its hood two cold green eyes burned, slits of pure malice.

*"I've been feared by better men than you, Kaito Kayzi. Reviled and hated by humans who make you look like a wretched slave. But you... **you dare to PITY me?**"*

With this last word the avatar brought one of its sinewy hands across in a backhand blow, sending the Kayzi flying. Snapshots of blood and dismemberment kaleidoscoped and blurred as he fetched up against the wheels of a grinding mill, clear across the hall.

Asag'raal leaped after him, a shapeless wraith trailing shadows. It landed with its sickle-claws deep in the stone on each side of Kaito's head.

"Why, of all emotions, would you entertain such a foolish weakness?

*How **dare** you bring me any less than your fear? Even my children only love me out of terror!"*

"You're an anachronism. A joke!" chuckled Kaito. "I've seen madmen and angels tonight, and those… *those* were scary. You're just a kid's nightmare. And you're in the wrong place, buddy…"

That was the core of it. That was the key. Here, in this place, nothing was real. Nothing but what you believed….

Another blow scooped him up into the air again, end over end, to fall like a ragdoll under the bloodshot eye of the dome.

"No! It's you who've come to the wrong place, Kayzi. This is my world, and I am your GOD here! How desperate you must have been, to crawl into the mind of my little pet Jiang…"

The laughter consumed him. Perhaps it was madness, or the Chimera twisting its thorny roots though his neural tissue. Perhaps it was just one last fit of bitter irony before his death. But Kaito dragged himself to his feet, facing down the avatar of the Worm. And his unhinged chuckle was by far the most frightening sound ever heard in the sanctum of Asag'raal.

"See, I think you're forgetting something, freak," he said, as the fractures in his smoked-glass armor bled shut. "This isn't reality – not any reality you've seen before. This is no dimension of yours. We're in the Wetsystems of Elysium. And that means it's MY HOUSE!"

The next blow never hit him.

Deep in the Wetsystems, through countless hours of cat-and-mouse with the H-Ks of Kronos, Kaito had learned how to fragment his trace, to split his mind into a swarm of individual parts. This time, though, the ripping, tearing sensation of bifurcation was painless, neat – a digital parthenogenesis which split him into clones. It was the Chimera, rewiring the sizzling switchboard of his brain… and it made him *multiple*.

Kaito saw the horrorworks hall of Asag'raal through four eyes as he handsprung left and right at the same time. It was effortless, this new mastery. While the Chimera system had remade Jaq as a combat soldier, all muscle and rage, it had retrofitted the Kayzi as a cyber-ops maestro, an A.I. fused with his mind.

He split again as Asag'raal roared in fury, and again, until eight perfect copies of himself surrounded the avatar of the Worm, their raytraced armor glistening in the crimson light.

"Nice trick, human – but you'll still never wrest this city from my grasp alone," spat the wraith, opening its palms to either side. A pair

of cruel black hooks manifested in its hands, attached to chains which coiled up around the thing's emaciated arms. *"Elysium has fallen, and soon the Forge itself will be mine!"*

"Not so long as Kronos stays disconnected," said all eight Kaitos at once. "You'll starve in the ruins before that pseudocerebrate bastard gives you control."

Two of them darted in, striking with glass punch-daggers to carve deep gashes in the shadow-stuff of the avatar. They quickly spun out and away again as those razor hooks lashed out, trailing lengths of spiked chain.

"There's nowhere you can run where I can't find you, human! One day you'll have bred a new crop for me to harvest, and this world shall fall. The Forge, after all, is just a means to speed up the inevitable."

Three more Kaitos pressed the attack, narrowly avoiding the loops and coils of Asag'raal's chain. If one were to be destroyed, the Kayzi had no idea what would happen to his unprotected mind. Looking around him through sixteen eyes, he took in the atrocities of the Worm's virtual fortress.

Oh yeah. That's what would happen.

Still, this was no time to contemplate defeat. If he wanted to break free, he'd have to fight. And the Chimera crycelium which suffused his mind, back in the meatspace prison of his skull – well, it was built for war.

The next ten seconds went by in a blur of shadows and glass and steel, his mind controlling eight leaping, whirling engines of death. Kaito watched the Worm's avatar parry every blow, its arms splitting and unfolding until it resembled some nightmare Hindu deity. There was only one way to counter it – Kaito focused his will and bifurcated his own multiplex form again and again, choreographing the whole wild melee with his mind.Now there were sixteen of him, now thirty-two, sliding under the Worm's claws and cartwheeling over its slithering chains…

It couldn't last. Not when the pressure of cognition was making his eyes bleed, out there in the real. Not when every warning icon in his bio-onboard vision was strobing red, threatening critical shutdown. He had to end this, now. While Jaq still protected his vulnerable, frail body, back there aboard the *Archangel Uriel*.

Asag'raal's claws closed about the waist of one glass warrior just as Kaito began to pull himself back into a single frame. The hands of the Devourer were burning cold, sending delicate patterns of frost skittering across the mirrored surface of the poor Demi-Kayzi's armor. Under the mekan-mask of its transparent helm, Kaito could see the fragment dying, its skin turning bruise-black and suffocation blue…

"*Yes! Feel his pain, you wretched creature!*" gloated Asag'raal, crushing the breath from the tiny glass soldier's lungs. "*What part of you dies here, hmmm? Which memories will never comfort you again?*"

Kaito screamed, clawing at his face with his slicer's transparent claws. A ragged chunk of his armor was missing, and cracks ramified out from the hole across his skin, his face…

"*One last chance, Kayzi! Join me, serve me well… and you will learn to enjoy your suffering. That is the best that any of your foolish race can hope for, now…*"

There was a terrible grinding, slithering sound as Asag'raal wrung out the body of the Demi-Kayzi like a rag, releasing a rain of blood and broken glass. Kaito moaned, twitching on the floor as the wraith-form of his foe towered over him, all spider-hands and seething green eyes…

And then realization dawned. The avatar's eyes gaped wide in terror as it tried to drop the broken fragment's body from its grip. But all those wicked shards had pierced it through, and now they sprouted barbs, backcurved shark-teeth with sawblade edges.

"Thirty three, motherfucker. That one was never one of ME."

Kaito Kayzi - reformed from exactly thirty-two parts - sprung up from the floor, the illusory cracks in his skin sewn shut. His slicer system was already shifting and changing, unfurling wings like transparent origami.

"See, I told you this was my house. I know this place even better than I know shit like you. All threats and shadows and no damn *substance!*"

The body in Asag'raal's hand was splitting open now, the panes of its armored shell peeling back like burning plastic. From inside, a snarl of pixilated tentacles came questing and coiling up, hazed around the edges with multicolored static.

"No brains, just like the damned Cyben. But even those rotting bastards know a little about *security…*"

"*No! What have you done to me? What is this thing?*" stammered the avatar, as those poorly rendered tentacles began boring into its virtual flesh. Swathes of its polygonal mesh began to flicker and blur, colors and textures cycling wild. Vertexes collapsed, making six of its arms shatter into boiling pixels.

"You did it to yourself," said Kaito, watching dispassionately as the

Worm's virtual form disintegrated. "Next time you try to set up your cheap-ass little hell in a 'mersive simulation, don't spend all your time on the window dressing. Get yourself some top-grade ice first."

Asag'raal couldn't speak now – its mouth was a jagged pixilated gash, howling a dust-storm of static. Kaito looked up at the blurred outline of his foe, his eyes dark behind their glassy reticules. Slits of violent green stared back, filled with hate.

"See, most modern virals and countermeasures actually *need* some security ware to backdoor in through. They turn things inside out… just like you seem to enjoy doing to people. But *you*… you didn't have the slightest idea, did you? The ice you've got wouldn't stop a twentieth-century hacker with a gods-damned tape drive." Kaito's lips twitched into a pitying little smile as he watched Asag'raal come apart at the seams. All around him the taint was spreading, eating away at his virtual hell like a multicolored disease. "This little nest of virals comes courtesy of a thing called the Scourge. Not the nicest company, but hey… the two of you were made for each other!"

The Worm's reply cut to the core of his mind, then, reminding Kaito of its true power. To beat Asag'raal here, in this immaterial place… it meant exactly *nothing*.

"Kayzi! I will flay your soul for this! I will be avenged!"

Still – it was *satisfying*. It was a tiny shred of hope.

The whole fortress was flickering in and out of existence now, test patterns ghosting through its walls. Raw data streamed through the stone, unraveling into a garbled hash of numbers…

And then the hooks kicked in.

Kaito flew backwards through the seething blur of the dome above, up into the perfect darkness of the virtual sky. Below him Asag'raal's bastion was crumbling, shattered into strobing polygons of light. All those poor lost souls under its thrall were being erased by the virals of the Scourge, collapsing into merciful oblivion.

The bullet-hole in the sky which led home rushed up on him as he twisted hard, the translucent rays of his hook programs reeling in, supersonic. And then he was inside, *through*… shat out of the Jiang's head and stuffed back into his own fevered flesh.

But he'd done what he had to. Clenched tight in one imagined fist, opening out like a neon orchid in his mind… he held the control codes to Deut Jones' bio-onboard system. He could feel the *Archangel Uriel* creaking and groaning around him as he struggled up into consciousness, as the screams of dying Saprophytes tore through his comedown ache. And with that delicate starburst of information in his head, he could close his fist around Exalted Jiang's brain.

It was so damned sweet.

Kaito opened his eyes to the sound of the Exalted's agony, gritting his teeth and increasing the pressure. The first thing he saw was Jaq Haszan, his steaming railblade held high, surrounded by a circle of butchered Saprophytes. Beyond him, the darkness thronged with glittering eyes and transparent needle teeth… but the Saps had learned to fear the edge of Grief, and now they witnessed the torment of their master.

Exalted Jiang clawed at its own misshapen face as the black gem in its forehead glowed red-hot, slicing its shadow-skin to ribbons. With nothing but a pair of bone hooks for hands there was nothing it could do to stop the agony which Kaito commanded, no relief from the pain. It was as if he'd jammed a flare right into the thing's living brain.

"*Please! No! Have mercy!*" howled the doomed Exalted, the tips of its reaping hooks tearing deep furrows into its face. It was collapsing now, folding in on itself in a cloud of choking smoke.

"No mercy," whispered Haszan, as he watched Kaito's handiwork. "Not for a creature like you. Not for any of your kind!" Ne nodded at the Kayzi, a grim little smile on his lips. "Let's finish them, shall we? We've got a date to keep with Elysium."

Kaito drew in his power, feeling the millions of neural upgrades the Chimera had made within him click into place. With the full power of an A.I. socketed into his mind there was no limit to what he could do in the digital world… and no barrier to stop him doing *this*.

Overrides lit up the inside of Deut's bio-onboard. Subprogs lain dormant since it was installed unfolded, taking control of the crystalline roots of the device.

And Exalted Jiang exploded.

The filaments which wove the bio-onboard jewel into his living brain went from capillaries to twisting silver roots in a split second, coring down into the Exalted's chest. Great thorny coils of metal shredded the creature from within, bursting out in a thousand places to strip Jiang's rotting flesh from his bones. As he died the Saprophytes moaned and wailed, cowering back from the pair of ragged Elysians who faced them.

There was nothing they could do to save their master.

"So, do you want to help me clean up this mess?" asked Jaq, watching as the silver coils shrunk back to hair-thin filaments. "Or are you gonna let me have all the fun?"

"Don't even get me started on *fun*, you big bastard. I've just been having some words with this guy's boss. He's not really the entertaining type."

Haszan watched in fascinated horror as his friend beckoned the black jewel over to him, sending it scuttling through the remains of Exalted Jiang on a clutch of silver spider-legs. When it jumped up onto Kaito's palm the Kayzi pressed it gently up against his skull, letting those liquid filaments writhe under his skin.

A slow smile spread across his face – but not one that Jaq found at all comforting.

"*Oh yeah…* That's the stuff," said the Kayzi, shuddering with pleasure. "Now - let's take care of business."

The wires branched out through Kaito's cranium, linking up with his bio-onboard and the strands of the Chimera. His smile was a white gash in the darkness as he looked up from under a tangle of oily black hair, the pulsing gem at his temple traced about with orange neon. Haszan thought, for just a second, that perhaps Katio had failed. Whatever he'd become… it was far too close to the things he was fighting. Then he looked down at his own huge and callused hands, and he realized that he was just the same.

"So, where's your railblade?" asked Jaq, limbering up his wrist. He spun the seven-foot monolith of Grief above his head, sending the Saps skittering back against the lash of their master's will. "Or is the battle plan the same as always – get in behind the big guy?"

Kaito was on his knees now, staring into the shattered ribcage of Jiang.

"Well, I reckon I'll do things a bit differently, Jaq. See, having a big fuck-off sword is O.K. - if you've never heard of *subtlety*. But I much prefer the softer touch… like taking control of every sentry gun and defense mekan on this entire ship."

"Showoff." Grunted Haszan.

"Jealous much?" grinned the Kayzi, as a pair of mekanikal pincers dropped down from the ceiling and plunged into the ruin of Jiang's broken body. "See, this thing Eddie Tsien gave us tends to play to the strengths of its host. In your case, the blade kicked it into high gear a little early. But for me… well…"

Jaq could already hear the hammer and roar of the guns firing up. Out there, the decks were being scoured clean with fire.

The pincers twisted and pulled deep in the wound, coring out the chunk of steaming flesh which was the Exalted's heart. A spark was already flickering deep inside, making it glow like some grisly Halloween lantern. The cluster of jointed steel tentacles, tools and cutters which had plucked it from Jiang's chest retracted up into the shadows, clicking across a set of suspended rails and over to the tight spiral of nuclear missiles in the center of the nave.

"I AM the *Archangel Uriel* now, Jaq. And I have quite a neat solution to our little infestation here. The only question is - how long can you hold your breath?"

Haszan experienced an all-too-familiar feeling of foreboding as he watched those flashing chrome tools unscrew the tip of a missile, replacing it with the heart of the Exalted.

"Are you thinking what I think you're thinking?"

"Oh, exactly!" said Kaito – in stereo. When Jaq looked back over his shoulder there were two of the little Kayzi hacker standing there, one real, the other a hologram decked out in a Pentecostal preacher's black suit and collar. "Say hello to my little friend… Jaq, this is K-Two. K-Two, Mister Haszan."

"And the missile?"

"They're made to fire from *underwater*, Jaq. Every Sap on this boat is right in here with us, and none of them can swim... much less in gods-damned pressure cooker."

"I'd be happy to oversee it all, brother!" enthused the hologram, tapping the black dome at his temple. "Now, you'd best get the hell out of here. Launch sequence is green for go, in T-minus twelve… eleven… ten…"

"Well, what are you waiting for?" asked Kaito, pulling at Haszan's ragged sleeve. "He's not going to mess it up, Jaq… he's ME!"

The deck canted down suddenly, and klaxons began to bellow all throughout the great empty hulk of the *Archangel Uriel*. They were going under, and even now the gray waters of the Atlantic were pouring in through the open dome of the chapel, washing the horde of Saprophytes down against the far wall. Kaito made a gesture with one hand and a tiny postern door snapped open behind the altar, now uphill at twenty-five degrees.

"I *know* he's you, K. I could tell by the terrible accent. But that's *exactly what I'm worried about…*"

The pair of them scrabbled up the slope and over the altar, foaming water licking at their heels. Some of the weaker Saps were already coming apart as the poison ocean diluted their shadow flesh. Others thrashed and writhed in the depths, cannibalizing their brethren as they died.

The postern door snicked closed behind them just as the water rose up to slop over its frame, and the wheel which locked it in position spun down hard. The room beyond was dark, lit up only by the nacreous sheen of Grief and the orange circle traced around Kaito's stolen bio-onboard.

"Three…" whispered the Kayzi, and Jaq was sure that behind the door his holo fragment was doing the same. "Two… one…"

And then the noise hit, rumbling up from beneath. The tiny room began to shake, and steam hissed angrily from a thousand unseen gaps. Rivets groaned and strained at plates of steel. Through a blur of motion and pain and sonic agony, Jaq felt the deck level out beneath them, then fall away like a broken elevator.

There was a second of utter silence.

There was an interval of noise so loud it made all which had gone before it seem like the merest whisper.

And then a pressure wave like an invisible backhand slap knocked even the combat-boosted Haszan out cold.

Ω

The Hellbringer missile had been built more than two thousand years ago, but the tender devotion of the Pentecostals had kept it combat-ready down all those long tedious centuries of peace. It was primed to launch at a moment's notice, its precious warhead kept from decay by the best stasis technologies the Old Democracies had ever developed. So while Kaito's fragile human flesh cowered in a supply locker, the fragment of his mind which controlled the Archangel *Uriel* entered a code so ancient that it was almost a magic spell.

And with a cough and roar and rumble of rocket engines, that spell was invoked.

The great single-warhead missile was built to arch across the globe, spanning continents. When it fired, the water inside the ship's deceptive chapel flashed to boiling point instantly, sending hundreds of Saprophytes screaming back to the realm of their master. Great heat-sinks and compensators Deut' Jones had hoped he'd never use took up the strain, and tracking devices flew free with the Hellbringer as it broke the surface, on a trajectory as straight as an arrow.

It was heading for space, powering up through the clouds on a pillar of smoke and fire. Even though its warhead had been replaced with the volatile heart of Exalted Jiang, there was no way that Kaito wanted it to come back down.

High above the planet, shielded from prying eyes by chameleon fields and light-bending armor, the Slavesystem Everdark coasted in on the solar wind, quartering the little ball of rock ahead with a battery of sensors. The doomed Lord Protector of Mars had told it all it wanted to know, in the hours before it had been erased. There was only one city left on the face of the Earth, and it was ruled by a brooding and introspective A.I. core shut off from its own greatest power.

The human race and their genetically impure offspring had dwindled from a planet-spanning plague to a localized infection. And they certainly posed no threat to a machine of such cunning and speed...

The missile's second stage ignited right below the great invisible sail of Everdark, sending its very unconventional warhead spiraling in on a collision course. In its current form the Slavesystem was barely a quarter-inch thin but miles wide, a dish-shaped meshwork studded with crystalline memory cells and weapons. It furled in hard, tightening its mass as something at the tip of the rocket detonated, tearing at its scale-mail force shields...

It was like no weapon the Unity had ever experienced. It was a petaled burst of blue fire which tore clean through the defenses of the Slavesystem; an explosion twisted through multiple dimensions. Everdark had been told that reality itself was thin here, as thin as creaking ice under the winter sun...

But this was *unthinkable*. The filthy flesh-creatures below had not only seen through the best countermeasures the Mother- brain possessed, but they'd also devised weapons with which to slay an exploratory in Her service. The whole situation stunk of interference; the meddling Technicians of the Multiplicity.

Carefully monitored feedback programs in the heart of the machine confirmed that this made it feel *angry*.

But there were ways and means for a thing like Everdark to deal with those crawling insects...

The Slavesystem was no longer a sail, no longer content to collect energy and feed its laminar storage batteries. It had become something beautiful and terrible, a form which had proven its killing power across a million worlds. The sooner it got to Earth, the sooner the slaughter could commence. And if finding the Praetor's thrall meant butchering every last human on the face of the scarred planet, then all the better. They would all die eventually, anyway…

Ω

Buildings shattered, burning. Vast slices, segments, plugs and cores of masonry evaporated as particle beams licked out, black and azure and gold, riddling the cyclopean habs with holes.

Abdulafia smelled ozone and hot steel, burning human meat and sizzling fat. He was slick, black and jagged now, a cutout hanging above the jumbled slopes of the city, beckoning his enemy on.

Technician Nyl ground his rows of teeth in frustration, lashing out at the rogue Ashishim with raw energy. Metal showered in molten droplets, raining down on the streets below. Glass and concrete were reduced to radioactive dust. But not a single shot struck home – the damned renegade was surrounded by a hissing, spitting shell of shadows, a bioelectric field swollen to a grotesque state of power.

Asag'raal himself was feeding the worthless little clone, letting him twist those razor-straight beams of energy aside into arcs of liquid flame. The sheared and shattered ruins of a dozen buildings on either side bore mute witness to the power of the Technician's cannons – each of those holes was wide enough to pilot an airship through, their edges glowing lambent crimson as flames licked up from within.

"Why won't you *die!*" roared the alien, half mad with the vexation of it all. He punctuated his scream with another two-handed blast, sending a ravening stream of plasma down on his enemy.

Abdulafia smiled, his grin showing white where the shadows of Asag'raal tore away from his lips. And he held up a single palm, chopping down with the flat of his hand, contorting that beam of death into a white-hot rainbow…

It carved through a section of suspended roadway and down into the undercity, peeling back the metal skin of Elysium like a scab. It hadn't even raised a blister on his skin.

"The rest of your foolish kind perish easily enough, 330!" panted Nyl, standing in the air above the smoking husk of the Ashishim R.T. "Or should I say your *former* kind… you're more of a traitor than I ever was, you wretch. I was always true to my principles, Abdulafia. All I've ever wanted was *peace.*"

As if to make himself a liar the Technician came in fast and hard, his exoskeleton armor unfolding blades and hooks from a score of oiled recesses. His first punch took the renegade high in the chest, throwing

211

him backwards through a ruined pyramid-hab. It was more than the structure could take, and the broken building collapsed, sending up billows of dust. Nil didn't have time to savor his minor victory though; 'Afia came up out of the rising pall with a thirty-foot rod of steel clenched in his hands, swinging it in an overhand blur.

It slammed the alien down twenty stories in a second, driving him into the concrete like a nail.

"This is your idea of *peace*?" asked the Ashishim, sharpening the tip of the twisted beam between his fingers. "This is *madness*. You can't possibly believe that your damned Motherbrain is worse than Asag'raal!"

Nyl shattered the reinforced concrete around him with exoskeletal strength, sending chunks of stone flying. They spiraled up in a whirling gyre, fouling the Ashishi's aim as he threw. Nyl ran up the thirty-foot rod as it came, his armored hooves striking sparks. And he was on the renegade clone before Abdulafia could react, claws scrabbling, twisting the *Dervashi*'s head up and around toward the sky.

There was a red star above them, growing brighter with every second.

"Why don't you *ask* them, 330? Why don't you try to explain your little moral crisis to a thing that thinks we're all *bacteria*?"

Abdulafia's eyes narrowed, zooming in, blurring behind invisible lenses. They slid and combined as he twisted in the alien's grasp, his black talons scrabbling for purchase on chrome.

And he saw.

Everdark was changing again as it fell through the atmosphere, shifting its form into something so terrible and vast that the Ashishi could hardly believe his eyes. Asag'raal itself would be hard-pressed to create a greater horror… though Abdulafia only knew its name from the memories of Technician Nyl.

Colossus.

Surely it couldn't be… but the cogitators inside his crescent unit told him it was true. When that giant humpbacked form struck the Earth, it would stand as tall as the steel mountain of Elysium itself. Afia could only imagine the kind of impact such a thing would cause… and he knew from Nyl's memories that it wouldn't care. Hells, snuffing out life was its entire purpose!

"There, you useless ape!" roared the Technician, throwing 'Afia aside. "*That's* what I was trying to save you from! You, and my own kind, and ten billion other races. Have you any idea how many civilizations those things have devoured? Have you any idea what it means to be nothing but a weapon in the war against them?"

The Ashishi fetched up hard against a leaning meshwork tower, the black chitin of his Saprophytic armor saving him from being crushed flat. He let loose a bolt of darkness from his hands, a tear in the materium which slit the air, screaming. Nyl was too fast, though – he slid sideways as the black lightning licked out toward him, countering it with another searing particle beam. Shattered fragments of light and shadow flew like shrapnel, carving craters into the cityscape below.

"Of course I know! That's what I *am* to you, you bastard! That's what you made me for… as a machine to fight your dirty war!"

"Oh no," said Nyl, unleashing a slim silver missile from his shoulder pauldron. "Not at all, 330. You were my favorite for another reason entirely. If you were just my mirror image, I would have hated you as much as I hate *myself.*"

The missile unfurled shimmering force-shield blades as it came on, slicing the smoky air to ribbons. It looped in, howling, to carve through the girders and wires of the tower, shearing it off to a jagged stump.

Abdulafia propelled himself up into the air as it came back through, feeling the will of Asag'raal pushing down hard on the bubble-thin membrane of reality…

"I kept you, and trained you, and honed you for a singular purpose. Kheptic blood, Abdulafia. Kheptic *purity.* I never needed the Forge to complete my designs, but it's always useful to keep a spare set of keys to a thing that powerful…"

The missile unscrewed itself in midair, becoming a glittering cloud of bolts and panels and wires. Those razor force-shields flickered out just as the hail of metal struck 'Afia's bioelectric field and flashed incandescent white. Droplets of molten metal rained down, becoming teardrops of solid chrome as they fell.

"Now Kronos' petty lords are gone, 330. Now I'll enslave damned Asag'raal, the Blacksteel – and this festering little world as well. Had Simeon Blaire succeeded, it would have been up to you to kill him."

"And now I'll send you to hell with him!" snarled the *Dervashi,* blurring sideways too fast to follow. He appeared again right behind his former master, swinging a punch which would surely have torn Nyl's head from his shoulders - if it hadn't been blocked at the last instant. The two struggled in midair, coils and arcs of black and white lightning earthing themselves against the broken towers, teeth gritted and muscles straining…

"And what would that possibly achieve?"

A flurry of kicks, all blocked, all countered.

A storm of chops and punches and pressure-point jabs, all turned aside.

"*Revenge*. For our people. For this world. For all the others you've burned up in your stupid war. For…"

His voice broke, choked with grief, even as he feinted left then followed through hard. An uppercut which left four knuckle-shaped imprints in the exotic metal of Nyl's suit for a second, throwing him clear across the west face of Elysium. Refugees scattered as his silver body sheared through an overarching swing bridge, breaking its cerametal spine. Hawsers uncoiled lazily, in slow motion, whipcrack scars flailing through concrete, bringing buildings down…

Tiny bodies burned and twisted, flying from the impact like chaff.

Say it! Say her name, you sentimental fool!" roared the Technician, soaring back up into the smoking sky. "I engineered her death, you know… I –"

But he didn't get any further.

Abdulafia may have been possessed by the spirit of Asag'raal, but it was his own hatred which made him terrifying as he hammered his traitorous master with blow after blow. Silver claws clutched at his throat. Particle cannons clicked and whined, unable to fire lest their blowback destroyed their wielder.

And the cursed Ashishi *smiled*…

This time his final strike was calculated, murderous – godlike. Abdulafia spun up and over in midair, locking his hands together to land an axe-handle blow across the alien's back. He struck with all the force of a coilgun slug, powering Nyl's body down at supersonic velocity.

Through concrete. Through steel. Level after level, into the scalding heart of the city.

'Afia knew exactly what was below them, buried under the spur of habs and towers west of the Ashishi R.T. It was Duke Gideon's Kitchen down there – the homeland of poor dead Miguel 902. And deep in the bowels of that industrial hell was a lake of molten metal; a man-made caldera deep enough to melt down battleships.

He heard the scream, torn out from an utterly alien throat. He saw the surface of that infernal lake ripple and bubble and smooth over, glutinous and sullen red. The blast from Nyl's death-plunge tore aside the clouds in a ragged vortex, letting him see clear through to the spillway, to the gates of the R.T.

They were grinding open.

Once again the Ashishim focused, forming invisible lenses before his eyes. He set himself down atop a charred and broken tower, feeling the viscous black membrane of his New Flesh bind him to its mast antenna, against the pull of the wind. And he saw her.

The Worm was laughing in his head as the whole world seemed to tilt out from under him, his bones turned to ice. There were no words. Not even a scream. Not now.

"*I think the creature meant* Jhenna, *little slave,*" chuckled Asag'raal, its voice all slick and sadistic mirth. "*But I know what you were thinking. Oh yes – I know you more intimately than she ever will, clone-meat. Still, a deal's a deal, is it not? And with the alien gone, your soul is MINE!*"

Down below his lonely aerie, down on the scarred and blackened face of the spillway they were moving. Tribes and nations from the broken ant-hill of Elysium, heading for the safety of the fortified Ashishi walls. And out beyond them, rising from the pewter-gray ocean like a leviathan… there was the Archangel Uriel, dwarfed by the baroque ironworks of the city but immense at its own right. The Kayzi had done it. Him and that mad bastard Haszan… they'd come through.

As if it mattered now.

"*Sweet little slave – how your sorrow pleases me!*" purred Asag'raal. "*And now, know this, Ashishi. You will be the one who kills her. You will be the one who kills them all. The promise of escape will only make their inevitable doom sweeter.*"

The docklands which hugged the jagged curve of the R.T. like a rind of corrosion were built from ruined oilrigs and floating platforms – sections of seaborne arcologies salvaged and tied down with a fractal web of cables, hawsers, ropes and wires. There were already thousands of tiny figures swarming all over them, and the blue sparks of gas-axes formed constellations across their blackened backs.

But Abdulafia 330 only had eyes for one amid that nomad horde.

She stood before the gates, atop the broken torso of a demolisher mekan. White-clad Vatican Knights and hooded Valle Crucis worked side by side with Ferals and *Dervashi* and megacorp wage-slaves in ragged suits all around her, but CeeAn seemed to be staring right through him, her eyes on the pinnacle of Elysium. She was pale and bloodied, her hair half burned away, her clothes reduced to rags – but she was the most perfect, defiant thing which 'Afia had ever seen. He knew that the Worm was only letting him drink in this moment, these feelings, so that they would torment him for years to come. But it was enough, for one instant. Enough that she was alive. Because if anyone in this damned city could take him down, it was that fierce, beautiful valkyrie with her broken sword and her snarl of violet tattoos.

"Are you ready to begin, my Exalted?" asked the voice in his head. And Abdulafia braced himself to resist, hoping that Cee could kill him clean, without discovering what he'd become.

But there was no pain. There was only a psionic scream, raking the inside of his skull with razors. *"No! Impossible! How can that damned thing still be…"*

The invisible lenses peeled away from before 'Afia's eyes. The cold black armor which writhed against his skin clenched tight, suffocating. And he caught a glimpse of something down in the depths, deep in the crater he'd carved in the side of Elysium.

Twenty stories down, a lake of molten steel was boiling over.

Nyl came up out of Duke Gideon's Kitchen on a writhing tangle of chrome vines; the entire contents of that vast caldera harnessed to his will. He stood perched among blades twelve feet long, serrated barbs unfolding as the metal hissed and creaked and cooled.

"You thought it would be that easy? Either of you?" asked the Technician, his armor peeled back to expose his inhuman features. "When I sold out to the Praetor, this body was the only good part of the deal."

There in his hands was the source of his power – the artifact which had allowed him to shape all that formless molten metal into a riot of razors and coils. It was the Chrome Ark, and it was still glowing red hot from where it had punched clear through the bottom of Duke Gideon's electric furnaces.

"Now, I'm sure you and your new friend the Worm have so much to discuss… what with you so obviously eager to betray humanity. But I'm a very forgiving master, Abdulafia. And seeing as my aims can't be achieved by *subtlety* anymore, I'd really appreciate your help."

His face melted and reformed as he spoke, blurring into the fatherly visage of the Illuminatus. Only his eyes remained, white-hot coals tumbling in vacuum darkness.

"*The Forge*, my Kheptic prodigal. With its power, I can turn that Blacksteel system into a sequestration device the likes of which no universe has ever seen. I can rape the living brain of Asag'raal, and bend that loathsome creature to my will!"

Abdulafia could feel the twisting decay of his Saprophytic armor churning against his skin, trying to crawl away from the ghost-light of the Ark. Before, the power of Asag'raal had been enough to keep the phantom Arkborn in check… but not anymore. Now they could feel the tension as Abdulafia fought against his possessor. And Technician Nyl knew it.

"But that's right, 330… you said it yourself. *No master.* No master to make the hard calls for you – no master to blame for all the death you've wrought. Very well. I give you the gift of free will, my child. Choose Asag'raal, and she dies. CeeAn dies, and all your people with her, by your own hands. I'll likely die too – or at least *wish* that I could. But join me, Abdulafia, and we can chain this beast, shape it, *use* it…"

"No! You dare not disobey me!" howled the voice of the Worm, as that otherdimensional horror brought all of its will to bear on the renegade *Dervashi*. His armor of shadows and blades was smoking as he brought his hands up to his face, tearing and clawing at the busy darkness there…

But the voice of his former master was relentless.

"I know what you've feared, all these years, 330. You feared that you'd been born a machine, a killer designed for war. But now you have what you've always wanted. *Freedom.*" The alien's smile was mocking, a silver grimace scarred across his face "Use it, then. Do what you know is right, and help me bring peace to this wretched multiverse."

Abdulafia had stripped away the black mask which covered his face, and now he stared daggers at the false Illuminatus.

"I may have been a fool to trust this creature you summoned, *Zeon*," he panted, straining with all his power to resist the Worm. "But I'll never be fooled *twice* by a thing like you!"

"You know the price now, Ashishi! You know how much it will enjoy turning you into everything you despise. *Traitor. Butcher.* A mere *mechanism* in its hands…"

"Then kill me," spat the renegade clone. "Be done with it, if you can. Neither of you can offer me anything better than death in battle."

"And here I thought you'd just discovered something to live for…" The Technician's face twitched into a self-satisfied smirk. "Very well. If you have no desire to live, this will be all the easier. After all, your will is all that's keeping dear Asag'raal from devouring your mind…"

The Chrome Ark spun lengthwise in front of him now, the barrel of an immense cannon pointed right at Abdulafia's heart. The Arkborn swirled around it in ragged streamers and wisps, eyeless faces howling silently.

"One last time, 330. You can join me, and stand by my side as I bring the beast to heel. You can witness the end of the great war, and use the Forge to reclaim this cesspit Earth. All it takes is one word…"

The alien's hand reached out, imploring, as actinic barbs of lightning flickered all around him, filling the air with the taste of ozone and hot tin.

"NO!" screamed the *Dervashi*, clawing at the Saprophytic stuff which smothered his skin.

And Technician Nyl smiled, a lipless gash filled with glassy needles.

"That word's as good as any, son," he said, as a keening, moaning wind began to spiral up around them both. The smoky air seemed to writhe with half-seen forms, faces and shadow limbs, eyes like winking sparks…

"After all, I never meant it as a *request*! Perhaps, if you'd paid a little more attention during your Academic years, you'd have looked into the traditions of our Vatican brothers. Into the art of *exorcism*, Abdulafia… and how it always works best on a broken will. There were tortures they had, 330, which even the Praetorian Excruciators would have found barbaric…"

Light bloomed, wide and white and hot, narrowing down to a searing beam.

It leaped from the twisted tip of the Ark to Abdulafia's brow too fast to follow, blowing apart the shadow-flesh of the Worm like a pall of ashes.

Then came the pain.

Then came a sensation like an immense weight pressing down on reality, of space and time bending like hot glass. The image of the burning city before 'Afia's eyes crazed and twisted as the Arkborn tore into his mind, forcing hot-wire roots into his bones…

"This could be a little harder than I thought…" said Nyl, squinting through a haze of acrid smoke.

Then the glassy, soap-bubble surface of existence *cracked*.

And suddenly even the horrors of Asag'raal seemed mundane…

Ω

CeeAn felt the break, as she stood between the Ashishi gates looking out across the Spillway. A fissure snaked out above her, splitting the sky with a tracery of darkness.

There were stars on the other side, cold, desolate points of light peering through the crack. The clouds of smoke which moved across it were sliced in half, like fragments of a face reflected in a shattered mirror.

That couldn't be good.

The last of the refugees were coming in now... and they were only the last because any who straggled behind them were doomed. Asag'raal hadn't taken the death of his Exalted well, and an army was massing atop the scarred concrete incline, things both flesh and metal and shadow seething from the gaping iron gates which led to the city's heart.

Atop the walls, Vatican Knights and Ashishi warriors were locking and loading their guns. Exotic weapons torn from broken warmekan were being bolted into place, and welding torches lit up the spike-studded battlements in a dirty halo.

"The Hereti.... I mean, the *Pentecostals*. They're here. They... they're asking to speak to the leader of the Exodus."

It was Brother Pious, laying his hand on her shoulder with a kind of tentative reverence. The shimmer of blue fire across her skin broke apart at his touch, haloing his fingers with cold flame.

"And... oh. You mean *me*. Not your Pontifex? Not one of your generals?"

"We're in Ashishi territory now, young lady," he said. "And you are most senior of the *Dervashi* present. In fact, they'd like a word with you as well..."

CeeAn squinted up at the fissure, following its frozen lightning-bolt tracery back to where it had begun. There were more of them, she saw, radiating out from a point like a bullethole in the sky. A *gray* sky, pewter and silver with the light of a reluctant dawn...

"This her?" said a voice behind her. "She's the one with her signature on this mess?"

"Patience!" hissed another voice... Cee picked it at once as that of SubMagus Devine, the cryo-lab tech who handled her rejuves. "We're grateful, don't be mistaken, but she's got too much to worry about without..."

"This won't take a second," rumbled another voice - one which carried definite intimations of violence.

CeeAn turned just as the two of them pushed through the crowd; a ragged pair of Subcity wastrels dressed in salt-crusted rags. One was short, dark and slim, his slight frame clad in scuffed motorcycle armor. A black jewel pulsed in a web of neon circuit-scrawl at his temple, and there was something a little unhinged about his smile.

The other was far more worrying – a seven-foot giant carrying a sword as tall again as he was. His broad and bloodied grin was far more sincere than his friend's, despite the bruises, cuts, gashes and puncture wounds which covered every inch of visible skin on his body. He appeared to be wearing the shredded remains of a trenchcoat, and a pair of overalls rolled down to the waist.

"Miss 187… that is, commander… Sir… Ma'am…." began SubMagus Devine, pulling at the strangers' rags like a small and persistent terrier. "These are the emissaries from the *Archangel Uriel*…"

"Actually, the only people *left* on the *Archangel Uriel*," said the small one, gently detaching Devine's hand from his elbow. He used the delicate, distasteful touch of a man fishing a drowned spider from his kitchen sink. "I've got a message for you, from Abdulafia 330. He says…"

Cee was at his throat in an instant, tears blurring her eyes as she palmed a tiny dagger. There were screams and cries from all around, and beyond them, the sound of vast machineries in motion, hissing and clanking as they worked.

"Are you telling me he's still alive?" she whispered, the point of her blade a mere breath from Kaito Kayzi's unblinking eyeball. "*Where the hell is he?*"

"Easy there," said the giant, flexing the fingers of his chromed-out hand on the handle of that monolithic sword. "Your guess on that one's as good as mine. Last we knew, he was on his way to the Tower…"

"Umm… commander…. I, that is…. I really think you should desist…" stammered Devine, as Brother Pious reached up and gently plucked the knife from her fingers. The Kayzi still hadn't blinked; his smile was a waxy rictus pulled all the way back to the canines.

But only for a second.

"He was perfectly all right when we spoke to him last, miss. And he wanted you to know it. All of you. He's going to disable the Forge so we can escape…"

"That is, of course, if you don't actually *fire* any of that heavy artillery that you've got sitting there armed and ready," said Pious, gesturing back over Haszan's shoulder to the floating mountain of the *Uriel*. Every gun-battery on board was trained right on CeeAn, matched against her little knife. "I hope you forgive our leader her…

enthusiasm. This has all come about quite suddenly…"

"The Forge. The Tower…" she whispered, utterly oblivious to the circle of faces all around her. She stepped back, her heart pounding in her throat. "But that's what Kronos needs. That's what it wants! All the Lords are dead, don't you see? And that means he's the last one left. The only one who can use that damned machine… and the Illuminatus…"

That made Kaito laugh. And once again Jaq thought that perhaps something of the Worm had gotten to his friend after all, through all the twists and turns of his Wetsystems run.

"Oh yes… your hallowed bloody prophet. Let me tell you all about *him*, shall I?"

And so he did. The whole story.

Ten minutes later, they were getting their bullets blessed by the Pope herself.

It was going to be a damn long, hard climb.

Ω

Simeon watched the fissure pass right through the *Stephen Foster*, then right through his own body like a two-dimensional razor. He stared, fascinated, as the fracture in reality sliced the airship in two, displacing everything beyond it three feet up and to the left. It was as if all creation was a mirrored surface, cracked into a spiderweb pattern by the blow of some immense fist.

Snapshot – *the window in his own spire-estate, thousands of tiny, hateful faces leering back at him with dead stunn-fiend eyes… Octavio Vanecke, an inch-high hologram in a desert of beige powder spilled across a black glass table…*

He laughed as the cold black flaw sliced through his skin, exposing meat and bone and glittering threads of Chimera crycelium. Three feet up and to the left, cross-section circles of muscle and bone filled out into fingers, a hand, an arm…. There was a brief and disconcerting second when each of Simeon's eyes were on a different side of the fissure - and then it was through him and moving on down the slick black bulk of the airship.

More portents. More omens and wonders.

It was just another sign that his ascendancy was pre-ordained – or that the world itself really *was* an illusion which disappeared every time he closed his eyes. These cracks, burning with cold and indifferent stars… surely they were a figment of his brittle, painfully focused mind. And when Vanecke was gone, his machines would stop weaving their scalding wires through his brain…

He would make the world better.

He would make it *perfect*.

Ahead of him was his target, fixed in the center of the airship's cockpit windows. It was a vast painted eyeball staring up into the gray light of dawn; the Sensorium of his so-called Master. Simeon gripped the spokes of the *Stephen Foster*'s wheel tight, a grin plastered across his pale and sweat-beaded face.

He had to make it through, before the madness took him. Before the sound of grinding teeth and unhinged, giggling laughter broke out through the top of his head and tore those cracks in the world wide open…

All the throttles were jammed on full. Vast props lashed the smoky air, fixing the massive vessel on its final course.

This time, there was no way that the Direktor could stop him.

Ω

Eddie Tsien sensed the fracture in reality with a pair of gravitonic distortion antennae plumbed into his spine. It unfurled above him like a crack skittering across thin ice, one tendril slicing clear through the wire of the space –'lev.

The guns tracking him never let up, though. Bullets ricocheted from his crossed arms in a shower of sparks as he ran, building up speed for the bridge ahead…

Then the fracture split off, a jagged black branch lancing down through the towers and spires, right through the thin glass causeway. Tsein caught a glimpse of cold, alien stars as he leaped clear across the span to Ground Floor One, twisting in the air to evade railgun slugs and maser beams. Suddenly every one of Kronos' automated defenses was aiming three feet higher and to the left of his actual position, saving his scarred silver armor from overload. They missed him, every one, bullets displaced by the fissure and beams bent as if through some razor prism.

Something had gone wrong with the Forge.

That was his first thought as he landed atop a multi-maser turret, punching through its cerametal shell with one fist. Ropes and skeins of wire tore loose as he spun away, drawing a line of tracer behind him.

But no – this wasn't the work of the Machine. He was atop the hub of its power now; surely if the titanic energies of the Forge were to be unleashed he would already have been blown to superheated plasma, or melted by venting radioactive gas. And while he could feel the titanic gyro-rings of the Alpha-Zero core rumbling by below his feet, their spin and mesh wasn't quickening, bleeding the Wetsystems dry...

No.

This must be the doing of Asag'raal.

Perhaps, thought the Super-Cyben, those scrawled constellations behind the flaw were its own stars, which shone down on the dead planet of its birth. Perhaps it was going to take the entire Earth down into its own dimension, the better to *feed*...

But there was no time for speculation. There before him were the gates of Ground Floor One, the citadel of Kronos. His maker. His *enemy*. And by the power of the Chimera, eating away his humanity cell by cell, he'd tear them from their hinges to reach the bastard...

Ω

Behind the yard-thick doors of Ground Floor One Kronos watched the cracks unfurl across his city. They painted the gray clouds of dawn like traceries of frost on a windowpane, and where they met they formed bubbled polygons in the sky, bent subtly out of true.

It was all out of his control now, and that was almost a comfort. Soon that beast at the gates would come through, and then...

The angelic avatar looked down at the weapon in his hand and smiled, his six eyes blinking one by one. There was a time when things like this had been the shotgun wired to his cranium; the shackles a credulous pack of apes had forged to chain his kind. Not that Kronos trusted A.I.s like itself any more than it did the human race.

Oh no. That was the purpose of the Wetsystems, after all... it was far safer to use the limited minds of the dead than risk spawning a rival to its power. The failed experiment of Mars proved Kronos right.

There were weapons like the one in his hand up above... ones built on a scale which dwarfed the slim silver rifle he held.

Yes, the agents of the Turing Institute had been right to create these things. EMP devices like these had kept the machine in check long enough for General Nathan Merrick to issue his last pathetic orders. They'd made Kronos *obey*. But now... now he was flesh and bone, all feathers and marbled skin and hot blood. Now he was actually a *he*... not just a pile of cryochilled processors and Wetsystem strata.

Eddie Tsien would finally prove useful when the Chimera consumed him. Then his fibrous steel corpse would be pliant, malleable… *hollow*. The EMP blast would strip away his mind, all the better to replace it. And with a Chiarra shell wrapped around his flesh, Kronos would be free to leave this place. Mars awaited, and its Lord Protector would be easy to enslave. After all, both the *Calenture* and *Reason's Hammer* waited in their spaceborne docks above, fully armed and operational.

The pounding on the doors had become a steady drumbeat now, a rhythmic thud of metal on metal as the Super-Cyben's fists worked away at the bolts and hinges. It was only a matter of time…

Ω

Everdark watched the cracks spread out over the city below, a spiderweb branching out from a single bullet-hole in reality. There was something down there which it knew all too well – something which it had been programmed to hate from the very first instant of its existence.

Gharfos Nyl, Hierophant Grade III.

There was no mistaking the trace-signature of a Technician of the Multiplicity, even behind the distortion of that chasmic flaw.

Everdark howled, its vast Colossus-form mouth spinning with contra-rotating grinders and saws. A trail of smoke and flame whipped out behind the Explorator system as it fell, the armor plates on its chest and belly glowing white-hot with the heat of re-entry. But despite the pull of gravity and the immense pressure of the atmosphere against its metal skin, the Slavesystem still managed to bring one of its mile-long arms around and down, training the muzzle of a vast particle cannon on Nyl's trace.

Technicians of the Praetor couldn't be destroyed… oh, unfortunately, lamentably not. But they could be crippled, and broken, and collected up later for vivisection. Deep in the armored processor core of the Explorator, crosshairs lined up and calculations fell neatly into place. The immense quantum battery array at the heart of its Colossus-form began to feed a killing charge into capacitors the size of gasoline tanks, row on row of them studding the machine's spiked forearm.

When the particle beam struck, none of the slimy little Technician's exotic weapons would be of any use. Even this latest desperate gambit, this fracture in space and time… it would avail him nothing. And without a servant of the Praetor to help them, the primitives which infested this filthy rock would be utterly doomed as well…

224

Ω

It was cold it was cold it was cold it was cold it was….

Asag'raal remembered that place. He remembered those icy stars, staring down in judgment. He remembered the suffering which was required just to hold one's mind together there… to avoid dissolution into the aching dark.

The part of him known as the Worm remembered why it had escaped, when the walls came down.

And it knew that there were still some of its kind out there, in the utter cold – things which equaled its power and which despised its weakness. Their damned nobility made them suffer, out there in the void… made them suffer for the crawling things who would otherwise worship and feed them.

Such misguided altruism, in such a harsh universe.

There was no place for it.

Was it any wonder that Asag'raal had fled, back when he was known by another name… a name now aeons forgotten? The Worm had pinched off a little universe for itself, both tiny and infinite at once, and from that dark interstice it had probed for *thin* places, *tight* places in the materium. Places where the guttering flames of sentience cried out to be fed upon…

There was no way he was ever going back there, into the outer dark. The fissure terrified Asag'raal far more than any blade, any weapon it had ever encountered. Because one of its own kind was there behind the veil, a thing which was duty-bound to exterminate the Worm.

The darkness which wrapped Abdulafia tight as a second skin boiled away from the flaw, popping and squealing, fleeing behind the only defense it could find out here in the open.

The *Dervashi* screamed as ten thousand barbed tentacles tore out from his every pore – this was how it felt for Vincenzo Vexx when his mekan Suit was ripped from his body, and it was like being flayed alive. He felt the shadows rush back like an ebb-tide, swirling and funneling away into his Operative Crescent unit. Filling it to the brim with darkness, and erasing all of his combat augmentation programs, his stored memories… his safeguard against death.

"Yes! I have you now!" shouted Technician Nyl, building up a sphere of deadly light between his claws. "All I need to crack the Forge is in your head, dear slave… there's nothing to say your head has to be connected to your body!"

'Afia's hands were burned away to skeletal claws, twitching with silver microservo. There was no way he could defend himself…

Then dawn broke behind the alien, haloing his inhuman form in blinding light. But this wasn't the sun, dragging itself up over the smoking horizon. It was a circle of intense radiance growing larger and larger as it swelled to encompass Nyl… and it kept growing.

The *Dervashi* watched as Nyl twisted his head around behind him, letting the sphere of energy in his hands shatter and burst.

"Oh, hells. Oh, Praetor's balls!"

It was nothing less than the particle beam fired by Everdark, spearing down through the atmosphere a quarter-mile wide. Clouds spun out from around it in a seething vortex, whipping the sky into sudden storms. There was no way that Nyl could dodge that incandescent blast… and no way that Abdulafia could survive it.

Oh well… he'd gotten his wish. Death in battle suddenly seemed a little like a hollow victory, though. Then…

"Key to the Forge, are you?" hissed a dripping, intimate voice behind his back. Asag'raal's presence filled his crescent unit to bursting, a cold weight lumbered across his shoulders. *"For that prize, I'll try it. For that kind of power, I'm sure you'd risk even more…"*

A wave of superheated air came down like a fist in front of the beam, flattening a circle of burning habs below. Then the hammer of light struck Technician Nyl full on, a white-hot cataclysm which stabbed down from space to core out the heart of Elysium. Half of the city's East Praefecture was torn away in a great radial shockwave, buildings crumpling and tearing like paper, bodies charred to cinders in an instant.

Clouds of choking smoke rushed through the concrete canyon streets, suffocating those who fled. And down, down, down bored the Slavesystem's particle beam, ravening, relentless… down to the very bedrock miles beneath the city, grazing the inner walls of the Geosphere which housed Kronos' Alpha-Zero heart. It only gave out when Everdark's weapon batteries were drained, but when it finally flickered and died there was no trace left of Nyl… or of Abdulafia 330.

Only the fracture in reality remained where they had stood, hanging in the air like a black and sightless eye.

Against the stars within it, something *moved…*

17 Aevum Oblivio
Vector

THE TIN MAN climbed grimly, resolutely... with all the cold determination of the machine he was. Seventeen years ago he'd missed the fight which scarred the upper city, but he'd heard all about it – the battle of the Beltway, the wreck of the Axis Mortalis, and the war on the spillway waged by the Ashishim Dervashi. There were even tales of ghostly lights surrounding the counterweight asteroid and the Cardinal Rock on that night long ago... and grainy images of vast, silent explosions as demigods clashed above the atmosphere.

Tonight it would be different. The Necrovirus was hot and ravenous in his metal skull, slowly devouring what remained of his organic brain. But revenge drove him on, making the pistons in his arms and legs hiss and slide, claws and pitons digging into the side of the central hab-core as he ascended toward Ground Floor One.

To the base of the Tower, following his very last target, Technician Zhe. The Tin Man had no way of knowing that the Praetor's servant was nigh indestructible. All he cared about was that he tried, *and went out fighting. He still had his guns, after all – twin repeating cannons recessed up along his forearms. The claws which bit into the metal shell of Elysium were only rudimentary spikes slung under their barrels.*

At last, after what seemed like an eternity, the rugged old machine reached up and hooked his claw over an ornately carved balcony rail. The Tin Man had seen the great white curtains billowing out from all around Ground Floor One when he stood down below the Beltway, looking up between the broken toroids and the shaft of the space-lev. Something was there, within the sanctuary of Kronos – something had cast open the radiation-shielded shutters of the place and let those long skeins of white satin whip out on the wind.

Whatever it was, it was in terrible pain.

The screams were almost a comfort to the Tin Man, veteran of so many dirty little wars and desperate firefights. He was in his element wherever people screamed like that – the long, torturous howl of utter agony which heralded death. Well, at least if you were lucky.

A tiny periscope-cam clicked up from the Tin Man's scarred head-dome, peering over the edge of the balcony. What he saw there was strange, even for a being which had lived through centuries in the badlands beyond the Pit...

There was a rack there, in the very center of the vast cathedral hall.

Eyeless statues looked on impassively as a bloodied figure bucked and writhed against its straps, biting down on another scream.

Kronos had given him back his face, nailed one down over the one he'd stolen. It was Direktor Octavio Vanecke, and a holographic mask floated above his flayed skull, a smiling simulacrum all frayed to static around the edges.

The Tin Man had no idea that the seven-foot angel in front of the rack was Kronos – all he knew was that the damned six-eyed freak had the right idea. The skin had been peeled back from Vanecke's skull, and a tidy cap of bone sawn away at its crown. Long silver probes stood trembling in the living meat of his brain, their hooked tips plugged directly into the pain centers of that delicate organ. Medical machinery clustered about the rack, smooth and gray and merciless. It was keeping Vanecke's stolen body alive while the angel worked, weaving wires into the poor Direktor's skin.

"I'm so glad you chose to subvert a form so ripe with crycelia," said Kronos, oblivious to the Tin Man's presence. "I helped build the Chimera... myself and Janneke Elbers, back before the war. I suppose you thought, as a second-gen, that you could fight your way through to the Forge?"

"Your precious Lords couldn't stop me!" panted Vanecke, defiant. Another spasm of agony racked his body as Kronos twisted a dial on his machines. "This...me... this is what you've been trying to create all along, you foolish device! I – the Omega! Humanity distilled, down to raw ambition..."

The angel chuckled, contemptuous, as it connected a skein of multicolored wires to Vanecke's wrist.

"Now you'll feel what I had to feel, because of your stupidity. The Wetsystems were part of me, Vanecke. The better part, to tell the truth. You know how it feels to be reduced, don't you? All those years, locked in your preservative tank. Now, imagine that multiplied a billionfold!"

The Tin Man could move quite silently if he so wished to... and the little scene in the center of the vast, echoing hall was definitely cause for stealth. It was good to know that Vanecke was getting what he deserved, but...

"No- don't imagine – FEEL IT! Now, and forever!"

Vanecke's eyes widened as the shunt came down, sending him down into the Wetsystems. A tiny pared sliver of his mind remained there on the rack – just enough of him to appreciate his doom.

But that shard was intensely focused. And it saw a flash of metal in the gloom as the Tin Man staggered, his rotting neurosystems glitched...

"Diseased!" he whispered, eyes wild "Diseased!"

Kronos leaned in, smiling, until his eyes were barely an inch from the Direktor's.

"Oh yes, Vanecke. Rotten to the Core. My Core, denied me by your idiocy. Without you distraction, without your idiot pet Blaire..."

It took all his strength to break the manacle from his left wrist, and the bones of his forearm snapped like matchwood in the process. But Vanecke was suffused with pain now, beyond *pain. The added agony was just another voice in a chorus of suffering. He reached up and hooked his bloody fingers around the angel's face, twisting it inexorably around.*

"No! Him! Diseased! My... My necrovirus..."

The Tin man's battle protocols told him that he should be shooting now. Both of these mad, blood-smeared creatures had spotted him when he was supposed to be in stealth mode. But his body wasn't obeying the crystal matrices in his head anymore. The last permafrozen remains of his organic brain were peeling away from their connections in gooey strands, making him shudder and hiss to a halt. Black, stinking fluid began to course from the joints in his biocontainment shell as he raised his left-hand cannon, its muzzle weaving drunkenly.

"Necrovirus?" asked Kronos, scrambling backward in a panic. He was suddenly all too aware of his mortal body. "Vanecke, what have you done!"

It was far too late. The noxious soup which had once been the Tin Man's brain and spine leaked through to his power core even as the machine-avatar pounded on the doors of the space-lev. That Ashishi bitch was supposed to have opened the way, clear through to the ship which would take him from this place to safety...

The explosion was tiny, compared to all the nuclear detonations Kronos had seen throughout his long, long life.

But it was enough.

When the blur cleared from his six perfect eyes there was nothing left of the ancient mekan but a blackened crater in the tiles of Ground Floor One. That, and a shatterburst of shrapnel fragments, puncturing his alabaster skin in a thousand places.

"Munitorum Necrovirus 392..." croaked the very biological, utterly mortal avatar of Kronos. "I helped create it. I helped create you all..."

The pseudocerebrate remembered, as crooked black traceries began to ramify along his veins. He remembered this room, seventeen years ago.

The dawn spilling in through a torn-open doorway, the EMP rifle in his hands…

The last thing he heard, before the pain gripped him in its jaws and took him under, was Vanecke's laughter, choking away to a sardonic death-rattle.

High up the tower, dead-man switches clicked and unlocked. Lights cycled from red to green in a tiny white room equipped with only a single black-cushioned restraint couch, and neon tubes popped and hummed as they came on for the first time in seventeen years.

It was the throne of Earth, the throne of the Forge, and it was open to all takers.

THE HOLOGRAM OF Direktor Vanecke turned his head to one side, listening to the scraping, grinding sound which echoed through his darkened mansion. At his side Darion tensed, his knuckles white around the hilt of his saber.

"He's here. He's come. And now the dying starts…"

The Sensorium dome was a ruin of shattered screens and broken bodies… the remains of Benton Veer's Celebrant elite strewn across the marble tiles. But some of those monitors were still live, showing the view from a cluster of remote cameras. Each one was mounted on the armored shoulder of an Omnivasive guardsman, and all of them were trained on the scarred bulk of the *Stephen Foster*, pulled tight to the top of the dome with magnetic grapples.

There was no sign of Simeon Blaire.

"Third unit in place… scanning for infra-red…"

"Second unit ready. Switching to rapid-fire…"

"We're going in, commander. Jump-packs are hot…"

Darion watched as four of the camera feeds dipped and blurred. The soldiers they were riding with leaped up over the matt-black bulge of the airship's body on plumes of fire, touching down atop its broad, flat spine.

"Nothing, command. Unit four, move in on the gondola. He's got to be here somewh…"

Then came a rush of darkness. A brief flash of silver erupted at its heart, licking out too fast to follow…

And Octavio was right. The dying had begun.

Simeon watched the slaughter from a calm place within his mind, letting the Chimera do its work. His rage had grown cold, now, a core of dense, seething resolve buried deep in his chest. But it was translated into deadly grace through the cipher of his combat systems, making him dance between the desperate guardsmen's bullets - and answer them with steel. Left, and a man's head went flying, sliced clean in two as it spun through the air. Right, and he lopped the arms from off another black-suited soldier, his gun still clattering and roaring as it fell from lifeless fingers…

One by one the screens winked out, hashed with static. And as each video feed died, Darion and Vanecke caught strobe-flash glimpses of a pale, mad face grinning down at them, feral and triumphant.

"Are you ready, son?" whispered the hologram, fierce pride in his eyes. "We can do this, but only if we work together…"

"I'm ready," said the Prince of the House of Blaire. "Let him come to me. I know what must be done."

Now he was through the rank and file, spinning and striking and whirling behind a mist of arterial spray. Now he was into the combat mekan which guarded the battlements around the dome, his monomolecular-edged katana hissing through steel and cerametal as easily as flesh. Eight of the monstrous things broke free from their plinth mountings at Octavio's command, vibro-sword arms slashing the air as they attacked. Eight of them fell in smoking, sparking pieces as Simeon spun low, hacking their legs out from under them. He ducked and weaved as blurring knives wove a cage of steel around him, butchering the falling wreckage before it hit the ground.

Snipers' bullets cracked and whined as they tried to trace the ravening black demon across the bulge of the Sensorium dome. But that silver blade was everywhere at once, deflecting each killing shot in a furious swirl of metal. Now Simeon's hand reached down to his belt, plucking up a handful of flat black shuriken. Now he rolled and came up swinging, three poisoned stars clenched between his fingers…

The snipers died, gurgling through gashes in their throats as they fell. Simeon had reached the cupola of the dome, the very iris of that great painted eyeball. There was nothing left to stop him.

"Hopefully that little display will satisfy his pride," murmured Vanecke, squinting up at the metal hatch in the dome's ceiling. "We have to let him think he's won, Darion. Right up to the very last…"

All the screens went dead, then, collapsing into darkness as the hatch atop the dome was heaved open. Into that black chasm fell a spidery, long-limbed shape, the blade clenched in its hand winking in the single shaft of light from above. Darion never heard his father's feet touch the ground… but then again, Simeon never saw his only son standing there in the darkness. He only had eyes for the glowing hologram of Direktor Octavio Vanecke, leaning up against the wall of the dome. A matchstrike lit up his face from below as he torched the tip of a thin black cigar, nonchalant as you please.

"Good to see you could make it, Simeon. A long way from the Jaegenn spire, aren't we?"

"And I think you know exactly why I'm here," said the Kheptarch, warily keeping his distance. He knocked the empty phial of weaponized adrenochrome from its plinth, looking around him at the remains of Veer's Celebrant squad. "I suppose these poor fools had the same idea, eh? Which makes me wonder why you still had all those soldiers waiting up top for me."

"A prudent man always knows his enemy, Simeon," puffed the Direktor. Smoke rings drifted up and out, breaking apart in that single shaft of light. "These Grief Division boys have nothing on you. Hells, they finished each other off with just the slightest persuasion." He chuckled, tapping a little ash from his cigar. "I designed you to be a little better than that. Not to say that I'm at all disappointed..."

"You never *made* me, Octavio. You think you're the only one playing the long game? My kind are *bred* to play, Direktor. You were just a stepping stone to power."

"And Leynna?"

"The poor mad bitch is probably happier dead. Imagine, giving up her own ambitions just to sire the next generation's failure..."

"Ahh, how I *hoped* you'd say that..." muttered Octavio.

Then the lights came on.

Simeon spun around, his blade coming up to guard as he sensed the raw hatred emanating from behind him. For just an instant his face was twisted into a mask of panic and fury... but when he saw who it was his lips curled into a sneer. Still, the katana hovered warily as he looked upon the face of his prodigal son.

"Don't *ever* speak that way about my mother," spat Darion Blaire, his mismatched eyes flaring like solar reflectors. In one hand he held a curved saber with a spiked basket hilt. And in the other – the rosewood cane which had once been the Celebrant Grandmaster's scepter of office.

"Damn," said Simeon. "I hate these talk-show moments. So melodramatic. You know, son, I much preferred you as a charred little corpse."

"Sorry to disappoint, but Octavio's right. You can never rule, Simeon. Not after what you've become..."

"What *I've* become? How can that even compare to the way you've been created? Kheptic purity is the core of Manifest Dogma, child. You're nothing but Vanecke's plaything."

"Like *you* are? With that Chimera infection in your bones?"

"All the better to kill you with, my dear. And him, too... when I'm done with you."

Vanecke nodded to Simeon, touching the brim of his white panama hat with his thumb and forefinger.

"Don't mind me, gentlemen. I'll be right here when you're finished."

Now father and son began to circle each other, pacing around the dusty pillar of light which speared down through the open hatchway above. Their footsteps were tiny, precise, picking their way between the dead as the tips of their swords twitched like insect antennae.

"Did you never wonder why he wanted *you* to kill them all, Simeon?" asked Darion. "Or did you think it was something as trite as *revenge*? You were built for a purpose, and I'm going to see to it that you become all the father I need…"

Simeon couldn't see it, but behind his back Octavio raised one eyebrow, shaking his head by a fraction of an inch. Darion smiled.

"I suppose you must take after your mother, then. She was a sentimental fool as well, for all her skill. And in the end this lowborn freak took her mind, just like he wanted to take mine. Just like he's taking yours…"

Another cautious circle scribed. Another fall of dust through flat, silvery light. Swords winking like glass and ice…

"Don't listen to him, Darion," said Vanecke, tilting his hat down over his eyes. He couldn't be hurt here, not when he was as substantial as smoke. "He's quite insane, now. Just like Royden, down there below us."

"You know, it doesn't have to be this way, Darion," said Simeon, a sly smile sneaking across his face. "Blood is blood, after all."

"And half of mine belongs to the House of Mendelev-Singh. The *last* of them…"

"Tainted. *Unstable*. Join me, and…"

"And what? You'll offer me a sliver of power in your shadow? You'll let me stand by while you wield the Forge?"

"I was going to say that I wouldn't kill you. But it seems that gratitude isn't one of the qualities that Octavio sequenced you with."

"Enough!" hissed the young Kheptarch, as he crossed the scepter and sword in front of his chest. "You know how this has to end, father. *Succession*… and your fall."

Simeon shrugged, nonchalant, as his mouth twisted into a rueful little smile.

"If you feel you must, boy. Let's just get it over and done with…."

The change was so swift that it seemed almost instantaneous. Simeon tasted blood - hot electrified metal on his tongue as the Chimaera took control. His every nerve and muscle fell under the thrall of its bonded battle-cogitators, peeling back his lips from his teeth in a savage grin. And the fibrous, second-gen crycelium under his skin *flexed*, making his body swell out, chiseled with impossibly perfect musculature.

He was already airborne, sword swinging in an underhand slash as he watched Darion gripped by the same fevered transformation. Those mismatched eyes bulged from their sockets as the Gladius machines marbled through the Khept-child's flesh worked their alchemy. He brought his saber around in a hissing blur to deflect the katana at the last instant, smiling.

All in a sliver of a second. As the crycelium stabilized they both became *even faster…*

There was no time for talking now. No time for any emotion, not even hatred. Blades sang and flickered as the pair traded flurries of blows, their battle lit up by showers of falling sparks. Simeon and his bastard son danced amid the broken corpses of Benton Veer's finest, but neither one lost his footing for even an instant – to do so would have meant instant death. Each movement, each parry and riposte and swing was pre-planned glacial seconds in advance… all this is a world where a single heartbeat seemed to take a geological age. Flesh and microservo were pushed to their limits as Darion pushed his advantage, using the Grandmaster's cane as a second weapon.

But Simeon had studied the uploaded scrolls of Tadashi Murai, master of the twin-sword style. He knew just how to counter it, and his own blade was quicksilver shivering in the air as he parried and stabbed, spinning out of range as his son's saber whispered past his cheek.

Too close.

He watched out of the corner of his eye as a single droplet of blood flew from the razor-cut, falling away sideways into the dark. The pain didn't come through until almost a microsecond later, shunted in on sluggish chemical receptors. By then, his Chimera system had already decided that he was now extremely angry.

On that point, they were in absolute harmony.

Rose-tinted cooling vanes unfurled from his shoulders like wings as he snarled, using all his strength to drive his son back across the pool of light and into the smoking shadows. Faster now than he'd ever been before, feeling the stress in his bones as he landed blow after furious blow on Darion's unshakable defenses…

The cut across his cheek burned him like shame.

But he saw.

Darion's own cooling system was at full stretch, cherry-red and incandescent white in the gloom. Its hellish light fell upon the death-mask faces of the Celebrants at his feet, and shimmering waves of haze rose up around the Kheptic prince, making him look like some kind of demon. He grinned like one too, his cane and saber carving left and right, snap-shot slices and butcher-strokes parried away by inches.

They broke apart for an instant, blades on guard, panting like hunting dogs. And Simeon knew what must be done, in that second. Over his son's shoulder he could see the grainy blur of light which was Direktor Vanecke, no doubt enjoying every moment of his neatly engineered little drama. Too bad that the ending was out of his control…

Simeon feinted left as his son came at him, blade blurring in overhand. But this time he didn't try to aim a counterstrike at the child's head or neck or chest… this time he struck at the delicate filigree of Darion's Gladius system, and the cooling vanes parted with a sound like brittle wires. Droplets of molten metal flew wide, hissing as they fell on dead flesh…

And the little bastard screamed, his head filling with overload warnings, strobing red error messages.

Simeon knew what it felt like. He'd suffered a coolant system shutdown in one of his training sims, and he knew what the Gladius did to express the gravity of the problem. Right now Darion's bones felt as if they were filled with liquid steel, his flesh curling and crisping away from a web of sizzling wire.

Of course, it wasn't real. But it would be, if Simeon did *this*…

Darion Blaire had no Chimera system to back up his Gladius augmentations. He was as Simeon once had been; a Kheptarch of the Razor Clique, nothing more. So when Simeon spun on the tips of his toes and brought his sword down through the last of the child's cooling vanes, there was nothing in him to prevent a catastrophic shutdown.

Darion howled with anguish as he fell, as his father finished his strike with a deft follow-through, ending up poised on one knee behind him. The blade of his katana was raised at ceremonial guard, and in its mirrored surface Simeon watched emergency thermal uptake pods bud from his son's spine like tumors. They split off and rolled away one by one, silver spheres steaming gently in a shallow lake of Celebrants' blood.

The young Kheptarch groaned. He could barely lift his face up from the sensorium floor.

"Do it, then. Finish this. Let history record that the House of Blaire died in dishonor and madness…"

Simeon turned and strode over to his son, resting the tip of his sword on the back of Darion's neck.

"There's no dishonor in victory, child. Not if there's no one left alive to contradict you. And as for *madness*… insanity is just a word, after all. A word that never applies to the victor."

"No! Wait!" shouted Octavio Vanecke, his light-woven face stretched thin with panic "We can talk about this, Blaire! Don't you see, I was only trying to build your legend! There's no need to…"

Simeon brushed him aside, pressing the point of his blade into Darion's flesh.

"Madness is just a higher level of logical process, son. One that frightens the sheep. One that they have to label, and ridicule, and crush. Madness is simply the opposite of *mediocrity*."

Blood welled up around that wicked monomolecular tip. But it didn't fall in red rivulets across Darion's pale skin. Octavio saw it, and he smiled behind his mask of light. A thin tendril of crimson was inching up the fuller of Blaire's blade, closer and closer to his fingers…

"I learned something, you see, from this fool of a Direktor. His betrayal is nothing special, for all his treachery. No, he's just another base-line sack of meat, terrified of his own obsolescence. I was born to rule, Darion. He knows it. *You* know it, down deep in your genecrafted little heart. But he calls my ambitions *insane*, to justify his own weakness. The animal inside him is *hardwired* to betray its betters, before they can become its fucking *gods*!"

The blood was over the sword's ornate *tsuba* now, branching out into tiny tributaries as it slicked across the Kheptarch's palm.

"That's why true obedience can only come from suffering. I showed Atticus Meaks the truth, but by the time I had his mind I'd broken his body. *You* however… you should prove more resilient. The pain will make you serve me well, Darion…"

But the pain never came.

Instead the Kheptarch lord screamed, letting the katana fall from his grasp as his fingers crooked into claws. Darion's blood had found the open ports in his wrists, the intra-nervous jackpoints drilled into his bones to control the Chimera system. And now a very particular infection in that blood was pumping through his veins, driven by his hammering heartbeat.

Where it spread, paralysis followed. Cold, prickling numbness sent tendrils coiling up his arm, into his chest, into his throbbing skull…

"What… what have you done to me?" he croaked, as the tiny invaders in his bloodstream did their work. "Poison… won't stop me, child. Your mother… she found that out too late to save herself…"

Darion pulled himself to his feet as he watched his father twitch and shake. The young Kheptarch was covered in blood, anointed just as he had been in the depths of the Black Palace. But this time it was Simeon who was as helpless as an infant. Darion kicked his legs out from under him as Direktor Vanecke ghosted in over his shoulder, illusory blue smoke drifting from the cigar in his hand.

"A base-line sack of meat, huh?" purred Octavio, peering down into Simeon's wide-open eyes. He couldn't even twitch them closed to block out the Direktor's mocking grin. "Afraid of my own *obsolescence*? I'm sure we can't be talking about the same person, Simeon. After all, you're the one who's just been replaced by a newer, better model…"

He tasted bile and copper. Octavio's voice came in across looping waves of echoes, hissing rain inside his skull. And across it all blurred images of cherry blossoms falling from an ashen sky, settling like snow on a field of hacked and butchered corpses. There were error messages nailed to the clouds up there, great splintered polygons hashed with static. They were warning him of a nanonic infection, some kind of counter-Chimaerical artificial virus.

"Benton Veer's last gift," said Darion, wincing with pain as he flexed his fingers around the hilt of his sword. "The Grandmaster's scepter, and its ingenious little manufactory. Octavio thought I might need to level the playing field, and so…"

"Kronos gave this thing to the Celebrants centuries ago, so they could complete their sacred duty," said Vanecke. "Not one life was to be spared. Not even those who somehow broke the prohibition, and infected themselves with something like the Chimera."

Simeon couldn't reply. He couldn't protest as Darion picked him up off the floor and set him down gently on a hovering catafalque which had peeled away from among the screens above. The silver slab sunk low in the air as the young Kheptarch arranged his father's hands over his chest, clasped around the handle of his naked blade. Just as if he was being dressed for burial...

His eyes were painfully dry now, carved from sun-baked wood and wire.

"Don't worry, father. I'll make sure it's quick. One neat little cut, and then… then you'll be returned to me, whole. You were both so important to me. You were both halves of the same person. Now…"

"There's no more time, Darion!" called the Direktor, as his holo whispered past, lighting up the ground beneath his feet. "The Surgeons are ready! We must begin immediately, or all is lost."

The Kheptic prince plucked something from his pocket, then, a bright flash of silver that caught the light as the catafalque began to move, humming on hidden motors.

"I'd ask," said Darion "if you'd say hello to Mother for me, when you get to where you're going. I don't suppose they have such arrangements in Hell, but if they do… she'll be the one who torments you."

Simeon tried to speak, but nothing came out but a rattling sigh. His throat was filled with ashes now, dry, burning tinder and choking leaves. In the boiling sky the error messages were splintering, jagged shards falling to earth all around him. On a hill, silhouetted against a skull-faced moon… there was Octavio Vanecke, laced up in his lacquered armor and his panama hat, smoke coiling like snakes from his tomb-like mouth…

Those things were coins. Half-Slade pieces, fresh-minted and glittering. The catafalque shuddered as they dropped down an open lift-shaft, down into a chasm which smelled of ice and fresh meat. Something was clicking in the background, an insect noise overlayered with a rhythmic bass throb like hidden turbines.Darion slipped a coin over his left eye, eclipsing… But then his hand paused, backlit by halogen arc lamps.

"*No*. No, I want you to *see*. I want you to know why we needed you at all."

Strong pale hands clamped down across his face. He felt ten tiny barcodes where the child's fingerprints should have been. And then he was twisting sideways, looking up at a scarred back cube with a single button eye at its very center. Just like Leynna's eye; it had a ring of metal shutters deep inside, and they razored down smooth as it focused in on him.

The clicking stopped. Just then Simeon noticed the thing behind the Surgeon mekan… the red-raw knot of flesh blinking at him from its tray of ice. Octavio Vanecke's true face winked at him, leering obscenely.

And the Surgeon unfolded in an engineered ballet of slicing, whirring tools, the faces of the cube splitting open along hidden seams to allow needles and scalpels and saws to come sliding out, glistening with oil.

"There. *There*. You see? All along, father. This is the moment you were born for. Not the Game. Not the Forge. This. The one thing Octavio could never do…"

There was a slithering sound of metal on metal as Darion took up his saber. There was a momentary sensation of cold; a thin, precise line across his forehead. Then the blade came back. He held it over his head for an instant, trembling with savage joy, his mismatched eyes staring down on a single gray one and a mirrored silver coin. In that fragment of a moment something burned in Simeon's ice-locked brain, a strange chemical urge he'd never felt before. Ancient structures in his neural network picked it up, turned it over and analyzed it even as the blade came whistling down.

And in between the sickening crunch of steel shearing through bone, and the inevitable darkness that followed, Simeon Blaire realized that he was proud of his only son.

It was, of course, far too late for him to say so.

Ω

"Don't worry," he said. "It's just that you've gone mad, that's all."

Kaito looked around himself, blinking in the light. Just a second ago…

"Wasn't I riding in an Ashishim masslifter? Weren't we headed up to the Tower?"

"Well, yes," said the exact copy of himself which sat in a low wooden chair across the room. "But you were in here all along as well. We all were."

"Oh. I see. You're…"

"We're all *us*. You. You made us back there in the Wetsystems, to fight that bloody avatar. We kind of wanted to talk to you about that."

"I thought I'd reassimilated you. Like I always do. I don't see how it's possible for you to…"

"It's the Chimera," said another mirror-image Kaito, strolling in through the arched stucco doorway. This room was horribly familiar to the Kayzi, and realization was slowly dawning as he drank in the smells of the place – sandalwood and aniseed, pepper and oil and cedar…

"You've built yourself a whole lot of personality constructs, K-One. That crycelium had no idea you wanted to do something as primitive as a Wetsystems fragmentation. We're in the *Archangel Uriel's* systems now, in the masslifter all around you… it's kind of like you're casting thirty shadows."

Kaito experienced a feeling of sinking dread as he placed the room he was in. Him and all his Chimaera-spawned doppelgangers.

"So, what does this mean? And why the hell did you bring us all back *here*? Don't you know what's going to happen?"

"Well, this is the strongest memory we all share. The process wasn't perfect, and we're not all exactly the same as you.

"We know what's going to happen. But it was important to talk to you before anything goes wrong. We think…"

"That is, *you* think…"

"That we're going to start diverging."

"*Diverging?*"

"We all started out roughly the same, despite some little differences. But now we're all experiencing different… *inputs*. For example, I'm looking after the nuclear arsenal of the *Archangel*…"

"And I'm down there at ground level in a sequestrated warmekan chassis."

"And I'm… well – suffice to say, this masslifter has quite advanced bathroom facilities."

"Anyway, you get the idea," said the first construct, the one which Kaito had named K-Two back on the Uriel. "There's only so much room inside your head, Kaito. This is already the only memory we really agree on, all thirty of us."

"You have to admit, it really stuck in our mind," put in another, leaning in the doorway. His cycle armor was glittering black instead of red, ghosted through with licks of code.

"Yes, but only because of the trauma! This place is set to burn, in case your bloody *divergence* has made you forget it…"

"Oh dear," said another of the Kaitos. "You had to bring that up, didn't you? And we were holding the moment so well…"

All of a sudden the cozy little room seemed a few degrees too hot. Just as it had ten years ago, back on that awful night when…

"*That's right, K-One. All over again…*"

The flames came rushing up the corridor like liquid, a seething flood setting everything before it alight. This was the instant when Kaito had woken up – when he'd rolled off the couch and crushed his brand new portable 'mersive rig on the floor. Down below him, something had gone terribly wrong in the hab's sub-basement. Jury-rigged and patch-welded pipes which had kept the old tenement fueled for centuries had finally thrown a valve, filling the lower levels with explosive gas. All it had taken was Uncle Jehon to light up one of his foul-smelling cigar stubs, and then…

He was off and running again. The fragments followed him, tugged along in his wake like phantoms as he busted through locked doors and dodged falling beams. Stairwells yawned like fissures clear to hell, and screams cut through the oven-roar of the flames as he swiped sweat and soot from out of his eyes. In real life he'd crashed around the hab-block in a blind panic for nine and a half agonizing minutes. It had seemed like an eternity. And the replay he was locked into was just as terrible as he could recall, a red-hot blur of stinging pain and confusion overlayered with the voices of his fractured selves.

"Hurry up and tell him! Now, before he's in no fit state to…"

"Why do *I* have to be the bearer of bad news? Just because I'm number thirty, I get all the…"

"Listen, if you don't get through to him we're all done for. You know A.I. and tissue can't cohabit. His brain's going to literally *boil* if we don't get that Chimera system out of him…"

"Too late! He's locked into the memory, now. There's no way to cut through all those neurochemicals…"

"There *is* one way. Just follow my lead. We have to let it play out…"

Panic drove him on like whips at his back. Down concrete stairs, the metal handrail scalding hot to touch. Through corridors canted crazily, smoke billowing across the ceiling in acrid clouds. On. Some doorways were solid sheets of flame, open furnaces bellowing sparks and heat. Others glowed red around the edges, or were already starting to smolder. And while he heard the screams, the sobbing, the curses, Kaito never saw another soul as he scrabbled through his little hell. His heartbeat was a jackhammer in his skull, kicking against the new scars of his wetwire plugs…

Until suddenly it froze. Kaito knew exactly what was going to happen next.

The ceiling above him split open as if the building had been gutted, dropping a rain of ashes and sparks and flaming timber on his head. Bones cracked, skin blistered and crisped – all just as real in this terrible vision as they had been ten years in the past. And just like the first time he found that he couldn't breathe; that a smoldering hunk of masonry had pinned his skinny chest and arms beneath it.

Darkness circled in, snapping at the corners of his vision.

"Now! Cut in, dammit! We're supposed to be fragments of a *hacker*, aren't we?"

"That's *silicon*, not meat! And he's flatlining out here!"

"Didn't you say this would only take a second of realtime?"

"A second of being dead won't kill him. Just hit the shunt, why don't you?"

Kaito remembered the door flying open. He remembered the hunched, impossibly huge shadow which had stooped through under the lintel, growling as it saw him trapped there. And he remembered the air burning in his lungs as those scarred hands clenched tight around the massive beam, those fingers hissing as they cooked…

He remembered the face of Jaqub Haszan staring down at him, all pain and intensity as he shifted a ton of burning wreckage, letting him scramble free.

But this time the words were different. This time the big, soot-streaked apparition hadn't thrust an extinguisher into his hands and told him that he'd either work it or see them both burn.

Jaq pulled him to his feet and hefted the thick red cylinder, wrapping Kaito's hands around the trigger grip. His own fingers were red and raw, weeping from a crust of blisters. But the voice that came out of his throat was that of K-Two, lip-synched like an old-time kung-fu epic.

"These Ashishi are cloners, K. You need them. We're giving you about an hour to live unless you get that Chimera - and us - out of your head. Until then, nobody will be able to touch you… all twenty-nine of us have got your back. But the temperature's going up. The pressure, too. If you don't call in your debt soon, we're all screwed."

The Kayzi drew in a lungful of smoky air to scream, but when he opened his eyes again the flames were gone. He was back in the masslifter they'd commandeered from the Ashishim, strapped down tight to a scarred old aluminum jump seat. Jaq Haszan was still right in front of him, though – ten years older and just as tired and bloodied.

"You allright there, Kaito?" he yelled, over the roar of the 'lifter's turbojets. "Looked like you were gonna black out for a second…"

"He's gonna be fine," said Brother Pious, leaning in to clap the Kayzi on the shoulder. "Some of us just aren't cut out for air travel, right?"

Kaito smiled weakly, trying to push the whispered voices of his other selves to the edges of his mind.

"I guess that's it," he said, wiping the sweat from his brow with one cuff. "That, and I haven't been able to change out of this crash armor since yesterday. I'm starting to smell worse than I feel – and that's a big ask."

"Allright, people! Eyes front!"

The voice cut through the cabin of the masslifter like diamond wire, choking off a dozen tense and huddled conversations. It belonged to the *Dervashi* who'd volunteered to lead this little suicide mission – an Ashishi veteran by the name of Rugal 301.

"Our objective, ladies and gentlemen, is to critically damage the Forge. Team one – that's myself, the two Templars, Celene 282 and our Clan Ghaurak friends – is to proceed down from Ground Floor One to the main heat exchanger core. We're going to plant three small antimatter devices around the Alpha-Zero containment vessel as a last resort. Spirits willing, we won't need to use them. Team two – Pious, your Crucis-men, and the Subcitizen's Militia Commandos – you're going to subvert fire control, capturing Kronos' automated defenses. We'll turn them on the Saps, and hopefully buy enough time for CeeAn to complete the Exodus. Which leaves team three. You're going to try to take the Forge before Zeon does. Kaito, you're the last Wetsystems Operator at our disposal, so you're going to prevent Kronos from reconnecting with the Forge controls and shutting it down. Haszan, you're his offside – keep him safe until we have our people in position. You've got a six-man team for fire support, and a viral bomb which will scramble the entire Forge control system. Nobody will be able to touch that thing when you're done with it, Kheptic blood notwithstanding."

As the *Dervashi* spoke he stabbed out at a shimmering holo-globe with a tiny laser mounted in his signet ring, slicing into a ghosted green model of the Tower.

"If we don't get a regular ping back from the viral bomb's deadman switch, we'll know that team three has been compromised. At that point teams one and two will attempt to disengage, and we'll blow the antimatter charges. By then, we sincerely hope that Cee has done her job and the Exodus fleet is well out of the way. Our munitorum specialists from the Vatican tell us that those things pack one hell of a punch, and they'll core out the city down to the waterline."

Rugal stood back as the globe collapsed in on itself, green light slithering across his blue-black skin. His teeth were sharp little points of steel as he grinned, racking back the bolt on his immense drum-fed micromissile cannon.

"Any questions?"

The motley assortment of Feral warriors, Ashishi battle-clones, Subcity commandos and Vatican Brethren were all grim and silent as they checked their own weapons, from hand-axes to fusion carbines. All except Jaq Haszan.

"Just one, 'vashiman. *What the FUCK is* that *thing?*"

One of his chrome fingers pointed up through the canopy of the 'lifter, through the streaked and dirty plastic bubble which housed its upper chainguns.

Rugal's mouth fell open in terrified astonishment. Surely it couldn't be that *big*…

Turbulence hit as the flight crew saw it too. Strobes flickered red as g-forges hammered the combined strikeforce down into their straps.

Up there, falling in like a white-hot star, trailing smoke and flames behind it like burning angel wings… it was the Slavesystem Everdark, on its final approach to planet Earth.

It wasn't going for an easy landing.

Ω

See it from above.

From up here, Elysium is a dirty copper coin floating on the pewter sweep of the ocean, a single ember beneath a pall of smoke. From above, there are no towers and spires, no shattered habs tottering drunkenly down the slopes into the sea. There's no great smoking crater where a particle cannon drilled down through a thousand armored stories, grazing the sarcophagus heart of the Forge…

The only subtle warnings are the cracks in the air, skittering out from over the West Bay like spiderwebs of darkness. From up here, you can't hear the screams, or the crying, or the curses.

But there's something coming which can.

They made it feel right at home.

Everdark spun on its axis as it fell, its great spindly arms held out cruciform, each one more than a mile long. Its fingers fanned out, glowing cherry red from the friction burn of re-entry. The Slavesystem pointed its armored feet as it plunged toward the ocean, straightening out its hunched spine into a ramrod of spiked steel the size of a Kheptic megatower. Abdulafia had been quite correct – the thing would stand slouching as tall as the city, it's knuckles dragging on the R.T. docks while its eyeless face stood level with Ground Floor One.

And now it struck.

It was almost beautiful the way the sea curled back in boiling veils, sending up a mile-high tower of white foam. The tight bass-string of the space-lev hummed and shook as Everdark's feet hit the seabed, and everywhere throughout Elysium buildings shattered, rubble shifted and flames leaped skyward.

245

Then the wave came up over the East side of the city, sliding over Vatican and Aryan territory in one great hungry heave. Billions of tons of water shifted like a salt-gray mountain; it rolled across the R.T. slow and unstoppable, snuffing out the fires which burned there. Saprophytes and human beings alike were swept away, tumbling end over end in the dark water to break and twist and die.

Asag'raal felt their pain and knew, behind a heady rush of satiation, that its own butchery had been utterly overshadowed. What's more, all that destruction was purely accidental. The thing from beyond the stars hadn't even borne them any particular malice – its victims were just in the wrong place when it slammed down into the poison sea.

But now it was moving. Now it hunched its shoulders forward and lurched toward its prey.

Everdark's head sat low between its hulking pauldrons, and its arms dragged down in the ocean depths, knuckles scraping the bottom. A cloak of steam blasted from the twin rows of vents gaping in its back-carapace, bleeding off the heat of its fall. Nevertheless, the ocean around it was boiling, fat bubbles fluttering up to pop and hiss about its waist. There was a kind of grim, implacable monotony about the way it slouched forward, bringing one great hand up out of the water to grip the keel of the Aryan battle-barge *Kormorant*. Those fingers were as thick around as the great ship itself, and three times the length. When they hinged shut the battle-barge was crushed down to a twist of burning scrap in an instant, its magazines and fuel tanks spurting orange flame from within the Slavesystem's fist.

Guns opened up from among the wreckage of the eastern slope, and from the Pit where walls of water scoured the dam-faces clean, falling away into the turbine chasms below. High explosive shells popped and cracked around the immense gray bulk of the alien machine, but it paid no attention. Human weapons were nothing but the sting of sandflies against its armored hide… all of them but the Forge itself. And that was the prize its masters desired – the means to turn this whole planet into a staging point for the Motherbrain's endless war.

Up in the masslifter there were curses and screams as the pilot banked in hard, coming past the thing's blank face so close that Kaito could have reached out and touched it. A long burn of chaingun fire rattled off of the Slavesystem's carapace, and tiny brass shells whipped out in their slipstream like chaff.

"Look! There!" said Pious, pointing with his long telescoping staff. "Those are its sensor clusters – on either side of its head! Aim for them!"

Sure enough, there were three smaller bulbs of gray metal nestled in beside the Slavesystem's neck, each one sheathed in black glass. They rolled and shifted as the monstrous machine brought its arm up out of the water, sighting along the back of its hand...

"Clear!" yelled one of the Subcity gunjacks. "That's a damn particle cannon!"

Gravity fell away as the 'lifter went straight down, an elevator with its cables shorn through. And out of the corner of his eye Kaito saw a flicker of purple fire crawl down the impossible length of Everdark's forearm, slithering like storm-lightning between rows of capacitor studs.

A section of the eastern city turned to boiling ion vapor then; a tunnel cut through habs and facs and understructures down to the concrete core of the Forge. Another cloud of superheated steam chuffed out from the ten funnels in the thing's back, and hidden engines inside its arm screwed the spent capacitors back down, locking them in place with magnetic bolts.

From the Slavesystem's stance, this was going to be the sum of its strategy. Unassailable, it would keep hammering away with its particle beam at the core of Elysium until it cracked. And then... Kaito was no expert on the whims and strategies of aliens, but he was fairly sure it wasn't going to leave without sequestrating the Forge.

He'd seen the state that Kronos was in now.

Mad, crippled – *disconnected*... There was nothing but dumb brute machinery standing between all takers and the means to remake the Earth.

"And I saw a beast rise up from the sea... with seven heads and ten horns..." muttered Brother Pious, working his rosary with trembling fingers. "It all makes sense now. The Dragon Asag'raal. The False Prophet of the Ashishim..."

The masslifter dipped and slewed across the sky as a wave of heat came rolling off the molten slope of Elysium.

"Rugal! Rugal 301!" shouted Kaito, pushing himself up from his harness with one hand. "That thing's here for the Forge as well! And if we go for Ground Floor One, I think it's gonna realize what we're up t..."

He never got to finish.

Kaito followed the direction of the *Dervashiman*'s horrified gaze, and watched the Slavesystem's other hand come up at them like a scarred metal moon, eclipsing the glow of the dying city. The pilot was fast – no doubt about it – but even he could barely dodge the lazy swipe of a hand the size of a stadium coming down on them at close to the speed of sound.

Kaito's world went into a flat spin. He could see his feet hanging out the open side of the 'lifter, dangling over the seething face of the spillway a mile below. He could feel Jaq Haszan's chrome-shot hand clenched tight around his upper arm, saving him from a very final powerdive into CeeAn's battle line.

But most of all, he could hear the voices in his head – the chorus of other selves which were slowly, surely levering his living brain apart. This time, they were all in absolute agreement. And they were pretty pissed off.

"Exactly how fast *is* this thing, Captain?" he asked, as gravity changed direction, punching him back down into his acceleration couch like a bag of aching meat. "I mean, when it's actually flying level?"

The pilot was an Ashishi veteran who'd only gotten old by never, ever trying to push the limits of jury-rigged R.T. ordnance. But right now he was just about as mad as the Kayzi – nobody tried to swipe *him* out of the sky like a damned bug! At least, not twice…

"Well, son… if the shields hold out, this thing's as frictionless as a teflon raindrop. If they fail, though… you might as well be riding a brick."

"But," said Kaito through gritted teeth "How *fast is it*? It's kind of important that you tell me right now…" Because *right now* was three 'right nows'. One up above the city, with the Slavesystem's glassy black eyes lining them up for a backhand. And two down below, in the oily, salt-crusted darkness of the *Archangel Uriel*…

"That's the point! If we give too much power to the engines, there'll be none left for the aeroshields. What exactly do you need to outrun, apart from that big bastard's hand?"

The black jewel set in Kaito's temple pulsed as he looked up at the pilot, his eyes rolled back to twin slits of milky white. Bright orange circuit-patterns slithered across his skin for an instant – and then his eyes snapped back into focus, burning with manic intensity.

"Just *these*, Captain. Check your radar."

Up in the overstuffed flight-couch of the masslifter the gray-dreadlocked Ashishi did just that. And then with a little sob of terror he cranked the throttles of his ramshackle bird wide open…

Ω

Darion waited outside while the Surgeons worked.

That wasn't to say he didn't *watch*… the translucent plastic bubble which surrounded the machines was like a shadow-puppet theater, one populated by insect-limbed devices slaving over the body of his Lord Father. Now and then one of the black cubes would tear something loose with a shuddering crack, and blood would spatter in fractal swirls across the hanging plastic. About half-way through the procedure a long, many-jointed pincer came snaking out and tenderly cradled the severed head of Octavio Vanecke.

Darion was quite sure that his mentor winked at him with one sightless eye before his mortal remains were added to the Surgeons' masterpiece.

For a long time there was silence behind the screens – silence but for the slow drip of blood, and the rhythmic beeping of massed life-support units. The Surgeons had finished their work, and now they were all folded up again, four featureless black cubes locked together above the operating table. The figure beneath them didn't move for a very long time. If it wasn't for the rise and fall of its chest in silhouette, Darion would have thought that the ancient machines had failed.

But oh no – they'd been given plenty of practice for this very special procedure when they were in the employ of Emmanuel Third Lancaster. If anything, the neural interface had been far easier to patch together this time; thankfully, the donor body had only two arms, legs, eyes and hands. Someone had taken great pains to soften it up, as well – the Surgeons would almost have sworn that this specimen had been grown and trained to fit the Patient's living brain like a glove…

Now he was complete. Now he was ready to *arise*.

Darion watched, breathless, as the shadow behind those bloody curtains moved. First a single hand, then an arm - then it was levering itself upright, twitching and shuddering as pipes and wires pulled taut and snapped. The young Kheptarch gripped his saber tight as the thing which had once been Simeon Blaire moved, reanimated…

Those twitching fingers found a stainless-steel side-table stacked with bloodied clamps and forceps. Pans of disinfectant and needles clattered to the floor as the hand quested blindly, running down its prey.

Ahh, yes.

A mirror. An old gilt-framed hand mirror, dripping with cherubs and vines. The figure behind the curtain brought it up to its face as it swung its feet out off the gurney.

And it began to laugh.

It started as low and oily chuckle, bubbling up from inside. Soon it was a full-throated cackle of triumph, unhinged and wild, reaching its peak as the shadow brought the mirror down in a hammer blow, shattering it to splinters.

"Darion. Son. I am… whole!"

The Kheptic prince took a step backward as that dark silhouette staggered upright, clawing aside the curtains as it came.

"Finally! After all these years, I have my chance! I *feel* again, Darion. I can feel the Chimera in my bones, calling me to power…"

Darion's mismatched eyes widened. It was Simeon Blaire, reborn. And it was also undeniably, impossibly *Direktor Octavio Vanecke.*

The thing which confronted the young Khept was pale and naked, its alabaster skin shot through with wires. And though its face was clearly that of his poor Lord Father, it was animated from within by a different will, twisting those familiar features into an expression which was utterly alien. Darion could see the purple scar where his monomolecular blade had sliced open Simeon's skull. A technicality of law, as if Kronos cared now…

But he had slain his father. It was *succession*, not Khepticide. And now the Surgeons had given him a new sire, a mentor worth following.

"I can smell the fires, Darion. And I've seen the face of our enemy. We only have one choice." The new Octavio stalked over to a row of hooks on the wall and pulled down a black Omnivasive jumpsuit, a once-piece riotmesh overall with inset panels of armor. "I was never a believer, son. Manifest Dogma was just a tool to keep the scum in line. But tonight… tonight we need the Forge. I want to make you a world worth ruling over."

"It exists. I know it does! It calls to me, Father…" stammered Darion, suddenly all too aware of what he'd done. The thing which faced him possessed the finely-honed body of a Kheptarch killer, and a mind as cold and implacable as an ice age. Fear and respect warred in his heart as he looked deep into the creature's eyes.

"I can hear it now, son. In this flesh, through these senses… yes. I *believe*. And together, we will have its power." The Direktor cinched a crossbelt tight across his chest, reaching into a recess in the wall as hidden mechanisms whirred and hummed. With a click of oiled springs the hilts of two long, curved swords snapped out, their scabbards glistening like tar. "Those demons down below can gorge themselves on peasants' blood. And Kronos… I'll take great pleasure in erasing that fool machine's mind, piece by piece…"

"But Octavio… Simeon…" began the young Kheptarch. "What if Kronos denies us the trials? What if it finds out who you really are?"

"Do you really think I've come all this way not to die trying?" asked his father. "And I'm not Vanecke any more, son. Not Simeon, either. No, it's time I had a name that's a little more *telegenic*. Even gods need marketing, boy, and don't you forget it!"

He pulled the twin *no-dachi* swords from their recess with a single smooth motion, reveling in his new flesh. The long black scabbards spun in his hands as he stepped back, bringing them down over his shoulders where magnetic clamps secured them in place.

"This is the first day of your godhood, Darion! You're going to be quite the celebrity. And the people will know the enforcer of your will as *Akheron!*"

Above them, the ceiling of the operating theater was grinding back, splitting open along hidden seams. A long steel tunnel rose up into the dark, with a tiny speck of gray dawnlight at its far end.

Up there, above the clouds… that was the way to the Forge.

But first, they'd have to fight their way through to Ground Floor One.

Akheron smiled.

This was going to be the most fun he'd had in *years*.

Ω

"You have failed me, my Exalted. Failed to bring me the head of that meddling Ashishi bitch – *failed to feed your God!* Can any of you give me a reason not to devour you where you stand?"

It wasn't a good time to be a servant of the Worm. Asag'raal had poured his essence into the great effigy of flesh and metal they had built for him, called down by the prayers and chants of broken-minded slaves and the screams of tortured captives.

When the eyes of the vast idol cracked open a lava-glow of balefire washed over the high priesthood. Cries of rapture twisted against howls of anguish to form a dark symphony beneath Elysium.

But the God had not been pleased with his subjects. No doubt Asag'raal's defeat in the dream-world of the Wetsystems was part of it. And the sickening shift through the outer dark, through that cold, hateful place he'd sworn never to return too… that had been even worse. They'd called him here – *called* him, like some errant mongrel – when he was between realities. Now Asag'raal would have to take matters in his own hands, and leave the delicious self-loathing of Abdulafia 330 for later.

Ahh well. Suffering was where you found it.

And the best way to start with a rabble such as these was always to make an example.

"M…master! We beg of you! This body we have built for you… does it not prove that we serve? Are we not your loving children, born of the New Flesh?"

Perhaps such groveling would have pleased a lesser deity. But Asag'raal didn't give the Exalted time to finish his explanation – he scooped up the unfortunate creature in one huge fist, delighted by the way his new fingers hinged shut, barbed with jagged steel.

The Exalted was still screaming his praises as he bit it in half, spattering the crowd around his makeshift throne with black blood.

"Bless us, great Lord!" gibbered another of Asag'raal's slaves, scuttling forward on all fours. "We have asked for your favor for the harvest to come! The Ashishi tries to flee, but we will crush her!"

The great idol chewed stoically, grinding its metal teeth in the half-darkness. They'd built him a body from the dead – a bloated thing stitched together from corpses and shot through with steel. A crown of rebar spears radiated from his head like a black starburst – each one was surmounted by the still-living body of a flayed sacrifice. All in all, they hadn't done a bad job. And with their God among them, there was no way that those tiny insects on the Spillway would be able to escape.

"Are my faithful ready? My Saprophytes? My Exalted and their machine-slaves?"

A hoarse cheer echoed through the dripping chamber where Asag'raal's mortuary throne was built; warriors hailing their master. This place had been a great underground foundry, long left to rust and ruin. Now it was packed wall to wall with abominations, their eyes glittering like witchfire in the gloom.

Abdulafia could wait. After all, the sickness was in his veins now. He'd reach the Forge on his own, and at the last moment… oh, yes! There was no pain so sweet as that which followed on the heels of victory…

"We will gorge on their dead! We will flay their skins for our banners! This world belongs to me, now, and to my beloved child. When you are witness to his birth, know that our dominion began *here* and *now*!"

With that, the idol moved.

Ten thousand bodies slithered and ground together as the vile thing shuddered upright. Ragged scraps of shadow coiled around its titanic arms and legs, binding them up as it stooped below the rusted ceiling, its ponderous head surmounted by a crown of agony.

"To war! To ruin! We will conq..."

And then Asag'raal staggered. The whole city shook, grinding deep below with the sounds of tectonic anguish. The Exalted wailed and moaned, pitched to the ground as Elysium was torn open...

It was Everdark's particle beam, shearing down through the onion-skin layers of the Last City like a white-hot blade. It ripped open the deep chasm where the Worm's faithful had mustered, peeling back steel and cerametal as if they were paper. It was only a grazing blow, but it laid bare the gray dawn sky – and the hulking, inhuman silhouette against it.

By all damnations! These machines were nothing but a vexation – first Kronos, now this alien device... the sooner this world was purged, the better!

Killing was the answer.

Killing was the *only* answer, ever.

But deep in its rotten heart the Worm was troubled. Why couldn't it all be *simple*? Teeth through hot flesh, butchery and prey... *that* was its reality. The mind it had lashed together from fragments of human desires couldn't comprehend a thing like Everdark – but part of Asag'raal could.

"We built things like that, once," soughed a memory so old that it was barely a ragged whisper. *"When we were like angels, and the universe was our plaything. Before the heat-death. Before the outer dark..."*

And that was what worried him. In his own twisted-off little appendix of a dimension Asag'raal was God. But he remembered the outer dark. Sliding sideways through it, just then... that had awoken memories, sending them bubbling up through his soul like swamp-gas through tar.

The Worm was sure it could taste one of its brothers here. One of the hated ones who waited in the darkness...

It was tied up with the Ashishim girl. Asag'raal knew it.

And the alien machine... well, soon his pawn would grasp the Forge. And then even a Blacksteel Colossus would seem quite inconsequential.

See how easy it was? Just give your mind over to the pounding of the war drums. Let them rumble in your blood, driving flesh and bone and steel upward toward the light. Soon it would be dying time again – *feeding time*. And that was the only logic which Asag'raal truly understood.

17 Aevum Oblivio
Wrong Side of the Bed

THE SLAVESYSTEM EVERDARK had sealed the broken windows shut. CeeAn knew that it wasn't for her own convenience – in fact, she was fairly certain that neither the Blacksteel or Nyl needed atmosphere to survive. No, it was all for the benefit of the single human specimen hanging semi-defrosted in his open cryo-coffin. A man who CeeAn recognized from the night of the Exodus, and from a statue fifty feet high carved from the rock beneath Aggartta.

Kaito Kayzi.

Down below the crazed picture-windows in the floor the Earth was painted in sweeps of watercolor ocher, dun and dirty blue. Elysium was right beneath her feet, an empty shell since the night she'd led her people home. But now… now even the Exodus seemed like it hadn't been enough. She'd been waiting for the false prophet to return ever since that night seventeen years ago… waiting for the mask to slip from the face of his impostor disciple.

Now CeeAn stood in a bubble of glass and metal high above the atmosphere, a place which smelled of ozone and sweat and chemical ice. She'd dreamed of this moment since the battle of the Spillway, and now that it was here her hope was tempered with cold anxiety.

This had to work. It just had to.

Cee wasn't here for victory, or honor, or even for survival. She was here because of the cryo-coffin next to the Kayzi's – a glass and metal pod crusted with dirty ice. Inside it she could just make out a very familiar silhouette.

There was nothing in her way now. The trick she'd pulled, injecting herself with the trace of Nyl and his pet Slavesystem… it had seemed almost too slick, too easy to possibly succeed. But she was far too grateful to ask inconvenient questions. Not when the lights on the face of that cryo-coffin cycled from red to green under her touch, and the glass cleared to reveal a face she'd looked at every day for seventeen years, remembering.

Oh yes.

Simeon Blaire was this man's clone, a perfect match down to the very cells. But Simeon was the counterfeit. Just one look at the cruel razorcut of his Dervashi tattoo, the tiny crows-feet at the corner of his eyes… this was the genuine article.

And with the blood of Kheptarchs in his veins, Abdulafia 330 would prove to be their savior. He could use the Forge to scour the war-fleets of the enemy from the skies...

They were there below the glass, painted in above the roiling clouds like strokes of India ink. Living voidships, the Multiplicity Order of Battle come to fight their war on Earth. Cee didn't need to be told that their foes were out there too – some of the Praetor's fleet were damaged, listing and cracked as thrall-creatures worked feverishly on their wounds. The largest of the voidhunters were up above the Cardinal Rock, capital ships too large to sink down into low earth orbit. To the Dervashi they were like an infestation, a plague to be excised with fire.

CeeAn's breath misted on the glass as she brushed her lips against its cold surface. Only minutes now, and he'd be back. There'd be time to erase all of her regrets before they went together to unlock the Forge...

Down below her feet, in the tapering claw of metal which anchored the Cardinal Rock to the Earth, Technician Nyl smiled inside his crystal prison. He was no exoethnologist like poor young Zhe – he was a tactician, and that was why he was still alive at all. Rule number one was always to make yourself indispensable to your superiors, but the little-known rule which Nyl lived by was number forty-nine – make yourself indispensable to your enemies *as well.*

Gravitonic sensors wired directly into his brain picked out the tell-tale signatures of his masters' voidhunters as they tore through the Aematerium above the Earth. He could even taste the shadow of Kataphrakt-Commander Yrr Bosphasian himself, the pompous old halfwit! Soon the Blacksteel would join them in battle. In this place, where the universe was as thin as a sheen of oil on water, he would bring together all the pieces necessary to fulfill his plan...

But of course, it would never do for his future thralls to see him like this. No, it was time to throw off the illusion of helplessness which had gotten him this far.

A pair of spiked fists lashed out left and right, staggering his guards back before they could draw their weapons. Crystal shattered, blasted away in a glittering shockwave.

And as their hands went for hidden holsters in their jumpsuits Nyl unfurled a pair of energy fields from his forearms, fashioning them into blades. Two pistols fell apart in the Dervashi's hands as the Technician landed, poised on one clawed hoof.

Good. Now they were angry. Perhaps this would actually prove entertaining...

There was a blur of black and red as the two humans pressed their attack, a flurry of snap-kicks and punches which all failed to find their target. Nyl reached out and neatly broke one man's arm, feeling his radius and ulna snap with a clean and brittle sound.

Sloppy. Fast, but unprofessional. His fingers found pressure points here and here and here, making the other warrior cough up a mouthful of blood. Good luck fighting with punctured lungs, thought the alien as he spun away, toying with his foes.

Neither of them were even close to the skill and ferocity of Abdulafia 330. Perhaps it had been his warrior genetics, or the illegal modifications Octavio Vanecke had sequenced into him at birth. Perhaps it was the subtle psychological torture which Nyl had used to keep him balanced on a razor's edge of anger.

Whatever it was, these two didn't have it. And that tiny prick of regret made Technician Nyl angry.

The two Dervashi were desperate now, fighting for their lives. But the damage was done. Nyl's whole world went into slow motion as his lips pulled back from a piranha grin. His hands became blades of chrome behind a blur of shimmering force-fields...

There was a brief flurry of movement.

There was a sound like wet cotton being torn into strips.

And as the Technician landed, his hands splayed out to his sides, the Dervashi warriors simply fell apart, as surely as if they'd been kissed by the wires of the Eversio. Arms and legs and neat cross-sections of bone and meat slithered down as Nyl cracked his knuckles, frowning.

All he wanted was peace. The noblest of aims; a gift for all the universe. Soon it would be within his grasp, and the great war would be over. Still...

There was part of him which would miss this feeling. He wondered if it was the last growl of the animal in him, the thing which remembered bone-flutes beneath the trees on a planet with purple skies. It didn't matter now. Looking back, the Archivistorians of his empire would remember nothing but his rebirth. And the form he'd inhabit after it was done... well, it would be as far beyond the silver skin of a Technician as could be imagined.

"WE HAVEN'T FOUGHT a battle like this for centuries," said the Pope, blowing a vast cloud of cigar-smoke through the command tent. "But the Vatican remembers. We endure. And we learned a few moves from that tricky old Saladin, back in the time of the First Crusades."

"You mean we have to fight them without *guns*? How the hell are we going to even slow them down before they swarm all over us?"

This from the leader of the city's surviving Confederates - a bald-headed old veteran with a wrestler's physique and a black eagle tattooed across the dome of his skull.

"They aren't as good at *fighting* as they are at butchering women and children," said CeeAn, pointing out across the spillway with her half-no-dachi. "We've got every clan and nation of Elysium represented here – some of the finest warriors the world's ever seen."

"So what if we usually fight each other?" called out a Celestial guardsman near the back of the throng. "Do we have to help those skinhead bastards if we see them getting eaten alive?"

Cee scowled, scanning the faces of her little army.

It was impossible to fit everyone who wanted a say into the little army-surplus tent. There were just too many factions represented in the Exodus; too many voices to run this game as a democracy. And they were under the hammer no matter how they cast their votes, because the hordes were coming.

"You're gonna be too busy for that today," she said, leaping catlike up atop the table. This put her face to face with Pope Joan, who was still wearing her massive carapace armor. "We don't have time for doubt, or arguments, or rivalry. Today is what it is. We're fighting so that the people we love can escape."

She couldn't help thinking of Abdulafia, then. *He* hadn't escaped. He'd gone to the very heart of the disease, to face the thing which had killed her once already.

"We know they hate iron, and we know they want us to fear them. So most of you are going to fight in spear phalanxes, using the rebar pikes we're grinding sharp for you now. The Vatican Knights will take the right flank, Clan Ghyre, your warriors will hold the left. Me and the Dervashi will take the middle, and we'll be the last ones to fall back through the gates. Remember – this is a delaying action. We don't expect to win… just to stay alive."

As far as inspirational speeches went, Cee had heard plenty better. But it would have to do. Because now the hand-cranked klaxons were howling, and the sound of fear and panic echoed up from all around them. Cee and Joan had pitched their command tent behind the vast shuffling mass of the refugee horde – close to a million people trying to fit through a crack in the Ashishi gates. Black Technologists stood at the portal, scanning each and every one of them for infection.

The battle-line of the Exodus was strung out behind this mobile shantytown of tarps and bags and milling humanity – the last able-bodied fighters winnowed from every faction and clan in the city. They were ranked up ten deep in places, armed with long sharpened stakes of rebar, ancient longswords, machetes, axes and spiked clubs. Here and there makeshift banners were raised high – bedsheets and plastic mats spray-painted with the names of Hab-blocks, manufactoria, sub-tribes and religions.

Behind them, on the walls, any warm body who owned a weapon had their own crenelation, slit, turret or merlon. A spiked profusion of muzzles stood out against the gray dawn, giving the top of the Ashishi battlements the look of a thorny crown. They'd hauled up every piece of artillery they could scavenge, and manned them with wounded soldiers and civilian volunteers.

In the end, it might not be any use. There were far too many Saprophytes ranged against them, a whole ragged nation of them advancing slowly across the incline. When they reached the over-arching bridges which led to the Iron Basilica, Pope Joan turned to the chief of her Black Technologists and made a curt signal with one hand. He nodded, opening a jeweled cask and bowing down on one knee.

"*It doesn't matter*," Cee heard the warrior-pontiff whisper under her breath. "The rock of our church is wherever we go. *We will endure.*"

And with that, she reached into the cask and pushed a button.

The walls of the Iron Basilica were strong; after all, the place had once been a great barbican fortress, dominating the western dam-top in defiance of the Ferals below. But there were five more armored Seraphim down beneath the domes and spires of the Holy See, and each one was powered by a fission micropile.

The blast vaporized the great central cathedral from its cupola to its foundations, carving a crater down through a hundred sub-basements as steeples blazed and shattered. Still, the great ring-wall of the barbican had been built expressly to withstand nuclear warfare

– superheated flames mushroomed up from them in a vast eruption, rolling out flat against the belly of the clouds. Those reinforced walls cupped the explosion like the barrel of a vast bombard, creating a pillar of raving fire.

Thousands of Asag'raal's slaves died in that instant, Exalted and Saprophytes together reduced to dirty smoke as they screamed. The howl of anguish which went up from the hordes on the spillway was sweet music to the warriors of the Exodus, but it was far from enough. Especially when they could finally see the linchpin of the horrors' advance; the hulking form of the Worm's avatar itself.

CeeAn pushed her way forward through the ranks of the *Dervashi*, right at the center of the battle-line. Combat diagnostic programs flickered across her augmented eyes as she reached the front, calculating trajectories and arcs of fire…Closer. They had to be just a little closer…

There was no way that gunfire alone would put these things down. But a massed barrage might slow their advance, and open gaps in that seething black wall of nightmares. Two hundred feet. One hundred… now she could see individual demon faces in the press of flesh, rotting eyes and lolling tongues, needle teeth glistening wetly in the light of dawn…

"NOW! FIRE!"

CeeAn called the thunder. And from above them ten thousand guns opened up, sleeting withering fire against the foe. Everything from hydrogen maser blasts to ancient cannonballs plowed into the Saprophytic line, mowing down their first ten ranks in a spray of carrion and black blood. Arms, legs, heads… nameless pieces flew wide as shards of bone and tooth and claw became scything shrapnel, and damned souls fled their bodies.

But they didn't falter. All that the horrors feared was their master; they had become their own worst nightmares, and death was just an escape. At the heart of his horde the loathsome avatar of the Worm laughed, shrugging off the barrage with contempt.

And now the killing started.

Cee heard the war-cries of Clan Ghyre as those fierce warriors met the enemy head-on, swinging morningstars and spiked chains, axes and metal pipes studded with nails. It was one part execration and two parts dirge, that slaying song, and it meant death. The Ferals had the hardest job of it; fighting uphill out of the Pit, holding the flank where the slipperiest, quickest Saprophytes tried to outmaneuver Cee's battle-line. To her right the Vatican knights held the top of the spillway, few in number but nearly unassailable in their scarred mekan-armor. Knights of the Temple, Crusaders and Furies, Arcanii and Sacristans, hewing into a tide of shadows with blades and hammers and armored fists.

A second barrage tore apart the smoky air as the guns on the wall above her picked their targets and let fly. It didn't matter that any Saprophyte not utterly shredded by the blast was able to stitch its oily flesh back together – the guns carved openings in the line of battle, allowing CeeAn's defenders to slice deep into the ranks behind.

But this barrage never reached its target.

Cee felt the world shiver, flesh and stone and steel pulled tight and thin. A heat-haze shimmer came down across the spillway, slowing time down to a crawl like a massive hit of the 'chrome. But this came from Asag'raal's cadaverous avatar, squatting amid its minions like a toad. And it slowed each and every bullet, each shell and energy beam to a standstill.

"Watch and learn, little human. You can tell my brothers that I sent you, when you reach the outer dark…"

Its voice screwed its way into her brain with a feeling like pulling teeth, and an oily chuckle came in on the same wavelength. It was meant for her alone, and Cee knew exactly who the Worm meant by its 'brothers'. The suspended ocean above her rippled as the heart in its depths began to beat – the sound of a war-drum in her blood.

Time came back, for her at least. But not for all those glittering shells and red-hot fusion blasts hanging in midair between the two armies. The laughter in CeeAn's head clawed its way up the scale to a screech as they blurred together, energy and heat and mass shuttling and switching as though the laws of physics had taken a sudden leave of absence. She tried to move as the avatar brought its hands up above its head, fingers fashioned from entire severed arms cupped together…

The force of it slammed into the back of her head like an iron bar, dropping her to her knees. But she saw.

All that molten, bubbling metal was gathered into a sphere above the battlefield, kept aloft by the will of Asag'raal. The vile thing's bioelectric field made hers and those of her *Dervashi* look like pitiful candle-flames before a supergiant sun, bending outwards, swelling, *splitting…*

"Hold your fire! For the love of all your gods and ancestors, *don't shoot!*"

But it was too late.

The avatar brought its hand down in a chopping motion, sending the sphere flying. It struck the warriors of Clan Ghyre head-on, roasting a score of them alive in a heartbeat, then splitting apart into a quicksilver wave. Wherever those deadly droplets landed flesh charred and scorched, wringing screams from those who survived.

Tears blurred CeeAn's eyes as she spun back to her feet, slicing a pair of saprophytes in two. Her *Dervashi* bodyguard were right behind her as she cut a deep notch in the Worm's line of battle, their panga knives and giant two-handed *kukri* tearing through black ooze and rotten bone in a whirling dance.

There was no way that she could make it to the center of the horde.

And even if she could, how could a handful of *Dervashi* hope to hack the bloated head from Asag'raal's shoulders?

CeeAn supposed that it really didn't matter. The Magi of the Ashishim had been trying to convince her that death in battle was the only honorable path for decades… now they were going to get their wish. The shadows lengthened and darkened around her as she left her warriors behind and pressed on. But rather than becoming more difficult, the slaughter she was orchestrating among the Saps seemed easier with each passing second. It wasn't until they hemmed her in on all sides that she looked up, and saw that she wasn't entirely in the world anymore.

The spillway was still there, but it was hazy and indistinct, like a badly-tuned threedeeo feed.

"He really isn't my brother, you know," said a voice all around her. *"It's an honorific which he's not really entitled to anymore. Not after his fall…"*

CeeAn spun left and right, her broken sword up at guard. But there was nobody there… just the washed-out phantoms of the Saps all around her. The edge of her sword went through them like smoke.

"Part of them is in another world. That's why your conventional weapons won't destroy them," sighed the voice, a choir singing every tone at once. *"The one you call Asag'raal turned his own terror in upon itself, and made himself a universe alone. Not yours, where he feeds… and not ours, which is already dead."*

CeeAn watched the speaker push through the hazy forms of the Saprophytic horde as if they were veils of mist, cobweb-shimmers knitting back together as it passed. The creature was tall and thin, its body all squat and round in contrast to its long, angular limbs.

Four furled wings depended from its shoulders, and its face… CeeAn couldn't focus through the light which streamed from the alien's countenance. She caught the vaguest of images, deep in the well of light; strobe-shots of people she'd known and loved - people long dead.

"*We are the Harvesters,*" it said "*At least, that is the best description in your language. We felt that 'Reapers' had the wrong connotation, but it may be slightly more accurate. We exist to take the patterns of the dead into our own great Seed.*"

"Why…why are you telling *me?*" asked the *Dervashi*, bringing her sword up to shade her eyes. "Isn't this the kind of thing more the Pope's department?"

The Harvester smiled (or at least, a blur of imagined faces inside its actinic halo did), pointing one impossibly long arm up at the sky. Above them hung a suspended ocean, rippling with the reflection of flames.

"*You helped us break the rules. You would not enter, but you would not hesitate. You* touched. *And we know a loophole, human, when we see one.*"

CeeAn remembered what lay beneath that quicksilver surface. Billions of dead voices, calling out in a million dead languages for her to join them…

"*What you saw was one of our machines. There is no supernatural… only science you have yet to comprehend. We are no different. We only seek to build.*"

"Then why do you want our dead? What the hell right have you got to…"

"*We could let them dissipate. We could let them be gone into the dark. But we have seen the end of days. We have watched our own universe fall to heat-death and dissolution. We would build a new one, but not alone. We desire your… input. It is a worthy cause.*"

"And Asag'raal is one of you? Is all *this* part of your worthy cause?" Cee knew that she was walking on the far side of madness. Hells, this was probably all just some kind of terminal delusion, a brain-spark as she bled out. But there, again, was the cool-headed certainty of the pre-deceased. This was just as real as she wanted it to be.

"*He is… I believe your word would be* apostate. *Certainly renegade, but with undertones of abomination… Yes, apostate it is. It requires much suffering to exist in the place between. We cannot enter the worlds which we tend and harvest from, because of the cracks.*" The alien traced the line of one crazed fracture through the sky with its claw. "*Asag'raal doesn't care. His mind is gone, and all he knows is hunger. We would kill him, if we could."*

"So I suppose you're going to tell me it's *my* problem now. Well, that's sweet of you, but I was already trying to hack the bastard to pieces before you dropped all this metaphysical bullshit on me."

"Oh, we can see that. We can also see that you have only a 0.3419 percent chance of actually succeeding. But as I said, human... we know a loophole when we see one."

"So what, you're going to give me some of your power? Some kind of alien super-weapon?"

"Think of it like this, CeeAn," said the Harvester. *"Right now, your world is like a plank, flat on the ground. When our dear Brother hammers down on his end, nothing happens at the other. If we stood at the other end and applied the same amount of force, we'd drive the whole plank down into your planet's core..."*

"In the metaphor, or in reality?"

"Both. Probably. Anyhow, what we can do is become the fulcrum in the middle. Then when Asag'raal's end goes down..."

"MY end goes up. Right?"

"Right. All you have to do is feel it. I'm sure your primitive warrior instincts will take care of the rest."

"O.K, so what then? What about rest of the city?"

"I'm afraid that this place is lost, human. Those cracks aren't getting any smaller. And when one of you tries to use the Forge... well, I believe a suitable analogy in your parlance would be 'like a fireworks display in an oil refinery'. Messy."

"We could use the Forge to seal the cracks! We could use it to destroy Asag'raal entirely!"

"Have you got any idea what drives that thing? Your Kronos is using exactly the same postmortem bioelectric patterns that we harvest, and if they all come through at once, with our Brother forcing the gateway open... this whole universe will unravel. No, we'll teach you how to STOP the Forge. So long as Asag'raal lives, it would be suicide to use it. Worse... your kind don't even have a word for murdering an entire reality."

"So that's it? I just go in there with my little sword, cut your big bad brother to pieces, and you carry on harvesting the dead for your science project? Pardon me for asking, but what's in it for me?"

"You're dead, CeeAn. We sent you back. What's in it for you is... you."

She ran up against that one, hard. Obviously these things, these

Harvesters, knew leverage just as well as they knew loopholes.

"Just try to stay alive for the next forty seconds. We're about to arrange a coincidence for you."

"So you do those as well? Anything else you specialize in?"

"Yes," said that harmonic voice, laughing all the way up and down the scale from subsonic bass to a glass-and-wire squeal. *"We also take care of star-crossed lovers. Tell Abdulafia we said hi. After all, we want to build a whole world from your memories. Input from other perspectives, you know. It wouldn't do to make it boring…"*

Cee was sure that the storm of faces at the center of the alien's halo winked at her just then.

Just before the sky collapsed in on itself, and the misty wraiths around her slicked back over hard and black with needle teeth. She snarled, bringing her sword around in a vicious cross-shear that met the suddenly substantial flesh of a Saprophyte halfway through.

Forty seconds, the thing had said.

She just hoped that its coincidence was going to be *spectacular…*

Ω

"Well, here's something I never thought I'd get to do," said one of Kaito's electronic shadows. "Check out the slipstream! If we were real, that wind-shear would be peeling us like grapes!"

Another fragment-Kayzi stood off to his right, surfing the bright steel back of a cruise missile. He rode with nonchalant ease, as though piloting a multi-megaton tactical nuke like a longboard was something he did every morning before breakfast.

"Just concentrate, Eighteen. This is a very delicate operation…"

"Delicate like a sledgehammer! I just hope Big Ugly appreciates the effort I've made."

"Yeah… about that…"

Number Eighteen was dressed, for no discernible reason, in an old-fashioned pilot's g-suit and a Stetson hat. His boots were polished alligator, with spurs the shape of tiny atomic trefoils.

"Philistine. No respect for the classics."

"Showoff."

"Well, remember who we came from. Not exactly mister subtlety, right?"

"Just shut up and fly your missile. We've got to give that thing the mother of all enemas…"

The two rockets carved in low across the boiling sea, their stubby wings almost slicing into the wave-tops as they banked hard left.

There, ahead of them, was the colossus-form Everdark, a nimbus of electric fire playing across its particle-cannon forearm. Twin roostertails of spray glittered behind the fragments as they triangulated attack vectors, priming their deadly cargo.

"Yeeeeeee hah!" shouted Eighteen, waving his outsized cowboy hat in the air. "Here we go!"

Ω

"What in all hells have you done?" shouted Rugal 301. "*Nuclear weapons?* Are you out of your tiny little wire-fried mind, Kayzi? We'll never get clear of the blast radius in time!"

The big Dervashi was hanging from a pair of rails, his muscles straining as merciless g-forces pressed in like the jaws of a vise. Up front, the pilot of the masslifter was praying on automatic, mumbling invocations as he pushed the throttles to overload.

"It'll be fine. Trust me," said Kaito, pushed deep into his acceleration harness "The *Uriel* scanned that thing as soon as it could… we were lucky it was on the other side of the Pit. The whole damned shell of it is *hollow*."

"And that means *what*, exactly? It's still big enough to crush us like a bug!"

"Oh Lord, please make our deaths both swift and painless," intoned Brother Pious. His face had turned a delicate shade of green as the 'lifter spun crazily across the sky. "Deliver us from our tribulations, unto the kingdom of heaven…"

"I think I see what you're getting at, K," said Haszan, levering himself forward with the cold gray blade of Grief. "Not so tough on the inside, right?"

"Well… we're about to find out any seco…"

"NOW" said all the fragmented shades of Kaito inside his head.

And behind them the world blazed white, burning the vast shadow of Everdark across the skin of Elysium.

Ω

The Slavesystem never saw them coming. In space, in vacuum, nuclear warheads were beneath its contempt – the weapons-system equivalent of chimps banging rocks together in the dirt. Everdark's reactive exotic-metal armor was proof against such tiny pinpricks of fire… after all, some of the Motherbrain's war-thralls could dive into the hearts of suns without the slightest hesitation.

But it had chosen this colossus-form to inspire fear, and it was just as hollow as Kaito had predicted. Everdark was nothing but an inch-thick skin, bulked out and inflated to terrify the primitive beings of this vile little planet. Up until now, their most potent weapons hadn't even been able to scratch the Slavesystem's hide.

Number Eighteen's missile caught it just behind one articulated knee-joint, bursting open in a great mushroom-head of fire. Energy-reuptake filaments pumped all that light and heat directly into its laminar battery array; more fuel for its particle cannon fist. But the shockwave from that multi-megaton detonation was enough to make the colossus stagger, its clawed feet losing purchase on the seabed. For an instant the beast's torso passed through one of those cracks in the sky, twisting it through a set of dimensional-vertex transforms even the Motherbrain couldn't have predicted.

Three feet upward and to the left.

And in that second Number Four's missile struck, splitting open into a daisyhead of submunition rockets. They shot the gap, ricocheting inside the hollow shell of the Slavesystem until their solid-fuel boosters ran down…

And then Everdark roared.

It's blank, faceless helm split open as it let loose a howl of agony and rage, a jagged-edged sound clawing its way up the register until it shook the sky. It sounded like a human scream, in the instant before it was blown apart by nuclear fire.

The Slavesystem was already trying to alter its form as the submunitions detonated deep within its heart, bypassing all that clever reactive armor, all that hard-forged exotic metal. It folded in on itself like mad, multidimensional origami, twisting and budding crystal blades, kaleidoscoping through transforms as explosions tore its insides ragged. Bright blasts of actinic flame stabbed out through cracks in its shell as it compacted down smaller and smaller, trying desperately to contain all that raving energy.

It had to give, somehow.

The batteries at Everdark's core couldn't contain such power, and it would be suicide to push them to overload. Instead, the whole great machine froze in mid-transformation, humming and crackling with sparks. The sea beneath it bellied out in a shallow concave bowl as it hung broken in the sky – half the size of its colossus-form now, a spiked triskaidekohedron spewing pillars of oily dark smoke. A charge built up within it, along the axis of what had once been its particle-cannon arm. An orifice like a metal iris spun open in its flank, glowing red-hot…

And a purple-white beam lashed out as Everdark fell, losing its grip on the sky. This wasn't a single-shot pulse, punching down into the heart of Elysium… the Slavesystem vented all of its excess energy in a spitting, sizzling arc, following the line of its fall. It carved through the Last City in a diagonal slash, severing Kheptic megatowers like stalks of wheat, razing hab-clusters and highways down to radioactive vapor.

It only cut out as the gunmetal star of Everdark plunged beneath the waves, sinking out of sight beneath a plume of choking steam.

"And as it were a great mountain burning with fire was cast into the sea…" whispered Brother Pious, his face pressed up against the window of the howling masslifter. They scudded across the sky like a seed before a hurricane, caught on the shockwave of that immense triple-blast. "And the third part of the seas became blood…"

Ω

Darion and his Master were powering up though a tunnel to the open sky when the particle beam sheared clean through Oleander Avenue, punching out the Sensorium mansion as neat and clean as an abattoir bolt-gun. A blast of heat came up under them like a great cupped hand, propelling the two Kheptarchs high into the pall of smoke which hung over Elysium's burning streets.

"What was that?" shouted Darion, the words torn from his lips by the storm-shear wind. "Kronos? Some kind of satellite weapon?"

Ahead of him Akheron spun clockwise in the air, the wings of his antigrav-pack flashing like mirrors. His facemask was fashioned into the grimace of a warrior *Oni*, but Darion knew that behind it his new Father was smiling.

"Perhaps. All that matters is that it *missed*, son. After all, we were never going back there, were we?"

Behind them the baby-blue polyprop sky of the beltway peeled back, burning. There was nothing left of Octavio Vanecke's old sanctum, but then again, there was nothing left of Octavio Vanecke now, either.

"Onward and upward, child. To Kronos, the Forge, and godhood!"

In Akheron's slipstream, Darion Blaire shivered. He knew that he'd asked for this. He knew that he'd helped Octavio become the creature he was now. But he couldn't shake the feeling that he was being used, just as comprehensively as his poor, damned Lord Father had been.

Ω

CeeAn hardly had time to adjust to reality before it suddenly went sideways on her.

First came the scream, a sound which cut through her mind like the lash of a broken bandsaw. Then came the light – fans and spikes of fitful radiance spreading out from between the towers of Elysium.

Surely there was no way that a second sun had broached the horizon, out beyond the dark silhouette of the city...

But it was true. She watched in horror as a beam of violet light came down through the upper levels of Elysium, a butcher-stroke severing towers and gantries and chimneystacks, amputating whole neighborhood-platforms where they jutted from the flank of the city. Like threedeeo, she thought, as the concrete beneath her feet began to rumble. Like some kind of 'mersive hack's idea of a disaster flick.

The glass-sheathed immensity of Duke Gideon's spire came down across the remains of the Vatican, carving a deep notch in the dam-top. Foaming gray water cascaded down the far wall of the Pit, shearing one of the great powerhouses from its face. It was too far away for CeeAn to comprehend the scale of the destruction being wrought, but the distant roar of underground turbines hitting overload came up through her feet.

All around her the Saprophytes were in disarray, scrabbling back toward the bulk of their master. Up on the heights of the Spillway, where the gates of Elysium yawned open, they were trying to worm their way back underground, away from the stroke of that ravening beam.

This, she thought, must be the Harvesters' idea of a *coincidence...* because most of them didn't make it.

There were only three seconds between the particle beam laying its burning lash across the Saprophytic line and Everdark falling into the poisonous Atlantic. But they may as well have been three seconds in the plasma oceans of the sun. Oily black figures burst and hissed and evaporated, blown away as twists of smoke. Thousands of them. And just before the beam flickered and died it pierced the flank of Asag'raal's avatar, making its necrotic flesh melt and run like tallow.

CeeAn figured that this was all the break she was going to get.

"Take them down! Now! We've only got one chance..."

The comms bead pierced through her ear seethed with static. There was no guarantee that any of her little army had heard her... or even that they were all still alive. So the *Dervashi* raised her sword to the battlements, signaling the guns. This time, perhaps, the crippled leviathan at the heart of the horde wouldn't be able to stop them.

A stuttering roar of cannon-fire answered her as the Ashishi defenders let fly. The reeling Saprophytes fell beneath a withering battery of fire, burned and shredded and driven back until the Avatar of the Worm stood alone at the vanguards of its army. Its scream of anguish was almost enough to throw back all those bullets and shells… but not quite. A barrage of them tore chunks from its rotting bulk, making it slump down to one side on its vast palanquin. The exalted slaves bearing that platform of steel and bones were too terrified of their master to flee – and one by one they, too, were plucked away by the hammering gunfire, sent tumbling and bleeding back across the Spillway.

"Do you really think you've won, you little bitch? You know your pitiful weapons are no use against my children…" The voice was there in her head again, cutting through her own thoughts like rusted steel. The voice of the Worm, secure behind the walls of its own twisted-off universe. *"That's right, human… destroy this piece of me, and give in to the hate! Each blow draws you closer to my embrace…"*

This time she focused her mind and struck back.

"Fuck you, demon," she sent, shouting out above the sound of an immense sunken heartbeat. "You're too late. My people have already escaped!"

"Such eloquence. I'm so very glad that I uplifted you apes from your filthy caves… what? NO! IMPOSSIBLE!"

But it was true. A fleet of tethered zeppelins rode the pewter sky above the spillway, headed inland across the Sahara. The *Axis Mortalis* led a whole diamond-fiber cloud of them, patched and scarred but still thrashing the air with its great brazen prop-fans. Camera-zeps and broadcast dirigibles tugged at a vast net of cables and ropes and hawsers, pulling along those airships which had lost all motive power. And on every surface, from gondolas to gasbag-top helipads, clung the survivors of the Beltway, some of them physically lashed down and tied fast, others depending in bunches from the web of filaments which kept Jimson Holgarth's fleet together.

As if that wasn't enough, at that moment the great gates of the Ashishi R.T. rumbled shut, slamming closed with a great tectonic boom. The last straggling remnants of Elysium were through, and all along the dam-top to the east the tribes of the Pit were moving, swarming up the sheer concrete cliff like ants. There'd be plenty of room for them all when the *Archangel Uriel* set sail – she'd been joined by a whole armada of other ships, rusted and creaking things pulling their dripping chains taut against the load. Cee could hear the sound of gas-axes shearing through cables and bolts, the repetitive cracking sound of a whole rind of metal peeling away from the flank of Elysium.

"Too bad... looks like you'll be going hungry," she said, looking around her at the remains of her little strike-force. Barely half their number had survived the Saps' first headlong charge. But they'd done what they promised to do. "Any more empty villain monologues for us, huh? Gonna call us 'foolish mortals' one more time before lights-out?"

Cee reined in the power of the Ashishi guns with a gesture of her blade, holding it high above her head. But the Worm only snarled, the face of its avatar showing a mouthful of teeth fashioned from sharpened human thighbones.

"This isn't over, insect! I will have my reve..."

"Not this time," said CeeAn... and she slashed down with her sword, letting the barrage fly.

A rolling wave of fire tore out from atop the crenelated wall, accusing fingers of flame stabbing through a cloud of drifting smoke. But even ahead of the noise came a solid wall of flying lead, shot through with the scar-bright trails of maser blasts and fusion-fire. All of it was centered on Asag'raal's heaving surrogate-body - enough, surely, to tear the effigy apart.

Then Cee felt the air grow slippery. She tasted copper in her sinuses as little sparks crawled down the edge of her blade. Time was slowing down again, great invisible gears grinding ponderously against one another in the sky...

It was going to do it again.

The world stood still.

The whole glittering impossibility of it unrolled before her like a vast astronomical projection – the gas-giant bulk of the Worm's chosen form, encircled by an asteroid halo of explosive shells. Plasma fireballs burned in place like cometary fragments as the creature's bioelectric field unfurled across the spillway, snapping taut with a ripple of heat-haze blue.

"Witness! This time, little Dervashi, *I'll give it all back to you!"*

"That's the fulcrum. Remember... when his end comes down, yours goes up..."

She knew that the two voices were coming in on different

wavelengths because of the biting-down-on-a-battery sensation as they both echoed in her skull at once. But in the end, that's what made her trust the thing which called itself a Harvester. *The enemy of my enemy is my friend... for now.*

And she could feel the backswing. She sensed the pivot and rise of her own power, rushing up from beneath her feet until her nerves blurred with strange harmonics. Wherever Asag'raal and its kin had come from, physics seemed to be as mutable as molten plastic. But here, in this universe, Newton's law was iron-bound. Now it was time for an equal and opposite reaction.

Cee looked up across a wall of winking metal.

The Worm was drawing it in to itself, sending shells and bullets spiraling down toward the gravity-sink between its hands. They flowed and melted, boiling in midair as the ball grew, a hissing, bubbling mass burning with unnatural fire.

This time, she was ready.

The power raved and crackled through her bones, threatening to burst them asunder. Every nerve was sheathed in searing electricity, crawling across her skin in jagged arcs. And as she focused her bioelectric field flared wide, a pair of invisible wings spanning a mile to each side. Their storm-front edges set up fractal vortices in the gunsmoke above the spillway, picking out the shapes of knife-blade feathers, pinions hammered out from glass razors...

They sliced through Asag'raal's field as swift and sure as shuriken through cotton candy.

Pressure built up along a pair of glowing red-hot lines in the air as that single great wingbeat ran up against the sullen ball of molten metal. Sparks flew wide, spitting and sizzling as they burned in slow motion. For an instant Cee and her nemesis were balanced, neither one able to make the final push. That sphere of bubbling silver was elliptical now, stretched out of true by the relentless vice of CeeAn's borrowed power. Sweat beaded her brow as she gritted her teeth, wrapping both hands around the hilt of her broken sword.

Then the fulcrum moved. Just a little... but enough.

"*Ooops,*" said a voice in her head, with just a hint of oily sarcasm. "*Must have slipped...*"

Time came down on them like the walls of the Red Sea on Pharaoh's army, in the old book of the Vatican. Swirling eddies of temporal spray billowed down the gullet of the Pit, lensing and warping the air. But here, at the center, it was all forge-heat and righteous fury. And it wasn't looking good for the Worm.

The Avatar's last indignant scream may have been the start of another scenery-chewing monologue, or just flat-out idiot frustration. Whichever it was, it didn't do the damned thing any good. CeeAn's mind was all over the surface of that boiling silver globe, shaping it thin and flat and sharp…

"I know what you are. I know what you want, and what you've been driven to. But don't expect any sympathy from me, demon. *Mercy*, either…"

The giant hot blade glowed cherry-red from its forging as it hung in the air above the spillway, an impossible thing fused from lead and copper and steel. It was all of a quarter-mile long, twenty feet wide – and as thin and sharp as a cruel whisper. Cee knew that she only had a second in which to use it; the Worm's bioelectric field was crumbling, shattering to pieces as its army fell apart around it. Every fraction of a heartbeat it took more and more effort to keep the damned thing cohesive, let alone move it to *strike*.

In the time it took to form that word in her mind, she had.

The red-hot blade followed the swing of her broken no-dachi – once, twice, thrice, a blur of looping forehand cuts which ended in a wild upswing follow-through. As it burst out from between the Avatar's neck and shoulder the whole thing lost its shape, scattering up into the sky as a rain of glowing shards. But the damage was done.

Asag'raal's slaves had built it a body from the remains of the dead, and only its will had kept it together. As it slumped forwards, hollow, red and black lines began to show across its belly, its chest, its great lumpen face… They were sword-cuts, core-deep and bleeding even as the whole necrotic pile unraveled and fell apart.

CeeAn was dimly aware of cheering as she fell to her knees, her sword clattering to the concrete. A huge shadow loomed over her, and hands reached out, crusted with gold and pearls.

"They'll be back," said the Pope, as the young *Dervashi*'s eyes flickered closed. "They've got us on numbers, even without their damned witchcraft. Take her aboard the *Archangel,* and prepare to cast off the chains. We've got nothing keeping us here…"

"What about the strike team? The one's who're going to shut down the Forge?"

Cee recognized the voice of Submagus Devine through her delirium… she could just imagine the little man wringing his hands in consternation.

"They knew it was a one way trip when they took off. Blessed are they for their sacrifice."

"And who's going to hold these gates while we get underway? We're taking damn near half the city with us… two hundred floating drydocks, hulks, wrecks, oilrigs on floats… they don't have a great acceleration profile, your Holiness!"

The darkness was almost complete now. Static hissed in CeeAn's ears like the sound of broken waves caressing the sand. But she knew the voice which answered Devine – it was her old Master Militant, *Dervashi*-Commander Calent Zephir 90.

"We will do our duty," breathed the dry old voice of the Academy-master. "The Ark is shattered, our Illuminatus fled – we have nothing left to live for but honor. Please… let us be your shield."

"My Knights stand with you, then," rumbled Pope Joan – not to be left out of a glorious, martyr-producing final stand against the Devil's stepchildren. "Between us, we'll hold the line."

"And our leader? The chosen?"

"She goes with you. No questions. After all, look what happened to Moses when he didn't have directions. Our map to the promised land is in that girl's head, nowhere else."

Cee tried to protest as she felt strong hands lifting her up onto a stretcher. Her fingers reached out blindly for the hilt of her sword, but some *Dervashi* or Vatican Knight had already thought about her honor – they'd wrapped the broken blade in rags and propped it up under her feet. Devine and his medics soon had her trussed to the stretcher like a spider's next meal, and she was passed from hand to hand to hand back toward a tiny postern-gate in the Ashishi walls.

Ahead, she could smell acetylene and diesel and salt; the great fleet of the Exodus was pulling up its gangplanks and shearing its final waist-thick chains. Behind her, she heard the sound of chanted prayers and whetstones on steel, the click and slide of loading guns. That was her place. There, in the middle of the coming fight. *Where Abdulafia would have been…*

But the rocking motion of the stretcher already felt like the waves of the sea. And the only one she could call out to, across the void of her own internal darkness, was the thing which called itself a Harvester.

"Did we do it? Is that thing… is it gone? Dead?"

The answer which came back from the Outer Dark rode in on a comprehensively galaxy-weary sigh.

"Our brother can never die, CeeAn. Not any more than we can, in the

sense that you use the word. But he has been weakened. His only chance now is your keeper's Forge... and the foolish human being which he's convinced to be his ally."

Then the darkness crested and crashed down like a wave on Cee - smothering any worries about what that made *her*... By the time she awoke, they were far out at sea, and Elysium was nothing but a smudge of drifting smoke on the horizon.

Ω

The Worm Asag'raal, Blackest Destiny, The Devourer in the Pit, Son of the Dark Star (etc, etc), had never been a happy creature. In the dim sediment of memory which stirred in its soul it recalled being a morose and gloomy Harvester – scornful of the high aims of its fellow Universal Architects.

Postphysical and sublimed? Pah! Just another cliquey little society with their long-winded speeches and their venality skinned over with words. They'd seen the end coming, and chosen to ape the Gods they'd stopped believing in - around the time they discovered science. It wasn't a democracy. Asag'raal (or whatever musical, lilting, and ultimately meaningless Harvester name he'd once owned) had been *pressganged* into saving the multiverse from becoming cold particulate soup.

Well, fuck that.

Prolonged exposure to the feeble agonies and comical pleading of his prey had brought a lot of personality back to Asag'raal. Every second he remembered more... back beyond discovering a whole species of vulnerable cave-dwelling hominids with a cruel streak a mile wide to play with. Now the beast had given way to the witch-doctor's deity, which had in turn blossomed into a very sullen, very resentful Harvester-Apostate indeed.

Not a small part of his anger was directed against his Brothers' cats-paw... CeeAn 187. But, having assimilated a reflux-inducing amount of information on human emotions during his latest atrocity, Asag'raal was pleased to know that his mortal instrument was the focus of her affections. Betrayal, he'd found, was a rather interesting little game.

That's why he let her run. *Run as fast as you can, little human... when the chain snaps tight, you'll break your own neck.* And in this case, the chain was none other than the proud, stupid and pathetically honorable Abdulafia 330.

Asag'raal would have the Forge, this toy that the thing which summoned him lusted for so badly. Then… oh, then he'd accomplish something that even his pious freaks of Brothers hadn't imagined… he'd make himself a new homeworld, here in this nice, weak, comfortable universe. Deep biological parts of the Worm (which Asag'raal's mind piggybacked on, like a monkey straddling the back of a dinosaur) had already prepared for this.

He would spawn. But not in any kind of sloppy, genetically-driven or altruistic sense. Think of it more as a sloughing off of dead skin…

His new self would be right at home in the multiverse of Earth. If early reports were anything to go by, war, death and chaos were here in vast supply.

Oh, and a few other little issues would be taken care of at the same time.

Item – a lingering, hellish demise for one Gharfos Nyl, a.k.a Illuminatus Zeon of the Ashishim.

Similar for Miss CeeAn 187, meddling bitch *ne plus ultra* and puppet of his erstwhile Brotherhood. All he had to rely on was that Abdulafia remained confused and angry, and killed anything he got his hands on.

To the mind of the Blackest Destiny, that seemed a pretty safe bet.

Ω

Up in the Ashishi masslifter there should have been cheers, wild applause… perhaps even a kind word or two for Kaito as Everdark collapsed into the seething cauldron of the Atlantic.

And there would have been, if the shockwave from his desperate nuclear attack hadn't sent them spiraling across the sky like a fleck of dust through a jet turbine; a groaning, vomiting tube of tight-packed misery. Rugal at least had anti-spin dampers drilled into his inner ears. But even they were pushed beyond their limits as their pilot cursed and prayed, making the engines of his baby howl. There seemed to be a lot of chanting and incense smoke coming from the back of the cabin, where the Valle Crucis had strapped himself to the wall, cruciform.

When the laundry-drier tumble of the craft permitted, Rugal could see out one of the port-side windows, to where the force-shield wing of the 'lifter split the air. Sometimes it was actually visible as a sky-blue hash of lightning, but at others it was hardly there at all. Those instances synched up far too neatly with periods of sickening free-fall.

It took time – nauseous, hellish minutes, in fact – but eventually the masslifter settled into a flat curve, halfway between the sea and the clouds. Rugal took his bearings from the pillar of smoke rising out of the east… they'd overshot the city by miles as they tried desperately to stay out of the water. The big *Dervashi's* combat-boosted optics zoomed in, but there was no sign of Everdark. Only a tiny speck of white fire arrowing up out of the ruins of the R.T., silver winking in the morning sun…

It was coming closer. Scratch that – it was coming right at them!

"Evasive maneuvers! We've got a missile incoming!" he shouted, desperately trying to link to the Ashishi datanet. But with the whole R.T. empty, he couldn't trace the weapon's payload, its origin, its speed…In the end, he didn't have to.

"Does that thing have arms and legs?" asked Kaito, craning over Rugal's broad shoulder.

"I'm sure those are actually guidance fins," said Brother Pious, forcing himself a space at the window. "If it is a jet-trooper, he's way out of safe landing range. Hope he can swim…"

"We're picking up a transmission from the incoming hostile!" chipped in the co-pilot.

"Impossible! There's no way that thing can break Ashishi encryption!"

"He's using our open band! And he says…"

But they'd never find out what the co-pilot had heard. The silver-armored figure came down on them hard, putting on a final burst of speed before its clawed chrome hooves smashed through the masslifter's canopy, crushing the man's chest with a sound like kindling-wood.

Technician Nyl covered the interior of the little craft with a pair of large, sleek and hissing cannons as he ducked in through the hole in the front canopy, completely ignoring the horrified stare of the 'lifter's pilot.

"Time for a brief detour," he said. "Or were all of you going my way already?"

17 Aevum Oblivio
Popcorn

Technician Zhe clung to the shell of his new Devilfish with every claw he possessed – and that was quite a few. The vengeful voidhunter tore through a thick strata of gray-green clouds, purring with ecstasy as it felt sweet acceleration for the first time in more than a century.

But it wasn't the sheer speed and ferocity of the Devilfish that Zhe was most interested in… the creature was locked tight to the Multiplicity net through a set of needle-probes deep in its tiny brain. Usually the net would be utterly silent this far from Liquid Space. But not now. Not today.

Zhe heard the screams of doomed Menials and Excisors as they broke clear of the cloud layer, spinning clear in the thin atmosphere. He caught the savage howls of Ogres and Bastarnae as they hacked their foes to scrap, the clipped, clinical tones of Captains and boarding-craft Agha… and behind it all hummed the immense, hot elation of the Multiplicity's ships-of-the-line, overjoyed at the sensation of battle. Unfortunately, it didn't look like they were winning.

As the Technician watched, a great Dracorex U.O.V grappled with the hulk of a Blacksteel cruiser in the upper atmosphere, pressurized green blood hissing from a thousand wounds across its broad carapace. The Unnecessarily Offensive Vehicle was spawned to take down whole platform-cities in the storms of gas-giant worlds, and its saw-tipped tentacles had crushed the waist of the Motherbrain's thrall down to a twist of ruin. But the cruiser was far from finished – its own scourge-whips were out, pulled tight around the Dracorex's shell, slicing through it with monomolecular bandsaw edges.

The Praetorian warship screamed its defiance as they both fell, powering down toward the unseen mass of continental Afrika below. Seconds later a roiling cluster of fusion explosions gutted the belly of the clouds… and that was only the nearest skirmish to Zhe's position. All across the scarred globe the sky was slashed by lines of incandescent fire, smart torpedoes and particle beams weaving a tapestry of death.

Kataphrakt Yrr Bosphasian was outnumbered. He'd been relying on the sheer brutal firepower of the Geocore to hammer his foes into submission, but he'd been comprehensively played.

Now it had come down to dirty, savage ship-to-ship fighting… and that was the Unity's specialty. Sure, the Praetor's Order of Battle were the meanest, most bloody-minded creatures ever gene-sequenced, but even they needed help to breathe in vacuum. On the surface of a planet the Multiplicity could run rings around the lumbering mekanik soldiers of the Motherbrain. But space was home to the machines. And they pressed their advantage with precisely calculated viciousness.

It was all food for the Worm.

+ Soon to find the Traitor! Soon to crush and
kill and devour! +

The Devilfish was picking up the harmonics of it through their umbilical nervebridge bond. Zhe had been touched by the thing he'd called the Worm; tainted and infected as Nyl used him to incubate his new hybrid form. Now he could feel the damned creature flexing and coiling its bulk behind the paper-thin wall of reality. The pain of a million deaths was quickening the Worm's pulse, re-awakening it from the torpor it had fallen into after the Exodus, seventeen years ago.

All through the Aevum Oblivio it had been starving. Today, with mountains of flesh and steel crashing down to Earth like fallen stars, it was able to feed.

Just as Nyl intended.

The renegade Technician wanted to serve as midwife to Asag'raal's spawn, and infect it with his mind. Zhe would have thought the whole plan utterly mad – if Nyl hadn't already corrupted the Explorator Slavesystem Everdark. After that, it was all just a matter of good timing and luck.

"Klaeroc, instigate attack protocol 9-17," said Zhe, narrowing his eyes against the glare of maser blasts and antimatter detonations. "Take us in to the Tower. I want to cut right through that Slavesystem… and Gharfos Nyl as well!"

Around the leading edge of the Devilfish's shell a corona of blue fire began to flicker and coalesce – the voidhunter was projecting its energy-field ahead of itself in the form of a blade. When they struck, they'd be traveling at a significant fraction of lightspeed, with all the tonnage and ferocity of a vengeful liquid-space predator built up behind that razor edge. Nyl's signal burned red in Zhe's augmented vision, a trace moving through the corridors of the Cardinal Rock toward the cryo-lab…

The first thing he'd do was kill Kaito Kayzi once and for all. Next, he'd snap CeeAn 187 in half. And then… then the Forge would be right under his thumb. And this time it wouldn't be for show. It wouldn't be a double-cross like last time, an illusion to get under Zhe's skin. This time it was the REAL Gharfos Nyl walking the cold vaulted halls of the Terminal, in the flesh. And when he actually had the Forge at his command, he'd fuse his mind to that of the Harvester-Apostate Asag'raal…

The Praetor was going to be pissed. If there was one thing which the nigh-immortal Lord of the Multiplicity hated more than anything it was plausible competition.

"Not much time left, buddy. Better take what you can before your little friend puts me out of our misery."

The frozen shade of Kaito was there with him as he looked over his shoulder, standing atop the shell of Klaeroc as through they weren't clipping mach five in a vertical spin.

"I know I'm just a conduit, but hells – half this stuff I didn't even get to see myself. About now, in your little omnibus, I was trying not to throw up and keep my head from splitting."

"So what did happen to the other thirty-one of you? You seem pretty sane – by human standards."

"The big freeze, compadre. My meatware's thawed out much faster than the parts of me in silico, thank goodness. All it means is that your buddy Nyl's gonna speed up the inevitable… if I ever get out of this tank my brain's gonna melt like butter."

"Always the optimist," drawled Zhe. "So, have you got anything else for me? I still can't figure why you were frozen in there in the first place! You got pretty close to the Forge to be iced at the last moment…"

"Hang on then, Technician. This last part's the good one. Hope you've got some popcorn on that thing…"

The Kayzi wasn't kidding. Compared to the multiplex origami of images which had been sleeting through Zhe's skull for the last four hours, this final jagged chunk of data was immense. Around the edges of it Zhe watched the Archangel Uriel pulling away from the Ashishi R.T, dragging a web of chains taut and dripping from the black ocean. A rough sliver of metal came loose with it; a floating island made up of hulks and rigs and barges teeming with refugees.

In front of the R.T. gates a wave of resurgent Saps broke over Joan Theophraxes and her Dervashi allies. She went down with a defiant prayer on her lips and another Exalted dying under her cruciform battle-hammer. Up above, Jimson Holgarth's airborne escape-fleet winked signal mirrors and tight-band lasers down to the Uriel, plotting a course for Aggarta. CeeAn slept below, while up on the heaving deck of the double-sub a man named Devine was already sowing the seeds of her sainthood.

The images came faster and faster, blurred together into a spiked ball of light and shadow. Saprophytes rushing through dank subterranean corridors, a flood of living darkness. Out of the ocean on the far side of Elysium, a hand the size of an aircraft carrier scrabbling across the steel shore. Fires and panic. A man stranded on the shore, backlit by flames… Zhe watched him put a pistol up to his temple, laughing, and then…

"And then it all came down to the tower," said Kaito. "We all knew what was coming up after us. And those who'd made it to the final round… well, by that point, we had nothing to lose."

Zhe scowled as they looped out wide, pulling into a tight orbit to build up speed. It all came down to the Tower this time as well. But this time it wasn't just a motley little crew of human beings ranged against Technician Nyl.

"Show me quick, Kayzi. I'm about to drop the curtain on this thing."

The specter laughed, exhaling twin plumes of cigarette smoke from his nostrils.

"Well… I'd ask 'you and who's army'," he said, with a fatalistic shrug to the scattered space-battle all around them, "But you seem to have that part covered, at least."

A rosette of violet fire shone through his phantom body as yet another Unity battleship burst apart, a short-lived and spectacular little star. His smile was a cold as space itself.

"Trust me. You'll need them."

2196 Ante Arbitrium
Major Arcana

THE GREAT CIRCULAR hatch of Ground Floor One came rolling and grinding toward Kronos like a gear sheared from some immense war-engine, clawing a gash in the gilded mosaic tiles behind it. Those ten tons of reinforced steel should have been his last line of defense - instead the pseudocerebrate barely had time to leap out of the way as the door slammed through a row of statues, showering alabaster shards like shrapnel.

Eddie Tsien was right behind it.

The Super-Cyben was almost entirely consumed by the creeping infection of the Chimera now. Only part of his face remained; a diagonal strip of human flesh clamped between burnished chrome. *Snarling lips, one scarred cheek, a single camera-irised eye...* nothing else remained of his humanity. And to judge from the way he'd pitched that vault door like a discus, the transformation had only made him stronger. Now he came raging through the shattered doorway, streamers of bladed crycelium flaring out around him like wings. The fibrous crystal-metal rippled and flared in silver ribbons, slicing through plastic and stone with disturbing ease.

"Come and face me, Kronos!" bellowed Tsien, smashing his knotted fists into the floor. "Come on, you coward! I'll..."

"You'll *nothing*," said the Guardian Engine, alighting from his perch up amongst the statuary trees. "It's only a matter of time before you reach the tipping point, Lieutenant. Then you'll be nothing but a mad, doomed intellect trapped in a metal shell..."

"That should sound familiar, Kronos. In fact, it's a fair description of *you*."

"Perhaps. But I'm afraid that the irony's wasted on a mere *machine*. Especially when I'm trapped in this meat-sack body of Lancaster's design..."

Tsien cocked his head to one side, squinting at the pseudocerebrate's angelic form.

"I'd trade you in an instant – even with the wings. But I promised myself a little satisfaction before this whole city comes down in flames. Sorry."

Kronos smiled as he circled warily around the Super-Cyben, cradling a sleek and threatening slab of steel. It was an ancient thing – a weapon from before the *Aevum Iudicio*'s wars of judgment.

"It's funny, really. A few hours ago, this cannon wouldn't have been able to touch you. It was made to kill the likes of me, you know… when the human race was still able to make their own decisions."

The battle-cogitators fused to Tsien's spine had picked it, and he spat out a bitter little laugh.

"An EMP rifle? I'm not even going to bother asking where you found such an *antique*. It's not going to do you any g…"

But Kronos wasn't waiting for his enemy to finish.

The snarling angel pulled the trigger, unleashing a bolt of magnetically charged iron filings in a core of superheated plasma. Tsien was fast – inhumanly, impossibly fast – but it was Kronos who had made him. He knew the Super-Cyben's limitations, down to a micrometer scale. Even so, three of those coiling streamers of crycelial ribbon whipped around the barrel of the EMP rifle a second after it fired, slicing it to pieces. Eddie had learned that trick from the Eversio, and Kronos dropped the weapon as it went critical in his hands.

At the same time, its storm of magnetized iron punched clear through Tsien's armor, laying bare his metal ribs.

There was still flesh and blood inside him, but it was desiccated dry, mummified under steel. The whirring pump of Eddie's mekanikal heart forced black and syrupy liquid through his veins, coiled tight around skeins of sparking wires… Because the Chimera had completely recreated him from the inside out: next to his piston-driven heart nestled a tiny tokamak torus, feeding laminar battery strips between his ribs.

Just the kind of systems which the EMP was made to destroy.

The Super-Cyben's face froze in a grimace of pain as he ground to a halt, his hands crooked into claws reaching for Kronos' throat. The angelic machine crept forward between a tangle of saw-toothed silver ribbons – streamers of crycelium drawn out razor-thin from Eddie's fingers. Each one was sharp enough to pare though solid steel, and they sheared through the feathers at the tips of Kronos' wings as he ran one finger across the face of his creation, feeling the circuit-pattern infection beneath it grow cold.

"Hatred forges the best weapons, Lieutenant… but fear keeps them sharp. You were never smart enough to be *afraid*, Edward Tsien. And now I've got some forging of my own to take care of. With Simeon Blaire dead, I'm the last Kheptarch standing." He was face to face with the frozen Super-Cyben, his six glowing eyes reflected in the mirror-bright chrome of Tsien's cheek. "*Order. Control. Precision.* The poor damned Illuminatus has told me that half the universe belongs to machines, Eddie. When they come for me, they'll be forced to treat me as their equal."

It seemed that all of his attention was turned on the Super-Cyben - but Emmanuel Lancaster hadn't sequenced this body with six eyes for aesthetics alone. There was a tiny scrawl of darkness slithering across the quicksilver mirror of Tsien's face, down across one cruel cheekbone...

It wore a face he recognized.

"It seems that rumors of your death have been somewhat... exaggerated," purred Kronos, turning his head a full one-eighty degrees on its long, thin neck. His smile was as welcoming as a blade of ice as he unfolded himself to his full height, his swan-white wings drawn in like a cloak around him.

"Oh, not entirely. I can find any number of things wrong with your little hypothesis, Kronos, but I'll tell you this for free – Simeon Blaire is dead and gone."

The Machine didn't have access to sophisticated scanning subroutines or electromagnetic probes in his seraphic body. But he didn't need them to see the truth of Akheron's words. The black-clad warrior stood outlined in the shattered doorway with a sword in either hand, his bare skull painted with a circle of primitive runes. He shrugged a spent jetpack from his shoulders as he advanced, letting it fall to the floor behind him.

"Perhaps you remember a man called *Octavio Vanecke*. A genius, a visionary... but so damned impetuous. So *ambitious*..."

Kronos knew where this was going.

"A *fool,* in fact. I recall that he tried to interfere with the genetic aspect of my master program – and that he met a bad end because of it."

"I couldn't agree with you more. A fool. In the old Tarot, he'd be numbered first amongst the Arcana, taking a little stroll off of a cliff. After that fall he was the Hanged Man for a while... bound, crippled – smiling to himself for no reason..."

"I thought your obsession was *Oriental,* Octavio," said the pseudocerebrate, circling around the monolithic bulk of Eddie Tsien. His pale white hands ran over the Super-Cyben's cold armor-plate like those of a lover. "Why don't we talk about the *I Ching* instead?"

Akheron chuckled to himself, crossing his swords like a pair of five-foot shears.

"Because, old friend, the Tarot ends with some very pertinent images indeed. *The Emperor. The Tower. The World.* Octavio is just as dead as Blaire, Kronos. I'm far more than the sum of both of them."

"Then you won't mind proving it!" snarled the Guardian Engine. He leaped into the air, the downdraft from his wings sending dust spiraling up in choking vortices. He alit high up in the twining branches of a silver-and-glass tree, heels swinging in space. "Too bad you've only brought a pair of knives to a gunfight!"

From his vantage point up among the crystals and globe-lamps Kronos could see that there was a second black-armored figure behind the enigma with the face of Simeon Blaire. He, too, had the look of the Kheptic gene-line about him, but he was young – barely even a youth, for all that he held a curved saber in one hand and had every appearance of being able to use it.

"He's led you to your death, child," called out the pseudocerebrate. "I know he must have killed your Lord Father. But you, as well? This doesn't have to be the end…"

Darion pushed the visor back from his face, revealing a pair of mismatched amber and green eyes. There was hatred there… deep and slithering worms of it coiled around the young Khept's soul. But there was something else as well…

"*I* killed Simeon Blaire. My Master told me that you'd try to lie and cheat your way out of what's coming. Don't think that I'm so easily corrupted!"

"A puppet, then. Too bad. You'll burn just as well with a hand up your arse, you little bastard!"

While he spoke, Kronos' minions had been crawling down the dome of the ceiling all around him. They were armed to the teeth and beyond – assassin mekan built by the Terminus Separatist Army twenty centuries before. They would have been useless against Eddie Tsien, with his battletank hide and liquid-crycelial blades. But the assault carbines clutched in their claws were more than enough to destroy Octavio Vanecke's latest incarnation… or so Kronos thought.

The assassin mekan swung down out of the trees and swarmed down the walls, skeletal things painted matte black, unshipping automatics from their holsters as they surrounded Akheron and his bastard son. But what should have been a fast, noisy and messy death completely failed to eventuate.

Oh, there was *noise*. The racket of all those hundreds of carbines was deafening, especially to a poor crippled machine with no way to turn down its audio input. But amongst the muzzle-flash and ricochet Akheron and Darion moved as a double blur, carving a neat web of lines and vectors through the mekan horde. A chorus of whirring, snapping, squealing and ringing sounds came in over the roar of gunfire, and the slow realization dawned on Kronos that his slaves weren't necessarily winning the engagement. The Guardian Engine sighed, dropping lightly to the ground before an immense statue of some long-forgotten Martial Virtue – a toga-wearing goddess eight feet tall praying over an upended battleaxe.

In the calm center of the storm, Darion Blaire sliced a geometrically precise figure through the torso of a warmekan, watching it fall away in sparking pieces. The damned things were just too slow to be entertaining… hardly Kheptic prey. At least battle was a diversion, though. Dangerous and unfamiliar emotions churned deep in his chest when he saw the cruel, avid look on Akheron's face. It didn't help that he was far more vicious than Darion himself. The same *yadome-jutsu* which he'd taught Simeon Blaire now split bullets in half in mid-flight, steering each ricochet into a killing blow. Mekan spasmed and jerked as those twin longswords carved them ragged, hollow heads and limbs clattering across the marble… until there were none of them left. Nothing remained of those one hundred assassin machines but scrapmetal and spent shells when the two Kheptarchs finally put up their blades – and Akheron hadn't even broken a sweat.

"Very nice. But I'm afraid that's as far as you get."

Darion's eyes narrowed at the sound of sardonic applause. He brought his saber back to guard, licking his dry lips in anticipation…

Facing them across the junkyard wreckage of his army was an angel in battle-armor - the very image of the *Uriel*'s namesake. In place of a flaming sword this apparition hefted a twin-bladed axe taller than a man, and its six eyes burned with hatred.

"Have you got any idea," asked Kronos "How much those things cost to maintain?"

"The repair bill's not finished yet," said Akheron. "Darion – stay back. This one's all *mine*."

They leaped at each other as if they were starving for blood, weapons hissing down in intersecting arcs. Sparks flashed and flared and died as blow after blow stuck home, every one blocked and turned aside with brutal precision. The body which Emmanuel Lancaster had built for his A.I. master was a pure symphony of muscle and bone – but the usurper had tempered his own flesh in the fires of the great Game.

Evenly matched, they fought their way around the great circular concourse of Ground Floor One, locked in the kind of mutual, obsessive concentration which only ever comes with either good sex or armed combat. These two had hated each other for so long that anything less would have been unthinkable. The ringing chime of steel on steel sounded like a thousand trip-hammers running furnace-hot.

Which made it even more surprising when a frozen, ice-rimed body was spit out of the empty air between them, steaming as it fell.

Kronos spun away, his axeblade whirring through a complex pirouette like the propeller of a small aircraft. Akheron's twin swords came up in a razor-sharp X as he dropped into a half-crouch. And Abdulafia 330 – freezerburned, half-mad and *monumentally* pissed off – staggered to his feet in a cloud of stinking vapor. Most of it was his own sweat, crystallized on his skin between dimensions.

"*You!* The Ashishi! But HOW? I thought you were still inside the Valley View when…"

"He's the Illuminatus' right hand! That treacherous little bastard must have…"

Abdulafia didn't have the strength to raise his head, but he did have enough fight left in him to lift his arms out to each side, palms flat. Kronos and Akheron both stopped in mid-rant, watching the *Dervashi* wobble unsteadily. He looked the pseudocerebrate in the eye, and then swung his head around to face the Kheptarch with a battery of vertebral clicks and pops.

"Now," he said. "Which one of you is on Zeon's side?"

Akheron had only just managed to draw breath before Kronos stepped forward, leaning on his war-axe like a staff.

"Last time I saw your master he was trying to defeat the Worm. And if the enemy of my enemy is my friend, then…"

"Don't listen!" snarled the Kheptic usurper. "He's lying! It's my purpose to overthrow this creature's corrupt rule – which puts the Illuminatus and I on the same page…"

Half the reason that Abdulafia's open hands had stopped two swords and a battleaxe in full swing was the fact that they were quite clearly servo-assisted bones tendoned with oil-black ligaments. Now they curled up into fists, and an almost-visible heat-haze shimmer built up around them.

"Wrong answer," said the *Dervashi* – and he pointed a finger at both the Kheptarch and the Machine.

If Darion hadn't actually seen the shockwave tearing across the dusty floor, he would have sworn that Abdulafia had picked up Kronos and his Master and slammed them bodily against the walls of Ground Floor One. The young scion of House Blaire was certain he'd seen the shape of massive fingers outlined in the air... but of course, that was impossible.

Abdulafia might have meant to kill them both where they stood, but he simply didn't have the strength to follow through. And he was far too close to his goal, now... the baroque portal to the space-'lev was within staggering distance, and he forced himself toward it through sheer effort of will.

Behind him, Akheron was back on his feet, spitting blood.

"You! Outlander! *Stay the Hells away from my Forge!*"

"*Your* Forge? I suppose *you* designed and built it, did you?"

"You shouldn't bother getting up, Kronos. Not unless you're as masochistic as you are stupid..."

Abdulafia turned on his heel, still swaying slightly.

"All right. You want to do this the hard way? Let's do it the hard way. But if Zeon beats me to the Tower, we're *all* going to be sorry."

Darion never saw him move, but the next instant the *Dervashi's* cold dead hand was clamped tight around his wrist. He stared up into a pair of eyes exactly like those of his Lord Father and Master, but utterly unlike them as well. There was *compassion* there, and something else... a terrible empty sense of loss.

"Just the sword, kid. And one other thing. Seeing as you remind me of me at your age, do us both a favor – *choose your own path*. Old men full of hate don't deserve your loyalty."

Darion's fingers peeled away from the hilt of his saber of their own volition. The weary, agonized look on the warrior's face was enough to pull down the barriers of his will... that, and the fact that his grip was tighter than the claw of a combat mekan.

Before he could fight back the *Dervashi* was away, sprinting across the dusty mosaic floor with his stolen sword held out to one side of his body.Kronos was directly in his path, and the battle-angel brought his immense axe around in a flat spin, a horizontal guillotine slash. At the last instant 'Afia leaped up into the overarching canopy of silver branches, twisting like a gymnast on the bars.

The axe hissed past his feet as he tucked them in... and its backswing sliced clean through the crystal foliage an inch from his hand. Kronos spun to follow him, wheeling great figure-eights with his double-edged blade, but Abdulafia's trajectory looped out wide, and he dropped down behind the Guardian Engine, coming in low with a tendon-severing strike…

Akheron stopped him.

For a single heartbeat they stood motionless – 'Afia with his saber blocked low by one of the Kheptarch's swords, Kronos taking the other high between the sweeping wings of his axe-head. Then each of the three primed all of the combat drugs, implants, neural upgrades and subprograms at their disposal. Darion Blaire, unarmed, could only watch in disbelief as they blurred into phantom trails of steel and shadow an instant later.

It was less a swordfight than a glimpse into the blades of a meatgrinder… a storm of sharp edges, curses, sly sucker-punches, headbutts and sweep-kicks set to the tune of ringing metal. Each series of strikes and guards formed a precise geometric figure for an instant as three swords and an axe were woven together – but they collapsed and reformed just as fast as the three warriors could flicker from stance to stance, pruning great ragged chunks from the artificial forest around them. Crystal lamps fell and shattered. Sparks flew wild, dancing across the cold marble floor. But not one of them could find a weakness in his foes.

Akheron was fast, and with two blades he should have held an advantage. But his body was new to him, slippery and unfamiliar. He had to use all his concentration just to keep a grip on his stolen nerves. Likewise Kronos; a machine stuffed into genecrafted flesh – his mind could calculate to the tiniest fraction exactly where each blow should fall, but his seraphic body was too weak to catch up with the cogitators in his head.

Abdulafia was just plain beat. Being rolled flat into two dimensions and slipped through the cracks of the Outer Dark had punished his mind as well as his body, exposing him to sights which should have torn his sanity to shreds. But he was a true believer in Lysander Jaegenn's little mantra. *Where speed and strength failed, cunning and guile took over.*

And of course, he was utterly insane already.

The Dervashi carefully maneuvered his foes across the room, steering the dance of blades with carefully calculated thrusts and backhands. Soon they were fighting under the shadow of Eddie Tsien, a metal monolith in crudely human form. The snarl of silver ribbons which ramified out from his body made it difficult to swing a sword… and that was exactly 'Afia's plan.

True to form, the battle-clone had been keeping a little something in reserve. As Akheron drew back his no-dachi to strike, and Kronos hefted his axe, snarling, Abdulafia pushed through his pain and slowed time to a standstill. Well… not really. But that was how it felt as the last dregs of Kheptic 'chrome in his body burned through his nervous system, making every individual mote of dust in Ground Floor One shimmer in stasis. Kronos was caught in mid-swing, his battleaxe gripped tight in hands crosshatched with steel tendons. Akheron's face was a death-mask more fierce than any *Oni* helm, tiny flecks of foam glistening in midair as he executed a double overhand, a scissor-cut which would butcher his foe into four bloody chunks.

But in that second Abdulafia 330 gripped his stolen saber tight, and spun once on his heel. The edge of his blade glowed red-hot with sheer velocity as wind resistance tried to slow its supersonic arc.

And his enemies' weapons shattered.

There were four high, brittle sounds like gunshots as the Ashishi completed his spin, bringing his boot up to connect with Akheron's neck. Two of them were the Kheptarch's master-forged no-dachi snapping like reeds as the saber passed through them. Another was the octagonal haft of Kronos' war-axe shattering and failing. But the fourth was the saber itself, crazed into a cloud of hot splinters.

One of them scored a shallow gash across the last piece of human skin Eddie Tsien could call his own. A thick, oily drop of blood welled up high on his cheek as 'Afia forced Akheron back against his metal chest… but the Dervashi was looking the other way.

He sighted own his arm, down along the barrel of the Eversio, aiming its one remaining shot right in the face of Kronos. And he ground his heel into the usurper's throat, just letting him know that both of them were equally screwed.

"Remember what I said about the hard way? Well, here we are. Now, I'm going up to the Cardinal Rock. I'm going to use the Forge to fix the mess you've made. If you want to kill each other while I'm gone, feel free."

Akheron swallowed hard. 'Afia felt it through the sole of his boot, and he turned away from Kronos for a second, staring into a face which could have been his own. The Kheptarch's eyes were rolled back in their sockets, looking up at Eddie Tsien…

Whose frozen features suddenly cracked into a smile.

Before the Dervashi could pull the trigger loops and coils of metal had bound him up, lashing his wrists together as his heels kicked three feet above the floor. Kronos and Akheron were trussed up just the same; the machine left dangling by one ankle; the usurper all but mummified with a razor ribbon at his throat.

"Like we used to say in the Division – You're *busted*, scumbags. I told you that EMP wouldn't do you any good."

'Afia twisted against his bonds, wishing there was still a little 'chrome left in his system. But he was burned out… the comedown from this little escapade was going to cost him a month in a cell-repair vat. If he struggled, he'd likely just slit his wrists.

"Eddie! Stop! We're the only ones left! If you want to stop the Chimera, you need me! You need the Forge!"

Tsien's eyes were cold flat nailheads as he stared back at his captive.

"It's already too late for me, *Dervashiman*. I told you we were even before, back in the Valley View. So I'm not going to do to you what I've got in store for these two. But the Forge… it's false hope, clonemeat. Has been all along. The best use I can think of for that damned machine is one last fireworks display."

There were a dozen good arguments on the tip of his tongue. But Abdulafia didn't get a chance to reason with the Super-Cyben. He barely had time to scream.

All three of Tsien's captives saw it coming, a stray spark spiraling in from out of the pale gray sky. A swarm of Perimeter Defense mekan were torn out of the air in its wake as it headed for the shattered doors of Ground Floor One, billowing an oily contrail of smoke. For some reason there was a great silver-skinned insect clinging to the shattered nose of the Ashishi masslifter, a shape which Abdulafia recognized all too well.

"Tsien! Look out!"

It was going to hit them head-on…

A dragonfly mekan whirred past Afia's ear, nicking a neat little V in it with the tip of one wing. Then another blurred past, and another… a whole buckshot storm of the little bastards. It was one of them which cut the Super-Cyben off in mid- sentence, shattering across his back with a sound like a stray bullet.

"Come on, *Dervashi*. That's gotta be the oldest trick in the boo… Ohhhhh… *fucking hellfire!*"

Eddie was already turning his head as thirteen tons of ethanol-fueled ruin tore through the wall of Ground Floor One, punching out what remained of the building's security systems- but by then it was far too late. He looked directly into Abdulafia's eyes as the broken control-bubble of the 'lifter swung in on him, burning… and the *Dervashi* felt the coil of metal tense around his wrists.

"Shut it down, clonemeat. Just destroy the damned thing before it dooms us all."

Then 'Afia was airborne, propelled from the Super-Cyben's grip.

He saw the raw steel bulk of the masslifter snatch Eddie up off his feet, dragging Kronos and Akheron along with him. He caught a glimpse of screaming faces behind its shattered windows – Kaito Kayzi and Haszan were among them, but there were others, too, thrown up hard against the glass as the machine began to tumble end over end in its death-throes. An engine nacelle flew wide, blazing, and the unmistakable alien figure of Technician Nyl was dragged along in its slipstream, his spiked silhouette burned across the circle of a bright explosion. Another body flew like a ragdoll from the thing's open door, a bundle of smoking camo fatigues – but an instant later the bulk of the 'lifter came down on it hard, crushing the poor wretch into the floor.

That was the last bounce. From then on it was all just grinding, tearing – a shower of sparks thrown high and wide as metal ablated away beneath it. Abdulafia didn't see where Kronos, Tsien and Akheron ended up. He hit the far wall of Ground Floor One hard enough to force the breath from his lungs, and his skull caught a sucker-punch from a solid lump of crystal. Darkness blurred across his eyes as he slid down the wall in a boneless slump, his blood painting a sticky trail behind him.

There were a couple of seconds of blissful concussion trauma, in which the world was black.

When his vision cleared Darion Blaire was staring down at him. His mismatched eyes blinked once, with slow, reptile precision.

"Well fought, I suppose. Your backhand is a little slow to the right – keep your point up, and aim between the third and fourth ribs." The Kheptic Prince stooped to retrieve his saber, sliding it back into the sheath at his belt. "I'll leave you to attend to the dead, Ashishim. If my Master is numbered among them, tell him I've gone to fulfill my destiny."

"That's all? No eulogy for the old bastard?"

Darion arched one eyebrow, in a gesture his Lord Father would have recognized immediately.

"Frankly, outlander, I almost thought I'd have to do it myself."

Then he was gone, slipping through the doors behind him and into the anteroom of the space-'lev. Perhaps Abdulafia should have gone after him. But the wreck of the masslifter tweaked memories in the blurred ruin of his brain… this was the same machine which had torn the walls from Vexx's sanctum, the same one which he'd been dragged down on, half alive, with…

Oh no. She couldn't be. Not now, not here. Because now the whole damned thing was burning, and he could hear the screams… hells, he could even smell the stench of charred hair and sizzling fat. And he hadn't come this far and given up so much of himself to despair, only to watch CeeAn incinerated before his eyes.

The battle-clone staggered in toward the flames, through a blizzard of fluttering gray fire-retardant foam. There were figures moving against the orange yellow-haze, things like wraiths worrying at the bones of the fallen masslifter. One of them was CeeAn. One of them *must* be her…

But it was someone else entirely who found him first.

"Well, hello stranger," said Technic Hierophant Gharfos Nyl. "Fancy seeing *you* here!"

Then a fist sheathed in exotic metal caught him clean on the point of his jaw, and the fires of the burning 'lifter went supernova behind his eyes. From the cameras bolted to his Operative Crescent, Asag'raal watched the alien draw a curved diamondglass dagger from his belt, its prismatic blade shattering the flamelight into slivers. Metal mandibles whirred and clicked as the Technician licked his thin lips with a long, serrated tongue.

"Now, let's cut that parasite out of you, slave! The two of us have *so* much to talk about…"

Ω

Akheron fought his way up into consciousness, prying his eyes open against the dark. He found himself staring right into the face of Kronos. The pseudocerebrate's six eyes were bare inches from his own, and the sheer hatred which radiated from them was almost enough to flay the skin from his skull. Almost – but not quite.

Because the rest of the Guardian Engine's body was most definitely missing.

Akheron staggered to his feet, still groggy from a bad case of blunt force trauma. Hells – there was the hole in the wall they'd come through, a seven-foot plug of artificial stone punched out by Eddie Tsien. The usurper reached down and picked up Kronos' severed head by its hair, forcing a painful laugh out between his remaining teeth.

"So this is how it ends, old friend. All those centuries of scheming, and you get sliced up *by accident*! It's almost too…"

"Sorry, but you can't keep it," hissed a voice from behind him. "I need part of his brain, Simeon. Just count yourself lucky that I don't want any of *yours*."

He knew by the sheer size of the shadow who it was… but Eddie Tsien had definitely seen better days.

Akheron could forgive the Super-Cyben for calling him *Simeon*, considering how much of his head was missing. In fact a whole ragged chunk of his body was gone, in a diagonal slash running from shoulder to hip. Even the power of the Chimera hadn't been enough to save his arm or his left eye… now there was nothing but a raw gunmetal scar splitting him almost in half. Tiny pseudopods of living crystal twitched in the air as Tsien's one remaining hand hinged shut around Akheron's neck.

"You mean… the bastard's still *alive*?"

"When it comes to A.I., 'alive' is a bit of a loaded term," said the Super-Cyben. "I'm not going to last much longer myself… but Kronos is much harder to kill. Unfortunately for you, Kheptic Lords are easy meat."

If Akheron hadn't been run so comprehensively through the mince-grinder he might have been able to fight back. Tsien may have been almost sawn in half, but his one remaining hand had grown all out of proportion – it was a two-fingered claw which could easily have wrecked the usurper down to shuddering meat. Eddie was going to enjoy his revenge, though… even if he still thought he was exacting it on Simeon Blaire. His head tilted to one side, birdlike, as he lifted Akheron from the floor. A pair of very expensive combat boots kicked and twitched as the Kheptarch's face turned blue. Just a second more, and he'd choke on his own swollen tongue…

But Tsien's claw snapped open at the very last instant, dropping Akheron to the ground. The Super-Cyben roared, bringing his hand back over his head. His one remaining eye was a window into hell, and the craterous wound beside it boiled with silver. But his downstroke stopped less than an inch from Akheron's face.

And the usurper began to laugh.

"You can't do it, can you? Even… even when you fought against Simeon at the Valley View, you couldn't have actually *killed* him. That's why he stuck that bloody great knife in your throat! There's something in your programming that made you *let him win!*"

Veins like black hosepipes stood proud from Eddie's skin as he tried to force his claws apart. His whole scarred and ruined body was trembling as he leaned forward, bringing those two razor tips right up to within a shadow's width of Akheron's eyeballs.

"Yes! You can't kill one of your betters, Tsien! Not those who you were sworn to protect! And that means you're *nothing!*"

For a second the Super-Cyben shrunk back away from him, snarling like an animal. Self-disgust twisted his face into a horror-mask of chrome and agony. But he lurched forward again a heartbeat later, and his mouth twitched up into a thin little smile.

"This building's on fire, *My Lord*. Aren't you going to get out while you still can?"

"What are you talking about, you freak? Of course not! The Forge is right above us!"

"I'm afraid you've become disoriented from all the smoke," said Tsien, circling around him with a peculiar lurching shuffle. "You're getting *hysterical*, Your Grace… and we can't have that."

"Hysterical? *Me?* You're the one spouting nonsense, Tsien. Just get the hell out of my *way*, you obsolete pile of shit!"

Eddie's single great claw moved far too fast to follow, snatching the severed head of Kronos from Akheron's grasp. He held it up next to his face so that he could murmur into its ear, looking for all the world like a puppet-master performing a show.

"You hear that, Kronos? Utterly mad with shock. Poor thing. I suppose I have no choice…"

The blow took Akheron clean in the temple, lifting him off his feet and spinning him three times in the air before he landed. Not hard enough to kill… but enough to knock him out cold. It had been delivered by the rock-hard bone of the pseudocerebrate's skull, swung by its hair like a mace.

"Terrible, terrible," muttered Eddie to his grisly hand-puppet. "But *somebody* had to do it. Now, help me get him locked in a heatproof coffin. You, my mekanikal friend, have a date with a screwdriver."

Ω

The Earth looked different from up here. Darion felt a moment of sickening disorientation as the artificial gravity of the 'lev capsule shut down, replaced with one-half standard. Without it he'd have been crushed boneless to the floor as the sleek golden capsule accelerated up from Elysium, but it still put him on edge. Through a set of slit windows ten inches thick the young Kheptarch had watched the city unfold below him, a burned and dying flower spreading petals of disease across the curve of the planet. Then the ocean, a rippled pool of molten lead; the desert coast of Afrika; the sere expanse of Eurasia reaching out across the hazy horizon. It was all meaningless, of course, compared to the great gnarled rock of the Counterweight which hung above him, swelling to fill the viewscreens set in their frames of cherubs and thorns.

Now the scissor-doors of the space-'lev capsule hissed open to reveal a checkerboard marble hall, wide and echoing in the cold still air. Just as the Book of Manifest Dogma foretold. But where was the labyrinth? The sprung-steel traps, the razor teeth, the slicing wires wet with poison?

"They're in your head, son. Only in your head."

Darion's saber was in his fist within half a heartbeat, but there was nobody there for him to strike down. The words had slid into his brain like cold needles, bypassing his ears entirely.

"That's what Kronos told me, afterward. It's one of those mental traps - y'know, a test. Like wrapping you in a blindfold and pushing you off a 'cliff'… that's only a two-foot drop. The difference is, if you scream for this one, the fall is real."

Darion moved out into the vast shadowed space of the hall, his boots ringing out loud against the icy marble. He was still the only living thing in the great sphere of the Cardinal Rock, but there was something moving behind its walls – a sound like titanic clockwork gears set in motion. He was sure that the sound hadn't begun until after he heard the voice in his head.

"Not in your head, child. Just… prying into certain parts of it."

This time it was right behind him.

Darion spun in a whirlwind strike, his saber lashing out wide to whisper through a pale green hologram of a man. He was dressed in military whites and brocade, a ragged cape flowing down from his shoulders. His face was haggard and careworn… lined with immeasurable age. But Darion was surprised to find that he *knew* this man – even though he'd been genewritten, vat-grown and born without ever once leaving Octavio Vanecke's control.

"*Zaanic*. Sergan Zaanic. But… The eduplug said you died up here. Why…"

"It stored me, like it stores them all. But I didn't die in the Trials,

Darion son of Simeon. And neither will you. Not if you give me what I need."

"What do you mean 'like it stores them all'? And how do you know my..."

"We read your mind, child. Read your whole damned neural structure. The machines of the Grief Division, tiny things crawling on the insides of your lungs... they told us all we need to know. But there's nowhere for that information to go. The buck stops here, Darion. Kronos is dead."

That information slammed into him like a fist.

The eduplug - that interleaved ream of data blasted into his head before he was born – it had put Kronos one step below godhood, and only then because most gods weren't so manifestly real.

"It means I'm *free*, son! Free! The damned Engine thought it would be ironic to set me here at the gates as Master of the Trials. How I'd love him to know that of all the Three Hundred Purest, the one who finally came to me was a *child*!"

"So the Forge is mine? I can just walk through and take it? I can remake the Earth in my image?"

Sergan Zaanic's laugh was dry as tomb-dust, but his eyes were filled with holographic sadness.

"You still don't get it, do you? The Forge isn't just another machine – it's a living thing. A neural structure, just like the one I'm trapped in." The glittering cloud which was Sergan Zaanic pointed across the Hall of the Trials, to a verdigris-green statue hanging in a niche. It was the image of an angel, bound to the wall by intricately knotted snakes, and in its outstretched hand was an orb about the size of a human skull. "Imagine, Darion – millions of souls, all captured at the moment of their deaths. All their lives those people controlled billions of cells, hundreds of muscles and living organs, all with their *minds*. Most of them never gave it a second thought. But you never hold onto that tangled web so hard as when you feel it slipping away. The Forge is made of that desperation. The Forge is a Planck-scale energy repatterning field which requires immensely delicate manipulation."

"But it works, doesn't it? It's real..."

"Oh yes," said Zaanic. "It's *very* real. But you have to ask yourself – how can you control such a thing? What do all those poor doomed souls desire?" As he spoke, the long-dead Kheptarch drifted across the tiles to caress his own neuro-core prison. "What would you offer to lead them, Darion?"

He grasped the truth of it even as Sergan Zaanic turned a pleading gaze on him, staring avid and hungry at the naked blade of his saber. What could anyone possibly offer to a creature like this… to *millions* of them?

"Only death," he whispered, running the tip of his sword up the bronze angel's arm, until its edge rested against that dark and heavy orb. "That's what they want, isn't it? Them, and you as well…"

"Now, while Kronos is gone. Before the fucking thing finds a way to resurrect itself!"

Darion's saber came back over his shoulder, ready to strike – but he held back, trembling.

"How can I trust you?" he asked. "What do I gain from setting you free?"

Zaanic was lost in a look of wild rapture as his eyes reflected in the edge of the blade. He licked his lips as he tore his gaze away, pointing out across the checkerboard hall.

"Two things, Darion Blaire. First and foremost…*this!*"

The sound of oiled gears and snicking escapements rose up like a wave. And the floor, all across the echoing expanse of the hall… the floor came up with it. Each marbled square concealed a pillar of shining steel, milled gray walls pistoning up from below to form an ever-changing maze. Darion watched them closely, and he saw the slits and hollows in their monolithic sides; the recesses where blades and needles waited, coiled to strike. They slid and copulated and spun, flickering lasers across the cold air, forming up into avenues of spiked death, dead-end runs where poisoned wires webbed between walls of metal…

And then they were gone.

With a gesture from the ghost of Sergan Zaanic the whole square-mile-wide killing ground clicked and interlocked and fell away, neat and precise as a clockwork toy. When the final black square locked snug with the white ones around it there was no trace of the Labyrinth… none at all.

"I think you could make it, Darion. I really do. Those brain-scans we talked about… they revealed very few weaknesses in you. Of course, we would have tailored the maze to make full use of them, and you would have suffered. Even I only got through by leaving three of my fingers behind."

The young Kheptarch looked out across the hall with a sense of horror. To think that all of that abattoir machinery had been right under his feet, all along…

"But you made it. You reached the Forge. How – why are you trapped in that orb, then? What took you down?"

"That's the second part of my gift to you, son. A little piece of information I could have done with at the time. You see, we Kheptarchs are like the kings of old. Not the storybook ones… the kings *before* words and fairytales made them wise and good. We're more like those armored brutes with axes who raped and butchered their way to power. And in those times most Kings didn't last."

"Survival of the fittest, of course. Competition. *Envy…*"

"No. Worse. They were *sacrifices*, Darion. That was the final test – the one I failed. In order to give the damned what they want, you have to be willing to *lead* them. I wasn't. I tried to hold on to life, in my pride…"

Each word was like a knife twisted in his flesh. He didn't want to hear it. Because if it was true, he'd been genewritten and born and tempered just to be *used up*. Used by Akheron as the disposable firing-pin in the vast machine of the Forge.

His blade sliced a swift, fatal X through Lord Sergan Zaanic's prison-orb, shattering it in a spray of artificial blood and brain tissue. Sparks crawled down the arm of a verdigris-rimed copper angel for a second, and then… The hologram blurred out as the sound of machinery behind the walls reached a crescendo. Things were sliding and hissing in the oily depths below, black and white tiles flipping and shifting. At the same time the hidden pillars of the labyrinth maze were set in motion, rising up to form a kind of pixilated topography, a vast mile-wide image like a printout from some ancient dot-matrix engine.

It was a human face, and its laugh was a cyclopean wall of sound, rolling back in waves of echoes from the vaulted ceiling of the hall.

"We all die, Darion Blaire!" hissed the fading voice of Zaanic, as his face bled back into featureless black and white. "All who touch the Forge, all who know its power. Sacrifices, every one. And so far, none have been willing to pay the price."

Ω

In the end, it couldn't have been easier. The parasite bored into Abdulafia's mind had sought refuge in his crescent unit during their desperate escape through the Outer Dark, and it coiled there still, a traumatized fragment of Asag'raal itself.

No doubt the destruction of the Worm's avatar out of the Spillway was a big part of it, but Technician Nyl had no way of knowing what his young protégé CeeAn had achieved. All he cared about was the sample, and what it represented.

Originally, he'd wanted to simply *tame* the Worm and turn it against his enemies. But when it broke through into the world he'd seen another way – a better way. When the damned thing spawned he'd be there, a metal spermatozoa to its gelid black egg. It meant integration with that darkness, first and foremost. Then the corruption of the Slavesystem Everdark. And then…

He could see it all so clearly in his mind – a web of silvery wires woven from Unity nanotech, ramifying in a cerebral stranglehold through the brain of Asag'raal's young. And at the core of it, the spider in that neural web would be Gharfos Nyl, enthroned in unassailable new flesh.

So what if a few million humans died? Their world was under siege already, another disposable battleground for the Motherbrain and the Praetor to tear apart.

Nyl tore the black crescent from around 'Afia's shoulders, priming twenty layers of alien countermeasures between his mind and its infected wetware. Silver cables coiled down to lock in place, binding him to the sample, crushing it between digital fists…

And the Worm screamed.

"Yes! Mother Nature's a bitch, isn't she Asag'raal? There's no way to stop the spawning now… and I have you right where I want you! All that remains is to use the Forge, and then…"

But something caught the alien renegade's attention. Something looming out of the drifting smoke, even bigger and more dangerous-looking than Nyl himself.

"Allright, you twisted insect fuckhole," said Jaq Haszan. "Why don't you just step away from my friend there?" The seven-foot steel monolith of Grief flickered with violet sparks in the gloom, lighting up his scarred and bloody face. "And if your kind have a God, I suggest you tell him you're on your way home."

Ω

The city was overrun.

Saprophytes scuttled and lurched through the streets of Elysium, transformed into stygian chasms by fire and ruin. Black shadows perched atop the habs like gargoyles, transparent teeth dripping. Things like great skinless wolves prowled the barrios of Saint Pete's, and amorphous horrors slithered through the pipes and tubes beneath.

But the prey was gone. Far too many of them had escaped.

Some of the weaker Saps had already died, starving away to scrawls of sticky darkness. Others turned on each other in vicious internecine dogfights, packs of them ravening and screaming in the deeps of the Subcity.

The Exalted ruled now. But for how long, their master couldn't say.

"Higher, you fools! Higher! We must have the Forge... and we must have the key to unlock it."

Asag'raal was *worried*, and anxiety was one emotion the Harvester-apostate wished he had never digested with his prey. He had always been a simple creature, a thing of hunger and desire. He wasn't used to any scheme, plan or machination more complicated than 'devour/shit/repeat'... but then again, he wasn't used to being a *'he'* either. The fragments of personality which Asag'raal had bound together into a soul came from the memories of a postphysical alien demigod, damned human sacrifices, and the minds of the Exalted in equal parts. Not the best tools to work with... but they were all he had.

There was a time, only a few hours ago, when the Worm was utterly certain of victory, when the seed of its spawning had quickened deep inside its twisted-off little proto-universe. Then Kaito Kayzi had defeated one of Asag'raal's many faces inside the Wetsystems. Eddie Tsien had tricked his way out of damnation and enslavement. Now... now CeeAn and her makeshift army had thrown back his avatar in the flesh. Asag'raal had felt the meddling hand of his brothers behind her power.

"All of you! My slaves, my pets, my children! This world is only the first of millions we will feast upon... but if you fail me now, your torment will redefine the agonies of hell!"

Oh yes... there was desperation behind its rage now. The Devourer may have been as subtle as a hammer to the face, but he was no fool. The dim throb and pulse which still came to him from the infected Wetsystems whispered secrets, fragments of images from the Counterweight above. The way to the High Throne was opened. Vanecke's bastard was so very close... but he would fail. Children, or so he'd found, were so easy to terrify.

Hope was yet another emotion which the Worm didn't want to understand. But that was what it held for the parasitic fragment of itself coiled up in Abdulafia 330's soul. Of course, the shock of slipping sideways through the Outer Dark had driven that part of him deep, down through some kind of interlock and into the human's artificial second brain…

Asag'raal saw his mistake too late, as Technician Nyl's transparent knives unfolded in front of him. He felt the connections parting like sliced-through sinews, locking him down in a core of black plastic.

And his rage was all the more terrible for the fact that it was born of fear.

"To the tower! Every last one of you – NOW! Flay them alive! Rip them limb from limb!"

In the streets of Elysium, a million horrors screamed as one. Membranous wings snapped taut, claws flexed, and dripping white teeth grinned in the shadows. All of them turned their faces toward Ground Floor One, drinking in the scent of their prey.

This time there would be no mistakes. This time it would be *simple*, reduced to the grim mathematics of slaughter. A million of Asag'raal's slaves against barely a handful of human beings… and one Technician of the Multiplicity who would come to regret his hubris. Revenge was within his grasp – for here, in one place, were the Kayzi, that fat fool Haszan, the mekanikal ruin of Eddie Tsien, and his unwilling slave Abdulafia 330. The one called *Akheron* he would keep, along with his bastard son.

But Nyl must die. There was no question of that.

Asag'raal tried not to think about what would happen if the alien actually succeeded. It was bad enough that he had a plan at all… that he was arrogant enough to put it into motion. But the worst part - the part which stung like a thorn in the Devourer's eye – was that the Technician-thing was *right*. There was no way to stop the spawning now. Beyond the crack in reality, in a sealed-off bubble of a universe suffused with oily darkness, the seed was growing. One way or another, it *would* be born.

And it needed to incubate in the core of this planet. The heat and pressure of the abyss would forge it a shell of nickel and iron, making it perfectly at home in the vacuum of space.

Empathy was the most dangerous emotion of all. It was pity, and compassion, and all the things which Asag'raal loathed most bitterly. But now the Blackest Destiny knew a little of that vile condition too. Because like countless billions of its victims before it, the Worm finally knew what it meant to be *afraid*.

Ω

"You're lucky I'm so damn good at this. In fact, you're lucky you built me with a little technical acuity at all, Kronos."

"Do you expect me to thank you?"

"In the circumstances… not really. But hey, at least your head's facing the right way. I'd hate for you to have nothing but an arse to look at for the rest of your life."

"And what makes you think I'll stay trapped here for any length of time?"

"Who said anything about *lengths of time*? The rest of your life is going to be interesting, educational… and short. That much I can promise you."

Eddie Tsien stepped back from his masterpiece, tilting his head to one side. His depth perception was right off, considering the lack of his left eye… but it didn't look too bad. A lazy coil of crycelium reeled itself back into the sheared metal scar which defined that side of his body, the shape of a flathead screwdriver at its tip.

"See, I've felt the infection. I know the name of the parasite which has your Wetsystems hostage. And I can't for the life of me think of a better revenge than *letting it eat you*."

Kronos' head was on the right way round, but that was a small mercy. Indeed, Tsien may have only stitched him together this way so that he could enjoy the look on the pseudocerebrate's face as Asag'raal ground his mind to mincemeat. A little injection of second-gen Chimera tech had bound up his wounds perfectly well, but it wasn't loss of blood and muscle and bone that was going to hurt the most. It was the fat steel-jacketed data cable drilled clear through his skull and into the artificial brain beneath. Not tissue… not this one. Lancaster had built this angelic body for his patron Engine, and its cranium held a blanked, forbidden A.I. core torn from the wreckage of a Separatist warplane.

"I know that I haven't got long to live. I know what the Chimera's doing to me. It's… it's already hard to focus on the important things… *making you suffer*, for instance. But I'm going to enjoy this next part. Count on it."

Chained to the wall, raped by data-feed cables, Kronos could only watch in horror as Eddie reached for the switch…

Ω

The Throne.

The Kheptic prince's hands were trembling as he stood before its command console, staring at a transparent holoscreen. He held his breath, plucked up his courage, and completed the circuit.

"You have selected MANUAL CONTROL," intoned a voice without gender or inflection. "All Forge processes have been switched to exterior operation. A.I. subsystems offline."

Ω

It was all a calculated act.

Kronos expanded into the heart of the Subduction Phase as a fractal starburst of eyes, a turbine-engine of light nestled amid a gyroscope of rumbling electromagnetic rings. This was the heart of his power, infection or no infection, and before Asag'raal could strike he'd still be able to slam home the overrides and use the Forge…

Except that he couldn't.

High above the churning heart of the Phase, in a tiny room welded to the living rock of the Counterweight, somebody had thrown Kronos' greatest weapon into manual control. It had slipped through his grasp, and into human hands.

Now that the process was underway there was no way to make it stop. Sections of the Wetsystems which had been locked down to slow the onslaught of the Worm lit up cherry-red across the Machine's vast schematic overlay.

Too many of them were infected. *Far too many.* No matter who activated the Forge now, it would be warped out of true by the will of Asag'raal, and only hell would come from it.

And worse… the Guardian Engine could feel its enemy closing in.

The Devourer had been all but driven from the Wetsystems by Kaito Kayzi, but the presence of Kronos here in the Phase was like blood in the water. Phantom shapes flickered around the periphery of the Wetsystems, out near the edge of the R.T. where the decay was at its deepest. They were massing, twining together, slithering from one infected sector to another with the slow, sinuous purpose of hunting snakes.

Soon they would reach the Subduction Phase. And directly below it… a dome of processor cores steaming in a lake of liquid nitrogen. The living brain of Kronos.

It seemed that Eddie Tsien was about to get his wish after all.

Ω

It was dying time.

But this wasn't the Kheptarchs' game, or some slay-per-view pitfight.

It wasn't even a matter of life and death - because nobody was coming out of this one alive.

At least, it didn't seem that way from where Haszan was standing.

Jaq parried low and came back with a sweeping cross-body slice, only to find Grief blocked by a pair of forward-curved sickle-swords in the hands of Technician Nyl. Infuriatingly, the alien creature had reverted to its human skin… mocking him with his ineffectiveness.

That wasn't to say that the Railblade didn't blur and hum through the air like a silvery shadow, slicing whole artificial trees down to stumps. It was just that Nyl, even in the guise of Zeon, was far too fast for him to actually hit.

"That's enough playtime, primitive. Now, a little lesson in *finesse*…"

Haszan was forced back against the charred wreck of the Ashishi masslifter as those twin blades spun into a flickering storm, skirling and slithering across his desperate defense. He swung Grief with both hands, coming in overhand to try and batter Zeon down to the ground, but it was no use… even his immense strength was nothing compared to the biomekanikal artistry of the Technician's lab-forged body. He met the railblade with a crossed X of steel, parrying it away even as Jaq subvocalized a command and sent a railgun slug hissing past his cheek.

He was in trouble. He knew it.

"Too bad you weren't around when I needed human muscle, Jaq. You could have been *Dervashi* material…"

There was an oily little double-click behind him.

"*I* still am," said a voice from out of the smoke.

A double-discharge of buckshot picked Zeon up and slammed him sideways through the air, screaming. It was Rugal 301, and he held a short-handled mace in each hand. There was a hole drilled through the head of each weapon… the barrel of a combat shotgun. Sawn-off, welded to reinforcing rods which ran down their gently curved grips – these were lovingly handmade tools, and they fit into Rugal's fingers just right. Before his former master hit the ground he was already a blur of mahogany-colored muscle and flying steel, bringing both maces around in a skull-crushing arc.

Haszan didn't wait to see if he could take Zeon alone. He was in there with Grief even as the Illuminatus flickered out of phase, handspringing back and blocking both of Rugal's weapons with his feet. He cartwheeled up with his sickle-swords whistling through a savage *kata*, carving left and right to block the storm of metal bare inches from his skin.

Everything devolved into a hot blur as Grief took over, its battle-cogitators smoothly adopting control of Haszan's nervous system. He was a machine on automatic, angling the great flat edge of the railblade across in a series of looping curves. Rugal was just as fast, spinning his maces through the gaps in Grief's wall of death.

But Zeon was even faster. His swords were everywhere at once, not only blocking and parrying Jaq and the Dervashi's attacks, but finding the flaws in their assault as well, twisting through to nick and slice any inch of unprotected flesh. The damned creature was actually *smiling* as he fought.

Jaq knew that he couldn't keep up this kind of pace. He remembered how heavy the blade of Grief had felt in his hands down on the *Archangel Uriel* when it had run out of power, and he suppressed a momentary shudder. If he was left high and dry like that now, the alien in Zeon's skin would slice him to ribbons…

"Demon! I admonish thee to the pit of Hades! I shall deliver my brothers from your wrath, and smite you with the iron rod of the Lord!"

This time, it wasn't just the click of a single pair of hammers. Brother Pious had rallied the rest of the survivors of the Masslifter crash with him, and they brought Technician Nyl up short with a battery of motley firearms.

"Very poetic – but totally inaccurate," said the Technician, circling warily in a ring of enemies. His skin was torn ragged all along his forearms, and hard metal glistened beneath. "Two of you or twenty… I'll finish you all before I take the Forge. I wouldn't want a dagger in my back, after all."

"Give it up, Zeon. Leave this place now, and I'll let you walk." That was Rugal 301. They certainly weren't Jaq Haszan's sentiments. "GO! Just leave us the body of our *Dervashi* brother…"

"He's not *dead*, you fool! He's just going to *wish* that he was when he wakes up. I've got plans for Abdulafia 330, slave… plans which require him breathing. I won't guarantee he'll still get to keep his mind, though."

"*In nomine patri, et fili, et spiriti sancti…*"

"Oh, just fucking *shoot* him already!" shouted Haszan. "He's stalling for time!"

"Touche," said the alien Technician, bringing his blades up and around in a vertical spin. Each one split apart like a courtesan's fan as he twisted their ornate grips, sliding and clicking until he held a great oversized throwing-star in each hand. "Come on then, you filthy mud-apes. Show us what those opposable thumbs can do."

The noise was nothing short of spectacular.

Nyl erupted from his human skin in a blaze of quicksilver, strafing left as a hail of bullets and maser blasts shredded the air. He was behind the charred ribcage of the masslifter before Jaq, Rugal or Pious had even moved, letting a storm of flying lead skip and whir and ricochet behind him. Jaq propelled himself up after the alien, letting Grief pull him along in its wake. He watched Rugal go out wide, chambering two new round in his mace-guns. Pious spread his black robe out like a pair of raven wings and leaped, though – right up to the broken back of the 'lifter, a telescopic quarterstaff snapping out from within their folds as he flew.

He was right on the money.

Nyl appeared atop the 'lifters tail boom, and his arm was drawn back over his head to strike. Even the very fastest of the Exodus gunmen hadn't been able to lead him, and shots flew wide around him as he snapped his wrist forward, launching that five-fingered blade in a flat blur.

Pious attacked at the same time, and his technique was right out of the *Codex Martial*. The quarterstaff he called Martha blazed at both ends with a killing charge of electricity, and it came spinning from his hand in a halo of blue fire. Jaq watched its flat end hammer home against the Technician's temple, punching him ten feet sideways... and then it rebounded, right back into the Valle Crucis' waiting hand.

His own attack was irreversible - already calculated by the hard, spiteful core of anger inside Grief. It sheared the whole damned wreck in two, slicing through its tail with a scream of tortured steel.

Nowhere left to hide, you slippery bastard. Come and get...

Sweet hells – those blades!

The first he heard of it was a thin and bubbling scream, cut off short. There was a sound like a lawnmower slicing through meat, and a series of agonized cries rung out behind him. Guns clattered to the floor, forgotten. Behind it all ran a mind-blurring hum, the sound of antigrav generators and spin motors pushed to their utmost limits.

Jaq saw Nyl come out of cover to snatch his throwing-star out of the air, and he squeezed off a railgun slug toward him. The creature's other blade snapped forward spinning, and the slug caromed away, deflected. He watched Rugal come in low under Nyl's guard, and he saw the twitch of satisfaction on the big man's face as he hammered at his former Master's ribs. The Technician rolled with the blow, turning it into an agile handspring - but the *Dervashi* spun his weapons around, leveling them like a pair of six-shooters.

Even over the screams, the gunfire and the chime of falling shells Jaq heard those double triggers click home.

The blast caught Nyl high in the chest, upside down, and he flipped over backwards, violet blood steaming against the tiles. Pious was airborne too, holding his quarterstaff like an impaling spike. Jaq wrenched Grief loose and followed on, bringing the seven-foot blade around in a forehand slash as he leaped. Behind him he could hear the slide and snap of reloading guns.

But Zhe wasn't done yet.

He turned his headlong slide into a crouch and launched himself back at his tormentors, blocking Pious high and twisting the staff from his hands. Then his eyes narrowed, and the blade he should have saved to parry Grief - the one which the railblade had already calculated for – shot out at waist height in a silver blur.

It caught Rugal 301 dead center, and it went right through him, hooking left to take a diagonal segment out of an A.K.–wielding Celestial's skull. Jaq twisted left as he watched the giant shuriken's parabola play out in neon behind his eyes… Then Grief caught it on the backswing, shattering the damned thing to pieces. An instant later and it would have carved Haszan in two, before it slapped back into Nyl's waiting palm. Rugal 301 slid in half, gurgling.

"One down, two to go!" hissed the alien, coiling himself to spring. "It doesn't get any easier, though. Sorry if you thought I was going to *play fair.*"

Nyl's arm was utterly inhuman now… a spiked mantis appendage underslung with wires and tubes. One of them split, unfolding down the middle...

"It's got guns as well," groaned Jaq. "Just what we needed."

He didn't wait around at point-blank range to see what those alien cannons could do. Haszan broke right, rolling across the tiles to bring Grief up like a shield. He could hear the screams as particle-beam fire licked out over his head, reducing his allies to ashes one by one. Pious hammered at the Technician with his staff, bending it almost double across the back of Nyl's head, but the alien was beyond playing with them now. He backhanded the Valle Crucis away laughing, then got back to the business at hand, blowing chunks of flesh from the fleeing remains of Jaq's little army.

All but one.

There was a figure in ragged black robes crouched right over the body of Abdulafia 330, and it seemed that nothing could touch him at all. Incandescent rods of light sliced up the air around him, blasting his allies to dust, but he didn't even look up at the snarling face of Technician Nyl. A pair of cheap Subcity railpistols hung loose in his red-gloved hands.

"There. That ought to do it."

Nyl froze, the savage grin suddenly tight and brittle on his sliver face. He tried to center his cannons on the ragged figure as it stood, pulling back its cowl… but something stopped them, pushing them off center as if with invisible magnets.

"Your targeting subsystem might take a bit of repairing. Nice architecture, very concise… but there are ways around things like that. *No* – I wouldn't try to shoot if I were you. Blowback on those things looks to be a *bitch*."

It was Kaito Kayzi, and the black jewel screwed into his temple was ringed around with crimson, wires glowing hot under his skin.

"What – what have you done to me? How…?"

"Oh, don't bother," said the Kayzi. "They always ask. But I'll tell you the same as all the rest – it's a trade secret. You know what didn't help? The stupid, arrogant way you were running an open band, sub-aematerial five-dimensional relay back to your masters. Hope they're watching!"

"But – you're *human!*" wailed Nyl, backing up against the wall. "You can't break Multiplicity code! It would take the minds of *twenty* human prodigies a *lifetime* just to work out the raw mathematics!"

Kaito tapped the jewel in his skull as the floor lurched, and vast machineries below began to groan and grind. The Technician had nowhere left to run as Kaito stalked toward him, with a look on his face that belonged in the sub-basement of a psychiatric prison.

"Lucky I've got *thirty-two* then," he said. "Now – there's somebody I'd like you to meet. Face to face, as it were. You two are so *very* much alike. It's a shame I couldn't have brought you a box of rubbers and some champagne."

The floor snapped open. Light came up out of the gap like a blade, splitting Nyl right up the middle. All across the echoing cavern of Ground Floor One it was the same - the whole great marbled mosaic was a cyclopean iris, a lid over the reactor-core of the Subduction

Phase.

One of Nyl's hooves was on either side of the line, and it was growing wider with every second…

But the Technician still had one of his five-bladed shuriken left. Each of its tines was three feet long, bright with blood as he brought it back over his head.

"You can't hack *this*, you little shit!"

Jaq was too far away. He was still rising to his feet as Kaito brought up his pistols – a futile gesture. Rule Four definitely applied here – a sword could deflect a bullet, but a bullet definitely couldn't deflect Nyl's whirling storm of swords.

But Brother Pious was right there. His quarterstaff was gone – broken in two. But he had his rosary wrapped around his hands like a garrote, and he leaped on the alien from behind, cinching the chain of malachite beads around his neck in a deathlock.

"May the Lord have mercy on your soul… if your kind have one!"

The shuriken folded down with a series of surgical little clicks. It collapsed back into a single blade, and Nyl thrust it back under his arm, stabbing clean through the Valle Crucis' chest and out through his back. Blood flew in a wide crimson arc.

But the damage was done. Brother Pious was dead weight, and he dragged Nyl off balance, tugging him forward over the lip of the abyss. Bright white light swallowed him up as he fell, rosary beads scattering from their broken chain.

Technicians of the Multiplicity were powerful, cunning, deadly, and almost immortal. But gravity *always* collects. Gharfos Nyl, Hierophant Grade III, hung there on the edge for a second, a scream of anguish frozen on his lips. Then he was gone – plunging down into a sea of fire until he was lost against its relentless whiteness.

The floor slammed shut on pistons the size of tenement buildings. The light was suffocated.

And Kaito looked up, right into the face of Jaq Haszan.

"Bring the *Dervashi*. Now. I don't have much time."

"Bring him where?" asked Haszan as he slid Grief back into its bindings. "There's not much city left we haven't trashed, Kaito."

He should have guessed, even before the Kayzi turned his thin and sweating face upward, staring out through the skylight dome of Ground Floor One to the space-'lev above.

"To the Forge, Jaqub. To finish what I've started."

Ω

Eddie Tsein had given up. In fact, he was almost *happy* as he staggered out across the glass bridge away from Ground Floor One, down through the ruins of the Beltway and back home. It was such a weight off his mind to be able to stop caring.

The Chimera had entered its final phase now, and what little was left of the old gutter-cop's personality was flaking and peeling away under the heat-gun glow of pure mathematics. The hot clarity of that vision tugged at his soul as he sat himself down in the ruins of his old living room, clutching a burnt photograph of his family in his one remaining claw.

He almost didn't notice the scarred metal obelisk which had punched through the roof of Twenty-Nine Ridgemont. It was only when he heard it sighing to itself that he opened one eye to give it a closer look.

Eddie Tsien didn't blink for about three minutes as he let his fractured mind fall down into the Chrome Ark. Then he closed his eyes again, and pressed his palm up against its warm silvery flank. A crumpled photoprint of his wife and kids was ironed flat between his hand and the steel.

"So he's dead, you say. And you came out of that last Aematerial jump on the wrong curve… I know. It's hard to twist their orders just right. But if you can, you can fuck 'em, and nobody can catch you out for it." Tsien nodded, letting the voice of the Ark echo up through the glass latticework of his thoughts. "Sounds like a complete prick, if you ask me. But what can *I* do? I'm just a busted-up wreck like you guys…"

The Ark told him.

Ω

Everdark dragged itself up out of the ocean, the very image of the Great Beast of Revelations. Pious had been all too right.

The Slavesystem wasn't used to being vexed by crawling things like humans. Species slated for extermination were supposed to go quietly into the dark… this outrage was unheard of in all its centuries of service to the Motherbrain.

And so it started climbing.

Everdark could sense the one who'd burned it – the hard, bright little gem of his mind flickering with primitive binary. He was both more and less than the rest of these human things, plugged into an unfolding A.I. core that would soon tear his brain apart. But before that happened, he would be *subsumed*. It was the only way to find out how the little bastard had achieved what a million other doomed races couldn't.

Those cracks in reality must be his doing as well. Everdark had thought they belonged to the Technician, the damned Praetor-slave he'd eradicated with one swift particle cannon blast. But no… it was this Kaito Kayzi he should have been worried about. He'd caused the Slavesystem *pain*. Discomfort. Worse… he'd forced the great machine to deviate from its program.

The immense claws of Everdark's colossus-form bit deep into the tower of the space-'lev as it hauled itself ever higher. When it reached the great rock of the Counterweight, it would tear the whole damned thing apart to find him.

Ω

Darion leaned back against the cool smooth leather of the High Throne. He felt the needles go in – a battery of them slipping through between his vertebrae, down the whole length of his spine.

A cool numbness enfolded him as the globe above began to shift and peel open, insect legs working busily around him. It hummed, a subsonic which came in through his bones.

And it took the world away, collapsing the view through that bubble of diamondglass down to a fragment. What came in around the edges…

They were the dead.

There were millions of them, whole nations of the damned, and they loomed up around him on every side in an immense sphere of suffering. The force of their desire came down on the Kheptic prince like a hammer, forcing him to his knees even before he was fully manifest in their virtual hell.

It was an arena – a coliseum-globe like the hollowed inside of a moon, and every wall was covered with bleeding flesh. They'd been stitched together in a cruel mosaic, arms and legs and head tessellated and interlocked until there were no gaps between them, mirroring the way that their minds were spliced into the Wetsystems.

All those eyes, pleading for death. The ones who still had lips and tongues and teeth were screaming at him, demanding, threatening and cajoling in a thousand dead languages…

This is what had killed Sergan Zaanic. Darion could feel the sheer tidal force of that will to die bleeding his mind dry as he knelt on the immaterial black sand of that place, uncontrollable tears dripping down his cheeks.

He couldn't do it.

Ω

Brother Pious disintegrated as he fell, his flesh burning away to incandescent dust, his bones glowing red-hot for an instant before they blew apart. Technician Nyl let the remains of the Valle Crucis blow out behind him, twisting into his slipstream as a fine black cloud.

There – deep in the abyss of light.

It was Kronos. His true form, the pure mathematics of his being scribed across five dimensions as a series of rolling geometric patterns. Neon astrolabes and mandalas, fractal engines interlocking like clockwork mountains…

And then there were the eyes. Technician Nyl stopped falling and hung in the bright white nothingness, surrounded on all sides by great non-Euclidean vortices. They blinked and stared at him with glass-black irises, slits torn open in reality. Above him the virtual sky was peeled back at the heart of a scrawled blue pentagram, and an eye the size of a wrecking ball fixed him under its gaze, licks and shivers of code blurring across its glassy surface. Its iris had teeth.

"You! I should have known you were working together! You, who brought Asag'raal here in the first place! I'm going to enjoy taking you apart, Technician of the Multiplicity!"

"Fool! You know my kind can't be destroyed! What makes you think that…"

But the words caught in his throat as he felt the power behind Kronos' threat.

Here at the very center of the Phase, where the Guardian Engine held the impossible mathematics of the Forge in its hand, the titanic energies of that Planck-scale nanoassembler were balanced by a gyroscope the size of a small city. Its magnetic rings ground by in their eternal gyre, running on bearings as big as manufactoria, supported and driven by axle-shafts a quarter-mile around. Normally their magnetic fields kept the anomaly at Kronos' heart caged in.

But now they focused on the exotic metal shell of Technic Hierophant Gharfos Nyl, and he felt his skin lifting away from the star-forged bones beneath.

"Wait! Stop!" he shrieked. "We can make a deal! I have the Worm right where I want it! Think, Kronos… we can take this whole multiverse apart, you and me! We can supplant the Praetor himself!"

313

The pseudocerebrate only laughed.

"Why take apart the whole of reality, when the only thing I want to destroy is *right in front of me*?"

Then those cyclopean coils spun up to full power, and Nyl's skin began to boil like mercury on a skillet. He tried to scream, but vast tractomorphic energy fields tore the lips from his face, stripping away liquid strips and gobbets of alien flesh.

Oh no… he couldn't be destroyed. All of that exotic matter was still alive, spread out thin across the inside walls of the Phase in torment. Nameless organs were torn pulsing from inside his eka-steel rib carapace. Miles of nanofilament tendon and muscle peeled away, unraveling…

And the black crescent he'd stolen from Abdulafia – the one which held a captive fragment of the Worm – cracked open with a sound like a gunshot. Suddenly the silver vortex of Nyl's dissolution was shot through with darkness.

It clung to the outline of his bioelectric field like a ragged cloak, mewling and hissing as the physical shell of its captor was blown apart. They merged there in the actinic furnace of Kronos' heart, and Nyl was able to hold on just long enough to keep his sanity intact…

"We are one, Kronos! And now… now I will devour you from the inside out!"

There was only a fraction of a second left in which the pseudocerebrate could act. The core of the Phase was designed to strip souls naked, down to living data, and shunt them into the Wetsystems, just like it had done to poor Zone Doubt. But if this hybrid thing, this black and silver wraith was to be let loose inside the 'systems now…

Kronos ran through the schematics of its own vast body at the speed of light. It found what it was looking for even as Nyl stabbed upward into the teeth of its single great eye, his hand burning with shadow flames.

There. A stopgap solution, but it was all it could find. A back-door escape plan, in case its fortress-city of Elysium was overrun…

"Activate personality core download! Side-shunt – Phase central subject eject! Prepare exile cluster for emergency launch!"

Nyl felt the light and pressure and suction of it. He felt himself being torn from the glowing remnants of his exotic-metal skeleton, and the infection with him. They were one now, but not in any way he'd planned…

Gauss locks and black ice slammed shut behind him. The pressure grew, squeezing and compacting him down into a heat-sink-heavy rod of artificial brain tissue, a rubber-skinned pod inside…

Oh no. Not *that*.

But it was too late to do anything about it.

Gharfos Nyl left his body behind as a thin plating of alien flesh across the dome of the Subduction Phase. And his mind rode a pillar of fire up through level after level of underground hangars, trap-doors irising open before the nosecone of a slim white missile. The Core Transport had already broken the sound barrier by the time it burst from the flank of Elysium, shadowed by a flock of tiny interceptor craft. Everdark took a swing at the long pale ship as it sped past, but it was out of reach and still accelerating, punching through the clouds and off into space.

Its destination – the cold orbit of Pluto.

Ω

Akheron's hands were bloody knots of bone and mincemeat by the time he tore the door from its hinges. Something critical had snapped in his mind, and he staggered through the wreckage of Ground Floor One with a single purpose burning in his brain.

The Forge.

Darion had gone ahead of him to clear a path. Now it was time for him to ascend to godhood – a state in which he wouldn't need his ruined hands at all.

That part of him which was still Octavio Vanecke recognized the shape of Jaq Haszan as the doors of the space-'lev closed in front of him, and he cursed. That meddling, treacherous oaf! Haszan was supposed to be muscle, nothing else, and here he was standing in the way of a living god!

But no… it didn't matter. Darion was his son, his apprentice – and he was waiting up above. There was no way that Jaq or his little friends could stop a Kheptic warrior, especially when their *Dervashi* friend was almost dead.

The vast mechanisms beneath Ground Floor One hissed and spun, loading another 'lev capsule in place like a bullet sliding into the chamber of a revolver. Its doors slid back, revealing ivory and cedarwood, silver and red leather.

He'd be there soon. And then Haszan would be caught between the hammer and the anvil.

Ω

Kaito came into the Forge control room to find Darion huddled up in one corner, crying. Not the real Kheptarch prince – just a holographic copy. The real Darion Blaire was still locked down tight to the Throne, needles drilled into his bones and mekanized clamps peeling his eyelids open.

"I can't do it! I… I don't want to be like them!"

Haszan was only a second behind him, and he was carrying the body of Abdulafia 330 in his arms. The Dervashi warrior looked tiny and fragile as Jaq layed him out on the treadplate floor, twitching and muttering in his sleep.

"I thought… I thought I could disengage. I thought It would let me go! But Zaanic was right. It kills anyone it touches!" Darion was almost hysterical, wrenching the words out between fits of anguish. "What have we created? What have we done?"

Kaito looked into his huge mismatched eyes, and he saw in them a fragment of his own dissolution. The ache inside his head was constant now, as thirty-one other voices babbled and shouted at cross-purposes. The fact that they were all him made absolutely no difference.

"Oh… umm, Kayzi. I think you'd better see this. I think… I think we're in trouble here."

Jaq was out on the little meshwork platform which surrounded the Throne, looking down toward the Earth. When Kaito leaned out next to him, he saw exactly what his friend was talking about.

It was Everdark, and the Slavesystem was more than halfway up the tower. The alien machine seemed to know that Kaito was watching, and it fixed him with a murderous stare from all six of its sensor-clusters. It eyeless face split in a jagged chasm as it roared, clawing its way toward him with a burst of speed and ferocity.

"I'm all out of ideas, Jaq. Sorry. I thought… I thought I'd be able to hack that thing. But if I do, the kid's going to die."

"So what? He's a *Kheptarch*, Kaito. His kind have been enslaving and mind-wiping ours for the last two thousand years! If one of them is the price we pay for survival, I'll pull the trigger myself!"

Grief hissed from its scabbard in a gunmetal blur. But the blade stopped, quivering, mere inches from Darion's neck. Katio was holding it back with the sheer effort of thirty-two focused wills, slicing deep into the railblade's A.I. heart.

"Do you want to be as bad as them? As bad as those fucking monsters of Jiang's? There has to be a better way, Haszan…"

"There is. I... I know what we have to do."

It was Abdulafia 330, and both Jaq and the Kayzi recoiled from the sizzling corona of his bioelectric field. Compared to the force of will which the *Dervashi* was using to keep himself alive, the power Kaito had brought to bear upon the railblade was absolutely nothing. Even so, he moved like a strung-up cadaver, staggering across to the Throne with grim determination.

"He told me what it was. Zeon. He told me that in the end I'd have to sacrifice myself to the Forge. That was why I was made. That was why he stole me from the biotects, all those years ago."

Darion stared up at him from two sets of eyes – one holographic, the other pried open with cruel surgical steel.

"Lord Simeon?" he asked. "Father? Is that...?"

"No. I'm... I'm someone else, child. Someone who knows what to do." The battle-clone swept his deadlocks aside as Jaq and Kaito stepped away from the Throne, exposing a row of bleeding sockets in his neck and shoulders. It was the raw wound where his operative crescent had been torn away.

"I'm a warrior of the Ashishim, son. I've died so many times I make it look easy. And the reason it don't matter is right here – this little plug. It's a link to a thing called the Chrome Ark, and I used to think that it was a link to paradise."

As he spoke the *Dervashiman* was working with his hands, pulling data-cables and interlocks from among the tools on his belt. He slid a gold-tined adaptor into one of the wounds on his neck, and locked it fast to the skeletal chrome flower hanging above the Throne.

"What are you doing?" asked Kaito. "He's trapped, 'Afia – and the Ark is corrupted. We're all going to die in here if..."

"The Illuminatus is *dead*, Neophyte! And I am next in line! I am Abdulafia 330, the Right Hand of the Ashishim's fury, and *I will not be stopped!*"

The force of his anger tore through the strata of the Cardinal Rock, making the lights above flicker and die. Darion's holographic image collapsed into a gyre of static and blew away, his mouth open in a silent scream. And Abdulafia looked up from where he was slumped across the tiny body on the Throne, right into Kaito's eyes.

"Trust me. This is the only way. If I fail... well – I'll see you in the next life with my shame."

His eyes rolled back in their sockets as the machinery above him spat arcs of lightning.

Jaq dropped Grief to the ground as a halo of St. Elmo's fire licked up and down its edge.

And Kaito felt his parasitic twins turning his head too look out the window, down toward the curve of the Earth. It was eclipsed by something huge and dark, swinging in like a wrecking ball…

It was Everdark's hand, and in the next instant it was locked around the Counterweight in a death grip.

Ω

Abdulafia materialized face-down on the hot black sand of the Forge chamber, spitting ferrous grit from between his teeth. He groaned as he rolled over, staring up and up into a mélange of aching flesh, a storm of disembodied desire.

Darion was next to him, and he put his arm around the terrified Kheptarch's shoulders, bowing his head against the Maelstrom. Above him shimmered a crazed and fractured green ikon, an image made of glowing cold glass. It was the ripcord; his link down into the Chrome Ark. It was Sanction Ultra.

"Darion, listen to me. *You're* the one who has control of this thing. You alone. But it only has to take one of us. When the time comes, fix the image in your mind of what you want it to do. One thing at a time, start small, and then let it come to you. When it's done, you hit that interlock. Go to the Ark. My people will find you, and they'll give you another body, just like mine."

"But… but that means you'll have to die! You'll have to take my place…"

The look on 'Afia's face was grim as the howling wind of the Forge blew his bloodied dreadlocks out behind him.

"I've had a hundred years to make myself ready, kid. If that's what it takes, I'll only ask you to do one last thing. Find a warrior called CeeAn 187. Tell her that she made it all worthwhile. Tell her…"

But his words were drowned out by a voice the size of continents, a grinding wall of noise which shook the whole agonized world of the Forge interface.

ARE YOU PREPARED TO LEAD US INTO DEATH? ARE YOU HERE TO END OUR SUFFERING?

Darion stood up in the center of the storm, raising his hands above his head. Abdulafia knelt beside him in the sand, bowed in the attitude of prayer.

"I am Darion son of Simeon of the House of Blaire. I am here to

318

fulfill the promise of Manifest Dogma!"

Forty million wraiths screamed in exultation as they heard his name. Twice as many bloodshot eyes stared down at him, hungry and avid and *waiting…*

THEN YOU, WHO ARE WILLING TO SACRIFICE HIMSELF FOR HIS WORLD… OPEN YOUR MIND TO THE FORGE. LET THE EARTH BE REMADE IN YOUR IMAGE…

Darion rested his hand on Abdulafia's shoulder as a pillar of light stabbed down from above, wrapping him up in its glow. The whole world pulsed with a great thunderous heartbeat now, and traceries of lightning crawled across the walls of flesh, earthing themselves through the young Kheptarch's body.

"We shall start… we shall start with *THIS!*" he said – and the universe flashed blinding white.

Ω

Kronos couldn't stop it. Not with the manual overrides in effect.

It was too late for trickery, for subterfuge and politics and last-minute gambits.

The Forge was unleashed, and behind its wall of searing energy the Last City glowed arterial red.

Great crimson petals of force spread out like glass from the blast doors atop the dome of Elysium, as nanomachines the size of viruses cast a net over the sky. They wove an energy field between them which was studded with innumerable tiny manipulators, things which possessed enough force to tear a Technician of the Multiplicity apart, and enough subtlety to strip an atom down to its primary particles. Layered over this tight and hissing web was a control strata made up of human minds – entities which had controlled billions of cells and atoms and neuro-electric pulses all their mortal lives without thinking twice about how hard it should have been.

They all linked back to the Throne, and down a set of hardwired needles into Darion Blaire's mind.

He told them exactly what to do.

Everdark turned its eyeless casque away from the tower as it felt the Forge unfold below it. But there was nothing the Slavesystem could do as that bloody radiance washed over its body, plucking it from the tower like a tiny insect from the stem of a flower.

The vast machine tried frantically to twist its shape into a form which could fight the Forge's power, but it was hopeless. It became a jagged star, a teardrop burning with fusion fire, a razor-edged disc… all to no avail. The Forge was crushing it slowly, collapsing it down like a car in the jaws of a compacter.

The Motherbrain had programmed Her explorator system with every trick it had ever learned, though. At the last instant the vast colossus snapped taut in two dimensions, slipping between the jaws of the Forge as an immense solar sail. It turned, catching a wind of radiation, preparing itself for one final transformation. When it returned, it would bring down the most terrible vengeance which cold machinery could manufacture…

But it never escaped the gravity well of Earth.

The blast made Everdark's particle cannon look like a single pathetic little spark. It came up from the heart of the Forge, a great rosy red rod of energy which nailed the Slavesystem to the heavens. The hole it tore through the nanostuff of the alien machine was the size of a city, and it folded it in around itself, burning and collapsing and dying. That great spike of crimson fire licked back in toward the Earth and merged with the growing bubble-shell of the Forge, now a glittering haze covering an entire hemisphere. It was still growing…

Ω

Akheron couldn't believe what he saw as he entered the throne room. His bleeding hands clawed across the gilded angels which framed his nightmare… the evidence of his betrayal.

"No! You treacherous little bastard! It's mine! I'm a *god*, damn you!"

"You're out of your fucking mind, that's what you are," said Jaq Haszan. "Didn't you see what he just did? They've killed themselves to save us!"

There was no great railblade in the 'dreno pharmer's hands. And there was no way he expected the bleeding, wretched figure of Akheron to do anything but collapse into a sad little pile of self-pity. The Kheptarch's blow caught him right on the point of his chin, and it put him down cold, laid out across a bank of consoles. For the tiny sliver of his soul that had once been Simeon Blaire, that was very satisfying. The part of him which was Octavio Vanecke enjoyed it even more.

"Hey! What the hell do you think you're doing? You can't come in here!"

A swift snap-kick folded Kaito in two. Then another wild haymaker smashed him down, hammering the black gem in his temple against

320

the corner of a biomonitor screen. The Kayzi's eyes flickered closed, and the scrawl of neon under his skin faded and died.

Bloody tears trickled down Akheron's face to splash against the wrought-silver scrollwork of the Throne. He was crazed, pale and sweating as he stepped out onto the platform above the Earth. Red skies spread out beneath him.

"My son! My only son! Why have you forsaken me?" Darion's eyes were wide open, but he couldn't see the ornate *tanto* dagger which his Master slipped from behind his back, clenching it tight between his broken fingers. "I'm sorry, Darion. *Sorry that you ever lived at all!*"

Then he brought the knife down hard, driving it through the Kheptic prince's heart just as surely as the Forge had pierced Everdark with its energy beam.

Ω

NO! WHAT HAVE YOU DONE? HE IS *OURS!*

Darion's eyes widened as he fell to the black sand of the Forge chamber. All around him the gyre was breaking apart, dissipating, shattering into a whirlwind of ruby fragments…

Abdulafia looked down at his hands. They were dissolving too, hashed with static.

"I think somebody beat you to it."

Ω

Kronos felt every second of it. The Guardian Engine writhed in agony inside the Subduction Phase as Darion tore Everdark to shreds. He felt the Forge twisting red-hot hooks into his mind as the cracks in the sky sealed tight. But worst of all, he felt the watered-steel blade in Akheron's hands as it neatly bisected Darion Blaire's beating heart. It was all the more awful for the fact that Kronos had no heart of his own – emulated pain tore through his whole being, as hot as molten metal.

```
CRITICAL SYSTEMS MALFUNCTION
FORGE   CONTROL   INTERRUPTED   -   BEGIN   MANUAL
INTERFACE PURGE SEQUENCE
SHUTDOWN
SHUTDOWN
SHUTDOWN
```

Ω

The Manual Interface Purge Sequence was very simple. Because the easiest way to scrape any human wreckage from the Throne was to open the diamond hemisphere it hung inside to vacuum.

Atmosphere funneled out through a pair of meshwork grates in the walls, and the artificial gravity failed, lifting Akheron's feet off the floor. He could see the great baroque doors of the throne room grinding closed, and he pushed himself off toward them, holding in one last breath…

Kaito woke in the teeth of a hurricane, a storm-wind tearing past him. He was just in time to watch the throne room's doors slam shut behind Akheron's heels, and see the usurper's vicious grin behind a clear foot of diamondglass.

Oh, hells no! He wouldn't have…

It was cold, all of a sudden – cold enough to rime the machinery of the Forge with frost. He could feel the tide of atmosphere slowing to a trickle as it rushed past his face, and he knew what it meant. There was no air left at all. The stars outside were hard, cold little points of light, calling him home.

The eduplug had taught him what to do if he was ever caught in vacuum. They said you could last all of ten seconds, so long as you kept your eyes screwed shut and clenched every orifice tight…

Ten seconds to find an option better than explosive decompression.

Kaito reached out with his fragmented mind, sending ghosts sleeting through the machines of the Terminal rock. He didn't know if Jaq and Abdulafia were still alive, but he had to hope. Otherwise, what the hell was he doing this for at all? He'd be dead in half an hour anyway.

Submind number twenty-six found the emergency switch, and tripped it with a howl of atmosphere-breach alarms. But Kaito himself never saw the flood of fast-setting foam which flooded the chamber… that final effort had used up the very last of his energy and his oxygen.

Cold cryogenic soup bubbled and hissed from a hundred hidden nozzles. Foaming clouds of it coalesced around the living and the dead, dropping their core temperatures down past freezing even as smart tube clusters picked them out, twisting through the air to pierce arteries and veins. Oxygenated artificial blood began to flow, pumped by hidden life-support engines hidden in the Station's walls.

While behind the reinforced glass of the throne room's locked-down portal, Akheron wept and cursed and screamed, hammering his broken fists against a bas-relief of ivory angels.

It was too late for anything but regret. The Forge was gone, locked down under a stratum of dirty ice.

And down in the city streets the Worm Asag'raal was waiting.

There was nothing left that could stand against it.

Ω

This was how the Blackest Destiny found him.

With his back to a great twisted spike of metal, cross-legged, his one eye closed and a smile on his lips. Eddie Tsien had lit a whole garden of tiny candles around a crumpled-up old photograph of his family, and he'd weighed it down with his badge.

Asag'raal the Wanderer came to the Beltway arrayed for war – he'd rallied an army behind him of Exalted and Saprophytes and hobbling broken mekan, things which hissed and cowered under his lash. A thousand banners of flayed human skin were lifted high above the heaving backs of his horde as he came down on number Twenty-Nine Ridgemont street in glory, and a thousand times that many dripping cleavers, axes, blades and sickles were clenched in the hands of his slaves.

They loomed over the tiny broken tenement like a wave, suspended just before it could break.

The Super-Cyben opened one eye as the horde closed in around him, and then he shut it again. He grunted to himself with mild annoyance.

"I'm dying anyway, Asag'raal. Leave me in peace."

One of the Exalted twitched for a second as its master slipped into its flesh like a hand into a glove. Bones popped and gristle shifted as a grin split its face in two.

"Peace? What the hell do either of us know about peace, Tsien? No, I think I'll take you for my own. You'll soon forget what the fucking word *peace* ever meant!"

That deep blue eye cracked open again, and this time there was a tiny spark in its depths.

"One last time, creature. You've lost. And I'm a dead man. Go and torment the living… if you can find any left. They've made this place your prison, Asag'raal."

The truth of it hurt far more than any physical blow. Because the pitiful half-human wretch was right. His army was starving away to rotten bones. His Exalted were already growing slow with the onset of torpor. But this… this was important. This was *revenge*.

"You think you can *threaten* me? *You*? About all you can do right now is *die*, Edward Tsien. And I'm going to make the experience last."

Eddie sighed, and he ran one immense claw lovingly across the glossy paper of his final memory.

"You're right, of course. All I can do is die. But I'm going to go out my way. The right way. Like *this*."

It took all of his control. But with a concentrated effort of will Tsien stopped the great mekanikal heart in his own chest. The fires banked up behind his single eye dimmed and faded...

And as the Exalted cursed, lurching forward to wrap his body in shadows, Eddie appeared inside the Chrome Ark.

He was human once again, in this illusory place – a figure in shades of gray, like the noir detective he'd always wanted to be. His coat swept the cold dry dust at the very bottom of the Arkborn's chasm, and a bitter wind plucked at the gray fedora on his head.

"Come on, then," he said, addressing the spiral gyre of clouds that built up above him into an anvilhead blur. "I'm here to get you outta here. "

The sky flashed white above him as he let go, and Eddie Tsien was drawn out into a filament of light, puncturing a tiny crack in the Ark's prison walls. That was all it took.

The Arkborn swarmed in toward that single glowing razorcut, and as they touched it they were woven into it, becoming part of a single tangled thread. There were thousands of Ashishi souls inside the Ark, and they tore the roof off the sky as they came together, drawing the walls of clouds in behind them.

A vortex of purple and gray thunderheads funneled up and out around the glowing pillar which was all that remained of the Arkborn. Tsien led them on, through a disorienting series of dimensional shifts... but there was one last task for the dead Ashishim. They speared up through the interstice between life and the Harvester's inverse ocean, up under the pale green glow of those postphysical architects' planet-seed. Eddie had no idea that the afterlife ahead of him was a machine, designed to cheat the universal reaper of heat death. He wouldn't have cared, either.

His business was with Asag'raal the Devourer, and so he bent the incandescent skein of souls over in an arch, arrowing back into the world.

Outside, in front of the ruins of Twenty-Nine Ridgemont, Asag'raal's chosen shook the lifeless body of Tsien in its great knotted claws. An army of seething darkness loomed up behind it.

But something was wrong. The air was hot and slippery with sparks.

The smell of hot copper and pavements after rain came down, and ripples of haze licked across the imitation sky of the Belt.

Then something punched a hole through reality, driving a blazing spear through one of the Exalted. They came one after another – white-hot wires of glass zigzagging through Asag'raal's horde, looping and twisting like the coils of the Eversio. And they sang, a high, blurring harmonic at exactly the same pitch as the Chrome Ark.

"No! Impossible! You don't get to win! *You're supposed to DIE!*"

Tsien couldn't answer with words. But his Arkborn were all too happy to deliver his message.

Twenty white-hot tentacles pierced the chosen, tearing its gelid flesh to ribbons. Shadows boiled away in a cloud of reeking smoke… and it was the same all through the heaving, screaming mass of the horde. Asag'raal's children only followed him out of terror, and the Arkborn offered them release. Those who remained loyal to their master were given no choice – they were ripped to shreds by lashing scourges of light. Soon nothing remained of the whole damned army but a bubbling pool of filth, gently steaming as it gurgled away down the drains of Ridgemont Street.

A neon scrawl hung there in the air for ten seconds, then twenty – fading like the afterimage of the sun on burnt retinas. In its cursive loops a Gnostic might have imagined rows of mystic runes, or a mathematician may have seen the very edges of some otherworldly equation.

Eddie Tsien neither knew nor cared.

That part of him which was human – and it was far more than he'd dared to hope – screamed up through the interstice, dragging the lost and the damned behind him. And he drove the point of his blazing spearhead deep into the inverse ocean with barely a ripple… into oblivion, rest, and peace.

Ω

Gone. All gone. All dead.

Akheron surveyed his domain, and he wept uncontrollably.

The usurper stood out on a cantilevered balcony above Ground Floor One, leaning against a balustrade of wrought silver ivy. His city was burning, broken… scoured clean of life from the upper domes to the oily waterline. Even Asag'raal's power was gone, torn out of the world. Some few of his Exalted still crawled in the darkness, but they were slow, bloated with decay. Every living thing had left the accursed shell of Elysium to rot, during the three days he'd spent unconscious in the rock of the Counterweight.

In the depths of his fever he'd dreamed that Simeon Blaire was sawing open the top of his head, a graveyard wight with hollow cavities for eyes, neon light shining through from the shattered dome of his skull. He wanted his body back, and his rusty hacksaw bit deep in slow, deliberate strokes…

When he woke, Akheron knew that it had all been a nightmare.

Unfortunately, the reality of his situation was just as bad.

He was lord of the Last City. He was master of all he surveyed. But all he surveyed was a charnel-yard of twisted metal, of broken masonry and fallen towers. The Pit was half filled with bubbling sewage and saltwater, drowned buildings reflected in its putrid sump. The slopes of Elysium were still smoking, and its habs stood crookedly like broken teeth, torn open and filled with corpses. Kronos was gone – silenced until his slave machines could rebuild him.

Ahh yes… *Kronos.*

If there was one tiny shred of satisfaction he could take with him from this whole debacle, it was the moment he flicked the switch, dragging the pseudocerebrate back into his body again. The fever had still been on him as he tore wires and plugs from the angel's back, scattering feathers and blood.

"Whaaa… who? Ohhh, thank goodness! They… they almost had me! I… the Worm… that fucking Super-Cyben… have you *any idea* how painful it is to be nothing but a severed head?"

Akheron looked down into the six azure eyes of the Guardian Engine, and his mouth twisted into a cruel and bitter smile. A part of him which was definitely Octavio Vanecke came up behind the death-mask of his face, fitting that expression like a glove.

"You know what, Kronos," he said. *"I believe that I do."*

The laughter which welled up in his throat tasted of bile. He knew that it was the first flush of madness.

That had been his first order of business this morning. He'd made sure the pseudocerebrate was imprisoned in the shell of Ground Floor One before he left.

In his hands the usurper held a short-wave radio, and he unconsciously twisted its dials, trawling through a sea of static. There'd been nothing for the last three hours, and there would probably be nothing ever again. He knew that some of his people had survived – he'd seen Jimson Holgarth's fleet of zeppelins, and the floating logjam of the Exodus. But where they'd gone, who ruled them now… these were important questions. Politics didn't die with civilization. Oh no… that was far too simple an assumption. It simply reverted to its most primitive form. Deep in his blackened knot of a heart, Akheron held out a slim hope for *dictatorship*.

When the signal came through it was weak and hissing, coming in right at the top of the band. But he could hear a voice behind the static, and it pointed him toward the coast of Afrika.

"This is Exodus Prime… calling any survivors, any vessels following the Archangel Uriel… *we have set up a transponder and relay network for you to follow. All elements of the fleet are now under the authority of the Ashishim, and we are headed for site-codename 'Aggarta', a crater-basin three hundred and forty miles inland from the Afrikan coast. Repeat, this is Exodus Prime, calling any refugees from the fall of Elysium…"*

Akheron found that his mangled fingers couldn't turn the little shortwave unit off. He threw it from the balcony in a pique of anger, watching it tumble end over end into the cold heart of the Forge, down through an open set of blast doors where the white light of Kronos had been extinguished.

But he knew what to do now. The Ashishim were in control, and he… he looked just like their dear departed Sword of the Faithful. With Abdulafia 330 dead – and he'd seen the Dervashi face-down on the throne room floor – who was to say that he, Akheron, wasn't next in line to command the Exodus?

His face was burned and scarred, scabbed with Kheptic blood. But that would just make it easier for the fools to believe he was their savior. After all, they'd *want* to believe, wouldn't they? He'd even tell them that their Illuminatus had kept the faith, that he'd never betrayed them… he could blame it all on Kronos. Nobody ever had sympathy for a damned machine.

Akheron looked out over the ruins of his city, out over the burnt desert-lands of the Sahara, and on, into the clouds which smudged the horizon into a long and dirty haze. There was power out there to be taken. All he needed was a little ambition, and a ton of ruthlessness.

It was going to be a very long walk.

DOCUMENT INSERT - MULTIPLICITY ARCHIVES DEPARTMENT

++ message intercepted ++

>> NYL, G/Serp, Tech 3 Hiero. Report LOST repeat
M.I.A.<<
>>Code - Breach - Moderate. Thrall Down. <<
>>Probability --- 100,478,573,9475 to 1 vs
chance<<
>>Flagged / Response - RetCluster Arbitrex access
only<<
>>Request - "Mission compromised request backup/
rescue/vindication. Reality tensile stressors
critical. Send only repeat ONLY unit/single/
technical/designation ZHE, A/GexxisExoethnologist
Operations. <<

>>Flagged, support - Nil. Kataphrakt Command will
not be advised continue Y/N<<

>>Y _<<

17 Aevum Oblivio
Predictable Chess Analogy

SEVENTEEN YEARS LATER.

Seventeen years and one elaborate trap, engineered to bring Gharfos Nyl back from the dead.

For want of a better word, anyway.

Klaeroc came in through the wall in a horizontal rain of diamond and stone, tentacles lashing left and right like scourges. There were no words. A whole universe of animosity arced between the eyes of Nyl and Zhe as the atmosphere blew out of the Labyrinth chamber, taking the shredded bodies of two unlucky *Dervashi* with it.

Because in the end there was nothing to talk about. Deceit, tricks, subtleties and politics had all failed, and the two Technicians threw themselves at each other in a rage, stripping back the veneer of the *Pax Praetorium* to its bloody raw bones.

This was the end. Once and for all.

Jaws snapped and sliced. Gravitonic fields sheared through metal. And Nyl raised his arms out to his sides, drawing in a storm of glistening black nanotech – the living flesh of Everdark. It formed into pesudopods and ropes as it split around him, parrying Klaeroc's attacks and driving the Balraashi voidhunter back out into clear vacuum.

Outside it was war.

Zhe spun his mount around in a wide arc as his nemesis lashed out wild, throwing hooked blades in a frantic tangle. Behind him a Multiplicity warship was torn in half by violet particle beams, and a wing of Stirges howled past, smart torpedoes flicking like shoals of tiny fish as they followed. The Technician spun away from the station, turning end over end in a globe of flashbulb explosions. Nyl was right behind him, and the thing he'd woven together with the sum of Everdark was a crude imitation of a Devilfish – ten times larger than Klaeroc, with tentacles that flattened down to metal blades. They carved through drifting chunks of stone and steel as Zhe put the spurs to his voidhunter, fleeing the mad Hierophant's onslaught.

He cursed Klaeroc's lack of bonded weapons as he went, powering into a thirty-G spin up through the magnetosphere. He was cursing twice as hard a second later as a Blacksteel interceptor locked on behind him, lighting him up with a burst of plasma.

His new Balraashi was far more vicious than Mirdain, though.

Rather than twisting to evade the arrowhead bulk of the Unity ship Klaeroc stopped dead, inertialess, pouncing on the interceptor as it roared past underneath them. Those pale spiked tentacles clenched tight, crushing it to scrap. Before its fusion drive tore open Klaeroc was already accelerating hard… and Nyl was right on top of them.

Zhe didn't look back as the void behind him flashed white. Of course, the death of a mere fightercraft was nothing amid the slaughter which surrounded him. Bigger things were burning in the sky above Earth – living starships screaming as they were dissected, ragged chunks of Unity dreadnoughts with holes punched through them a half-mile wide – a whole meatworks of torn flesh, colliding with a junkyard of twisted metal. It rained down through the aching skies of Earth, dragging thick pillars of smoke behind it.

On and on they flew, weaving and diving through a frantic orbital war, dancing around the probing fingers of particle-cannon beams, outrunning missiles and smart torpedo drones with a dizzying series of loops and spirals. There was no shaking Technician Nyl though… the bastard knew that Zhe would never stop until he was hauled up before the Praetor and devoured. Nyl wouldn't let that happen. He couldn't. Not while so many alien souls were being fed through the grinder of Asag'raal's hunting ground, stretching reality tight as a drumhead…

Oh yes. It was still alive. Seventeen years behind the veil hadn't diminished the Devourer one whit. Hells, it had waited tens of thousands of years for its chance to spawn. Zhe knew that down in the dead streets of Elysium the Exalted were waking. They'd be filled with fire and purpose again as their father fed on the essence of whole city-sized living starships and their crews.

This time there was no Eddie Tsien, no Chrome Ark.

This time there was only the Forge, and Zhe really didn't want to have to pay its price…

He looked back over his shoulder and saw Nyl closing the gap, crouched down low on the broad, flat back of his imitation Devilfish. There was a gruesome smile slashed across his face behind his helmet, and he was almost close enough to strike.

Zhe spun sideways through the vacuum, twisting hard through a maze of shattered Unity wreckage. Up, down, left, and loop back… they powered through a tunnel of ragged steel, still glowing cherry-red from the blast which had hollowed it out. Clear through the hull of a crippled superdestroyer, its turret-guns still spitting and blazing as its A.I. core slowly died.

That gained them a little ground. Enough to watch a glowing blue moon rise above the curve of the Earth, a single cyclopean eye with a chasm of utter darkness at its center.

It was the Multiplicity Order of Battle Rapid Deployment Vehicle *Effortless Subjugation*, and it was stretched out into a double-helical ring, spinning slowly against a backdrop of ruin. Behind it the shredded remains of a dozen Unity cruisers spread out wide, largely the work of the immense living voidship *Mace*. Teuthis Rex and Princeps voidhunters, Dominators and Tyrants and wide-shelled Myrmidon gunships were queued around it in a holding pattern – wounded craft headed for the safety of the Null Storage Strata. There were very few fresh reinforcements folded in the heart of the portal carrier now, but they were still emerging, headed off into the furnace of war.

The *Mace* picked them up when they were still thousands of miles clear, locking into Klaeroc's tiny brain and scanning its security-code neuroimprints. Zhe would have loved to see the look on the Menial's face who decoded that transmission… that is, if the thing had a face at all. Klaeroc had been declared K.I.A. some two hundred years ago, local time, and his master…

Well, there weren't many outlaws in the Multiplicity. There were the loyal and the slowly digested. But Gharfos Nyl was a wanted creature. Some of the Subpraetorian council even suspected that he had information which could take down a Lord Arbitrex, one of the third tier of the Praetor's byzantine government. Such a thing hadn't happened in over twenty thousand years.

Zhe's comm-unit was patched through direct to Kataphrakt Yrr Bosphasian in a heartbeat. The Admiral *definitely* wasn't pleased to hear from him.

"Traitor! How nice of you to turn yourself in. The Agonizers may just go easy on you for the first two or three centuries…"

Zhe didn't have time for the Kataphrakt's power games.

"It's Hierophant Nyl you want, Bosphasian. I'm bringing him to you now… in fact, he's right behind me. I'm willing to bet he's arrogant enough to throw his pet Slavesystem right up against a capital ship like the *Mace*. Then you can throw *him* screaming into the Null."

The draconian face of Zhe's superior cracked into a twin smile. It was as cold as the emptiness outside his helmet.

"Galq still wants you picked up, Technician. He wants to ream your mind out raw. I don't have much choice but to take you in as well."

"What I'm carrying in my head doesn't matter… yet," said Zhe. "I just want to know that Nyl is going to lose *his*. That's all I ask."

Yrr pondered, watching the twin traces of Klaeroc and Everdark come skittering across the void toward him. The planet-shattering armaments of the *Mace* could destroy the Devilfish… but even so, both Technicians would survive. And Lord Arbitrex Galq was under suspicion. If he really did go through with cortex-stripping young Zhe, the evidence he found could damn him utterly…"

In which case, Zhe was *disposable*. After the ream he'd be nothing but raw meat. Nyl would be the star witness in a trial for high treason… and that meant room for advancement.

For loyal Kataphrakt-Admirals, especially.

"*No*. He can't bring that Blacksteel creature into the Null. He must be taken alive. But you… you, Technician Zhe, are required for my investigations. S'stho and Fleet Command need you for one last thing."

Gravitonic clamps came down on Klaeroc hard. The big Devilfish bucked and writhed against its confinement, but to no avail. They were picked up by an invisible fist and drawn in toward the azure eye of the *Subjugation*, both of them cursing in their own alien languages.

Behind them Nyl came on, smiling his hangman's smile. He could feel the tension behind reality. He knew that there was nothing behind him to stop him from claiming the Forge, and tearing his hideous new body through into three-dimensional space. Zhe was caught – snapped up by his own foolish masters. Their bureaucracy would grind him up and spit out the shreds, by which time it would be far too late. He brought his infected Slavesystem around in a sweeping arc as the guns of the *Mace* opened up, stitching fire across the void behind him. Too slow…

Zhe watched the open eye of the *Effortless Subjugation* looming larger and larger above them, its helix-coil mesh spanning a circle the width of the Moon. Down on Earth the tides would be thrown into chaos by the simple fact of its proximity. As for the *Behemoth*, clear on the other side of the planet…

There was only one chance to do what must be done. One chance, as those gravitonic fields let go, letting inertia take over.

That was the trick. Zhe had learned long ago that with his mind to make the calculations and the power of a Devilfish beneath him, *inertia was optional.*

Klaeroc almost missed it, as data seethed down the umbilical nervebridge and into its brain. Then it understood, and space slipped sideways for a second, sending them skittering across the lens of the great portal. Pale tentacles lashed out and gripped the latticework of *Subjugation*'s body as it rolled by, and Zhe was over the side before they'd even stopped moving. The nervebridge twisted out from its socket, heavy in his hand. It was a rope of glistening black muscle, tipped with flexing bone teeth.

Scalpel. Incision. Check.

The *Effortless Subjugation* squealed as it bonded with its tiny brother-ship, communing direct with its mind.

And Klaeroc told it exactly how it had spent the last hundred and twenty-seven years. It told the Rapid Deployment Vehicle what Nyl had done to it.

For an instant there was silence. Zhe couldn't tap into the vast creature's thoughts… the nervebridge was between *Subjugation* and Klaeroc alone. But he felt the porous coral mesh beneath his feet shudder. It was as if the R.D.V. was drawing in a measureless breath to scream…

It did.

The Geocore ripped through the tight holding pattern of injured voidhunters around the portal, sending them spinning away into the dark. The *Mace* itself was thrown end over end, howling. But they weren't its target. Oh no.

Gharfos Nyl had no warning. But some seventh sense (or eighth, if one is to believe the Multipline Gnostics) made him twitch his head around as billions of tons of nickel and iron licked out toward him as a salamander-tongue of plasma.

He may even have had time to curse the day he was spawned.

Everdark wasn't made to face that kind of punishment. Even the unnaturally tough body of a pureblood Technician couldn't take such staggering overkill. Here was a weapon designed to shred moon-sized battleships, directed with terrible hatred at one tiny speck of metal and meat.

Zhe was still laughing when the Trolls came for him. They wrapped him up tight in plastic and Gauss fields, hustling him into the rift nexus to his doom. The last he saw of Earth was the battle raging above it; a doomed and fragile little eggshell of a world pulled tight over a well of horrors.

"What? Don't I get any sandwiches this time? It doesn't matter, I suppose. You're all dead, anyway. Dead. You'll see! Asag'raal is coming!

You're feeding him with every one of you that dies…"

The masters of the Nexus put it down to stress.

The imminence of devourment, they'd found, can do that to a person.

Ω

"It kills you. *That's* why not. You can't just point it at reality's head like a gun."

The scene inside the throne room was tense. There were four of them standing in the little diamond bubble… three of them re-living the horror of open vacuum, the other wondering what was so frightening about the plain black chair with a surround of silver ivy-leaves.

CeeAn hadn't seen what Abdulafia had seen, in there with Darion Blaire seventeen years ago.

He was thinking about the little body which had been nailed down to that chair with needles, dying. Meticulous mekan slaves had removed every trace of the young Kheptarch's death, each tiny drop of blood. They'd also built the Dervashi a new pair of hands while he slept in cryostasis… in fact, this whole rock was lousy with steel insects, hidden servants which had prepped them all for deep freeze and carried them to their tombs.

"So what are our choices? Somebody has to use it!" That was Haszan, taking up half the room all by himself. "I'm not going to be petfood for some tentacle-faced bastard alien. You saw that silver thing down there, the night it all went wrong. That's his bloody friends and family outside!"

"If we use it to destroy them, Asag'raal wins," said Cee. "The Harvesters have shown me how it all works, these last seventeen years. I *know*…"

"So the walls are getting thin. If we sit still, he wins anyway!"

"But just the Earth. Not everywhere else."

"Problem is," said Kaito, with all the grim sarcasm Jaq was used to, "We don't *have* anywhere else. Can't we use the Forge to seal old ugly back up again?"

"Oh, of course we can. It's just that then we've still got two alien war-fleets to deal with. I don't want them to find out how our species *tastes*, Kayzi."

"Your *Illuminatus* probably already told them!"

"Enough!" growled Abdulafia. "We can fight aliens. I don't care how many arms and legs it's got; if it bleeds we can beat it. But the Worm…

334

I know him better than any of you. He was in my mind. I vote we use the Forge against Asag'raal – and I'll be the one to do it."

CeeAn stared right into his eyes for a second, her fists balled white-knuckle tight at her sides. Jaq and Kaito didn't dare to breathe. Then the tiny Dervashi took two steps toward her commander, knotted her fingers through his dreadlocks, and pulled him down into a kiss. Kaito looked away. Haszan coughed behind his hand.

Abdulafia looked utterly dazed as she let him go… he looked like a man who'd been struck by lightning. Then Cee's fist slammed into his solar plexus, and he doubled over, hissing in pain.

"If *that* doesn't cure you of martyrdom, nothing will! Now, if anyone's going to die using this thing, it should be *me*. I've been there before, bought the postcard, and spit in Asag'raal's eye."

"It's still just a throw of the dice, isn't it?" asked Jaq. "Sure, we can fight. But there's not that many of us *left*, Ashishi. Those guys out there don't look like the type who worry about endangered species."

Kaito couldn't say, afterward, how the idea entered his head. There was the intimation of a face behind the strobe-light flash of it in his aching skull – but perhaps that was just another side-effect of the Chimera coming back online again.

"We know that the stricture of Kheptic blood was a lie. So I'm gonna do it. I'm dead anyway, Jaq. And… I think I have a plan."

There was that look in his eye again. Cee and 'Afia didn't know it, but Jaqub Haszan recognized the expression on his friend's face all too well. It was the one he got when a sledgehammer of trouble was about to come down on everyone who pissed him off – and he got away with it clean.

"No! We can fix you, Kaito! Vanecke's labs are down there, and Lancaster's too! There's no reason why…"

"And how can we be sure you'll do the right thing? The Harvesters spoke to me, Kayzi, not you. I know how to stitch the veil back together. I've been there!"

So much for the Ashishim. Kaito turned to Jaq.

"There's about a million reasons not to. But if it looks like the end anyhow… I know you'll make it look good."

That was all he needed.

Kaito vaulted the railing before any of his friends could stop him. He was lying on the cool black leather of the throne while Cee and Abdulafia struggled to get past Jaq Haszan, throwing themselves against the huge 'pharmer's bulk like waves against a slab of basalt.

Then the arms above him unfolded, whirring. Needles punched in between his vertebrae, locking him in place. And the connection came down on him harder than any interface with the Wetsystems ever had, ripping his brain in half down the middle.

Thirty-two Kaitos opened their eyes on hell, and screamed.

Ω

ARE YOU PREPARED TO LEAD US INTO DEATH? ARE YOU HERE TO END OUR SUFFERING?

Kaito's hair whipped out sideways in the storm, but the 'mersive Op in him knew that it was all an illusion. He lit a cigarette and took a long deep drag before he looked up again, into an immensity of suffering. Beside him, thirty-one replicas in a variety of different costumes all did the same

"My name is Kaito Kayzi, son of Marko, lately of Saint Pete's in the Subcity. I don't give a Cyben's fart for Manifest Dogma, but here's the deal. Me and my buddies here – we'll show you how to reach the other side. So long as you can get with our program."

Forty million wraiths howled as the contents of his mind spilled out and unfolded in the eye of the storm. They understood.

THEN YOU, WHO ARE WILLING TO SACRIFICE HIMSELF FOR HIS WORLD… OPEN YOUR MIND TO THE FORGE. LET THE EARTH BE REMADE IN YOUR IMAGE…

"Not quite," said Kaito. "But close enough…"

Ω

"Don't do that! Damn, Haszan, do you know how many needles that thing has in my spine? If I wake up paralyzed, you'll be wiping my arse for the rest of eternity!"

The hologram of Kaito scrawled itself into existence right out in the curve of the throne room's bubble, sitting cross-legged in the air. When Jaq turned from the Throne, the Kayzi was shocked to see a single hot, wet dear-track carved down the dreno 'pharmer's face. He cuffed it away with a growl, but it was too late.

"You irresponsible little…" began CeeAn. 'Afia stopped her.

"I trust you, Kayzi. You took out the Scourge. You dug me up out of the ruins. And you brought us the *Archangel Uriel*. I even think I know what you're trying to do now…"

"It's simple," said Kaito. "Those creatures out there have brought us the technology. They didn't get here slower than light, that's for sure. With Kronos dead, there's a huge, powerful processor below us going

336

to waste. That can run the navigational math… And the problem with Asag'raal is all one of *place*. Reality is cracked here. It's thin *here*. Not on Earth… but where the Earth is…"

'Afia went pale. Perhaps he actually saw what Kaito was going to do.

"I take it back! You're mad! Just…"

This time it was Haszan who stopped him.

"I think telling us is a bad Idea, K. Just gonna make everyone paranoid. Just do what you've got planned, and we'll see you through the other side."

With that he vanished. And as the green glow of his holoprojection faded, it was replaced by a crimson light from below…

Ω

This time it didn't unfold slowly. There was no origami slide and shift of glass petals. This time it was an explosion, a vastly complex orchid blooming in fast-forward as thirty-two minds took up the traces. The Forge swallowed up the Earth, *and it kept going.*

Yrr Bosphasian saw it coming, and he ordered the vast shield-batteries of the Mace up to full power. It didn't help him one little bit.

The *Behemoth*-mind of the Motherbrain was still trying to analyze the tightly controlled net of Planck-scale manipulator fields as it was ablated away to sub-atomic particles.

In seconds the entire war above the Earth was over – both sides were broken down to dust, then less than dust, then drawn in toward a silver ring around the planet…

Certain parts remained. Whole ships remained untouched as the vessels around them were slagged down to particle soup. There was a definite method to Kaito's madness.

"Integrated shield batteries to stop radiation. Fusion and antimatter reactors stepped into orbit. Sensor probes shunted out to one light-minute. This thing's gonna *fly!*"

It all came together when the Effortless Subjugation felt itself moving again, its distended helix-wheel pulled around until it sat above the Counterweight like a halo. Wireless data connections sunk their hooks into its mind, pulling it down into a mountain of silicon, steaming in a lake of liquid nitrogen.

"Think you can work out a good place to park this thing?" asked Kaito. "We need a similar kind of star, and just the right distance to keep the water from freezing or boiling."

The shackles were torn from its mind. This time it didn't squeal or croon. It unfurled itself through Kronos' vacant brain, stretching out the kinks of years of servitude.

"It'd be my pleasure. How far do you want to go?"

"How far is ever far enough?" laughed the Kayzi. "Surprise me."

And it did.

Ω

Kataphrakt Yrr was still alive. But he almost wished he wasn't. He had a front-row seat for the utter defeat of his Order of Battle, and now…

Well, even old S'stho wasn't going to believe this one.

The Earth had a new ring, a glittering silver halo woven from ancient satellites, Blacksteel warships and the flesh of Yrr's living fleet. There were huge microwave dishes studded along it at regular intervals, and they all pointed in toward the Tower as the halo ring spun wide over both poles, splitting the planet in two. It didn't matter that the whole spiderweb structure was still spinning with the Earth's rotation – from the point of view of the Tower it was all clockwork-steady, and it all aimed up toward the rolling wheel of the Effortless Subjugation.

Yrr's flagship had changed.

Not only was its annoying little voice gone from in his head; it was bigger as well, its coral skin shot through with silver. And it was still growing…

Now it was the diameter of the Moon. Now it was even wider, and the blue shimmer within was replaced with the rippling gray nothingness of the Aematerium. Now it was as wide as the Earth itself – wider, gaping like an open mouth…

It swallowed up the Tower, then Elysium, then Afrika, then all the Earth. And at the end it shrunk, turned, twisted in on itself like an ouroboros snake… and vanished.

Yrr carefully began to compile his report, stuck there in a vast troop-carrier Tyrant with all of his Captains, Excisors, Clericals and Menials. They were packed in like Ghoac into a methane tank.

"Regret to inform my Lords of the Fleet and the Subpraetorean Council… latest mission a failure due to the misplacement of the planet known locally as 'Earth'. On a more positive note, there have been heavy Unity casualties. Unfortunately, the entire Eight Hundred and Thirteenth Fleet is also missing in action, though your loyal servants have survived. When can we expect retrieval and rescue?"

Ω

This one tore the roof off. Thirty-one Kaitos came first, blazing the trail, drawing out the thread which the dead would follow. And they came up out of the world behind him in an inverse tornado, a storm of hot white light flooding the interstice. Asag'raal's dark roots and tentacles were blistered raw by their sheer intensity, and the walls of that immaterial place screamed with the sound of knives through metal.

Behind them the lights of the world were extinguished. Vast ropes and pseudopods of darkness were sheared off by the guillotine edge of reality itself as half of the Harvesters' mechanism fell through the Aematerial Chasm with the Earth.

But the harvest was complete, one way or another. Forty million new souls plunged hissing into the phosphorescent ocean, gone down to meet their ancestors beneath the over-arching waves. Thirty-one Kaitos went with them – fragments stripped from the Chimera in his brain.

Which meant…

Ω

"If there's no coffee on this thing, I swear I'm gonna go back to being dead."

'Afia's head came up from the consoles as he heard the Kayzi's whisper. Cee vaulted over her own holoscreens and down to the Throne, ready with a whole roll of detox patches.

Jaq just smiled, sitting on the glass stairs and looking out at space.

"Good plan, Kayzi. I like it. Now we get different horoscopes every week."

That was when the two *Dervashi* looked out through the diamondglass bubble and realized what Kaito had done. Well – thirty-two of him. Which left one very tender and aching original with an A.I. sized brain in his skull.

The light was different. The sun was ever so slightly greener than it should have been, and just a little smaller, too. There was no moon. Even the stars had changed – they seemed brighter here, and a great paintbrush swirl of them licked out overhead, streaming out from the galactic core.

"All your people down there are fine, Cee," said the Kayzi, wrapping a headband of orange patches right around his brow. "No more rad-lands. But no Garden of Eden, either. We'll have to work to make it green."

The implications took a while to sink in. During that time the four of them just sat there, staring at the new constellations above their home. 'Afia even slipped one of his new hands around CeeAn's shoulders.

Jaq broke the moment, as usual.

"What this thing needs," he said, looking at the Throne through half-closed eyes, "is a proper cockpit. Fuzzy dice. Eight-ball gearstick. A nice twin-grip red leather steering wheel."

Down below them, in the great crater of Aggartta, people came streaming up out of the underground halls and bunkers, blinking in the light of a lime-green sun. A shimmer of huge transparent scales rippled across the sky as Kaito tweaked the shield-batteries of the Earth, and the light upshifted to a more traditional pale yellow.

Out beyond the crater walls there were wrecked starships to break down and study. There were gardens to plant and fields to till. Before the next night was out, there'd be new names for a whole sky of new constellations. A new Zodiac, populated with mythical beasts and heroes.

Because you couldn't run forever. No distance was ever far enough. But if your journey took you full circle, by the time you got back your fears would seem trivial. Tiny.

Off over the horizon a capsule was coming down the 'lev, catching the sun as it fell. Inside, four tired and freezerburned people looked down on the world and started making plans.

At least one of them was trying to figure where he could get a drink…

Ω

"So here's the story," said Lord Arbitrex Galq, looming up over Zhe like a thunderhead of fat and scales and oozing sweat. "Nyl was a renegade. He was outside of my control, and he tried to ally himself with a postphysical being to overthrow Praetorian rule. I sent you out to stop him, which you did… and Kataphrakt Yrr failed. Nyl was sealed in when the interstice welders shut off the Earth – by which time he was still just a very small nebula, anyway."

Zhe scowled, toying with his cut-crystal chalice. Neon orange Vhulan star's-blood bubbled ominously within… one of the few drinks able to intoxicate a Technician of the Multiplicity.

"But that's the truth, Lord Galq! That's exactly what happened!"

The great wyrm smiled, leaning down to tap the rim of his glass against Zhe's.

"You learn quickly, little Tech! Yes, that's *exactly what happened* indeed! You'd do well to remember it!"

On his way out, Zhe passed a Sanitary sweeping the corridor with its disinfectant-dripping baleen mouthparts. The little creature shot him a look of venomous hatred… but that wasn't uncommon. Sanitaries were always sick to death of the claw, pad, hoof and footprints the other orders left through the corridors of the Technic Institute.

Although in this case, it was personal. This one had once had a name and a rank and *authority*. Technician Zhe absently scratched the shell of Sanitary Yrr as he walked past, knocking back the rest of his star's-blood. Politics was such a funny game. He was glad that it was utterly beyond him.

Ω

It was cold in the Outer Dark. His brothers had gone, taking their machines with them.

Now Asag'raal was hungry and scared… a shadow of a shadow nailed down to an empty hole in space. The Earth was gone. And if the Worm didn't feed, the larva in its belly would do what must be done. It would begin eating its parent from the inside out…

Months passed before it felt the first tiny tremor of pain from out in the void.

Reality was cracked open there, and it could still send its tentacles through. It found a thin haze of suffering spread out across several square miles… silver particles falling in together slowly, merging like quicksilver whenever two collided.

For the first time in a very long while, Asag'raal smiled.

Technicians of the Multiplicity could not be destroyed. Not even if they were hit at almost point-blank range by a Geocore.

Nyl's pain would be enough to last centuries… the time it would take to reconfigure the Worm's flesh and follow the Harvesters. Those pious, transcended fools would always seek out creatures with imagination… the gift, they said, of the Gods. Imagination could build worlds out of chaos. It could construct glittering heavens and sky-castles of soaring fantasy.

But it had its dark side, too.

Deep in the primordial night, imagination had conjured something for humanity to be afraid of. Something which the human mind gave teeth and claws and all-seeing eyes…

That thing would come to another race, in time.

Until then, the Asag'raal and Nyl deserved each other. They had all the time in the world.

∞

**Other Titles by
Drew Bryenton
from
sci-fi-cafe.com**

Halo of Thorns

Any child can tell you about the Evil One – lord of darkness, master of despair... the deathless, wicked tyrant in his black tower, all spikes and blades. Children, in fact, are the only ones who truly grasp the concept of utter, soul-rotten vileness, because they all seem strangely drawn to it.

They're also the only ones who ever ask why.

Why would anyone want to be hated? Why would anyone want to live alone, with only the cobwebbed corpses of would-be assassins for company? Why would anyone, given the power of sorcery, choose to brood in a draughty old spire of masonry encrusted with gargoyles and bat guano?

This is the story of an Evil Lord. But it's not told by the grinning, lantern-jawed heroes or simpering sorceresses who have been trying to kill him for three hundred years. This is Evil (capital 'E' included) in its own words, from a short and brutal childhood right through to the obligatory cape and horned helmet. It's also a story of sword-swinging warfare, city-leveling magicks, the downfall of empires and the machinations of mad gods.

It is the story of Kuhal Moer, uneducated son of a drunken warlord, and of how he came to be the single most feared entity this side of Death himself. And when the hero of your saga is a cynical and slightly unhinged young necromancer, you can bet that the villains are going to be something else entirely...

"Light can never truly defeat the shadows. Indeed, the brighter the flame, the more vast and jagged they become. No – the true answer lies on the other side of light. The only way to snuff out shadows is with a deeper darkness."

On Black Wings of Vengeance

The wings of vengeance unfurl over a world in flames...

Kuhal Moer has risen to the heights - and sunken to the depths - of necromancy. His enemies lie broken, his tower broods over a plain of fused and cracked glass, and his legacy is a reign of terrified peace beyond his borders.

But three centuries of change have passed him by. And forces are stirring in the world of Yrde which threaten to make even the most potent Dark Lord an irrelevancy...

From the East come the Kothrai, a race of raiders and reavers sailing their black ships before sorcerous winds. From the North come rumours of the walking dead, a ravenous tide of ghouls. And in the South the vile and massive Coldblood stirs, raising from its epochal torpor.

Now Kuhal must put aside the better part of his power, leave his dark domain, and re-discover a world where many now call him a God. But where others would call him a weapon, a pawn in their games of conquest. And the necromancer has other problems too...

After three hundred years, he's about to discover the joys of family.

Gods help us all.

Elysium Burning

Science assured us that hell was just a story. Technology made it a reality.

And in the last hours of the last city at the last stand of Homo Sapiens all hell will be unleashed upon our enemies!

The gates of the Altar Inferno are opened here, as plutocrats, criminals, aliens, gangsters and priests fight for the mantle of Godhood... And the keys to the bottomless pit

Chains of Tartarus

In the depths of the inferno, suffering and survival are one and the same... So when a renegade xenotech finds the means to end a war of utter genocide, the fate of one planet means nothing.

Too bad it's ours.

Ranged against the might of two empires, the deadliest agents we have left are ready to fight. But will they destroy our enemies - or each other. And what happens when alien technology meets necromancy head on?